The...

...ect
com... ...ith
a magical light.

What to do?

She couldn't announce it. She didn't know what would happen. What would people think. What they'd expect.

She trembled with awestruck fear. This jewel had been touched by the hand of Christ!

Stella mirabilis!

Wondrous star.

Come light one woman's way.

Her breath caught.

Light her way to what?

. . . AND LET THE MAGIC BEGIN.

STAR
* OF *
WONDER

Jo Beverley
Alice Alfonsi
Tess Farraday
Kate Freiman

JOVE BOOKS, NEW YORK

STAR OF WONDER

A Jove Book / published by arrangement with
the authors

PRINTING HISTORY
Jove edition / October 1999

All rights reserved.
Copyright © 1999 by Penguin Putnam Inc.
"Day of Wrath" copyright © 1999 by Jo Beverley.
"Starlight Wedding" copyright © 1999 by Alice Alfonsi.
"Last Kiss at the Loving Cup Saloon" copyright © 1999 by Terri Sprenger.
"Joy to the World" copyright © 1999 by Kate Freiman.
This book may not be reproduced in whole or part,
by mimeograph or any other means, without permission.
For information address: The Berkley Publishing Group,
a division of Penguin Putnam Inc.,
375 Hudson Street, New York, New York 10014.

The Penguin Putnam Inc. World Wide Web site address is
http://www.penguinputnam.com

ISBN: 0-515-12653-5

A JOVE BOOK®
Jove Books are published by The Berkley Publishing Group,
a division of Penguin Putnam Inc.,
375 Hudson Street, New York, New York 10014.
JOVE and the "J" design
are trademarks belonging to Penguin Putnam Inc.

PRINTED IN THE UNITED STATES OF AMERICA

10 9 8 7 6 5 4 3 2 1

Contents

Day of Wrath

✳✳✳

Jo Beverley

Dies irae, dies illa
Solvet saeclum in favilla . . .

Day of wrath and terror looming,
Heaven and earth to ash consuming . . .

Kent, England, December, 999 A.D.

Wulfhera of Froxton hurried along the narrow road between
the hedges of empty fields, frosted earth crunching under her
shoes, every sense alert for danger. The land around lay so
quiet, however, that she almost felt the world had already come
to an end.

Not yet.

If Christ did come to judge in this the thousandth year,
surely it would be on the winter solstice tomorrow, or on His
birthday, still days away.

Not yet.

Piously, she chanted *"Veni, Domine Jesu"* as she marched
along, though she didn't really want Christ Jesus to come quite
yet.

No, it was not the hand of God that silenced life. It was the
whipping, icy wind and sleet-threatening sky, and the Danish
raiders scourging the coastal lands. These had driven people
and animals under cover, and swept the sky of birds.

It was no day to be traveling, and no day to be alone on the
road. Part of Hera regretted leaving her companions, but she
did not have far to go to reach her home. The sisters fleeing
the convent at Herndon faced many more hours on the road
before they reached the safety of Canterbury.

Hit by a clawing gust, she paused to lean her sturdy staff against a rough fence and pin her brown cloak more tightly around her, saying a prayer of thanks for its thickness. Thank heaven, too, for the three layers of woolen clothing she'd put on this morning for the journey, and for thick stockings and sturdy shoes. Even so, her feet were icy.

She looked ahead. Not far now. Froxton should be over the next rise. Pray God it was safe. She crossed herself, grasped her staff in her mittened hand, and set out again, fighting dread that her home, too, might have come under unexpected attack.

Froxton had never suffered directly from the Viking raiders, not even years ago when the pagan Vikings had scourged the coast of Wessex again and again. Froxton lay a bit too far inland, and the Vikings stayed close to their dragon ships. Who knew what might be happening in these dread times, however, when all the world churned in disorder? After all, Herndon Convent had always been safe before, but now the nuns fled farther inland.

Yesterday, the first refugees had pounded on the big gates, demanding safety within, and last night the horizon had glowed with destructive fire. From the top of the feeble wooden walls, the nuns had watched the thatched roofs of Odswere village shooting sparks high into the night sky. Hera had fancied she could hear the screams of the raped and tortured, though she'd known she was too far away.

The Danes had not reached the convent last night—and thank Sweet Jesus for it, for the walls would be feeble defense. Morning light had shown nothing unusual except a distant circling of ravens and eagles—signs of death. Surely like the tides, the raiders would have retreated back toward the coast and their ships.

But who could tell in the thousandth year, when Antichrist should come, herald of the end? Many whispered that the Danish raiders were the Antichrist, and that decades of troubles had been leading up to this season.

The thousand years.

The end of the world.

The Vikings were certainly bolder now, venturing far inland, only weakly opposed by the king. It seemed they came at will to terrorize and demand tribute as if England were a free market, and if not appeased, they destroyed. They set up winter camps here, and sometimes even took land for their own and settled, and none seemed able to stop them.

She scanned the skeleton-treed horizon again, seeking movement. Any woman in their clutches would be defiled into death. She hesitated and glanced over her shoulder, weighing the distance back to her party of nuns against the distance to her home.

Enough of this! She wasn't scurrying back to join the nuns. She was going home. If Antichrist had come, and Apocalypse threatened, she'd face it at home, not among strangers.

She set off again. Not far, she told her aching, frozen feet, bruised by stone-hard ruts. Not far. At Froxton she'd find warmth, but more than that, she'd find her family.

For a while, since going to Herndon in the summer, she'd thought the convent was her life. She'd persuaded herself that she'd be happy there all her days. Yesterday's shocking attack had broken that spell. When Reverend Mother Gudrun had decided to send the younger nuns, the novices, and the postulants to safety, Hera had begun to doubt. On the road, once close to home, she'd known she could not stay.

She wanted to be home, not among strangers in Canterbury; but she also had a keening sense of trouble, of being needed. It was over a month since she'd had news. Anything could have happened, especially in times such as these.

Perilous times.

What did she fear most? The coming of Danish pirates, or the coming of Christ? As a good Christian, she shouldn't fear the latter—"*Veni, Domine Jesu,*"—but she was young. She didn't want her world to end yet, not even if the new one would be the glorious Kingdom of Peace.

Reverend Mother Gudrun said the only danger was the Danes, and she was wise. According to her, the archbishop said the same thing, and even the pope in Rome. Just because the thousandth year was looming, did not mean Apocalypse.

Many thought otherwise, however. The convent was not cut off from the world, and they'd heard how some people were praying and fasting, hoping to wipe away a lifetime's sins before the Last Judgment. Herndon had started to receive an astonishing number of special gifts accompanied by requests for prayer. Some of these had been from people giving away all their worldly goods, hoping to be poor Lazarus in the bosom of Christ, not wealthy Dives burning in hell.

Hera did wonder what would happen if the thousandth year passed and life trudged on as normal. She suspected some of the donors would be knocking at the convent doors, sheepishly asking for their property back.

Many people were looking forward to Christ's coming with song and joy, as they should, foreseeing the glorious day when death, toil, and suffering would cease to afflict mankind. Others, perhaps despairing of heaven, were seeking the glorious day now and indulging in every earthly pleasure while they could.

Most of the time, Hera believed Mother Gudrun, believed that God did not count in worldly ways, but as she struggled across the bleak landscape, fleeing soulless enemies, she murmured prayers—prayers for safety, and prayers that Christ not find her wanting if He came. She was almost a Bride of Christ, was she not? But she was a Bride of Christ who was running away from the wedding. She'd taken no vows, but she feared her flight was a black sin.

The road turned, and at last in the distance she glimpsed her home on the next rise. Froxton Manor, enclosed by a ditch and an earthwork topped by a spiked-pole palisade. Most of the buildings were hidden behind the walls, shown only by wind-whipped smoke rising from the central vents. The thatched roof of the two-story manor house was visible, however, blessedly intact, and the wooden watchtower rose even higher. She could see a figure in there, and soon the watchman would see her. He wouldn't blow his horn for a solitary traveler, however, and his silence meant there were no enemies hereabouts.

She relaxed a little, and her frozen feet became happier to make speed. To the right the church tower of Becksham rose where it should be. To the left, gusts of smoke, almost invisible against the gray sky, hinted of Tildwold being at peace.

Home, and all was well.

Deo gratias.

She'd never expected normality to taste so sweet.

Would she return to Herndon, to the religious life? She'd willed herself to have a calling, but in her heart she'd always known her motives were flawed. Truth was, she'd run away, run away from Raef, from the thought of Raef and Edith, from ever having to see him again, see him with her. . . .

She blocked off those thoughts. If Christ came, her anguish over Raef and her dilemma over her vocation were two of many worries He would take from her.

Froxton slid behind a bare-boned coppice, then came clear again. Not far now.

Perhaps the convent wasn't for her, despite the comforts of order and wonderful music. Six months had been time enough to heal and accept reality, so she should be able to live in the world again now.

Raef had been a lifelong friend, but clearly that's all he'd been—on his side, at least. He'd chosen Edith of Tildwold, who was kind, gentle, and pretty, and who would make him a good wife. Doubtless she was with child by now. Hera grimly said some prayers for Edith's health and safe delivery.

And that she'd never have to see her. See her and Raef together.

Or, if she did have to see them now and then, that she be able to greet them as if they were both just old, comfortable friends. . . .

The first thing Hera saw when she staggered into her father's hall was Raefnoth Eldrunson standing wide-legged on her family's central table, gilded by the nearby extravagant fire, ale horn in hand, leading a chorus of a bawdy song.

She stopped dead.

Dear Mary, even drunk he was the embodiment of her most wicked dreams. He towered like a god, teeth flashing as he sang, light dancing on gold armbands and buckle. His blond hair straggled his broad shoulders, his strong, clean features glowed in the fire's light.

A god or a beautiful devil.

She tore her eyes away to look around the smoky, raucous room packed with red-faced drunks. What was going on here? The place looked, stank, and sounded like a scene from hell. Searching macabre faces for her family, she did not find any.

Despite icy, painful feet, she marched over to the table and looked up. "What are you doing here?"

She had a hundred questions, but that one had spilled out. Immediately she thought back over it, praying it hadn't revealed the spear-sharp shock of seeing him.

The longing.

Pity her, but nothing had changed. His body was as strong and perfect, and her reaction was as fierce. His face was still as handsome, and his blond hair . . . His blond hair, she realized from up close, was tangled for lack of a comb. His cheeks were stubbled, and his bright blue eyes, which had always shone with zest for life, were strangely flat.

For a moment, he looked down dazedly as if he didn't recognize her, but then he leaped from the table in one bound. "Little Wolf! Come from the convent to save us all!"

Before she could react, he swept her into his arms and kissed her soundly.

He'd never kissed her before.

It wasn't a loving kiss. Despite the nickname that only he had ever used, it wasn't a kiss any woman would want.

She pushed at his chest with all her might, spitting out, "Let me go!"

He obligingly stepped back. "Ah, another sin on my damned soul. I've kissed a Bride of Christ." He turned to his grinning audience. "What's one more sin, eh, to those already on the greasy slope to hell?"

They cheered, and Hera stared at them again. She spotted some of Froxton's servants—their eyes slid guiltily from hers—and a few of her father's men-at-arms. There were too many strangers, however, and a lot of soldiers she didn't know. Were they Raef's housecarls—his private force?

Here?

Why?

His home was Acklingham, down the river.

"What are you doing here?" she asked him again. Then she added the important question, "Where are my family?"

The tarnished glow of jollity faded, leaving him shockingly haggard. She saw now that his fine clothing was soiled, uncared for over too many days. Only his gold ornaments shone clear.

He sat suddenly on a bench, his back to the table, and those around turned away. Quiet settled, an uneasy quiet they'd perhaps been keeping at bay with noise.

"It's not good," he said as soberly as possible for a drunk man. "Two weeks ago, the shire reeve called out the local forces to oppose the Danes here. Your father, my father, me. I was to take my ships to sea and block the mouth of the river.

But the Danes came ashore farther down. They took horses—''

"Horses!" Her tired legs suddenly weakening, Hera sat on the bench nearby. The Danes had always raided on foot. "No wonder they're coming farther inland."

He swiveled to face her. "Aye, the devils."

"And our men took a stand against them?"

"They did. And unlike many, unlike King Ethelred, they stood firm."

"They're dead"

She said it as fact. No one stood against the Danish Vikings and lived. That fact had broken the spirit of everyone, leading to armies fleeing, and kings paying the pagan devils to leave England in peace.

Until the next time.

"My father is dead," Raef said, taking her still-mittened hand. "Yours is not. But he lies sorely wounded at Sutton Priory, Hera. And most of the men perished at their sides, as is right." He pulled off her mitten and clasped her hand, but then said, "Hera, you're frozen!"

He dragged off the other mitten, and clasped both her hands between his big, callused warm ones.

She looked down at them, dazed almost to death by weariness and shock, and by his touch. Friends, she reminded herself. Despite a four-year difference in age, they had been friends as long as she could remember. Her brother Edmund, of an age with Raef, had not wanted his little sister along on hunting trips, but once she was old enough, Raef had never minded.

They'd touched often. He'd even let her swim with them in the summer river as long as she never told her mother. Distant, golden days . . . His touch shouldn't bother her now.

He let her now tingly-warm hands go and went down on his knees to pull off her leather shoes and rub her feet. "I don't suppose you can feel these at all. What was the convent thinking to let you walk here on such a day? Did they send no escort?"

She winced at the blessed pain of returning sensation. "The Danes were threatening, so they sent some of us to Canterbury. I ran away."

He looked up with a flash of humor that was almost like the old days. "Ah, my little she-wolf. I knew a convent would never hold you. I don't know why you thought it would.''

Because you married Edith, you stupid man! But she was grateful that he didn't suspect her feelings.

As unconsciously as if they were still children, he put his hands up under her layers of skirts and undid her garters, pulling off her double stockings, then putting her icy feet on his thighs and covering them with his hot hands. ''A fleece!'' he commanded, and at least one of his men was still alert enough to leap up and get it. ''And hot mead.'' Another servant ran to obey.

Slumped back against the table, Hera noted that he wasn't as far gone in drink as she'd thought, and neither were his men. Of course, Raef was above all a good thegn, a good warrior. So, what had been going on here?

''Where's Mother?'' she asked.

He was tucking the thick fleece around her feet and his thighs, trapping his own warmth for her. ''With your father at Sutton.'' He began to rub her lower legs. ''He's close to death, Hera.''

She closed her stinging eyes, hardly able to believe it. ''I was right to come home, then.'' She looked around the room again, wondering. It was almost as if Raef was in charge here. Why?

''Where's Edmund?'' she asked. Edmund was her oldest brother and should be filling her father's shoes.

At the look in Raef's eyes she choked back a moan. Not Edmund, too! But of course, Edmund had died at their father's side.

But Raef pulled a face and said, ''In Rome, if his journey went well.''

Hera began to think she'd collapsed on the road and was dreaming. First the kiss, now this.

''In *Rome*?''

''Aye.'' Raef took a steaming cup from a servant and pressed it into her hands. She cradled it, then sipped, shuddering with pleasure as the spicy warmth ran into her. Surely this was too vivid a delight for a dream?

Hands resting on her ankles, Raef said, ''About a month ago, Edmund decided to face the end in Rome. To be in Saint Peter's Church there when Christ comes to judge.''

''I thought Christ would return to Jerusalem.''

He shrugged and after tucking the fleece all around her warming feet, he stood to pick up his own ale horn and drink. "Rome. Jerusalem. Bethlehem. . . . I told him, God will find us, no matter where we are, but he was set on his plan, and intending to pray and fast on his way. As for me, I intend to greet Christ as I have lived"—he toasted her with his cup—"drinking and fighting."

She didn't know who she thought the maddest, him or Edmund. "Christ is the Prince of Peace," she said. "Do you want to face him with blood on your hands?"

He laughed bleakly. "Who's been free of bloody hands in this cursed land in our lifetime? The Danes are devils, sent to warn us of the torments of hell. I'll not be judged a sinner for killing devils. It hardly matters, anyway. I'm one of the damned."

Hera squeezed her eyes shut, then opened them again. Though nothing in front of her changed, perhaps this was a dream. Or a nightmare. "You? Damned? As you say, in this world men cannot help but fight."

He turned away to stare into the leaping fire. "Wait until Christmastide and see whether Christ places me on the right hand or the left."

"Raef, the world is not going to end at Christmastide."

He turned back. "Will you take all hope from me?" He seemed calm, but now she could see the dark void beneath.

Sweet Jesus, what was going on here?

In desperation, she quoted Reverend Mother Gudrun, in the nun's brisk tone. "It's impious to think God keeps to man's calendar. He can bring the end at any moment, and cares not for our earthly reckoning."

"So, He can bring it at the thousand years." He looked up as if scenting the wind. "Can't you feel it, Hera? Can't you taste it? It's on the air like the howl of hungry wolves—"

"That's the Danes!"

"Perhaps the Danes are the Antichrist, predicted in the Bible. And what of the dragon fire in the sky during the summer?"

Hera shuddered. That had been a portent for sure, throwing the whole convent on its knees. She remembered that time of awestruck terror, and how glad she'd been to be wrapped in a life of prayer and penance, and thus ready to meet Christ.

Now she was in flight from the holy life, and in danger of lusting after another woman's husband. A sinner.

If only he hadn't been here!

She asked the question directly. "Why are you here, Raef?"

"Acklingham was taken." He gave the shocking news flatly. "I was out with the ships, and most of the men were with the forces. When the Danes won, Acklingham was left vulnerable, and—" His abrupt stop suggested something strange. "It's in the hands of a man called Torkil Ravenbringer, who demands more gold than I have for its return."

She wanted to ask how such a strong holding as Acklingham had been taken, even with most of its armed men away, but she knew it must be a terrible pain to him. "Won't the king help?"

His lip curled. "Ethelred the Ill-advised? I suppose he might help me find gold. But if we buy them off again, they'll be back next year, and next." He turned fierce eyes on her. "We have to *defeat* them, Hera. To show them we can't be pillaged for their comfort year after year. We need a king who will fight."

"Our fathers fought, and see where that led."

"We need a full army that will stand firm. And ships to attack them on the water, as we had in King Alfred's day."

"Even King Alfred didn't drive them away forever." Hera sighed. "I've heard tell that the Danes seek to conquer us entirely, to put their own king on the throne. They already hold power in much of the north."

"They will not hold power in Kent, as long as I have breath."

The pain was like a fist squeezing her heart. "Raef, what does any of this matter if you believe the Last Judgment is coming within days?"

He looked at her with eyes that were frighteningly cold. "It matters. I'll face Christ as thegn and warrior, and with His strength, I'll face Him in Acklingham. Ragnarok."

The pagan word for the final battle between good and evil rolled from his mouth like a foul curse. He couldn't have turned pagan! "Raef . . ."

"I long for Ragnarok, Hera, and I pray Armageddon is here, in this very corner of the earth."

Hera was too soul-sick and weary to deal with this. She put

aside fears about the state of Raef's soul, and turned her mind to mundane matters—like the state of Froxton Hall.

Even in smoky firelight, she could see that no one had scoured a dish for days, and that the only ones clearing up scraps were the dogs. The stink told of vast amounts of spilled ale, and a fair quantity of urine mixed in with it.

Then she saw one man fish about in a bowl of stew, then pull out a lump of meat to shove into his mouth. He grabbed a jug to top up his cup and wash it down. People were eating meat and drinking ale and mead as if there were no winter to face! She should leap up and whip them away from the food like wild dogs, but she lacked all will and strength.

Someone should have been managing things better. Not her mother, since she was with Father. Not Edmund, off in Rome. Not Raef, for it was not his hall. Perhaps Edith, though she'd likely not have the fortitude for the task. Though sweet, she was not one to take on battles.

So, where was Hera's youngest sister—the only other unmarried one? This was her task, and as usual, she'd shirked it. "Where's Alfrida?" she demanded of Raef.

Immediately his face hardened. "Locked in her room. She's gone mad. Don't look at me like that," he went on roughly. "It's true. I'm sorry, Hera, but you've returned to a blighted place. Three days ago, Alfrida was seized by the Danes. She was raped. It's turned her mind." He ran a hand through his tangled hair. "Perhaps you can help her, for I can't. She needs a woman's care."

Hera stood, hugging her chilling cup, shivers running down her spine. Rape. Alfrida, with her rosy cheeks and riotously curling golden hair that matched her riotous high spirits? Crushed and broken by cruel men?

Rape was what the convent feared, the threat that had haunted her as she made her way alone across the countryside. She'd told herself that she was far enough inland to be safe from Vikings, but she'd kept every sense alert, and constantly sought out possible hiding places. In these times, there were English wolves as well as Danish ones on the prowl.

"How"—she cleared her throat—"how did Alfrida fall into the hands of the Danes?"

"We didn't know about the horses, so we didn't expect the Danes here. Even so, she shouldn't have been out alone, but you know Alfrida. . . ." He shrugged. "Whatever the reason, it happened."

No wonder Froxton was in such a state. The family was absent or wounded in one way or another, and Raef and his men had brought extra souls to care for.

It was too much. Hera didn't know what to do. She longed to throw herself into Raef's arms to be comforted, and if they were still just friends, she would. To her, however, they were not just friends, and she feared to betray herself. Anyway, Edith must be around somewhere, and Hera would do anything not to face Edith from within her husband's friendly arms.

"But why lock her away?"

"To save her from herself. She's not in her right mind."

"Then she needs help!"

Oh, what point in talking? Though she quivered at the thought of seeing her sister's state, Hera put on her cold shoes and worked her way through the crowded hall to the end, where the private rooms lay.

Her parents' room took up the center, with the separate chambers for the unmarried men and women of the family on either side. The man's side was empty now, she assumed, unless Raef and his housecarls had taken it over. Alfrida would be in the other side.

The door really was barred on the outside, with hastily constructed holders and a plank across. Hera glanced back at Raef, staring moodily into a blind distance, and wondered for the first time if he was entirely sane. Her sister couldn't be mad enough for this, and if she was, she shouldn't be left alone.

Perhaps she'd misunderstood, and she had her women with her.

Her eyes were lingering on Raef, however. Be he sane or mad, nothing in her had changed. Her feelings for him were as strong, as wild as ever, and now everything was worse. With his home in the hands of the Danes, he'd be here day after day. She'd have to see him, work with him to keep Froxton running. Have to talk. Touch. . . .

Worse. She'd have to watch Raef with Edith. Kissing, perhaps. Watch them leaving the company to go to their intimate bed.

She shook her head. It was ridiculous to care when the

world was falling apart around her, when it might be coming
to an end.

But she did care. She cared most deeply and bitterly.

She crossed herself and said a prayer for forgiveness for the
sin of envy, for the sin of coveting her neighbor's husband.
Then she asked Christ's mother, a woman who must surely
understand a woman's heart, to purge her mind of all painful
feelings for Raef Eldrunson.

Hoping prayers still had power, she lifted out the heavy bar
and opened the door to care for her poor sister.

"It's about time, you—"

Hera ducked and narrowly missed being knocked out by a
swung pottery jug.

Alfrida had doubtless checked the swing, too, for she exclaimed, "Hera! Thank Blessed Mary and all the saints!"

Hera found herself in her sister's fervent embrace, thumped
hard on the shoulder by a carelessly wielded jug. She struggled
free. "But Raef said—"

"What did he say?" demanded Alfrida, banging the jug
down on the small table. Even though she'd wound her curly
blond hair into a thick plait, much of it foamed around her
rosy, fierce face like a halo.

The hair suited her nature—Hera wondered what her calmer
hair said about herself—but surely even Alfrida wouldn't be
so undaunted by rape.

"He said you'd been raped by the Danes."

"Ha!"

"Oh, I'm so glad it's not true. But then why—"

"Why am I locked up?" Alfrida's mouth firmed, but she
glanced at Hera almost warily. Hera knew that look. Her
younger sister was up to something.

"Well?" she asked.

Alfrida pulled her plait to the front and nibbled the end,
beginning to glower. Oh, this must be bad.

"I wasn't raped," she said in the end. "But I was seized
by the Danes. And one of them did . . . did deflower me. I did
try to fight him off, Hera—"

"Then it *was* rape! Oh, Alfrida—"

"Even if I liked it?"

Hera sat on one of the three big beds. "You *liked* it?"

Glower squirmed into a very wicked smile. "Oh, yes. I liked it. I liked it a lot. And I intend to have more of it! That's why Raef imprisoned me in here. Because I wanted to return to Torkil."

"Then thank God he did! The shock has turned your mind, Alfrida."

Her sister rolled her eyes. "Besottedness has turned yours."

"Besotted? Me?"

"Besotted! You! Everyone knows you're mad for Raef, and that's why you ran off to the convent."

Hera covered her flaming cheeks with her hands.

"Oh, probably not him," said Alfrida. "Men can be so dense. That's why I have to get back to Torkil."

Hera saw something to leap onto. "Ah! So he doesn't want you."

"Well, he certainly did at the time. And he will again. I'll make sure of it."

"Alfrida, this is madness. I mean . . . I'm glad it wasn't terrible, that you're not wounded and hurt, but you can't possibly want anything more to do with a *Dane*. And it would be a sin. Doubtless it wasn't your fault the first time, but . . . You don't want to be in a state of black sin when Christ comes, do you?"

Alfrida gave her a look. "Not you, too. I don't think the world is coming to an end, but if it is, I want more time first on Torkil Ravenbringer's furs."

"But . . ." Then the name connected. "Ravenbringer," Hera whispered. "Alfrida! Not the man who's taken Raef's manor?"

Her sister shrugged. "That doesn't make it better or worse, does it?"

"It makes Raef's reaction more reasonable. You can't possibly—"

"I can, and I will." Alfrida spread her hands. "It's a time of madness, Hera. Can't you feel it? Why else are you here? It's a time for seizing fate."

Fate. Despite Christian teaching, there was always fate. Fate set the path, and nothing could change it. Fate would come, pray or squirm as humans might. Had she tried to fight fate by hiding in the convent, or had she opposed it by running back here instead of going to Canterbury?

But still. A Dane. A Viking. And Raef's deadly enemy.

"Alfrida, how can you long for a man with a name like Ravenbringer? Deathbringer. How many of our neighbors has he killed?"

"How many Danes has Raef killed?"

"That's not the same. The Danes are invaders!"

"And in the past, our ancestors invaded here and killed those who resisted. Men kill one another. That seems to be their fate. Ours is to love them despite it." Alfrida began to pick up objects—a comb, a cloak-ring, a pouch of herbs.

"What are you doing?"

"Preparing to leave."

Hera put herself between her sister and the door. "Oh, no. If you try, I'll get Raef to stop you again."

Alfrida's face crumpled into tears. Unlike Hera, Alfrida cried easily, big fat tears swelling in her eyes and trickling down her cheeks. "Hera. Please. You know what the Danes are like. They come. They go. How long will he stay in this area? I can't bear it."

Hera truly thought the whole world had gone mad, but she couldn't let this happen. Alfrida was her younger sister. Younger only by eighteen months, but younger and thus hers to guide.

"Alfrida," she said as calmly as she could, "you were seized by the Danish raiders and raped—"

"What's rape?" Alfrida demanded.

"Taken against your will."

Alfrida chewed the end of her plait, which was looking rather overchewed. "I didn't want to be seized. I was terrified. Torkil terrified me, too, at first. He's very big." This, however, was said in a rather dreamy voice. "I didn't think I wanted to share his bed. But . . . he persuaded me. By the time he did it, I wanted it. So there. And it was splendid. And," she added, with a toss of her head, "if he thinks he can do that and just dump me back here and forget about me, he's wrong. Very, very wrong."

"Alfrida! He's not a neighboring lad to be scolded. He's a *Viking pirate and raider*!"

"He's a Dane who wants to settle here."

"On Raef's land?" Despite her plaits, Hera's hair felt as if it might be standing on end.

"Fair conquest."

"It's nonsense and you know it. This Torkil doesn't even care for you. You said he dumped you here after he'd used you. He's doubtless raped a dozen others since then."

Alfrida smirked. "Since he only dumped me here yesterday, I doubt it's been a dozen."

Hera was tempted to slap her. "No wonder Raef locked you in. What are you planning to do? Run out hoping to be seized again?"

"Of course not. I'll ride to Acklingham."

"No. Even if you pleased him for a while, he's had his fill of you, and now he'll toss you to his men."

Alfrida smiled, a secretive, powerful smile. "I don't think so. I think he threw me out because he wanted to keep me. But," she added, "men have short memories. I have to return to him before he leaves."

Hera knew common sense about the man's feelings was powerless at this moment, so she tried common sense about the situation. "Since he's found comfortable winter quarters, I don't suppose he'll be going anywhere until the spring. You have plenty of time."

"Hera! We don't have all winter. What if Christ does come on Christmas Eve, or Christmas Day? Or even on the solstice tomorrow?"

"I thought you didn't believe such nonsense."

"But He might."

"Oh, Alfrida. . . ." She was thinking like a child, and Hera only wanted to keep her safe. "If Christ comes, He must find you on your knees in prayer, not in fornication."

Alfrida tossed her head. "If Raef asked you to his bed, you'd change your tune."

"I would not! He's a married man."

Alfrida stilled, mutinous anger fading from her face. "Didn't he tell you?"

It was like a wolf howl, a harbinger of desolation. Hera wanted to run and hide, wanted to find a burrow in the earth and be like an animal, with no thought more complex than food and safety. But she also had to know. "Tell me what?"

Her sister sat on the other bed, hands clasped in front of her. "Edith's dead."

"What? How?"

"She drowned herself."

Hera shook her head. "No. Why?"

"She *was* raped. Really raped. Raef thinks it was Torkil, but it wasn't. I know him. He wouldn't."

Before Hera could argue that, Alfrida swept on. "It was after Torkil took Acklingham. Edith was trapped there but escaped. She made her way here, but . . . It had already happened. We cared for her, but her mind wouldn't heal. When Raef returned from sea, that's what he found. Not long after that, she went to the river."

"He blames himself," Hera whispered. "I see that now. But for no reason. It wasn't his fault."

"Perhaps he said the wrong thing. Men do, about things like that."

"Raef would never be cruel. He wouldn't!"

"And Torkil wouldn't rape Edith." With a cynical twist to her lips, Alfrida asked, "Are all women blind to the men they love? Anyway, he hit me."

"Torkil? Then—"

"No! Raef!"

Hera looked for a bruise, but her sister was unmarked.

"All right," Alfrida said. "A slap. Still, he had no right."

Hera didn't even try to argue—she couldn't summon words—but surely even Alfrida had to see how this must affect Raef. Despite her sister's besotted fondness, it doubtless had been this Torkil who'd raped poor Edith and then, as with Alfrida, thrown her out. Edith wouldn't have the spirit to escape on her own.

She said a quick prayer for that uncharitable thought.

And here was Alfrida, raped and liking it, wanting to run back to the Viking monster who'd seized Raef's home and raped his wife. No wonder Raef thought Alfrida mad. No wonder he'd locked her up.

But poor, poor Edith. Hera could imagine Alfrida surviving even true rape as long as the physical damage was not too great. She thought perhaps she could herself. But she knew Edith never could have.

Doe-eyed Edith could hardly bear to see animals slaughtered for food, never mind hunt and kill them herself. She hid her body even from other women, and covered her ears when people told naughty riddles or jokes. Truth was, Hera had thought her a silly sort of woman, and that had made Raef's choice all the more painful.

As if picking up her thoughts, Alfrida said, "He'd have been better off married to you."

"Are you wishing me raped?"

"No, but it's the truth. And I wish you well bedded by a good man before the end. It's not something to miss."

"A good man? Torkil Ravenbringer, Danish Viking and pirate?"

Her sister tightened her lips. "He is. Good. In truth, there's little difference between him and Raef except that Torkil is better-looking."

That proved the madness of love. No one was better looking than Raef.

"He's even Christian," said Alfrida, adding a thoughtful, "More or less. The prow of his ship has a cross added to the dragon. And he doesn't kill or destroy where he doesn't have to. He hopes to settle here peacefully."

"On Raef's land. Alfrida, that makes him a mortal enemy!"

"Of Raef's, perhaps. Even of yours. But not of mine. He's the man I want, Hera, and I intend to win him." She bounced up from the bed. "Which I cannot do stuck in here! He probably has some other woman in his bed now."

"Well, then . . ."

"I don't *care* for that, except that it should be me!"

Hera gave up. Truly, this season was driving everyone mad. It only had to be survived. With the peaceful passing of Christmas, with the turning of the year, everyone would awake as if from a bad dream, and sanity would return. It was her task to prevent irreparable damage in the meantime.

She pushed to her feet. "I won't bar the door again if you promise not to leave." She looked at her sister's rebellious face and found a compromise. "Alfrida, night's settling and it's bitter out there. Promise to stay at least until morning, until we've had time to talk. We'll see then what can be done. Anyway, I need you." She rubbed at her weary head. "Everything's in such disorder. The hall's not fit for humans, and I don't know where half the servants are. . . ."

"They've been seeping away since father fell. To their family homes to be there when Christ comes. Or just further inland, away from the Danes."

"All of them?"

"No, but of those still here, half are in the chapel, waiting Christ's coming, and the new age of milk and honey. They don't see any purpose in work anymore. The other half—the ones who reckon they're damned anyway—are enjoying the things they've been deprived of all their lives."

The damned.

Like Raef.

Because of Edith?

Damn Edith!

"They're eating the winter stores," Hera pointed out. "That will make life hell on earth if the world does not come to an end. You should have stopped them."

"Well!" Alfrida glared at her with real affront. "I did waste a day or so grieving for Father, and then we had Edith here like a living ghost. But I tried. I went after a party who were sneaking off. That's when I was taken. As soon as I returned, Raef tossed me in here!"

Hera went to embrace her. "Alfrida, I'm sorry. That was unjust. Forgive me."

Her sister gave her a short, fierce hug. "Of course. This is a terrible time. But it's a time to break free, Hera. I'm so glad you've left the convent."

"I haven't left," Hera said. With Raef free but still uninterested in her, she'd have to return. "I felt called here. And see, I am needed. So are you. We have to put Froxton into good order. If Christ doesn't come, we'll need to eat in the future months. And if He does, I want Him to find me attending to my Christian duty."

Alfrida's face was eloquent. She didn't care about her mundane duty. She wanted this Torkil Ravenbringer, even if it meant facing Christ tangled in the man's bed.

"You don't understand anything, Saint Wulfhera," she said, swishing toward the open door.

Alfrida paused there, however, and turned to ask, "What do you think it will be *like*? The Apocalypse. If it happens . . . I mean, will Christ appear in Rome or Jerúsalem as a man, as He was a thousand years ago? Will word then spread out slowly? Or will He be everywhere, a hundred, a thousand of Him? How can that be?"

Hera had never thought to ask. Trust Alfrida, the practical one, to consider the matter so clearly.

"With God, all things are possible," she replied.

"I know. But I can't make it make sense. Perhaps we'll all be swept to Him for judgment."

"Perhaps—"

"But then it won't matter where we are when it happens, or the state of our homes!"

"Alfrida, God sees everything and knows everything. He hears and sees us now. He knows even our most secret thoughts."

"I don't see how anyone can control their secret thoughts." Alfrida frowned. "Perhaps the world really will come to an end—will become dust beneath our feet—and we'll drift like the stars in the sky either to heaven, or to hell."

Hera shuddered. "I don't like that."

"Nor do I. But it makes me all the more determined to have some very solid, earthly pleasures before the end. But not till tomorrow. I give you my word." She swung open the door. "Come, sister. I'll even labor hard by your side in the hope of gaining a pinch of God's mercy against my wicked end."

If salvation came through hard work, Hera thought when she collapsed into bed hours later, then she deserved a place with the angels. And they'd hardly started.

There'd been little hope of sobering the drunk, so she and Alfrida had sealed up the ale and mead and instructed two reliable soldiers to guard it. Hera had gone to the chapel and found that a number of the Froxton people were indeed in the small stone building, either praying or sleeping, placidly awaiting the coming glorious day.

She'd left them undisturbed, but had the braziers taken away. Cold would have most of them back to work faster than a lecture.

With Raef's help, she and Alfrida had driven the servants who were still capable of work to rake the foulest rushes out of the hall and cart them off to the midden. They'd scattered what clean stuff was available over the floor, then supervised the scrubbing of the benches and tables.

Once the place was bearable, Hera had left Alfrida to supervise the end of that work and arranged a simple meal, mainly for herself and her sister. Alfrida had not been fed since Raef locked her up and in these days before Christmas the convent fasted. During Advent they ate no meat and took only one meal a day, in the evening. In preparation for the journey, she and the others had eaten this morning, but it had only been gruel, and she was famished. Even Advent food of stewed vegetables and day-old bread was ambrosia.

Raef came to lounge nearby as they ate. He didn't mention Edith, so neither did she. Hera didn't know what to say, or whether what she said would come out right. She didn't know if he wanted to talk of it—surely his drinking, and even his edged bawdiness, was an attempt to cover pain.

Anyway, she was too weary and soul-sick to try, so the talk was all practical.

"Do you think the Danes will attack us here?" she asked.

"Why should they when they have a cozy, well-stocked winter home?"

She wanted again to ask how Acklingham had been taken, but his bitter tone stopped her. "So it would be safe for people to go out looking for food. To fish."

"I don't see why not."

"Perhaps we could send messages to the local hamlets, encouraging people to come back."

"So close to Christmas? Leave them to find what peace they can."

"We're short of servants," she pointed out, beginning to get irritated, "and now we have extra men-at-arms to feed and clean up after."

"My men are extra defense, too."

"Defense inside as well as out, I hope. You should have guarded the stores, not pillaged them. You should have enforced the Advent fast." She heard her voice turn wild but she couldn't seem to control it. "You locked up the only member of my family who might have been able to control things, and you let people eat or drink as they pleased!"

His cheeks turned ruddy. "What point in stores when the world will shortly end?"

She leaned over the table and grabbed his tunic. "And what are you going to eat if it doesn't?"

Suddenly, true humor glinted in his eyes, and she realized

she'd fallen back into older ways, when she was always scolding him for this or that.

Comforting. Foolish. Pointless.

Humor faded, and his words were as bleak as her last thought. "One way or another, I'll be past caring long before winter is out."

Her hand was still tight in his woolen tunic, the warmth of his chest so close to her fingers. Carefully, she let him go and leaned away. "Don't talk like that."

"It's fate, Little Wolf. No man can fight his fate, and mine is death and damnation. But I'll not mind hell's flames if I can take Danes to hell with me, especially Torkil Ravenbringer."

Hera saw her sister stiffen to respond but she flashed her a look. Nothing would be gained by a screaming match except Alfrida locked in her room again.

She'd kept the peace throughout the rest of the meal, but couldn't claim to have brought Raef to his senses.

Now, lying in her bed, exhausted as she was, she fretted over him. He seemed to have turned pagan, which would damn him for sure, and a death wish could lead to death, even though a love wish didn't seem to lead to love.

Raef's wife's death, and such a death, must be a terrible wound, one that would make death appealing.

She sighed and acknowledged her own wound from that.

Raef's devastation spoke of a love that went soul deep. Ah, that hurt because it said there had never been, would never be, any such thing for her. She admitted now that she'd comforted herself with the thought that Raef had made a mistake. That he hadn't really wanted Edith. That he'd realized too late that Hera was his true mate.

She grimaced wryly in the dark. The mind could make a fool of anyone. Despite everything, Alfrida's words itched. If Raef invited her to his bed . . .

There'd been a time when the idea would have made Hera giggle. Raef? Raef had been like a brother to her, and she could count off all his many faults any time she was asked, just as she could for her three noisy, squabbling, bullying brothers.

The change had crept up on her like a hunting dog, then pounced one day as they rode out with falcons, she, he, Edmund, and Alfrida. She'd watched Raef loose his bird in the sunshine, comfortably admiring his skill. Then, without warning, she'd been transfixed by his physical beauty—by his fine healthy body, his even features, and his good white teeth shown in a typical enthusiastic smile. Spilling after, like beans from a slit sack, had come lust, admiration, adoration, and a terrifying impulse to silliness.

She'd been harsh with him that day—cold and rude so he'd commented on it and tried to tease her into good humor. She hadn't let herself be teased because she'd feared that the slightest relaxation would make her do or say something revealing, something that would have them all laughing at her.

For days, it seemed, she'd hidden, being alone as much as she could, causing her mother to fret and make strengthening potions, some even with precious sugar in them. Slowly, however, she had settled into the new view of the world and found it magical.

Raef. She and Raef. What could be more perfect? They were friends. Acklingham lay close by, so she wouldn't have to move far from home when she married. Her parents would be delighted to marry a daughter to him. His family already liked her.

She and Raef.

Perfect.

She emerged from hibernation like a butterfly from a chrysalis—and found Raef bewilderingly unchanged. Once assured that she was well again, he treated her with exactly the same brotherly affection as before. She'd always been a tomboy, but now she began to select her clothes with more care, to rinse her blond hair with essence of marigold in the hope it would turn more golden, to pamper her neglected complexion with violet water. She even made up an herbal mixture supposed to capture a lover's heart and wore it in a bag around her neck.

Nothing had brought about any change. Knowing she was in danger of being ridiculous, she'd told herself that it would take more time, that she'd have to be patient. She was fourteen, and he but eighteen. With great care, she'd returned entirely to their earlier ways, waiting for the idea of marriage to come to him.

Waiting for years.

Then, a wary look in her eye, her mother had broken the news that Raef had asked to marry Edith of Tildwold, and all was arranged. Even then, in the first deadly shock, Hera had been grateful to her mother for telling her in private. And for not commenting on the obvious.

After a while, she'd found the strength to be polite, to smile, and to offer her own exciting news—her decision to enter the convent. Most people had not been surprised. After all, why else wasn't she married by twenty if not because she was called to the holy life?

Had Raef been shocked by her decision? In the face of his happiness, his belief that Edith was the most perfect woman ever created, the effort to hold to her own part had been so ferocious she'd hardly been able to see his reactions at all.

And now he was here, free again—but she'd learned something, surely? He didn't feel that way about her now any more than he had then. Look at how he'd handled her legs as if she were a . . . a horse! Or at best, a comfortable old friend. Even if he showed interest, she'd not be taken out of pity, or by a man seeking comfort for the terrible loss of another.

Would she?

The feel of his hands on her skin still burned in her mind. The feel of his strong thighs heating her feet. That kiss, unpleasant though it had been. Their first kiss. . . .

Exhaustion sometimes is a blessing. Despite it all, sleep saved her from further foolish, betraying thoughts.

Raef spent most of the night, as he generally spent his nights these days, blighted by wakefulness, lying watching the low night fire. It hadn't felt right to take over the family rooms here, so he and his men slept in the hall. All around, people snored and snuffled, shifted and turned. At least the lovers over in the corner had finally stopped their gasping and groaning and gone to sleep.

The black nights were full of Edith, and lovers made them worse.

What had he done wrong?

She'd been shy, but he'd expected that. Though it had taken longer than he'd expected, he'd enjoyed coaxing her into accepting him, and even into coming to like lovemaking.

A bit, at least.

Over time it would have come completely right.

They hadn't been given time.

God knows why, but in the darkest hours of the night, he always found himself trying to imagine what had happened to her, what it had been like for her. He didn't know who or how many, though apparently the physical damage hadn't been too bad. One lusty, unwanted man would have been enough to destroy Edith, however, and she had certainly been destroyed.

He blamed himself for not protecting her, but was sane enough to realize that it hadn't really been his fault. He blamed himself more for not understanding her wounds.

When he'd returned, her woman had said she was healed. She appeared much the same, though she'd lost weight and her eyes had been vague, as if she looked elsewhere. She certainly never looked at him for more than a fleeting moment. He'd only wanted to help her heal, but she'd flinched from his simplest touch and not seemed to want his company at all.

Should he have stayed away from her?

How could that have helped in the long run?

He'd not blamed her. What was there to blame? He'd asked nothing of her. He'd just tried to offer her the comfort of hand, arm, or voice, of the promise of his loving constancy. He'd tried to aid her slowly back to normal ways.

And after two days of his loving care, she'd risen early in the morning, before the household was awake, and walked down to throw herself into the icy river.

What had he done wrong?

How had he failed her?

Thinking it over did no good. It brought neither enlightenment nor healing. Yet this seemed to be his private hell—to revisit these thoughts and questions nightly for the rest of his life.

May it be short.

Now, into familiar bleak ice came a searing hot poker. Hera. Her steady eyes. Her courage. Her feet, icy on his thighs. His organ shamefully hard.

Hera.

He rolled his face down, head in arms. God protect him. Hera.

Had Edith ever guessed that he'd come to his senses too late? Surely not. He'd worked day and night to be sure that she never guessed, never felt less in his eyes. But had she? Women were sharp about these things. They had a special sense for them. Was that what had driven her into the river?

He rolled onto his back, arm over his eyes, but nothing could block the inner visions.

He'd kissed Hera.

There'd been nothing loverlike in it at that moment. She'd appeared, a witch from hell in a place where he'd hoped she'd never be again, like a weapon driven straight at his guilty heart, and he'd reacted. Defended. Tried to drive evil away.

Ah, Jesu, Hera was not evil. Hera was the sun in summer and the fire in winter, and he thought, looking back, that despite her interest in the religious life, she'd have accepted him if he'd realized in time.

He'd have had her, her vital warmth. . . .

He pushed away thoughts that still seemed sinful, even though he was now free to marry again.

He'd never be free. He'd taken the wrong path, and there was no going back. He was no longer worthy of a woman like Hera. Somehow he'd driven Edith to her death, and he would pay for it in hell.

Before Christ came, however, before he died, he wanted only one thing. To send Edith's tormentor, Torkil Ravenbringer, to hell ahead of him.

Used to the convent's hours, Hera awoke at first dismal light, though she noted that she'd not woken for the hours of prayer throughout the night. Truly, she didn't think she was suited to the convent, yet now it seemed her fate. Easing her body, stiff from the long walk and hard work, she braced herself to leave the warm bed and face the nippy air. Alfrida was still snuffling in the other bed. Let her sleep awhile.

She spent a little time trying to think of a way to persuade her sister of her folly, but failed. Alfrida had always been willful, and wouldn't accept a mere sister's command. And she was wildly desperate to go to this Torkil.

What sort of man was he to have such an effect? Despite her spirited nature, Alfrida had never been silly. Big, she'd said. More handsome than Raef. Certainly that was a package to turn any woman silly, but there had to be more to it than that.

Unless the world truly had turned mad.

She remembered her sister saying something about the man persuading her into his bed. Not a crude raider, then.

Though Hera knew exactly what men and women did together, and had even seen it in passing a time or two, she had little idea what a man might do to persuade a reluctant maiden into his bed. She'd never, thank the saints, been captured, and in her safe home, there'd only ever been one man who could have persuaded her.

And he'd never tried.

She squeezed her eyes against the sting of tears. She didn't cry, and she wouldn't start now. There were more important matters to grieve over, anyway, than the fact that Raef saw her as a sister. She would like to find a way to lighten his soul. To bring back his zest for life, to help him heal.

That wasn't likely to happen if Alfrida ran off to Torkil Ravenbringer. Despite Alfrida's denials, who else could have raped Edith? If the man hadn't done it himself, he'd allowed it. That made peace short of death impossible.

She shivered at the thought of Raef's death, and her thoughts moved to her father. Big, gruff, and fierce, he hadn't been the heart of her life, but he'd always made her feel safe. Soon he'd be gone, and until one of her brothers returned home, Froxton would be in a sorry state.

Indeed, it was wretched to be a woman in these dreadful times.

With a sigh, she forced herself out of bed, and hurried into many layers of clothes. There were simpler matters to tackle—ones where she could achieve something. She decided to leave Alfrida sleeping. She'd like her help, but as soon as she was up they'd be back to the matter of her foolish longing for that Dane.

Yawning and chilly, she went first to the guarded store-rooms and took careful inventory. It wasn't quite as bad as she'd feared, because people had eaten the luxuries first. They'd suffer later for lack of preserved fruits and honey, but there'd be enough beans and grains if everyone was careful. Half the hard cheese was gone, but the salted fish remained. The indulgent ones had been after quick food, not that which needed slow and careful cooking.

When she went outside, however, she found that they'd roasted half the laying poultry. Were people always feckless fools as soon as order broke down?

She continued her inventory, calculating how many people

they could feed for how long without needing to buy extra food—if any was available. When the weak wintry sun rose over the palisade, and some servants began to stir, she had one ring the bell to summon them all together. Standing on the steps leading up to the second story of the manor house, she eyed the sorry scene.

Too few, she decided, and half were hung over from drink, the other half weakened from fasting and prayer.

Not quite true. Raef and his men had obeyed the summons, and they were fit and alert.

"These are troubled times," she said, speaking clearly so all would hear. "Some say that the end of the world will come at the solstice today, or at the thousandth Christmas three days hence. But I tell you, the pope in Rome does not say this, nor does the archbishop in Canterbury. They say as they have always said that Christ could come at any time, and will come when least expected. On that day, we will all be judged on the state of our souls."

Some of the people fell to their knees and started to pray.

Suppressing a groan at their reaction, Hera carried on. "This means that, while prayer is good—very good—we will be judged on how we are performing our everyday duties. We will all gain grace by hard work, and by trusting in God's wisdom and mercy. Moreover," she added, not looking at Raef, but directing her words to him, "we will be blessed if we refuse the sin of despair. Christ died to save us. He can forgive any sin, and He will come again in mercy—in *mercy*, note—to save us all."

She was rewarded by some fervent amens.

"Therefore, we must all work in our apportioned way through these difficult days, and work hard. And we must remember this is Advent, the time of preparation for the feast of Christ's birth. If we do not fast, we cannot feast. Froxton will observe the Advent fast in these days leading up to Christmas. We will take only one meal in the evening. There will be no meat, and for drink, only water." Over groans, she said, "And then, on Christmas Day, we will feast as we have always done to celebrate Christ's ancient coming to save us all from Satan's power."

"But what if He does come again, here and now?" a woman called out. "What then, Lady Wulfhera?"

"Then we will greet Him with joyous song, Hilda, in a state of grace because of our work and fasting. Remember, if Christ does come to judge us, that will be the glorious beginning of a golden age. An end of pain and suffering, of loss and death, of hunger and cold. For the blessed," she added, looking around the crowd. "For the charitable and virtuous. For the honest, the chaste, and the hardworking."

Some looked downcast, but most seemed cheered by a simple prescription for salvation.

"So, be about your work. However, I know some of you have already fasted through the past days, and fasted foolishly, so you must eat of pottage and bread before you work."

"We might be ready for Lord Jesus, Lady," a man said, "but what of the Danes?"

"Our walls are strong, and we have Thegn Raefnoth and his men to add to our own. We will not be taken. Go! Go to your work, and prepare Froxton for Christmastide."

Obediently the people scattered, and Hera followed those who went into the hall to eat, to make sure that only those who'd fasted in the chapel were there.

"Well done," said Raef, making her twitch with his closeness behind her. She felt as if heat was creeping up her neck to her face.

"Thank you," she said without turning. "I expect you and your men to observe the fast, too."

"I'll see to it. And I'll enforce your will."

He sounded normal, and she wondered if his fatalistic despair had passed with the effects of drink, but she didn't dare face him to see. She just nodded and went to supervise the ladling of the soup.

Later, however, she had to seek him out. "Raef, we spoke of getting fresh fish from the weir. Is it safe to go out?"

He did look composed. Perhaps too much so for the Raef she knew, but then, grief must still weigh heavily on his soul. "There's no sign of Danes nearby. I have the place locked up mainly to keep more people from running away." He glanced at her. "Despite your scolding, I've not been quite as neglectful as you think. Even the feasting was to keep up spirits—lacking your skills with a sermon."

There was an edge to that, but she wouldn't let him pick a fight.

"I'll send some people, then. They can get more flour from the mill, too."

They discussed practical matters for a little while, and she was soothed by his manner. Shadowed, yes, but that was reasonable. There was no more talk of damnation.

She picked some servants to catch fish at the weir—people she thought she could trust to come back, and who were strong and agile enough to run back if the watchcorn sounded the alarm. It was only as she saw them off that she remembered Alfrida. The thought came with a jab of alarm. Her sister must just be shirking work, of course. But . . .

Hera rushed into the room to see an empty bed, to see that Alfrida's special possessions were gone.

She'd promised!

Thinking back, however, Hera realized that Alfrida had not promised to stay. The words had been something to do with her sister staying until they had a chance to talk. There'd been chance and more. Hera had simply forgotten, and Alfrida had taken advantage of it. Hera sent a servant to check, but her fears were confirmed. Alfrida and her maid had talked their way past the guard and were probably close to Acklingham now.

She ran her hands through her hair, cursing her willful sister then praying for forgiveness for the curse. Oh, but it could be such trouble. With God's mercy, the Dane would just send her sister home, chastened and wiser. The alternatives didn't bear thinking of.

The alternatives were more likely. She turned and raced in search of Raef.

"Alfrida!" she gasped, finding him grimly exercising with his sword against a man blocking with a heavy shield.

He paused. "She's gone?"

"You *knew*?"

"No, but I had her locked up for a reason." He returned to savaging the shield, almost knocking the bearer off balance with each blow. "I know the power of lust"—*thwack*—"no matter how foolish"—*thunk*—"or how wicked." *Thud.*

She jerked as if the blow had landed on her.

Lust.

Somehow, even though she'd accepted that he loved Edith,

loved her deeply, she'd never quite thought of him lusting after her. . . .

She thrust that thought aside. "You have to go after her. She can't have reached Acklingham yet. You have to—"

He stopped, shaking sweaty hair back off his face despite the chill air. "I don't have to do anything. I'm not risking men for her."

"Raef!"

"No." He turned cold eyes on her. "If you're not willing to imprison her, she'll be off again tomorrow and tomorrow. Love, lust, whatever it is, burns like a fire. It must be pleasant dwelling in your cold, unpassionate land, but it isn't where most mortals dwell."

Struck silent, she watched him hold back other words and stalk off, shoving his sword into its scabbard.

Cold and unpassionate? Why would he ever think that of her? Because she'd gone to the convent? Didn't he know that true vocations were passionate? And if he thought her unpassionate, it merely proved how dense men could be.

She saw, however, that she'd lacked passion in the convent. Herndon had been a peaceful place, a haven, but not a place or a life she'd truly embraced.

There was revealing relief in finally and completely putting it aside. Her place was in the world. But not with Raef—she must be clear on that point. His passion for a dead woman ran too deep.

What of Alfrida?

There, he probably was right. Short of true imprisonment, her sister could not be held. The best that could be hoped for was that she'd learn her lesson without too much pain, and come home again of her own accord. Heartsick and suddenly lonely, Hera climbed up to a watch point on the walls and searched the bleak countryside for a solitary figure.

She saw the servants heading toward the river, where the mill stood, wheel turning in the rapid water. A few other people from the area were out seeking foodstuffs—wild plants and even small animals unwary enough to reveal themselves by day. There was no sign of her sister, however.

Was it possible that Alfrida was right, and that Torkil Ravenbringer desired her, and would keep her? That offered little solace. An Englishwoman couldn't be happy with an invading Dane, and Raef truly intended to kill the man.

Faced with this desperate situation, Hera no longer even knew what to pray for. In the end, she crossed herself and said the simplest and best prayer of all.

"Thy will be done, O Lord."

After checking that all necessary work was being attended to, Hera went to spend some time in the weaving shed, seeking the company of the women there as much as the work. She picked up a basket of carded wool and a distaff and spun thread as work and words wove comfortingly around her.

No dismal talk here. No talk of Danes or of the end of the world. Instead, there was gossip, chatter of Christmas, and the occasional song.

After a while, one of the women said, "Sing us a song, Lady Wulfhera."

Hera did have an excellent voice—it had been much appreciated in the convent. A gift of God, not to be denied to others. She looked around and smiled. "What should I sing?"

"Something of Christmas," another woman said.

"A happy song."

"'The Star of the Magi'!"

Amid a chorus of agreement, Hera laughed and put aside her spinning. She had no instrument, so she took up an empty wooden box and beat a rhythm on it with her fingers, as she began to sing.

The Star of the Magi was an old tale—some said it went back to the Bible—but she'd put it to song a few years before, and it had become a favorite at this time of year.

It told of the coming of the wise men, the Magi, to the Christ Child's stable in Bethlehem, bringing with them gifts of gold, frankincense, and myrrh.

> *Stella mirabilis, come from afar.*
> *Stella mirabilis, come where we are.*
> *Stella mirabilis, shine night and day.*
> *Stella mulieribus, come light one woman's way.*

The last line didn't make sense until later in the song, but the women liked to join in with everyone. They loved the

song because it was all about women and power. Of course,
women knew they steered the world, but men didn't like to
think of it that way, so there were few enough songs that gave
the women's view of things.

Hera stood with her makeshift drum to dance as well as
sing, as her joy grew in the singing, the company, and the
message.

The first part was all about Bethlehem, and the Magi's arrival, especially Melchior, who brought gold to Christ. When
he approached the baby Jesus and bowed over the manger, the
fine pendant he wore swung down and attracted the baby's
eye.

This pendant, so the story went, was made of gold shaped
like a star, and in the center sat a mysterious blue stone, polished smooth but magically holding within it the image of a
bright star.

Of course, the Holy Child reached out to such a glittering
object, and brushed it with His tiny fingers. Immediately, Melchior moved to take it off, to give it to the baby Jesus, but
Mary leaned forward to stop him. As if the child spoke through
her, she said that it was now a special gift for women, and he
must take it home and give it to his youngest daughter.

> *Stella mirabilis, come from afar.*
> *Stella mirabilis, come where we are.*
> *Stella mirabilis, shine night and day.*
> *Stella mulieribus, come light one woman's way.*

So, Hera sang, Melchior returned to his northern homeland
with his pendant jewel. Of course, the Bible described the
Magi as wise men from the East, but many also called them
the Three Kings of Cologne. Hera had happily changed the
details to make one of the Magi a leader in England, so the
song would mean even more for her people.

They certainly loved it. Some of the younger women put
aside their work and rose to dance with her, hips swaying,
hands clapping, and bracelets jingling.

> *Stella mirabilis, come from afar.*
> *Stella mirabilis, come where we are.*

Stella mirabilis, shine night and day.
Stella mulieribus, come light one woman's way.

Hera sang the sad story of Melchior's youngest daughter, Miriam. She had been scarred as a baby when she fell into the fire and so, despite her warmth and wisdom, no man courted her. Even the man she had come to love did not see her as a potential bride.

For a moment, Hera almost lost the song. She was not scarred, but she was blighted by a man who could not see her as a woman, a woman to desire.

She pushed that thought aside and carried on, dancing and smiling, to tell how Melchior returned to his home to be greeted by his loving family. How there he placed the pendant, with its precious blue stone, around the neck of his beloved daughter, thinking it would give her solace in her single state.

But, lo! Within days, the neglectful suitor saw Miriam with new eyes, and soon he asked for her hand in marriage.

Stella mirabilis, come from afar.
Stella mirabilis, come where we are.
Stella mirabilis, shine night and day.
Stella mulieribus, come light one woman's way.

Miriam married Alric, and his courage and strength was enhanced by her warmth and wisdom so that their lands were a haven of peace and prosperity. Their deep and special love spread like a light around them, bringing harmony to the country and the world.

Stella mirabilis, come from afar.
Stella mirabilis, come where we are.
Stella mirabilis, shine night and day.
Stella mulieribus, come light one woman's way.

Then—Hera stilled the dance, producing a roll of thunder on her drum—one day Miriam and her husband crossed the sea and a great storm came up. All feared they'd be cast into the deep. Miriam clutched her first baby to her, and held the star pendant in her hand, praying to the special child her father had spoken of, the one who had sent her such blessings.

Their boat was driven to the shore, but lodged on the rocks long enough so all could scramble off. In the struggle, however, the pendant chain broke and the jewel fell twinkling into the dark and stormy sea. Alric would have plunged after it to try to get it back for her, but she stopped him. It had blessed them and saved them, but now she knew it had completed its work for her. It was for some other woman, somewhere, sometime, who needed to find her own true love so as to be able to bring peace and harmony to all around her.

> Stella mirabilis, come from afar.
> Stella mirabilis, come where we are.
> Stella mirabilis, shine night and day.
> Stella mulieribus, come light one woman's way.

Smiling at all the bright-eyed women, Hera spoke the ending, the traditional ending of the story, without the drum.

"And it is said that the Star of the Magi was swallowed by a fish, that symbol of Christ, and that it rests there waiting for the time when it is needed again. A special time of great need, when another woman must light the way for men. This, my sisters, is why we eat fish at Christmastide, especially on Christmas Eve, and most especially on the last Christmas of a century. For that, the story says, is when the Star is most likely to come to bless us all."

After an appreciative moment, the women applauded. One young woman, flushed from the dance, asked, "If the Star's most likely to come at the turning of a hundred years, Lady Wulfhera, what of the turning of a thousand?"

Hera thought it just a charming story, but clearly some of her audience believed it. "Then," she said, "it is a hundredfold more likely, and a hundredfold more powerful."

Perhaps young Heswith longed for a man who did not see her, for she fervently said, "Then I will eat lots of fish!"

Raef leaned against the wall of the weaving shed, close to a window, both eased and racked. Hera's voice could never do anything but ease him. Another gift he'd taken for granted and thrown away. If he'd been a wise man, he could have had her singing company all his days. At least her gift was back in the world for a while, and not hidden behind a convent's walls.

He loved the way she told the story, too, in song and words. He wished he could believe it. Had there truly been a time when Christ and His mother could touch the world's pains in such a direct way?

If so, the sins of Man had driven away that gift, along with so many others. Now the world was steeped in darkness, riven by discord and violence, and a man had no choice but to live in dark and danger until death sent him to hell.

He could try for a bit of light now and then, however. He pushed straight and went to the door. "Lady Wulfhera, could I speak with you?"

She was chatting to a group of young women, and turned, suddenly flushing. He thought perhaps she was angry at being interrupted, but she came over quickly enough and stepped outside with him.

"If you truly wish it," he said, "I will go after Alfrida and bring her home."

She stared at him, but then shook her head. "It's too late. It was doubtless too late when I first realized. It is her fate. When she returns, though, Raef, be kind to her."

It stabbed like a rough-edged blade that she might think otherwise. "Of course. I was trying to be kind before."

"I know." Then she frowned in thought. "She seemed to think that the Dane wanted her, but sent her home anyway. Is that possible?"

The last thing Raef wanted was to peer into Torkil Raven-bringer's foul mind, but for Hera he tried. "I know nothing of him except his reputation as a mighty warrior, but why would he throw away something he wanted?"

Wanton blindness, he thought, wondering what would happen if he pulled Hera into his arms and kissed her. Kissed her properly, not in the cruel parody he'd wielded like a weapon yesterday.

It was not possible. She was as good as a nun, and he was no longer a man for any good woman.

He rubbed his hand over his face, wishing he could wipe away a year and be back where having Hera was possible. "Likely he simply tired of her," he said, trying to make sense of it for her. "Perhaps she made tiresome demands. Alfrida could tire me."

"But Alfrida's not a fool. If he *did* care for her, would he still send her away?''

"Perhaps," he said, almost inhaling the sight of Hera's clear skin, honest eyes, and slightly parted lips. "Perhaps he has a wife he tries to be true to.''

Hera's mouth opened a little more. With dismay. "Oh, no!''

He'd said too much. "By Saint Peter, Hera. There can be no question of them marrying!''

"Better to marry than to burn."

Only if a man marries wisely. Oh, God, this was torture, this was hell on earth. He couldn't live like this with Hera, talking to her day by day.

"He won't marry her," he said curtly. "He'll doubtless throw her out, and she could be in danger. There are roving bandits these days, English as well as Danes. Perhaps I should ride over there with a few men and be ready to escort her home.''

"No!" She put her hand on his arm. "Raef, there's no point in a few men huddling and freezing in case they're needed, and we need you here. I see no sign of danger nearby."

Her hand felt like sunshine, and he covered it with his own, trying to trap it there. "I want to do something to help you, Hera.''

A strange expression flitted over her face, as if there was something, but she did not want to ask.

"What is it? What can I do?''

"Nothing. Truly." She pulled her hand free. "Thank you though, Raef. And . . . Alfrida told me about Edith. I'm so sorry."

"You didn't know? I assumed you would. . . ."

He immediately realized that had been stupid. It had been recent, and her parents were not here to send messages. He'd foolishly assumed she would know anything of importance about him, and he about her. He didn't. He didn't understand, for example, her strange impulse toward the holy life. It didn't make sense to him. Her running a home fit better, but it seemed she intended to go back.

"I had no news," she was saying, and now—cruel pleasure—she took his hand. "I know how painful it must be, Raef, but don't let it darken your soul. Especially not now. You were not to blame."

He pulled his hand free. "Don't speak of what you do not know."

"I know this. Christ can forgive *any* sin, and the blackest sin is to doubt that. Even if you carried Edith to the river yourself and threw her in!"

Shockingly, he itched to slap her. "I loved Edith."

Her hand was over her mouth. "Raef, I didn't mean that. Not . . ."

But he was walking away, fleeing her words. He'd loved Edith, yes. In a way. Not enough, yet too much. Talking to Hera, he'd suddenly realized that he *had* driven Edith to the river.

It was so clear now.

Edith had lost all liking for men.

Perhaps she'd never liked men much anyway. She'd never liked the physical side of marriage, and he'd deluded himself by thinking that she was beginning to get pleasure out of it. Once the terrible pain of her maidenhead was over, he saw now, she'd tolerated him, saying appropriate things but gaining no true pleasure. He didn't understand it, but he feared that even when he'd stirred a physical response from her, she hadn't liked it.

He'd wanted a lusty, enthusiastic bed partner and she must have known that. She'd probably done her best.

After the rape, he saw, all she'd wanted of him was absence. As long as he'd been away, she'd survived, reasonably comfortable with her women companions. But his return, his insistence on spending time with her, on talking to her about the future, on touching her, had shattered her fragile peace.

She'd fled him, fled her intolerable duty to him, and found the ultimate peace of death.

He stopped in a private corner, pressing his hands to his face. Did it count that he had only ever intended good? Was it any excuse to have been stupid?

Stupid to have married her.

Stupid to think she'd become the wife he wanted.

Stupid not to understand her pain.

He should have placed her in a convent for care. She'd doubtless have stayed there all her life, and could well have found happiness. Instead, driven by his own guilty dissatisfactions, he'd tried to force their marriage back together again with kindness, concern, and flinched-from touches.

No, good intentions didn't count, and stupidity was no excuse. He looked up at the dark-clouded sky. The end couldn't come soon enough for him.

Hera watched Raef walk away and for the first time sincerely wished herself back in the convent. He'd loved Edith. She knew it, yet she'd said that terrible thing. She'd not meant it that way, but she'd said it, wounding him grievously.

There was no dealing with this. No road. No possible accommodation when every time she tried to speak of painful things, she made them worse.

She saw the gates open to admit the returning servants carrying strings of fish and sacks of flour. Work! She grasped it with relief and hurried off to supervise the preparation of the evening meal. She'd carry Froxton through these last mad days of the millennium, then when madness passed, and when her mother, or—by the grace of God—her father returned, she'd go back to Herndon, where at least she would do no harm.

She organized the setting up of a long trestle table outside the kitchen sheds so the fish could be cleaned and prepared. Then she went to make sure the new flour was put into clean bins in the granary, and that all the stores were still properly guarded.

She wondered where Raef was, but knew it was wiser not to know, not even to think of him. To make sure of it, she hurried to help with the fish. Work defended against sin.

It did help, even if cleaning fish was a task she particularly disliked. An excellent Advent penance, she told herself, and penance for speaking so cruelly to Raef. If anything could teach her to hold her tongue, it was handling cold fish and pulling out their slimy innards.

Even so, she had to struggle not to pull a face as she slit the fat belly of the next fish. Years ago, she and Alfrida had come to an agreement that Hera would prepare small animals, and Alfrida would do fish, and she'd forgotten just how much she hated this.

Even the smell. A sort of wet, muddy smell. . . .

She hastily turned her mind to other matters. Perhaps her earlier "sermon," as Raef had called it, had done some good, for even those servants who thought the end near were working hard—with occasional glances at the sky to see if Christ was coming yet.

It was the solstice, after all, when night and day were equal, and the great wheel of time turned. A likely time.

Most people, however, had their attention fixed on old Thorgytha, gnarled hands working with speed and skill, who was telling one of her funny stories—the one about the miller with his foot stuck in a bucket. Hera focused her attention on that as she slit the fish, and scraped out another disgusting mess, looking at it as little as possible.

She touched something hard, however, so she had to look down. Sometimes a fish had a stick or even a hook inside, and a person could get hurt. This item seemed quite large, however.

A coin? She'd felt a point. An arrowhead?

If it was an unusual item, especially a valuable one, it might be seen as a good omen and help raise everyone's spirits even more. Setting aside her distaste, she cut into the stomach and pulled the tissue away from the object.

Something glittered, and she smiled.

Gold.

That would be a find to celebrate. There were many stories of fish with rings and coins in their stomachs, but she'd never found any such thing before. This was bigger than a ring, however, and she saw a hint of blue glass.

Or perhaps not glass.

Her heart started to pound and she glanced around, wondering if she'd fallen asleep and was dreaming.

The Star of the Magi?

Folly.

But this didn't feel like a dream.

Now she looked around to detect if anyone was watching her.

Thorgytha was coming to the climax of her story, and she was a skilled storyteller, so everyone's attention was fixed between their busy hands and her.

Hera looked down and pulled the object completely free, finding that the blue stone was indeed not glass, that it glittered deep within with a magical light. Concealing it with her hands, she wiped away membranes and blood with her thumbs to reveal a golden circle with star points, and that deeply glowing blue stone in the center.

What to do?

She couldn't announce it. She didn't know what would happen then. What people would think. What they'd expect.

A quick glance showed that still no one was watching her, though the man next to her, waiting for the next fish to stuff, flashed her a curious look.

She had to get away from here to think.

The pendant was almost too large to conceal in her hand, and she needed her hands to finish the fish, anyway. Grimacing slightly, she tucked the still-soiled jewel up under the snug cuff of her sleeve and looked down at the fish.

Was this a sacred fish that should be treated with reverence? She couldn't see how unless she announced her find, and fish were surely created to be eaten. After a moment, as Thorgytha ended her story and everyone laughed, she finished cleaning it and slapped it down in front of the waiting servant.

Then, with a word about other duties, she left the line of workers. No one would think it strange, but she felt as if everyone was staring as she washed her hands and hurried into the hall. Once out of sight, she almost ran to the maidens' room, where she slammed the door and slid the piece of jewelry out.

It hadn't changed. It was still, she was sure, the miraculous Star of the Magi. She went to her leftover washing water and cleaned it properly, scrubbing away all trace of fish.

Cradled in her hand, it was certainly a very valuable piece of gold jewelry worked with the highest skill. Finer skill than anyone had today, even though there were many fine goldsmiths. She tried to tell herself that the stone in the center was glass, but she'd seen no glass with such depth, or with the magical effect of light trapped within.

Stella mirabilis, shine night and day.

She hadn't invented that line. It was part of the original legend, linking the jewel with the Christmas star which had led the wise men to Bethlehem, the star in the sky which had shone by night and day.

She rubbed the stone, as if rubbing would wipe away that mysterious light trapped inside. Of course it didn't. This was the fabled Star of the Magi, brought to her by a fish, now, after not only a century, but ten centuries.

She trembled with awestruck fear. This jewel had been touched by the hand of Christ!

Stella mirabilis!

Wondrous star.

Come light one woman's way.

Her breath caught.

Light her way to what?

These were dark times, in truth, but . . .

But other thoughts danced in her head.

She was trying to be reverent, but all she could think of was Miriam attracting the man who had not seen her in that way, the man she loved.

This must mean that Raef was finally to be hers!

She sat with a thump on her bed, clutching the piece of jewelry to her heart and saying a fervent prayer of thanks, and not just for Raef. If ever a world needed healing, it was the one around her, and perhaps now she could do it, and heal Raef at the same time.

She and Raef.

She and Raef.

How long had it been since she had allowed herself to think that?

With trembling hands she found a piece of leather thong and threaded it through the ring on the jewel. Then she tied it around her neck, tucking it down under her clothes, next to her skin. She half expected it to burn with magic power, but it just lay there, slightly heavy, hard against her chest.

She couldn't wait. A faint tremor running through her—she felt like a hunting hound on a hot scent—she went to find Raef, to test the jewel's power.

For a panicked time she thought he'd left the manor, but then she heard from one of his men that he was in the stables. She entered to see him watching as a horse was treated for a swelling.

"Raef?"

He turned, not evidently pleased or displeased to see her. Not struck by magical change.

"Is there a problem?" Then he stepped closer. "Hera? What is it?"

She couldn't imagine what she looked like, but she tried to seize control of herself. What had she expected? Instant, magical adoration? Of course it took time. "Nothing in particular," she said. "I just suddenly felt a need to talk to you."

He moved closer and touched her arm. Did she shudder? "This is a bad time, I know. Your father . . . and now Alfrida. Truly, it's better that we make no fuss over her."

"Why?" She had to say something. Were his eyes warmer?

"If he sends her home, she'll be safe. If he keeps her, then when the king's forces come and we take back the place, she'll be free. If he thinks she's a valuable hostage, however, she'll be in more danger."

"Oh, that makes sense." It did. Even her tangled mind saw that.

He suddenly drew her into his arms. *Precious baby Jesus, it's working!* "What is it, then? Some other trouble?"

She rested against his strong chest, breathing in his scent, which she would recognize anywhere, though she'd not realized it, feeling as if their bodies were two parts of a whole, split and now rejoined. "Nothing special," she muttered. "Just everything."

"True." He rested his head against hers. If she turned her head up, would he kiss her? Properly, this time?

"I wish . . ." he began, but then fell silent.

She did look up at him then, at lines that hadn't been there six months before, at beauty that was eternal. "You wish?"

Kiss me, Raef.

He gazed at her a moment, but then he firmly pushed her away from him. "Wishes are for children, and we're neither of us children anymore. Anyway," he said with a twisted smile, his eyes sliding away from hers, "we've worked so well to lessen the fear and panic here. We don't want people seeing us clutching one another like that."

Hera saw the stablemen watching, grinning. "I don't think they think we're clutching one another out of fear."

"What else?"

It was flat, absolute, and blocked any response. It shouted that he still didn't see her as anything but a friend.

Feeling fifteen again, with her hair plaited with ribbons and her prettiest gown on and still ignored, Hera tried to rescue her pride. "They don't know that," she said with a joking smile. "But you're right. Can't show any panic or fear."

"That's my wolf." He turned and went back to the horse.

Hera very carefully did not watch him, and turned to stroll

casually toward the hall, willing tears to stay inside, and lips not to tremble.

She *never* cried!

In the first private corner, she leaned against a wall and squeezed her eyes tight against impossible tears that threatened anyway. Why did she never learn? Raef thought of her as a sister, and that would never change.

She clutched the jewel under her garments. What of this, then? Was it to bring her some other man? Never! She didn't want any other man. If she couldn't have Raef, she'd stay unmarried all her days.

What of the Star, then? Why had it come to her?

She needed guidance, and hurried over to the small stone chapel, a holy, peaceful place. She put one of the thick pads on the ground in front of the altar, and knelt to pray.

Is this the Star? she asked.

She could answer that herself. It must be.

What am I supposed to do with it?

She began silent, familiar prayers, letting them open her mind as she waited for an answer.

Then, it was as if a voice spoke. A woman's voice, soft and gentle. Mary's voice?

You must take the Star to Alfrida.

For a moment, Hera rebelled. No! It was *hers*. Hers to capture Raef.

But then she bent her head and accepted bitter bread. She didn't need a heavenly voice to tell her that Raef was not for her. She'd just tested it, hadn't she?

Of course the star was for Alfrida. If she'd been here, Alfrida would have been cleaning the fish.

Furthermore, Alfrida was in a better situation to bring peace to this area. If the Dane fell in love with her and married her, he'd want to make peace with her family. That meant he'd have to surrender Acklingham. Which would help keep Raef from killing him, especially if Raef could be convinced that Torkil hadn't raped Edith.

Even though he must have.

She was beginning to think these tasks beyond even a miraculous pendant, and formed a simpler picture.

Once out of Acklingham, the Dane would leave this area. Perhaps he'd go to Sheppey, where the Vikings had their principal winter encampment on this side of the sea. That would separate him and Raef, though it would presumably mean that Alfrida would have to go and live with the enemy.

She began to try to plot ways around that, then realized this was hardly a pious response. She had to trust in God's mercy and wisdom.

"Thy will be done, O Lord," she said, crossing herself and rising to bow to the altar. "Dear Mother of God, pray for us all."

She left the chapel, only then realizing how difficult a task she faced. *You must take the star to Alfrida.* All very well, but how? Was she to walk into a nest of Viking pirates, and deliver it?

It was just the sort of thing Christ and His mother expected of people. She swallowed panic and muttered another, "Thy will be done, O Lord."

One thing was certain. If Raef guessed her plans, she'd end up locked in her room like Alfrida!

The day had cleared a little, but the sun was low. Not long to full dark on the longest night of the year. If she was to travel to Acklingham today, she must leave now.

She couldn't help searching the sky like the peasants, looking for a hint of Christ's coming. She shook her head. Silly. Would Christ's mother have told her to take the jewel to Alfrida if within hours her son was coming to bring the Last Judgment?

Safe from that, at least, she hurried into the hall, keeping an eye out for Raef, the only person likely to interfere with her movements. He must still be in the stables, and she must trust Mary to keep him there. Deep inside was direct fear of the Danes, but that wasn't something she needed to face now, and she tried very hard to put true faith in God. Her task was to get out of Froxton without raising the alarm.

She dressed in her warm cloak and mittens, then headed toward the gates. No one guarded them when they were closed, for the watchman would alert everyone if people approached. She should be able to unlock the smaller portal and leave with no difficulty.

When she was close, however, she met the laundrywoman, a basket of wet washing on her back. "Going out this late, Lady Wulfhera? Dark's coming."

Though her heart started to flutter nervously, she'd prepared for this. "Just down to the mill, Hilda. A problem with the flour we just received."

"That miller. Bone idle, he is," the woman muttered. The laundrywomen were generally in a foul mood at this time of year, and with reason. It was hard to get things dry, and working with wet cloth in cold weather was penance work. Hilda said a God-go-with-you, however, adding, "You take care not to be benighted out there, lady."

Hera hurried on, feeling guilty for making an unfair accusation about the miller, even though he was lazy and too fond of drink. She'd make reparations later.

In moments, she was through the gate, and crossing the wooden bridge over the ditch. She walked briskly down the track toward the river and the mill. If anyone was watching, her mission would look innocent.

Near the watermill, however, the road forked. One branch led to Tildwold, and the other to Acklingham, further down the river. There were a number of coracles tied up below the mill and she thought about taking one. The river was running fast, however, and she wasn't particularly skilled with the small, round leather boats. Near Acklingham, the river was tidal, too, and she didn't know when the tide came in.

No, she would have to walk, and make haste.

She set off, breath puffing white into the cool air. She prayed that the watchman wouldn't see her, or wouldn't find it strange and alert Raef. If only she'd been able to take a horse. As it was, if he came after her on horseback, she'd have no chance.

She couldn't help hoping he'd come after, hopeless though it was.

Though the weather had stayed dull, it had warmed a little and the ground wasn't so hard beneath her feet. In places she even had to skirt puddles of mud. The land around her was still deadly quiet, however, apart from the harsh cawing of the crows.

She knew the deserted feeling was nothing unusual. It was a quiet time of the year, and any people who'd been out in the fields and woods were heading home before dark, especially with Danish raiders in the area. Still, as the light slowly faded, she felt dismally alone in a harsh world.

Clutching the pendant through her clothes, she prayed to the Blessed Virgin for protection. It was she, after all, who had sent Hera on this mission.

It would take an hour to walk to Acklingham. Time—too much time—to think of a future as bleak as wintertime in Kent. If she survived this, what was she to do? It was more than her soul could take to live here with Raef nearby forever, perhaps watching him take another wife. And yet, she had no true devotion to the religious life.

With a wry laugh, she thought she could understand Raef's bleak outlook. At times, the end of the world seemed positively attractive.

Then, Acklingham came in sight, a solid, wood-walled manor set near the river. Again she wondered how it had been taken, even with Raef, his father, and most of his men away with the king. Some trick, she supposed, but they would have had a system to guard against that.

Had the Danes come by water? The river was navigable to here. As she speeded her steps, she glimpsed boats anchored on the river beyond the palisade. A few small fishing boats— and two Viking longboats. Proof of what she had to face.

A bend in the road gave a new angle, and she saw that the dragon prows indeed had crosses on top of them. She didn't think that would make much difference to her fate. Christian men seemed as able as pagans to be cruel.

Her faith in the Star of the Magi faltered and her steps slowed. Was she really planning to walk into a den of Viking raiders?

She stopped.

In her own silence, she heard thunder behind her and whirled to see Raef hurtling toward her on horseback. Her purpose surged back in full strength, and she thought that perhaps her purpose was as much to escape Raef as to reach the gates! After a quick, frantic glance around, however, she didn't run.

That would be pointless.

Instead, she waved at Acklingham and screamed, *"Help! Help!"*

A moment later, Raef was off his horse beside her and had her tight in one arm. "By Saint Peter's Keys, what do you think you're doing?"

"Going to Alfrida."

"Why?"

"I have a reason!" She pushed against his unbreakable hold. "Let me go, Raef."

"Never." He began to drag her toward the horse. "Is everyone in the world mad? Or are you just mad for Danes like she is?"

"Don't be ridiculous." She kicked, she squirmed, she fought, all without daunting him. "I have a *purpose* there!"

"What purpose?" He turned her roughly toward him and for the first time in her life she saw true, burning fury in his eyes.

For the first time, she feared him.

She feared for him twice as much. He was unarmed except for his sword. No shield. No mail. "Raef, I called for help. They'll be coming."

"Then they'll come to my sword."

"No! Leave! This is nothing to do with you."

"Only if we leave together."

"I can't do that. I have a holy mission."

He focused on her for the first time. *"What?"*

She didn't want to tell him, but she realized she must. He was holding her so her back was to Acklingham, but she thought she heard the distant sounds of men gathering or emerging.

"The Star of the Magi," she said rapidly. "I have it. I have to take it to Alfrida. The Blessed Virgin said so."

Anger left him, but pain remained. "Oh, Hera. Not you, too. What is this madness that flies around like a contagion?"

"It's not madness!" The sounds were growing louder. "Go, Raef! Leave me here. I'll come to no harm. Mary will protect me."

Instead, he picked her up and flung her astride the wild-eyed horse, leaping up behind her, arms around her to the reins. Seeing the riders coming, she tried to slide off, but he had her in a pincer grip. "Raef. Stop this! Let me go to my own fate."

"Never." He'd dragged the horse around toward Froxton, but then, insanely, he turned it back. "If God is kind," he almost purred, "this is Torkil Ravenbringer."

"Raef . . . !" Madness like contagion indeed. He couldn't mean to face six men alone.

Of course he could.

Doubtless the big, red-haired man on the leading horse was Alfrida's Dane, but he was followed by five others, carrying ax or spear. Sick with dread, Hera stopped struggling so that at least Raef could defend himself.

She began to pray.

He drew his sword, but the Vikings surrounded them beyond sword length.

Grinning through a thick beard, the leader spoke. "The woman cried for help."

Raef was controlling the uneasy horse mainly with his legs. Hera took the reins and helped.

"She is mad," Raef said. "I am taking her to safety."

The Dane gestured toward the wooden palisade. "Here is safety, close at hand."

"Safety from you, Torkil Ravenbringer."

"Ah. You must be Raefnoth Eldrunson."

They were like two snarling, circling dogs, except that one was in fury, the other amused.

Hera had her mission, and she knew what she had to do, though it would be like a spear wound to Raef. "I did cry for help," she said to the Dane. "I am Wulfhera of Froxton and I wish to visit my sister, Alfrida, to be sure you are treating her well."

It struck all the men silent, as well it might. It was an extraordinary claim, and must indeed seem completely mad.

Then Torkil threw back his head and roared with laughter. "Two peas in a pod. Of course you must be Alfrida's sister. Come then."

His approach was halted by Raef's sword. "Over my dead body."

The Dane remained calm, as well he might with such a superior force. "This one's yours, is she? Then you have my word she'll return to you safely. I have need of your manor, not of your woman."

"She is *not* my woman," Raef snarled. Hera knew it was stupid to be hurt by that, but she was. "She is simply under my protection."

Torkil's eyes turned to Hera, and she saw they twinkled with amusement. She'd never imagined that a Danish raider's eyes might twinkle. "What now, sister of my bedmate?"

"I need to go to Alfrida," she said, as steadily as she could, stuck literally in the middle of this male confrontation. "But you must not hurt Raef."

"He said you were not his woman."

"We're friends. We've been friends all our lives."

"Ah. And he was the husband of the timorous Edith."

Hera heard Raef growl and felt his body become hard, vengeful muscle. She wondered why men could be relied upon always to say the thing most likely to make a matter worse rather than better.

Perhaps they simply liked things worse.

"You didn't harm Edith," she said as a fact to the Viking. She didn't make the mistake of thinking him harmless, but she couldn't imagine this man raping a terrified woman, or even being interested in trembling Edith.

"Never touched her," Torkil agreed, but, she thought with a chill, perhaps something uneasy lurked behind his eyes.

"You lie," snarled Raef, and his sword jabbed out as if it might reach the other man.

"Why should I lie?" Torkil asked, lip beginning to curl in a snarl as well. "If I'd wanted her, I'd have taken her, and felt no shame at it. But she was *nithing,* that one. Why do you fight over her memory? She betrayed you. She gave me your manor out of fear, then whined at everything."

Hera expected Raef's enraged denial, but she heard nothing but another speechless growl.

Edith had surrendered Acklingham to the Danes?

"You should have married this one," Torkil said, with a nod of his head toward Hera, "or her sister. They're real women."

Raef howled and kicked the horse toward his enemy. Hera threw herself forward to clutch the horse's neck, both to hold on and to get out of the way of the swishing sword. Hell take the two of them!

She twisted her head to see what was going on. Torkil was backing his horse, but his sword was out, too, and soon he'd have to fight.

Enough of this.

Muttering a mixture of prayers and curses, Hera grabbed

her eating knife from the sheath on her belt. Then, with one hand tangled firmly in the horse's rough mane, she jabbed the mount in the withers with the knife. It squealed and reared. She managed to stay on. On the hindquarters, already unbalanced by the weight of the sword and his attempts to get at his enemy, Raef didn't have a chance.

He was good, though. Upright now, and struggling to control the horse, Hera saw him roll so his sword didn't harm him, and bounce onto his feet already beginning a mighty swipe at Torkil's horse's legs. Hera stroked the neck of her shuddering, foaming mount and watched as one of Torkil's men swung his spear handle to crack against Raef's head.

He crumpled to the ground. She thought perhaps he'd forgotten there was anyone in the universe other than himself and Torkil Ravenbringer, the man who had said such cruel things about his wife.

Cruel but true?

She slid off the horse and went to him. "Raef," she said, in despair, running her fingers gently over the wound. Under her breath, she whispered, "He's right, though. Edith was *nithing*."

It was a word usually used to describe a man who abandoned his lord in battle, who fled his duties out of fear. At heart, however, it meant "coward," and she saw now that Edith had always been not gentle, but a coward.

She'd doubtless gone to the river out of cowardice, though not, surely, for fear of Raef.

"Not his woman, eh?" said Torkil, his big boots appearing on the road by Raef's head. His hand under her arm raised her firmly to face him. Alfrida was right. He was big. Hera had to look a long way up.

"Come along, Wulfhera of Froxton, and let us see what we can make of all this."

At his command, Raef was tied hand and foot and slung over the saddle of his horse. Hera winced, but there was no point in protesting the rough treatment. She was put up behind him to make sure he didn't fall off. Once mounted, Torkil took the reins. Be he good man or bad, they were still his prisoners.

Raef came around before they were inside Acklingham—he groaned, but he didn't say anything. Hera tried to tell herself it didn't matter if he hated her. She'd assessed that danger before she'd spooked the horse. It might be a blessing, in fact, since she couldn't live with him as just a friend.

It didn't help.

She could only hope she'd not have to face him for a long, long time.

It was strange to enter the familiar grounds of Raef's home and find it invaded, yet unchanged. If Edith had opened the gates and let the Danes in it had been a dishonorable act, but one that had preserved the place. Hera was further eased by the sight of Alfrida running toward her, hair flowing in one wild mass, but clearly unhurt in body or spirit.

"Hera, you idiot!" Alfrida cried, sweeping her into a hug as soon as she was on the ground. "What are you doing here?" Then she looked beyond and her eyes widened. "Is that *Raef*?"

Hera turned to see Torkil's men cutting the bonds on Raef's ankles and setting him on his feet, more than ready for any attempt to trip them. He did nothing and stayed grimly silent. At one point, his eyes passed over Hera.

As if she didn't exist.

Hera shuddered. "Don't ask how we came to this state, for I don't know."

With another hug, Alfrida led her toward the manor house.

Hera went, but then she turned back to fix Torkil with a stare. "Don't hurt him."

He laughed, but for some reason she felt sure that Raef was safe for now. Of course, whether she'd be safe from Raef after all this was a different matter. She remembered the blind fury in his eyes. And that was before he'd truly fallen into a rage, and before she'd betrayed him as badly as Edith had.

Sweet Mary Mother, she prayed, *I don't think this was your plan. But guard him anyway. And guard him from hurting me.*

The chief hall here was one story, and as Alfrida led Hera inside, she asked, "What are you doing here? This is crazy."

In fact, it was beginning to seem so, and Hera half feared to find the Star gone, or to take it out and see a piece of iron set with glass. Perhaps she had imagined it all. But when she shed her cloak and pulled the leather thong out from under her dress, the Star was there, in all its eerie beauty.

"What's that?" Alfrida asked, lips parted with wonder. "It's beautiful!"

Hera found she didn't want to let it go, didn't want absolutely to give up her dream, but she pulled it off over her head and passed it to her sister. "It's the Star of the Magi. I found it in a fish."

"The . . . the what?"

"The Star of the Magi! You remember. Melchior, Miriam, Star!"

"*That* star?"

"That star. Look at it. Look into the stone."

Alfrida raised the pendant into the fading light. "Oh," she breathed. "It's like magic." But then she looked at Hera. "Why are you giving it to me?"

"It's meant for you. Don't ask why or how. I just know it. It's to make Torkil love you." She saw the big Dane come into the hall, so bit back the words about peace. Having seen him and Raef together, the idea of peace short of death was becoming ridiculous.

He strode over, bigger than Raef, but not more beautiful. Though he was not much older, his face was craggier and marked by a vicious scar on his temple. He casually plucked the Star from Alfrida's hand, and Alfrida did nothing to stop him.

Oh, no. Would the Blessed Virgin expect her to fight a Viking for it?

"A well-made piece," he said, assessing it with a pirate's eye. "And worth a bagful of money. What is it doing here?"

"Hera brought it for me," Alfrida said, not seeming to mind his taking it. Besotted fool! "A gift."

When he looked at Hera, Torkil's blue eyes were somewhat suspicious. "So, Wulfhera of Froxton, why such a hazardous journey to bring your sister a yule gift?"

Hera quickly thought up a lie. "It's a tradition of ours. The older sister gives it to the younger on the eldest's twentieth birthday." Surely there'd be no reason for Alfrida to deny the story, or to tell Torkil that Hera's birthday was in March.

Alfrida held her tongue, but the Dane still looked suspicious. And why not? It was a foolish tale. He put the pendant over Alfrida's head, however, so the Star shone brightly against her red gown.

Hera said a short prayer of thanks. She should have trusted heaven. Now all should be well.

"Happy birthday, Hera," Alfrida said, with a private, dis-believing look.

Hera decided she might as well play her part of concerned sister to the full. "Do you wish to stay here, Alfrida? I'm sure if you wanted to return to Froxton, Lord Torkil would not stop you."

"A Viking give up the spoils of war?" the Dane remarked.

Hera suddenly turned to him. "Did you tell the truth? About Edith?"

"You shouldn't question a man's word, woman."

"Very well. I believe you. So tell the truth about this. What did happen to Edith?"

He bellowed for ale, and it was rushed to him in a huge, ornate drinking horn which he half drained in one gulp. "That weeping, wingeing, whiffle of a woman. I never expected to take Acklingham. Raid a few of the outlying places. Perhaps squeeze a bit of tribute to go away. But no. At the first burning building, she orders the gates flung open and greets me on her knees, pleading that no one be hurt. What kind of behavior is that?"

Hera and Alfrida shared a glance. Hera wondered if Raef knew this story, or believed it. Surely he'd have to believe it. It was so typical of Edith. Not complete cowardice—it doubt-less had taken courage to face Torkil and plead for peace. More like stupidity. A weakness of mind that quailed over little sufferings and thus got mired in greater ones.

She also noted a distinct complaint in Torkil's voice. Was it possible that he didn't really want Acklingham and the trou-ble it brought him?

"But who raped her?" Hera asked, surprised to find herself talking to the Dane as if he were a reasonable man, astonished to find that perhaps she might like him.

"None of my men. For my own honor's sake, I kept to her terms. No one here has been hurt. Some of us, it is true, have found sweet bed companions," he said, with a smile at Alfrida, "but not by force."

Hera wanted to scold her sister for accepting such a descrip-tion, and she wondered when the Star would start working and make him fall in love. "Who, then?" she asked.

"She ran away," he said, finishing the ale and wiping his hairy mouth with his big hand. "I admit I didn't stop her. I'd planned to keep her as a useful hostage against the time Raefnoth came to attack, so we'd get extra gold before retreat. But by Woden, the woman wearied me. Not only did she not want rape here, she didn't want any unblessed unions. She was constantly at my feet, weeping and wailing and begging me to enforce Christian rules. As if this was a monastery, and we all monks!''

He looked not so much angry as bewildered. ''And she couldn't bear to see food that looked like an animal. No leg or rib, even. She screamed when offered a fish with the head still on, and fainted right into her dish when the cooks brought out a boar's head. Since the day she came to be lady here, or so they tell me, no one had eaten anything but sliced meats or stews. Mad. And her husband was witless not to have beaten it out of her.''

Hera had never realized Edith's squeamishness had gone that far, though she did remember once finding her throwing up because of the pigs roasting on spits for a feast. Had Raef known? Clearly his love had been strong enough to overlook all her faults.

''You're saying that she ran away because of this and was attacked somewhere between here and Froxton?''

''That's all I can say. My fault in it, if there is one, is in letting her go. But she should have been in little danger. You made the trip without harm, as did Alfrida. It's typical of that woman that she couldn't even walk a league safely. Even so, I gather she didn't die of it.''

''She did. It drove her to kill herself.''

''Women's talk. Her body recovered and her man was ready to take her back. What cause to hasten death? Enough of this. The thought of her sours my stomach.''

Hera could argue with him about the effects of rape, but what was the point? She believed his story, but she doubted Raef would. Was there any chance of ending this without bloodshed?

She'd try the direct way first.

''Thank you for telling me,'' she said. ''Now I have done what I came here to do, you can let me and Thegn Raefnoth go.''

He laughed. ''You think me as big a fool as Edith? You're two big fat bags of gold if nothing else, and you'll both spend the night here while I consider your price. But to show good will, Little Sister,''—he reached out and tweaked one of her long plaits—''I'll let you join our yule feast.''

It was definitely not the time to tell him Raef was determined not to pay a penny more to the Danes. What would happen when he found out, however? She sent a few more prayers for a miracle.

''Yule?'' she said, trying to think of a way to change things. ''I thought you were Christian, Lord Torkil.''

''Even for Christians, the wheel turns. It is nature's way, and there is no sin in celebrating nature.''

''But for Christians, it is still Advent. I am fasting.''

He smiled, but it no longer held a twinkle. ''It is not for you to choose whether to feast or fast here, Wulfhera of Froxton.''

''I am a true Christian, Torkil Ravenbringer. I will keep the Advent fast until Christmas Day.''

''I am a true Christian, too, Wulfhera of Froxton, and *we* celebrate Yule. And you will feast with us.'' He was no longer smiling at all.

''You cannot make me eat more than I choose!''

''I can make you eat your toes,'' he roared, ''if I wish to!''

Hera gulped and stepped back, making the sign of the Cross. How could she have forgotten what he was? She could well imagine him chopping off her toes and forcing them into her mouth.

''Torkil,'' Alfrida said, taking hold of his big, tense arm, and cooing at him. ''Don't let Hera anger you. She's a postulant to the convent at Herndon, and takes these religious matters very seriously. And you know,'' she said, placing a hand on his big chest, ''I'd be very unhappy if you mistreated her.''

Hera watched, expecting rage at this blatant manipulation, perhaps even a blow. But the big man melted. That was the only way to describe it. His bunched muscles relaxed, and the smile came back, making his thick moustache twitch and ripple as he looked dotingly down at Alfrida.

The Star, Hera thought. Now shining on Alfrida's breast, it was working. Blessed Mary be thanked.

But then another thought poked her mind. Would the Star

have worked for her if she had worn it openly? Would Raef have looked so dotingly—

"A nun, eh?" Torkil's voice broke into her wistful thoughts, and for all his sweetness to Alfrida, he didn't sound particularly mellow about Hera. "A nun and yet so fond of a man? What is Thegn Raefnoth to you, Lady Wulfhera?"

Hera knew her face was red. "A dear friend."

"You're a fool or a liar, woman. And you will not feast?"

She thought of giving in, tempted by pure weariness, but it would be a sin of cowardice. Like Edith. "I will not."

He snorted with displeasure, but it didn't sound vicious. "I'll have no long faces at my feasting table, Little Nun. Ho!" At his bellow, two burly men rushed up. "Seize her!"

Even Alfrida cried a protest, but he ignored them both.

"Advent is a time for penance, eh, Sister? Yule, the turning of the sun, is a good time to find out where your calling truly lies. Go spend time with the dear friend you overruled and betrayed. If he beats you, it will save me the trouble."

"What? No!" But Hera's screamed protests did no good as she was forced toward the hall door, feet scrabbling to run in the other direction. She threw a pleading look toward her sister, but knew Alfrida couldn't change this.

Her sister did run over, however, pulling off the Star. She flung it over Hera's head. "Pray Mary it protects you!"

"No, Alfrida!" Hera cried, terrified for her sister without the Star's powers, but she was already being virtually carried across the muddy yard toward a shed.

She looked at it with horror, heart racing with panic. They couldn't lock her in with Raef! They couldn't.

He truly might kill her for what she'd done!

They could. One big man easily confined her, while the other lifted the iron bar that sealed the door. There was already a third man standing guard, so when her captor shoved her into the dark shed, she had no chance to do anything except try to keep on her feet. The door thumped shut behind her, and the bar rattled solidly into place.

"Well, well." It was Raef's bitter voice. "The traitorous wolf."

The walls were split-logs, well caulked, but narrow vents had been left up near the eaves. They let in a glimmer of the evening light, showing an empty room, and his shape, sitting against one wall. Watching him as if he were a dangerous animal, she edged toward the opposite wall, as far away as possible, and sank down to sit on the earthen floor there.

All her life she'd never feared Raef, but now she knew she deserved his anger, even though she felt sure in her conscience that she'd done the right thing.

"I had to get the Star to Alfrida, Raef. I told you that."

"And now that you've done it, is the world a better place?"

"It's working. Torkil dotes on her." She put her hand, however, to the jewel now hanging around her own neck. Was Alfrida safe?

"Then why are you here?"

She couldn't fully explain. She certainly couldn't tell him of Torkil's strange words about finding out where her true calling lay. "I refused to join in the Yule feast, and this is his punishment." She rubbed the smooth stone between fingers and thumb, worrying about her sister. In the story, however, Miriam had let the stone go once all was right with her world. Did it only need to work once?

"With the help of the Star," she said, almost to herself, "perhaps Alfrida can persuade him to let us go. In the morning."

She hardly saw Raef move before he slammed into her, hands biting into her shoulders. Her head bashed against the wall as he drove her to the floor.

"Raef—" she choked out.

"Persuade!" he snarled, shaking her so her teeth clashed. "*Let us go!* If not for you, he'd be dead, or I would. Honorably!"

"Stop it! You'll live to fight again. To—"

"*I'm a prisoner in my own home!*" But he flung himself away to crouch nearby, hands over head. "Brought here bound and gagged," he muttered. "I'd rather be dead."

"Raef, I'm sorry. . . . " Hera sat up, wincing, rubbing her bruised shoulders, but with no solace for a heart in pieces. What had she done to him?

"But I can't wish you dead," she whispered, thinking perhaps she was as silly as Edith at heart. "I can never wish that. And . . ." She hesitated about saying it, but perhaps it would help. "I was told to bring the Star of the Magi here to Alfrida. I think it was the Holy Mother speaking."

He slowly pushed to his feet, facing away. "That's just an old story you put into a song."

"The stone does look as if a star is trapped inside." She lifted the stone and looked down, but the light had faded almost to nothing by now, and even the Star of the Magi showed no fire. She let it drop to hang against her chest. "And I found it in a fish."

He turned to her, and as best as she could tell his fury was either burned out or controlled. "Women's folly, Hera. Besides, if it was that magical Star of the Magi, and you found it, why wouldn't it be intended for you?"

Perhaps it was, she thought. Perhaps I didn't have the courage to wear it openly. She couldn't bear to tell him she'd tried it on him, and it had failed.

"I'm to be a nun," she lied. "I went to pray about it in the chapel, and Blessed Mary spoke, telling me to bring it here to Alfrida. That's why I had to come, why I couldn't let you stop me."

He slid down so he was sitting with his head in his hands, but at least he hadn't put the full room between them. "All is madness. I'd never have believed that you'd betray me."

She bit her lip and swallowed tears. "I had my mission." She knew she mustn't say that she'd wanted to protect him, too. "Your head must hurt." She rubbed hers, still sore from bashing against the wall.

He didn't even respond to that. "So, what does the Dane plan now?"

"Ransom, I think."

"I suppose your family will pay for you. Without Acklingham I have little, and I'll not give the Danes a penny more."

She hadn't imagined he'd change on that. "Then we'd better escape."

Though the room was almost completely dark now, she saw him look up, saw a hint of the shine of his eyes. "If you tell me there's no guard outside, I'll know the world truly has gone mad."

"There's a guard," she admitted.

"Who wouldn't notice us prying off the boards with our fingernails, or smashing through the gridwork?"

His sarcasm made her grit her teeth, but she tried to speak

calmly and reasonably. "They're feasting tonight. For Yule. Perhaps they'll be less vigilant."

"Hera, I'd *really* hate to think that Acklingham was taken by a weak leader and a fool."

"It wasn't *taken*," she snapped, irritation breaking free. "It was given to them by Edith!"

She braced for another attack, but after a moment, he wearily said, "I know."

She longed to go to him then and offer comfort, but that would be folly for a great many reasons. Instead, she asked the awkward question that was nagging at her. "Is that why she killed herself? Because you berated her?"

But he said, "I never mentioned it. What point?"

Then why? Why would a woman with Raef for a husband, with her health returning and her husband forgiving and cherishing her, why would she throw herself into the river?

"I shouldn't have left her alone in Acklingham," he said, so quietly she could hardly hear.

The shed was pitch dark now. Distantly, she could hear music, and perhaps singing voices. The feast. A clink reminded her that a guard still sat by their door.

"I should have sent her back to Tildwold, to her family, before leaving to fight."

"You didn't expect Acklingham to be so vulnerable. In fact, it wasn't. It could have held Torkil off with little damage."

"But I knew what Edith was like. I should have thought what would happen if it was attacked."

"She was trying to save your people from hurt." Why was she defending Edith? "She made Torkil promise not to harm anyone, and he claims to have kept his word."

"By heaven, Hera, there's more to life than avoiding hurt!"

She flinched at his new anger. That fury simmered under very fragile control. She'd perhaps be wiser to keep silent, to pretend to go to sleep, but she sensed Raef needed to talk, that she might be able to help.

"I know," she said soothingly. "I'm just trying to see it from her point of view."

"You couldn't," he stated. "Never in another millennium. She made no sense to me." She thought maybe he was shaking his head. "She even wept over a rat caught by a dog."

Questions frothed in Hera's mind, mainly the crucial one—

why, then? Why marry her? She fought them back.

He suddenly said, "You must wonder why I married her."

Hera made some vague sound, not sure now if she wanted to know.

"I don't know," he said. "Strange not to know such an important thing. She was pretty, of course. Her nervousness made me feel like a mighty god, and when I was tender with her, I felt like a saint. She adored me. I think that's the truth. Do all men secretly long to be gods?"

"I don't think women want to be goddesses."

"I think women like you are goddesses. Hard for a man to match."

She wished she could see his face, but if ever there was a time of honesty, it was now, as the world turned from dark to light, as the thousand years approached, and their lives hung in the balance.

"Are you saying you're afraid of me, Raef?" she teased.

Clearly she'd misjudged, for only silence replied. But then, he said softly, "Afraid of not being a god in your eyes. You know me too well, Hera. All my faults."

"And all I know is good." Oh, by the ancient gods, she was tired of living a lie. "I love you, Raef," she said. "I've loved you for years. Isn't that as good as being worshipped?"

He didn't say anything, and she'd have given her right arm for light then. What was his reaction? Surprise? Shock? Dismay? Embarrassment to equal her own?

"But," he said at last, slowly, "you plan to be a nun."

"No longer. I liked many things about the convent life, but that's no reason to take vows. I have no calling. Oh Raef," she burst out. "You can't be such a fool! I went to Herndon because you married Edith, and for no other reason!"

Then she put her hand over her mouth, wincing at her own scathing words. She'd been trying to be reasonable and pleasant.

"Oh, God . . ." Then he was by her side, touching her. "Hera, I am a fool. Are all men fools? I didn't know until you left. I didn't know what Edith was like until we married. . . ." His fingers found her cheek and traced up and down there. "I didn't know."

It seemed incredible to her, too. "Didn't you ever feel anything physical for me, Raef? I lusted after you sinfully and often.''

His forehead touched hers. "It felt wrong. You were almost a sister to me. You were young. I thought you'd kill me if I touched you in the ways I wanted to touch you. . . .''

Still scarcely daring to hope, she asked, "What ways?''

His hand slid to cover her breast. "This way." His thumb began to rub over her nipple.

"Oh.'' Her heart was pounding. "Any other ways?''

But then, abruptly, he was gone. Gone somewhere in the dark room, not touching her at all.

"Raef? What's the matter?''

"By heaven, Hera, this is no time for this! Did you think I would dishonor you here in this dank, dark shed, with my home in enemy hands?''

Sheer relief made her grin. "The thought did cross my mind, yes.''

And he laughed, though he choked it off. "Stop it.''

"Stop what?''

"Driving me mad.''

" 'Tis the season for madness, I think.'' She stood and moved forward, groping around for him. "Raef?''

He was silent, though, so as not to give his location away. Was it a serious attempt to avoid her, or a game? For Hera, this was no game, and she'd find him whether he wanted to avoid her or not.

"I love you, Raef,'' she said, sweeping the silent space with her hands, and hunting him with her words. "I trust you to marry me if it becomes necessary, and whatever happens to-morrow, I want you, here, tonight.'' Her fingers brushed cloth, but he escaped before she could grasp him.

In about the center of the shed, she stopped still. She'd never catch him this way.

There were other ways.

"I'm taking off my belt,'' she said, unbuckling it and letting it fall to the floor. It was leather with a metal buckle, and held her pouch and knife. It made a dull thump.

She waited, listening, and if she didn't know better, she could believe she was alone.

"Now I'm taking off my tunic.'' She pulled it off over her head. "I have my long gown underneath, and my shift beneath that. That's all except my stockings." She kicked off her shoes.

She heard rustling sounds and was tempted to lunge for them, but she knew he could evade her if he still wanted to. She would not chase. She'd make him come to her.

She hoped.

If this didn't work, it was going to be annoyingly embarrassing. She thought back to his words about frightening goddesses. They made no sense to her, but that was apparently why he'd married weak, silly Edith instead of her. Perhaps she'd be wiser to burst into tears and let him comfort her. Perhaps from there she could get what she wanted.

She contemplated it, and decided she simply couldn't. It wasn't in her nature. She so rarely cried that she didn't think tears would come to order. And it would be a horrible simulacrum of Edith.

Edith, whom he hadn't loved, or at least not for long.

It was wicked to feel such fierce joy, but she found that in this mad hour she didn't care about wickedness or virtue, only about Raef.

Here.

Now.

Almost in her grasp.

Despite the chill, she pulled off her thick woolen gown and dropped it on the floor. "I'm only in my shift now. It's cold. Warm me, Raef?"

More rustling noises, but no touch.

She turned again, trying to spot him in the dark, but it was too complete. She stilled instead, trying to hear his breathing, but he must be controlling that better than she was. Her heart was racing and her breath was speeding, too.

Ah, well. Might as well be hanged for a sheep as a lamb. She wriggled out of her knee-length linen shift. "I'm naked now," she said, and when the silence stayed unbroken, she twirled, whirling the garment around so it brushed the walls, and must skim close to the corners. So it might touch him—

It was caught.

Held taut.

Then slowly, naked and vulnerable, she was drawn toward him.

Toward what?

She sensed his warmth a moment before she was crushed against his body. His naked body.

She must have made a querying sound, for he said, "I can at least try to match a goddess, move for move."

Clutching him, his wonderful hard, hot, naked body, she said, "Don't make this a contest!"

"Why not? That was always the most fun with you." Then, hand trapping her hair, he kissed her.

It was like the tainted greeting kiss of the day before, but also profoundly unlike it. Whatever was happening between them now, it was at least honest and lusty. If that was all there was, she'd take it.

His penis was hard between them, and she pressed there, encouraging, welcoming.

"Don't worry. You're not escaping," he said, sweeping her into his arms.

By accident or design, his cloak was spread, ready for her. He put her there, but then left.

"Raef?"

"Just gathering clothing. No need to freeze."

In moments he was back beside her, and he spread their various garments over them to make a haphazard nest. When he lay beside her, she went into his arms as if it was the hundredth time.

Even while kissing her ear, her cheek, her lips, he said, "Someone might come, Hera. To feed us. To torture us. To kill us."

"I don't care."

He laughed. "Neither do I."

He kissed her again, hotly passionate. Oh, heaven, the world could come to an end now and she'd die happy, twined with Raef, sealed mouth to mouth with him.

Well, perhaps it could end not quite yet. . . .

But then he stilled and broke the kiss. "Are you sure, Little Wolf?" His hand slid up to cup her cheek. "It will hurt. Edith—"

He tried to move away. She held him closer. "I am not Edith. Take me. Now."

He stayed tense in her arms. If Edith hadn't already been dead, Hera could have murdered her for what she'd done to Raef.

She knew better than to relax her hold on him, but she tamed her own hungers. "Has there been anyone since Edith?"

"No, of course not."

"And not while you were married." That was a statement of fact. He would have been a faithful husband. Since he didn't seem to be pulling away, she stroked his hair. "Raef, I don't know how it was with her, but all women are not the same. I'm not."

He turned his head and kissed her palm, but it wasn't the sort of kiss she wanted. "She was the first—the only—virgin for me. You can't know...."

He suddenly rolled onto his back, escaping her lax hold, but then he gathered her and pulled her into a tender embrace. Hell take it. She didn't *want* a tender embrace.

"It was so terrible for her," he said, rocking her. "The first few times, even. More than a few. I had to do it. We couldn't not do it forever. She agreed. She didn't object...."

She just suffered, Hera completed for herself, suppressing a growl. And made sure he knew it. She could point out that Alfrida had lost her maidenhead to Torkil and come running back for more, but she didn't think mention of their captor would help at this moment.

"Many women are lusty," she said, "and they all lost their maidenhead at one time."

"But at least within marriage. We'll wait, Hera. We'll marry...."

"When? Perhaps Christ will come tonight!"

"Stop that. You don't believe that."

She eased across, so she was lying half over him. She didn't know what to do to overcome his reluctance, but she'd try. "I believe it's right for us to do this, Raef. I'm not afraid. I want it."

"Adults are not governed by wants."

"But they can grasp them if it's right to."

"It's not right. We're not married." His hands settled at her waist, controlling her, but she managed to wriggle a little closer. Her leg brushed against something and she realized he was still hard.

"You still want me."

"Of course I do! I've wanted you since you walked into

the hall. I nearly died of wanting while I warmed your frozen feet. I've wanted you . . .''

He thrust her off him, and in a moment she was alone with only his lingering warmth on the cloth beneath her.

For a few moments, she did not breathe at all. He'd been about to say that he'd wanted her during his marriage to Edith. She could imagine how much that must hurt a man of honor. A man of honor whom she ached for.

She sat up, gathering his cloak around her shoulders, seeking words that would break his resistance, his fears, and his sense that this was a sin. Perhaps his sense that his desire for her was a sin.

The darkness blinded her, however. It stole all sense of his feelings and his pain. Was he angry, or in despair? Was he longing or tangled in other matters?

Was he lost in memories of Edith, whom he must have loved at some point, and who had been his wife? Marriage alone formed a bond. Would Edith always come between them? Did thought of Edith's rape mix in with his desire for her, making it impossible?

An ache around her eyes gave her a new weapon. ''I'll cry.''

''What?'' She could imagine his expression of disbelief.

''I will.''

''You never cry.''

''I'm sure you cried over Edith.''

''That was—''

''Different. This is different.'' Suddenly she was speaking the blunt truth, all deception forgotten. ''The world's already turned. Father, Edmund, Edith, Alfrida . . . I've been saying cheerfully that Christ is not coming, but I don't know! Perhaps He is, and I suppose He'll take me to heaven. I've not committed too many sins, and I've spent the past half year praying and doing good works.''

''All the more reason not to—''

''But even if Christ doesn't come, *my* world has turned awry! And you're probably going to fight Torkil. And . . .'' Her voice genuinely broke. ''And I just want one thing right. I know it will be right, Raef. . . .''

She felt his closeness, then his hand touched her arm, and he drew her close. ''Ah, don't, Hera. Don't! If you cry, the world will truly have come to an end.'' His lips brushed her cheeks and she thought, she hoped, they found them dry, even though perhaps tears would complete her conquest.

She didn't want that kind of conquest. She just wanted Raef.

She held him as tight as he held her, kissing whatever skin came close to her mouth.

The heat of his body would have been enough, but she was tangled in the warmth and textures of their clothes—in linens smooth and rough, in wool and embroidery and the occasionally soft toughness of leather.

In the hall, a drumming started, and she kissed him to the rhythm of the drum, grasping various parts of his hard-muscled body.

Suddenly pressed to beg him not to put himself in danger, she forced the folly far back into her mind and concentrated on relishing every moment of this miracle. Raef, here, now. Murmuring his delight as he kissed parts of her she'd never imagined kissable. There was a burning need inside her that told her for certain she'd not be like Edith.

She breathed a prayer of thanks, rolling her head back, as she opened herself more to his exciting mouth—

The door slammed open and flaming torches dazzled her, the smoke soon making her eyes sting. She couldn't help but cry out with shock.

"Hell's fires!" Raef bellowed, sitting and swirling covers tightly around them both. "Get out of here!"

Torkil, huge in the doorway and torchlight, rocked with laughter, but he gestured the grinning torchbearer outside, so at least the smoke lessened. "I think you forget who rules Acklingham now, Thegn Raefnoth!"

Raef's indrawn breath rattled like a growl, and Hera flung her arms around him in the faint hope of stopping him from trying to kill the Dane with his bare hands. One thing was sure. Her chance to make love to him had probably just been smashed like ice on a puddle under a cruel boot.

May Torkil Ravenbringer roast in hell!

Only then did she think to be afraid. She looked up at Torkil again, wondering why he was here.

Torture?

Death?

Raef went still, too. "What do you want?"

Torkil spread his hands as if innocent of every sin imaginable. "What is it Christians say? Good will among men. Come to the feast."

"No."

Torkil's beard jutted forward. "It was not a request. I can drag you there naked. Both of you."

Hera realized the Dane was drunk, and thus even more unpredictable. Raef was dangerous through sheer, simmering fury. Even so, she couldn't think of a thing to say that wouldn't make matters worse.

"I will not eat or drink in this place," Raef said, "until it is mine again."

"Then I'll happily watch you starve!" Torkil roared, but then he glanced at Hera, almost pouting. "Blame your sister, Lady Wulfhera. She's been begging me to save you from this terrible man."

"As you can see, there's no need."

"Ah, but didn't you preach Advent to me, Little Nun? Shouldn't I save you from sin?"

"I'd really rather you didn't."

"Alfrida will not believe me. You must come to the hall. Dressed or naked."

The Star's power over him was truly remarkable. "Alfrida will not like to see me dragged into the hall naked, Lord Torkil."

"Yet I will do it."

Clearly that was his limit. Hera wondered what she could possibly say to get Raef to be reasonable.

"Go!" snarled Raef to the Dane. "We will dress."

At the tone, Torkil folded his arms. "We will stay."

"Then—"

Raef stopped because Hera had locked hands and squeezed his chest as hard as possible. It was only momentary surprise, however, so she rushed into speech. "Lord Torkil, I don't think Alfrida wanted you to provide this sort of show of me for your men."

The Dane glanced back at his grinning men, and perhaps he even reddened. He stalked out and slammed the door.

"Don't interfere again," Raef snapped in the dark, pulling out of her arms and standing up.

"I'll do whatever I can to keep us both alive." She was

scrabbling around in the clutter of clothes for the ones that were hers.

"I have no wish to live."

"Well, I want you alive." She realized she was trying to put on his shirt and shoved it toward where he was. He was closer than she thought, so she thumped him.

It felt rather satisfying, despite the sorrowful ache left by his lovemaking. May the imps of hell nibble his toes, and Alfrida's and Torkil's, and . . .

She found her shift and wriggled into it.

And King Ethelred who was letting the Danes run free all around England. And King Olaf of Norway, and King Svend Forkbeard of Denmark, who saw England as a free market-place. . . .

By the time she'd found and struggled into all her clothes, she'd wished pains on most of the rulers of the world, including the pope. Underneath it all, however, churned fear. As soon as Raef and Torkil were face-to-face, they'd be like snarling wolves again, and though her name meant "wolf herder," she doubted she could stop this all coming to bloodshed.

She remembered the Star, and pulled it out. There was nothing in the myth to say it could protect men from their own violent follies. But, she thought, holding it tight, didn't the story imply that the woman who wore it could bring harmony and light into her world?

After they were both dressed, Raef opened the door, flooding the small room with the flaming light of torches and showing Torkil waiting, arms crossed. Hera realized for the first time how much pride was at stake here. Raef's pride was deeply wounded, and Torkil would lose face before his men if he was too weak with these enemy prisoners.

She looked around and found her shoes, thinking there was no hope of a solution. Even if Torkil didn't truly want it, he could never give up a prize like Acklingham. Raef would accept nothing less.

Oh, Alfrida, if you hadn't tried to help, at least I might have had something to cherish.

Raef looked at her, then seized the Star. "Is this . . . ?"

Did he think himself magicked by it? "Yes."

"I thought you said you'd brought it for Alfrida."

"When Torkil sent me here, she gave it to me to protect me from you."

He closed his eyes for a moment. "Hera, you never need protection from me."

She looked at him, and even by torchlight she saw him color.

"I was not myself."

She touched his face. "You had reason to be angry. But now, I think, we must go to the hall. For my sake, don't force a fight."

"I make no promises." He wrapped an arm around her as they left the hut, but it was protective rather than tender. In fact, it was territorial. A claim made by one snarling wolf to another.

At least that was one thing she need not fear. Torkil had no physical interest in her.

Edith lay between the two men, making any kind of peace impossible.

The more she thought about it, however, the more sure she was that Torkil had told the truth. He hadn't raped Edith. Raef would never believe that, however, for who else could it have been? It was far too convenient to blame it on some wandering brigands that no one had seen or heard.

As long as Raef believed Torkil to be guilty, the Dane could go on his knees and beg Raef to take Acklingham back and Raef would still have to try and kill him.

The winter night's wind cut cruelly through her clothes, but the ice inside cut crueler still.

Their escort flung open the big doors to the hall, and a blast of heat, light, and noise hit them as they were hustled in and the doors slammed behind them. All the light here came from the central fire, but what a fire. They'd brought in the huge, traditional Yule log and set it upright to burn like a tree of fire, threatening even the high rafters. The smoke hole above had been enlarged to prevent fire there and to let most of the smoke escape so that the room wouldn't be stifling.

Four men played instruments, and some danced. Other men drank, laughing and talking, many with women on their laps. A few were more intimately engaged still!

Edith would have fainted for sure.

Alfrida leaped up from her place at the big table and ran

toward them in a fire of gold—gold bracelets and arm rings, torques and pendants. A pirate's woman, wearing his hoard. "Hera! Thank Sweet Jesus. Are you all right?"

"Of course. You know Raef would never hurt me." She ignored the memory of his furious attack. She had to add, however, "This might not have been wise, though."

Alfrida glanced at Raef, who seemed to have brought the winter chill into the hot room. "That wasn't my idea. I only wanted you here."

Torkil pulled Alfrida to his side, and considered Hera and Raef. "You still refuse to feast with us?"

Raef didn't answer, so neither did Hera.

"Very well," said Torkil, who clearly still had all his wits, no matter how much he'd drunk so far. "We will feast in another way. This is why I brought you here, Thegn Raefnoth. For my people Yule, not Easter, is the turning of the year, when the old is put behind us and the new begins. It is a time for making peace. And a time for starting new wars. Which is it to be, Thegn Raefnoth? Peace or war?"

"War," Raef said without hesitation.

"On what cause?"

Raef looked eloquently around the hall, but said, "You raped my wife, thus killing her. Or if not," he carried on, before Torkil could speak, "you permitted it."

"On my soul, on my wave stallion, I did neither." With a great bellow he brought silence and attention to the hall and strode into a central space where the roaring fire illumined him.

"Hear me, hear me! I, Torkil Gormsson, the Ravenbringer, swear on my Christian soul and on my great ship, my wave stallion—may it sink beneath me if I lie—that I never touched Edith, wife to Thegn Raefnoth, in any offensive or injurious way. I swear this oath, too, on behalf of all my men here gathered. That none belonging to me harmed her. If this oath will dishonor me, let the man who makes it meaningless step forward now. He will be given the gift of a swift death."

All around the hall stayed still and silent. Hera glanced at Raef, and saw a slight frown that might mean doubt. It certainly was a mighty oath that no man would take lightly.

"So," said Torkil, looking around the room, "who here can support my oath before witnesses, that truth shall be known?"

One man stood, an older man with gray in his hair and steady eyes. "Great Torkil, lord, ring-giver, I, Foter son of Erik, speak to support your oath. As you ordered, I did not stop the Lady Edith and her maid from sneaking out of this place, and watched them as far as my eye could follow. Though frightened, she did not move as one who has suffered any kind of physical harm. This I swear by Woden and by the White Christ, and on my oath to you, and on the ring I wear." He held up his clenched fist, showing the iron ring on his right hand, the sort usually given by men such as Torkil to their wild followers.

Another man stood. "I, Haakon son of Omry speak to support my lord's oath. In all the time Thegn Raefnoth's wife was here, I never heard her scream except in the hall over meat. This I swear by Woden and the White Christ. . . ."

And so it went, until twenty men had stood to speak in support of Torkil's claim.

After leaving another silence, Torkil spread his arms. "So be it! That is my oath, by the God on the Cross and Woden's beard, and I stand by it, to my death and the death of all my followers." He turned to Raef. "What say you?"

Raef's frown had deepened. None could doubt such oaths and witnesses. "She was attacked on the road?" he said. "It is no great distance, and no one saw any disorderly strangers about."

Torkil gestured to the head table, littered with broken meats and bread and stained with drink. "Come, sit. You do not need to feast, but sit and let us talk about this one thing of which I am innocent. This is Yule, and for Alfrida's sake, I would have the enmity between us be on an honest basis at least."

At an order, churls ran forward to gather the old cloth, complete with all its mess, and to spread a new one. Torkil and Alfrida sat on one side in the big chairs, Hera and Raef on the other on benches. The seating arrangement was inevitable, but it must be salt in Raef's wounds.

"We will still be enemies," he said flatly. "You hold my home."

Torkil leaned back, drinking. "I can perhaps be persuaded to give it up for gold."

"I will pay you pirates no more gold. I want you gone or dead."

"Your king does not think that way."

Raef just shrugged. "Let us talk of Edith, and see if we can find the truth there, at least."

Hera leaned forward. "Alfrida, did you speak to Edith? What did she say happened?"

Alfrida took the ale cup given her by a servant and sipped. "She didn't say much, or at least much of sense. All about Danes, and how they are foul and disgusting, and how men are foul and do disgusting things. She kept wanting to wash herself and wash herself."

"She did that here, too," Torkil growled. "Never seen such a waste of water."

Raef's hands clenched. "She was always very fastidious."

With her new knowledge that he hadn't really loved Edith, Hera shared his tangled hurt and struggle. She knew that even now he'd die rather than criticize his wife.

She looked at Alfrida. "Did your maidservant attend Edith?"

"Fleda? Yes, why?"

"Call her. Let's see if she can add anything."

Soon the middle-aged woman was standing nervously by the table. Everyone seemed to want Hera to question her, so she started, "Fleda, you remember when Lady Edith came to Froxton not long ago, having escaped from Acklingham?"

"Oh, aye, Lady Wulfhera. A sad day."

"Indeed. Did you see her as she arrived?"

"Nay, but I was called soon after to help prepare a room for her."

"And you saw her come to the room?"

"Aye, lady."

"You heard a man here say that when she left Acklingham, she did not move as one who has been physically hurt. What was her state when she came to the room in Froxton?"

The woman pulled a face, staring into the distance. "Weak, Lady. Exhausted like, which was strange since she'd only walked from here. She collapsed on the bed as if she'd sleep, but then immediately called for a hot bath."

"Did you see her undress?"

"Nay, Lady. Her maid attended her."

"Did you see any blood?"

"Nay, Lady."

"Fleda, in the weeks between Lady Edith coming to Froxton and Thegn Raefnoth returning, did you hear Lady Edith
say anything about what had happened to her?"

"She wasn't one for chatter, lady, and she mostly just had
her woman, Gytha, for company. But I heard from the younger
maids that she kept warning them to stay away from men. That
men would do foul things to them."

Hera sent the woman away, wondering how such stories
affected a man who had been intimate with Edith.

Raef, however, showed no emotion when he said, "Gytha
might know something, but she returned to Tildwold after
Edith's death. She can be questioned, but not now."

Hera considered what she was going to say, considered all
the implications. She couldn't not say it, however. "Did Edith
ever actually say she'd been raped?"

Raef turned to her sharply. "Of course she did. She said it
to me."

"Oh." Despite his anger and possible hurt, Hera said to
Alfrida, "What about earlier? When she first arrived."

"I don't remember. We all just assumed . . . After all, Vikings." She glanced at Torkil, and perhaps even blushed.
"You think . . . ?"

Raef seized Hera's arm in a cruel grip. "What are you saying? That she *lied* about it?"

Trying not to wince, she met his eyes. "Entered an unreal
world, perhaps. Raef, at least think about it!"

He let her go, but glared. "No one could make up something
like that!"

In fact, Hera thought people could make up almost anything
if the mental pain was great enough, but she wasn't sure how
to express her thoughts without hurting him further.

Torkil spoke. "Thegn Raefnoth, you must know well
enough how some soldiers run mad during and after battle. In
some it is glorious, and we call them *berserker*. In some it is
shameful, and we call them *nithing*. Some never recover, and
their words make little sense."

"Edith didn't fight," Raef snapped. "Edith didn't see any
bloodshed or violence. Edith just opened the gates to you!"

"But she opened the gates," Hera said, "because she was
so afraid. And yet, it took great courage to treat with Torkil."

"And once they were inside," added Alfrida, "she found

herself with no control over her home, surrounded by men she thought barbarians. Men of violence and lusty tastes who made no attempt to hide such things from her.''

Torkil grinned. "Is that a complaint, my plum?''

She poked him in the chest. "I've grown used to it, but I'm no Edith.''

"Thank Freya.''

Raef lowered his head for a moment, hands tightly clasped, then looked up. "Even if this is true. Even if Edith's mind was turned, and she came to imagine things that had not happened, she would live still, and be in peace, if not for you, Ravenbringer.''

"Are we all not but the tools of God? Fate lies in His hands.''

"It is your *fate* to hold Acklingham?''

"So it would seem.''

Raef swung to face away from the Dane, but Hera laid a hand on his tense arm. "Raef, can you not accept that it is likely that Torkil did Edith no direct harm. That her pain came from within herself. He would not swear such a mighty oath if it was untrue. Christian or pagan, it is the time of forgiveness. Can you not at least be at peace on that one thing?''

He closed his eyes, and she could imagine what he was thinking. That if Edith had gone mad in this way, he had failed her most grievously. After all, it was apparently to him alone that she had spoken directly of rape, perhaps using it as a shield.

But then he did turn back to the Dane, and held out a hand. "On this matter, I cry peace with you, Ravenbringer. For the good of my soul, I absolve you of fault in the death of my wife. It was her folly in letting you in here, and mine in not forestalling that.''

The two men clasped hands briefly, and Hera had the frustrated feeling that they could even be friends if a thousand things were different.

Apart again, Raef said, even with a touch of wry humor, "Now, leave Acklingham and we can truly be at peace.''

"Abandon such a rich prize without gain, Englishman? I'd be a laughingstock. You must pay, and pay well.''

"Never.''

Back to snarling, circling wolves.

"You must fight for it." The words came out of Hera's mouth without her intending them at all.

Before she could retract, Torkil shot to his feet, shouting, *"Glima!"*

The hall fell silent again, all turning in keen expectation.

Glima? Hera stared at the Dane. The world had truly turned mad. Glima was wrestling with no bloodshed attached. An entertaining sport. It could not settle a matter such as this.

And why had she suggested fighting in the first place? She put her hand up to touch the Star. Was it possible that someone holy had spoken through her?

"Why?" asked Raef, clearly as confused as she was.

Torkil put down his ale horn. "I have turned Christian, Englishman, but pagan blood still runs in my veins. Both sides tell me we live in extraordinary days. Perhaps we face Ragnarok or Apocalypse tonight. Or at Christmas. Whatever else it may be, this is the thousandth year since Jesus Christ was born, and I would start the new millennium aright."

"I thought you were innocent of everything."

"We all have our fate, and seek to evade it at our peril. I would put mine to the test. We fight for Acklingham?"

At that, Raef leaped to his feet, stripping off his tunic and shirt to stand naked from the waist up. "I am more than willing."

Hera knew a thirst for violence must have been burning in him for hours. Days, even. But glima?

Torkil laughed for joy, kissed Alfrida heartily, and began to strip, too.

Raef turned, and with almost a smile in his eyes, swept Hera into a passionate kiss. The hall erupted with whistles, shouts, and thumping hands and feet.

She emerged dazed, and put her faith in Christ and his Holy Mother, though she couldn't see how this was supposed to work out. At the end of the bout, they'd still be deadly enemies.

"We fight for Acklingham?" said Raef, hands on hips. "But what if I lose? I have nothing to stake."

"Not quite true," said Torkil, his eyes sliding to Hera.

Hera glared at him, then glanced at Alfrida, who was glaring, too. Did the Danes have the pagan practice of keeping more than one wife? If Torkil tried that, he'd likely find himself neatly divided down the middle . . . by a blade!

"The *pendant*," Torkil said, shaking his head. "Could I even try to handle the two of you? Alfrida has told me the story, that it was touched by the hand of Christ." He came over and reverently touched it. "With that around his neck, a man would be a mighty warrior."

Hera grabbed it away, almost protesting that it was a woman's jewel, not meant for men at all.

"It is Hera's," Raef stated, moving closer as if in physical guard. "It is not mine to wager."

Hera realized that she was putting her own thoughts and wishes first and made herself relax. *Thy will be done.* "I am willing for it to be a stake. It only comes to anyone for a brief while." She offered that as an honest warning to the Dane, but he just smiled. Perhaps he even winked.

Had she been right in thinking that Torkil did not want to keep his prize? Was this all an elaborate plan to give Acklingham back to Raef with honor?

Her suspicions were strengthened when he said, "I understand you have a song about it, Lady Wulfhera. Would you sing it for us, so that all may understand."

Hera was willing to do everything she could to help this plan along. She called for a harp, tuned it, then began the saga of the Star of the Magi. However, for the chorus, she changed the wording slightly.

> *Stella mirabilis, come from afar.*
> *Stella mirabilis, come where we are.*
> *Stella mirabilis, shine night and day.*
> *Stella mirabilis, come light one Christian's way.*

She even improvised a little toward the end, making Miriam's husband, Alric, a warrior made great by the love of his wife, so that he conquered many lands and brought them into Christian harmony and prosperity.

"And it is said," she completed, letting the harp go silent, "that the Star of the Magi was swallowed by a fish, that symbol of Christ. And that it will return at a special time of great need. And what greater need could there be than now, as the thousand years turn, and the end might be nigh?"

She put aside the harp and rose to walk down the long

feasting tables, holding the pendant out for all to see.

"Today, I tell you, the Star of the Magi, that magical pendant touched by the hand of Christ, came to me in the belly of a fish, and this is it. Christ's magic among us. But for whom? I found it, and yet I tell you true, Christ's Holy Mother herself spoke to me in the chapel and told me to bring it to my sister Alfrida, beloved of your leader, Torkil Ravenbringer. Alfrida felt driven to return it to me."

Men and women leaned forward to peer as she passed.

"There is a star trapped in there!"

"Magic."

"Power to the husband of she who wears it."

Some stretched to touch and pray. "Bless me, Christ Child."

One man, however, seized the pendant, and drew a knife to cut the leather thong. "By Woden or Christ, this belongs to my lord!"

Torkil's bellow had him releasing it, but Raef was faster, and his fist drove the man to the floor. Torkil hauled him up to face him.

"If I wanted to seize this thing by force, could I not do that for myself, Thorold Svensson?" He threw the man back down. "No, this will be put in the hands of the gods, old and new. Lady Wulfhera, return to the table and sit by your sister."

Raef rubbed her neck where the thong had bit. "Are you all right?"

"Of course, though I've been manhandled more this night than in my entire life, I think."

He rested his head against hers. "I'm sorry about earlier. Too much bitterness held inside for too long."

"And now?" she asked.

"Now? I feel very strange." He moved back and raised the pendant in his hands. "Is this really the Star of the Magi?"

"I believe so. And I think it can solve all this if we let it, Raef."

He looked into her eyes. "For the first time in an age, I hope it might be so. Hera, you are my sun in summer and my fire in winter, and my precious jewel at all times." Then he gave a strange laugh, and wiped her cheeks with his thumbs. "Hera? Tears?"

She sniffed. "I knew you'd make me cry one day, Raef

Eldrunson! Go and fight for Acklingham, for I want to live here.''

She escaped to the big chair Torkil had vacated, and not having taken Raef's vow, accepted water to ease a throat dried by singing. She hugged Raef's words to her, but couldn't help a niggling worry that they came from the Star, not truly from him.

She told herself again that the magic seemed to be permanent, no matter what happened to the pendant thereafter. Then she began to worry about how the prizes could be arranged. Surely usually, winner took all, and for there to be peace here, both must win.

"Now," said Torkil, standing in the central space, hands on hips, magnificent broad chest gilded by flames. "This is how it will be. I place this manor of Acklingham in the test. Thegn Raefnoth places the sacred pendant currently around his woman's neck. The winner of our bout will have first pick. The loser must take what remains."

Hera tried not to look as relieved as she felt, but she took Alfrida's hand beneath the cloth and squeezed it. Truly the Star was magical and Christ was with them. A solution had been found.

"Your Torkil is a very clever man," she said quietly.

Alfrida was practically eating him with her eyes. "Isn't he wonderful?"

"Will he marry you?"

Alfrida grinned. "He's going to have to. After all, the Star's power only goes to the wearer's *husband*."

Hera had to choke back a laugh. "It will probably return to the sea soon. What then?"

"Torkil doesn't truly need its power to be great."

"And you don't need it to hold him?"

Alfrida's look was astonished. "Of course not."

So, it was as she'd thought. Once started, the magic was permanent. Hera settled to watching the wrestling match almost with enjoyment. In glima, contestants rarely suffered more than a bruise or two.

The men took a firm grip of each other's belt with their right hands, then grasped each other's trouser leg with their left so they were locked together. Losing grip was an easy way to lose the match.

Thus locked, they began to move, trying to force a fall while never looking down at their feet. That was another way to lose.

The first whose torso touched the ground lost.

It was a game that even children played, but she knew pride burned in both to win, and she hoped fiercely that Raef would. The result would not matter. If Raef won he would choose Acklingham. If Torkil won he would choose the Star.

Torkil was bigger, but Raef was as tall and strong, and perhaps more agile. As they swayed, trying to hook their opponent's legs away, or twist to throw them off balance, the fire danced golden over sweating, rippling bodies. Torkil had a cross of red hair down his chest. Raef was smooth.

And beautiful. Definitely more beautiful.

Knowing she was probably devouring him with her eyes, Hera rested her chin in her hands and admired the strong, graceful movements of her beloved's body. She'd seen plenty of it in their younger games, but it was definitely different now. She couldn't help thinking of their tangled bodies, disturbed too soon.

If this all worked . . .

For the first time she truly realized that hope danced here.

Hope of survival.

Hope of peace of a kind.

Hope of a future for her and Raef.

Her and Raef.

She saw him flick his head, and almost be unbalanced. Both men should have taken time to tie their hair back, for it fell into their faces and stuck there, and they could not brush it away.

Hera glanced at Alfrida, and met understanding. They both took a ribbon from one of their braids—one blue, one red— and ran forward to halt the bout. With the men still locked, they combed back their hair with their fingers and tied it, finishing in both cases with a warm kiss.

The rapt audience cheered, and the bout recommenced.

A dozen times it seemed one or the other must fall, and yet they kept their feet—just—grunting with effort, cheered by the men who understood the finer points of this sport. Hera suspected that any awareness of Acklingham and the Star had faded from them both.

Both wanted to win.

She prayed that Raef would win—it would do so much for his bruised pride—but then she hastily reverted to the prayer, *Thy will be done.* God and His Mother were doing excellently thus far.

Raef loved her. Raef desired her. Surely nothing could come between them now. Her hand hurt, and she realized she was clutching the Star tightly.

Still, she wondered if Raef's love came because of the star.

It had only been after she'd worn it outside her clothes that Raef had told her, shown her, his love.

What might happen when she gave it up?

Suddenly, before her troubled eyes, Raef threw himself to one side, kicking out, and Torkil, after a bellowing struggle, fell to the floor with a hall-rattling thump.

Raef let go as the other man fell, and raised his fists in glorious triumph. Even though their lord had fallen, the hall rocked with cheers for the good bout.

After a dazed moment, Torkil leaped to his feet to shake Raef's hand, buffeting him on the back hard enough to stagger him.

"So now," he said to all, "Thegn Raefnoth has the difficult choice. A plot of land, or the pendant of power."

Hera braced herself to give up the Star, thinking that Torkil was as crafty as an entertainer making his audience believe in magical spells. But then she saw Raef looking at her hesitantly. She realized she was still clutching the Star, and hastily let it go, giving a little shake of her head. The man couldn't be stupid enough to pass up this chance!

He turned to the hall. "How can a man give up a precious item once touched by Christ's own hand?"

Raef! Hera braced herself to run out and knock some sense into the man.

"And yet," he added, with a believable effect of reluctance, "my family's honor gives me no choice. I can only hope that the fact that it has briefly rested in the possession of the woman who is to be my wife will grant me blessings."

He turned to Hera and held out his hand for the jewel. "Do I assume too much?"

He was giving her the choice, even now. Releasing a relieved breath, she took it off. "Of course not."

He put it around Alfrida's neck. "You understand," he said,

turning to Torkil, "this means you must marry her."

"I'd not let her escape me!" The Dane seized Alfrida's hand and pulled her around the table to face the hall. "Hear ye! This is Alfrida of Froxton, and now my wife, till death us part. My helpmeet, my mate, and my magical powers!"

His men cheered, not seeming at all put out at the loss of Acklingham. Probably they, like their leader, had been wondering what to do with a place that kept them landlocked, and required all kinds of care they had no mind to give.

"Do you all now pledge to honor and protect this woman, now my wife? On your oaths."

"Aye!" The great shout seemed to shake the hall.

Alfrida was glowing with happiness, but she looked up at him and said saucily, "It would have been nice to be asked."

"Do you forget you're my prisoner, woman?"

"Oh no, my lord," she said, wickedly demure. "Never."

The laughter told that all his men knew the true way of things.

"And I," said Alfrida to the hall, "am proud to call Torkil Gormsson, called the Ravenbringer, husband. He will have my honor and my care all my life. And whatever blessings the good Christ chooses to bring him through this magical pendant."

And now she went around the hall to show it off, and to let people touch it, Torkil escorting her with glowing pride.

Raef walked around the table, and with a distinct sigh of satisfaction, took his rightful place in one of the great chairs, next to Hera.

"Do you mind?" he asked her.

She took his hand. "Not at all. If there was magic in it for me, I have it. I have you."

He wound his fingers in hers, but his eyes were on Alfrida and Torkil. "What happens when one day it falls from her neck into the sea?"

"God will protect her."

"The Star of the Magi." He suddenly leaned back. "We live in extraordinary times indeed."

"But now," she said, "even if the world ends, I will be happy." Thoughtfully, she added, "Almost."

He rolled his head to look at her, smiling. "I know. Doubtless Torkil is using the lord's room here, but I'll gladly fight him for it.''

It was tempting as a hot honey bun, but at the same time it didn't feel quite right. ''If we wait till Christmas Eve, we could marry in a true Christian way. And I could celebrate it, for Advent would be over.''

He nodded. ''That is right. Truth to tell, this is too raw for me just yet.''

She knew what really troubled him still. ''You mustn't blame yourself over Edith. She was as she was, and it was her fate.''

''But if I'd opened my eyes sooner and married you, she—''

''She'd have married another. Clearly she didn't think of a life of chastity until too late. I'll not speak badly of her to you, but she always enjoyed her beauty and the attention it brought her.''

''Marriage didn't kill her.''

''But it didn't please her, either.''

''Perhaps with another man . . .''

''Raef, I'll admit I'm besotted by you, but it's still true that there can be few men on earth more willing to be kind and patient with a woman like Edith.''

He laughed and looked at her. ''Besotted. I don't deserve that.''

''Deserve it or not, it's your fate.''

''And I am besotted by you. . . .'' But then he straightened. ''By the thorns, I've just realized I'm free of my vow.'' He thumped the table with his fist. ''Ale! Food!''

Hera laughed and watched dotingly as her famished beloved made up for missed meals.

Hera slept in solitary splendor in the lord's chamber of Acklingham. Raef took the bachelors' room, and Torkil and Alfrida the maidens' room. Judging from the noises Hera heard coming from there, the name was not at all appropriate.

It kept her awake. Not just the noise, but the longings within herself. It was right, though, to wait. It was still Advent, when Christians should not wed, and she meant to keep her Advent vows of fasting and abstinence from meat. She knew, too, that Raef needed a little time to think about Edith and all that had happened.

She still worried a little that the thousand years might mean the end of the world, and that it might happen on Christmas Eve, just as she and Raef were making their vows, but before the consummation. She made herself put that thought away. She had been steered by holy hands thus far, and would trust them in this, too.

Thy will be done.

The next day, Raef agreed that Torkil and his men could stay at Acklingham as guests until Christmas Day, so Alfrida could attend her sister's wedding. Raef's men were divided between Acklingham and Froxton, until one of Hera's brothers returned to take things in hand.

They planned for the future, but still, every now and then, couldn't help looking at the sky and wondering. It was a time of miracles, after all.

"I wish we could go and see Father," Hera said at one time. "Perhaps he still lives, and it doesn't seem right to marry without his blessing."

Raef looked at her. "Why not?"

Hera went to ask Alfrida if she wanted to come.

Alfrida nibbled at the end of her plait. "Will they be angry? About Torkil?"

"They'll be angrier not to see you. And hurt. Will Torkil let you come?"

"Of course," said Alfrida, and to Hera's surprise was proven right.

The Dane came to see them off. "I'd come myself to pay respects to my wife's father, but a Dane abroad in the land might stir trouble." He stretched up, and Alfrida curved down from her horse's back for a kiss.

"Tell them," Torkil said to Raef, "that I'll care for their daughter all my days, and arrange for her to visit her home as often as possible."

"Hopefully," said Raef, "not with a raiding party at your back."

Torkil laughed. "I note you leave me here, trustingly."

"Am I wrong?"

"No. But perhaps one day you English will accept my king, and we can all be brothers."

"Never," stated Raef, but without heat. As Hera had pre-

dicted, the two men were well on the way to being friends, of
sorts.

They rode hard and reached the priory close to noon, to
hear the glad news that their father still lived. "Weak," said
the monk who led them to the infirmary, "and it's a miracle
he still breathes, but perhaps he waited to say farewell to his
daughters. Or perhaps," he added, opening the door, "he
awaits the glorious coming of Christ."

Their mother was sitting by the bed, looking worn down by
weeks of hard nursing, but she rose with a pleased cry and
gathered her daughters into her arms. Hera hugged her, then
turned to where her father lay withered, pale, and obviously
in pain.

"I've prayed for his release," Lady Elswyth whispered into
her ear, "but he lingers on."

Hera went to kneel by her father's bed, Alfrida beside her.
He opened weary eyes. "Ah, my daughters. A blessing to see
you before I die." Even his bushy, grizzled beard was gray
and thin.

Hera took his hand. "Perhaps you're supposed to live, Father."

"No, no," he said in a wispy voice. "But perhaps I'm to
wait until Christ's coming. It's the only explanation. And the
pain will make me ready for Christ's right hand." He'd always
been such a big, hearty man, but there was only half of him
here.

"You were always ready, Father," said Alfrida, rising to
kiss his sunken cheek.

His mouth twitched in a feeble smile, but then his eyes fixed
on the pendant swinging in front of him. "What's this?" His
hand fumbled to touch it. "Where did you get this, Alfrida?"

Hera told the story, which was fine until she arrived at the
part about Alfrida being in Acklingham with the Danes, and
the events from there on.

Her father's frown was fierce enough to remind her of his
earlier days, and her mother had her hand over her mouth.

"You went to a *Dane*?" he asked Alfrida, and if he'd been
stronger, it would have been a bellow.

"He's a good man, Father."

He looked beyond, to Raef. "You permitted this?"

Raef stepped forward. "Hera wouldn't let me keep her under lock and key."

Now Hera was pinned by her father's eyes that almost seemed as sharp as before his injury.

"We couldn't keep her locked up forever, Father."

"I'd have chained her to the wall till she turned gray." To everyone's astonishment, he sat upright, scowling. "I'll have no more of this."

Hera and Alfrida both moved back hastily, but Lady Elswyth ran forward to ease him down. "Don't distress yourself, love. Lie back."

"Lie back!" he bellowed, and though raspy, it was a bellow now. "You've been praying for me to die. I've heard you. So stop coddling me now!"

"Only because of your pain, my love. Your pain . . ."

Lady Elswyth stared at her husband, who was even beginning to get some color in his face. "Sweet Mary, Mother of Christ, it's a miracle!"

Hera crossed herself, but her father scowled. "Don't talk nonsense. I'm just feeling a bit better. In fact, I'm hungry."

Hera fell to her knees again because they'd turned weak.

The Star. He'd touched the Star!

"Father," she said, "it is a miracle. When we came in here you looked close to death, but now . . . It happened when you touched the Star of the Magi."

He scowled at the pendant as if reluctant to believe.

"Are you not free of pain now?" she risked.

After a moment, his frown eased. "I am indeed. A miracle? Here?"

"I think so. And I'm sure it was Christ's Mother herself who told me to take the Star to Alfrida, and who has guided me throughout this. So it must be the will of Christ that Alfrida marry Torkil Gormsson. Perhaps in the future they can bring peace to our people."

Her father let her ease him back onto his pillows, huffing out a breath. "A daughter of mine and a Dane. And what of you, Hera? Why aren't you in your convent?"

She decided to leave out most of the explanations. "With your blessing, Father, I'm going to marry Raef."

He nodded. "At least one of you is going to do the right thing. So who's taking care of Froxton? It must be falling into ruin. Get me some food, someone! I can't lie here like a weakling forever!''

Monks ran in to see what the shouting was about and fell to their knees in wonder at the miracle—though by silent accord no one told them about the pendant. Then there would be talk of shrines and a pilgrimage, and probably a war over whether it should go with the Danes.

Once her father was sitting up supported by pillows, and taking his first food in days, Hera went into Raef's arms.

"Perhaps this is Christ's coming," she said. "His clear presence among us through the Star."

"Perhaps. Certainly my world has changed in the past few days." He smiled into her eyes. "And tonight, beloved, we marry."

He was clean-shaven and neat, but more importantly, his eyes were bright and full of hope and joy. He was Raef, whole and complete again before her.

That night, at Acklingham, as close to midnight as anyone could tell, they said their vows outside before English and Dane alike. The Christmas star shone clear in the frosty night, but no brighter light split the sky to show the coming of Christ. He only came, as He did every year, in the memory of a baby in a stable, and a promise of peace on earth.

And afterward, Hera told the story of the three Wise Men, the star they followed, and the Star one took home with him, a little Christian magic captured for all time, to appear for a woman at the turning of times when it was most needed.

"That was very good," Hera said later, sprawled in sweaty contentment in the big bed.

Raef's hand roamed her body beautifully. "Truly? It must have hurt."

Even through the wonderful sensations, she'd known he was tense, afraid she was another Edith. She looked into his eyes. "It hurt. It was nothing. If you get kicked in glima does it make it less fun?"

He lowered his head to lick around her nipples. "Glima? You want to wrestle?"

"No. I want to cuddle." Tangling herself with him, she kissed his muscled chest, felt him naked against her head to toe. Hers at last.

Her and Raef.

"I think perhaps the world has come to an end, Raef."

"Why?"

"Because this is how I imagine heaven."

And when the spring came, Torkil Gormsson, called the Ravenbringer, carried his wife in his great sea stallion across the waves to Denmark, to show his family the prizes he had won, including the miraculous pendant touched by the hand of the White Christ.

But on the way back—on their way north to Dane-held lands, for Torkil would not raid Kent again—a storm arose, so all were in fear of their lives.

Then Alfrida took off the Star of the Magi, which now hung on a gold chain of great worth. "It is time," she said to her husband, whose first child swelled large inside her.

For a moment he frowned, but then he nodded. "It is time. It does not serve to be greedy with the gods."

So Alfrida took the chain and whirled it fast around her head in the storm winds, and cast it as far as she could. It flew like a shooting star, then sank, deep into the iron-black waters.

And as it sank, the storm lessened, so that soon the sea was in order and the ship sailed on its way, while below, the Star drifted downward, to wait until it was needed again.

Starlight Wedding

***

ALICE ALFONSI

To my sister, a woman to admire,
DR. GRACE ALFONSI CAPALDO.

In loving memory
of all our Christmas carols.

Prologue

Christmas Eve
Paris, France, 1793

Still exhausted from recent childbirth, Lady Anna Devon, wife of Thomas Court, Earl of Devon, slumped back against the hard stone wall of her prison cell. The Bastille's bitter cold was cruel to her lungs and she coughed violently.

With frozen fingers, Lady Devon drew her thin blue shawl more tightly around her torn muslin gown. The shawl was not unlike herself, she mused, a thing of useless beauty—impressively embroidered but too slight to dispel the rapidly plunging temperature of a winter sunset.

How she longed for Thomas's arms instead of this wretchedly expensive accessory. For the warmth of his passion, the solace of his green eyes, the soothing whisperings of his mind and heart . . . but the Earl of Devon was far from her this night. As far as all her hopes.

Lifting her weary blue eyes, Lady Devon looked toward her cell's small window. Grimly she watched as night's inevitable black closed in, killing every last vestige of twilight's regal purple—not unlike this bloody reign of terror, she thought, a merciless movement that had crushed every noble thing to ashes.

In truth, Lady Devon now feared the dying of her faith even

more than the failing of her weakened form. She wanted to
believe that goodness still existed in the world. But anger and
hate, betrayal and violence were so prevalent now . . . how
could she not think that the end of everything was coming?
That darkness had won?

That's when she saw it—a new sight revealing itself in the
sky. Beyond the window's grimy bars, within the frame of
descending dark, a pale point of light was slowly growing
brighter.

"A star," she whispered with wonder, brushing tangled
golden strands from her cheeks.

A Christmas star.

Perhaps it was a sign, she told herself. A sign to believe
again. Believe there was a heaven. Believe her one last prayer
would be answered—to keep her newborn safe.

Mere hours ago, while she herself was being arrested, her
three-day-old son had been secretly swaddled up by her maid
and swept out the back staircase. Now Jacques Court was a
child without a home, like another babe of long ago.

Moving to her knees, Lady Devon prayed to that divine
infant, hoping that his kingdom was filled with more splendor
and goodness than the late King Louis's crumbling court.

"Please to help *mon enfant* find his father across the Channel," she murmured in broken English, the language of the
husband she loved. "And, when it is over for me, find him a
loving mother—a woman who will raise him to be an honorable man."

In the heavens, the Christmas star seemed to sparkle for her
like the shining memories of her girlhood. For a moment, she
forgot the hardness of the floor and the breaking of her heart.
For a moment, she was transported to those happy days before
all she'd loved had been ripped from her; and, despite her
weakened state, she opened her mouth to sing.

The carol was an old French one, loved by children. Its
words were not especially brilliant or clever; it simply told of
a special star, a charm worn by one of the three Magi who
had come to honor the divine baby. Touched by Him, the star
brought love and peace ever after to all who found it.

She had not sung the song in years, but it provided her with
the comfort she needed this night—a night she knew in her
heart would be the last Christmas Eve of her life.

Like the snow, fluttering through the window's bars, the tune's purity swirled around the stone room. Then it slipped beneath the heavy door, inspiring another voice to join hers, then another, and another, until a frail but faithful chorus lifted its song to honor the coming of Christmas.

Lady Devon soon felt her remaining strength dissipating. She wanted to hold out, but sleep was inevitable for every living thing in this mortal world, and she was no exception.

For the last time, her eyelids closed. Yet, though the Christmas star left Lady Devon's sight, its joyful light remained in the sky and in her spirit—a radiant vision far too brilliant for anyone on earth to extinguish. . . .

One

December 13, 1799
South coast of England

The Honorable Miss Felicity Fairchild cursed all society.

With the heat of anger boiling inside her, she vigorously marched away from her brother's large estate. With reckless speed, her sturdy half boots swept through the barren streets in the closed-up village of Lyme Regis then tramped down to the Cobb, the curving pier that skirted the murky gray shoreline of Lyme Bay.

"Why?" railed Felicity to the cold choppy waters. "Why do people feel the need to be cruel?"

The sea's only answer was an icy puff of wet wind that nearly blew off her simple brown bonnet. Cursing softly, Felicity tied it more securely over her chestnut hair. The homely little hat was rather pathetic. On the other hand, it perfectly matched her plain beige gown and utilitarian brown cloak—clothes she'd acquired since her arrival in Lyme three days before.

Such was not Felicity's usual elegant attire, but fashion mattered little in this rustic seaside resort during the off season. She recalled that well enough from her childhood years here. Indeed, this was why she'd come. Not for society, but for the refreshing lack of it.

Felicity had hoped that Lyme's wintry sea air would blow away the stench of rumor that had oppressed her in fashionable Bath. But today, like a very bad perfume, the gossip had followed her—right into the home of her own brother.

". . . and they say he was quite taken with the girl, almost upon first sight. Miss Collins was her name. Yes, a Miss Collins with fifty thousand pounds. . . ."

Just twenty minutes ago, before heading out for her afternoon walk, Felicity had halted in the festively decorated hallway of Maidstone House, her long glove drooping half off her hand like an abandoned puppet. Beyond the partially closed doors to the drawing room, the voice of a distant female cousin was speaking rather loudly to Felicity's kind sister-in-law Jane—speaking of matters involving *herself*.

"Miss Fairchild has obviously left Bath to escape the gossip," carped the cousin, "and, of course, she would want to avoid Drury and his fiancée at all the holiday balls. It's quite a pity, and everyone I called on in Bath agreed that Mr. Drury has treated Miss Fairchild quite ill. Quite ill indeed. And, at her age, you know what *else* is said . . ."

How unbearable! Felicity had thought, clenching her teeth and wanting nothing more than to burst into the room shouting to her bibble-babbling cousin that she'd heard it on "good authority" that indelicate rumor-mongering gave women severe warts!

Instead, however, Felicity had bit her tongue, tugged at her flopping glove, and forced her legs to move with haste for the nearest exit.

With blind vigor, she now teetered down the Witches Teeth, the rickety stone steps that led to the pebbly sand, and began to stride angrily along the empty shore. *I do have my generous inheritance,* she bolstered herself. *And, of course, my family name.*

These things were true. But there were other truths. Bitter ones. Felicity well knew that women were shadows in this world. Their identities were assigned by asking one question: *What is she to the man in her life?* Mother, daughter, wife . . . or . . .

Felicity sighed. In the case of *no* man, she knew a woman was rendered beyond shadow. She became *invisible*.

"Spinster," she whispered, trying the word on the icy sea

air. The very breath she'd used to speak it formed a dissipating ghost.

To Felicity, the label seemed an especially cruel irony. As the eldest of an orphaned clan, she'd helped her uncle raise and settle her younger brother—now the Baron of Lyme—and her three younger sisters into wonderful matches and happy, cozy married lives. For this accomplishment she felt very proud indeed.

It was only *herself* she had neglected to consider.

And now that she did, it was far too late.

Felicity had never presumed to find true love. She could not even guess how such an emotion even felt. *But* she had always expected to live in society as a *married* woman! And now . . .

The echo of the dreaded word "spinster" resounded through her very bones, aging her in seconds, slowing her pace.

She could not blame John Drury for his decision to break with her—only for the coldness with which he'd severed their relationship. A coldness that betrayed a shocking lack of generosity, kindness, or honor. But even on that score, Felicity felt she had little justification to dwell. After all, no matter what Drury's character, she knew that no respectable man would take her as she was: at the advanced age of twenty-eight, and with recent ailments that left her with little chance of conceiving children.

Perhaps a widower with offspring already, she reasoned . . . but, in her heart, she knew even that was unlikely now. Bath society had already branded her Drury's "leavings." Added to that were shocking *speculations* on just *how* intimate they had become. The truth was an utter bore; for until she'd revealed her barren state to Drury, they'd shared nothing more than a few chaste kisses. The lurid gossip, however, had driven any chance for a decent offer into oblivion.

As the last turbulent waves of the eighteenth century lapped upon the sands, Felicity realized she was drowning in regrets.

"I have many good years ahead of me," she lamented to the snow-white gull keeping pace with her along the shoreline. "Is there no honorable man who would take what I have to offer. No one who wants what I have to give?"

The sudden snag of her boot's toe sent her tripping over her skirts and nearly tumbling to the ground. Regaining her balance, Felicity turned to see what had so unceremoniously re-directed her course.

It was a tangled piece of fishing net. Old and badly used . . . not unlike herself, she decided. Beneath it was a yellowish sparkle, like a tiny sun. Her gloved hand reached to take the chunk of light into her palm.

The piece of jewelry was roughly made and, on first glance, was not very attractive. But the smooth blue stone that sat at its center was quite remarkable—and oddly glowing with a kind of inner light.

The antique design was unique, as well, with bold, brilliant points that seemed to pierce the heaviness of her heart and drain away some of its sadness. Indeed, the golden points formed a shape not inappropriate to the coming day of Christmas. It was then she realized what she'd found . . .

A star.

Two

Merchant ship Destiny
Lyme Bay

"Ye got a little wife ye need to see right quick, eh?"

From *Destiny*'s rail, one mile off Devon's shore, William "Sea Hunter" Court glanced at the craggy old seaman who'd addressed him, then dropped his heavy bag into the rowboat below. "God forbid," he answered before swinging his leg over the side.

As Will's strong form descended the rope ladder, the *Destiny*'s tall first mate turned toward the older sailor. "The man's anxious to get back to his family's estate."

"Estate?" questioned the old sailor.

"Aye, man. You've been sailing with the new Earl of Devon. Brother's dead without legitimate offspring. Will here's inherited title and lands."

"Bloody hell!" exclaimed the sailor. "An earl! Well, now, happy rowing to 'im, I say. And Godspeed, as well."

Will nodded up at the first mate and the sailor above him before settling into the boat. Then he adjusted the tarpaulin hat on his shoulder-length raven hair and took up the oars. He was content to do so. He'd much rather use his own well-developed back muscles to traverse the mile across Lyme Bay rather than hire a horse for a long ride from Portsmouth. Ever the poor rider, the past fifteen years of sea service had taught Will to prefer water to land. He expected this preference would always be so.

"Hear that, Will?" the first officer called down. "Happy rowing to you!"

"Aye. And happy docking to you, Jack!" Will returned.

The first officer smiled as he turned to jest with the sailor beside him. "I say, I'll wager this is the first you've ever seen an earl, let alone a Royal Navy officer, do his own rowing."

"I was raised the spare, not the heir!" Will called to the men as he gave the first pull. "The sooner I untangle the family lands, the sooner I'll be back on the water."

"Amen," said the old seaman.

"Did I ever thank you?" shouted the officer to Will. "For the help with those French privateers?"

"Pirates, Jack!" Will corrected with a laugh. "Do not mince words when it comes to bloodthirsty French thieving!"

"Whatever you call them, we are grateful for your seasoned assistance in driving them off. Thank you, Lord Devon!"

Will took in a cold breath upon hearing his new title. It was the first time he'd heard it since his brother Thom's death, and it sounded strange to his ears. Will had never been a man to stand on ceremony, but he knew the importance of the peerage, and he knew he would learn to grow accustomed to it—and the additional responsibilities that went with it.

With his good, unpatched eye, Will glanced back up at the officer. "You are welcome!"

"Then Happy Christmas to you!" the first mate shouted in farewell.

Pulling on the oars, Will considered returning the expected farewell to the good officer, but instead he chose silence. The *Destiny* was already disappearing into the pearl-gray fog. And, since his twenty-first birthday, fifteen hard years ago, the words "Happy" and "Christmas" had never been uttered by William Court's tongue.

As far as he was concerned, they never would again . . . never in his lifetime.

"It is surely a family heirloom," Felicity Fairchild whispered to the white gull that had been following her along the chilly, wet beach.

There was no chain attached to the golden star she'd found, but there was a small loop where one might have been threaded. Clearly, some gentlewoman had lost it off a necklace.

Felicity quickly scanned the shoreline for another strolling gentlewoman like herself, but there was neither foot nor hoofprint in the sand. She stood completely alone—and much farther from the village than she had meant to walk. That thought unsettled her, and Felicity frowned with the sad realization that her youthful hikes along this shore had been carefree only because they had not been shadowed by a grown woman's knowledge of the world. Now that she had lived in London and Bath, Felicity knew what perils might befall a woman alone. It spoiled the sense of purpose her walk had given her, so she turned to head back.

As she set off, she considered how heavy the star felt in her gloved palm. The weight of the gold alone betrayed its high value.

"If only my hand in marriage could be as valued as gold," she whispered on a jest. As if in answer, a sudden booming crack of thunder rumbled across the gray clouds.

Oddly, the star grew warm in her hand, even as the thunder faded and another sound drifted toward her ears—a sound like a woman singing. A trick of the wind made the song seem as if it had descended from the same place as the thunder, from somewhere *above*. Yet in the next moment, the melody was coming from close by.

The voice was beautiful and, though the words to the carol were French, Felicity's well-schooled mind automatically translated them:

> The shining star up in the sky
> Is not the only Christmas light.
> The little babe reached out a hand
> To bless the Magi who gifted him. . . .

Felicity looked up to find the singer standing some distance away. She was a golden-haired woman strolling along the rocky sand.

But where, in heaven's name, had she come from? wondered Felicity. The woman had not been on the beach before.

Perhaps she is the owner of the lost star, came a sudden strong thought to Felicity's mind. *Perhaps she is here searching for it.*

"Miss!" Felicity called out.

The woman stopped singing and turned. Her pale face was beautiful, the white skin almost transparent, the blue eyes shining bright as fire. A shiver touched Felicity at the sight. The woman's white gown and finely embroidered blue shawl were far too expensive for that of a fisherman's wife, and her face held the genteel look of aristocracy—yet she had not even a cloak! On a day as chilly as this, the woman would catch her *death.*

The woman smiled directly at Felicity, then turned away and began to run down the beach, away from the village and toward *nowhere!*

"Miss! Wait!" called Felicity, starting after her and wondering if the woman was unwell in the head. "Do you need help? Wait!"

But the woman did not wait. So Felicity followed, concerned, this time calling after her in French. But still the woman would not stop.

Another booming crack of thunder rolled over the gray sea skies. Felicity shivered with alarm as a third crack split the clouds and sent an icy rain to sting her cheeks and a cruel wind to tear her bonnet free.

She tried not to panic as an eerie fog enveloped the darkening bay. The dense mist surrounded her with alarming swiftness, and she quickly lost her bearings, seeing barely more than two paces in front of her.

As the freezing rain beat down, and the wind howled, she could do nothing but slip the golden star into her cloak's pocket, hold herself into a tight ball, and grit her chattering teeth.

When the storm finally passed and the fog lifted, an exhausted, frozen Felicity did three things in quick succession: She rose to her feet, took in her surroundings, then cried out in complete shock:

"Where in heaven's name am I?!"

The fog had somehow swept Felicity *miles* away from her childhood home and into a landscape she barely recognized!

The gentle hills of her youth, which sat far back off the

beach at Lyme's familiar Cobb, had crept forward to become forbidding cliffs. The wide beach was no more. She now stood, dirty and drenched to the bone on a dismal strip of rock-strewn sand, walled in by the steep, uninviting side of a mountain. The gentle grass was stripped raw by the elements, and the exposed rock was jagged, skirting the edge of the shoreline and casting all things below them in threatening shadow.

"This place looks like Devon. But how?" she murmured as the winds continued to ravage her chestnut hair, pulling it loose of its tight pins. But before she had time to consider the answer, she heard the singing again. That strange golden-haired woman was just ahead.

"Miss!" cried Felicity, lifting her skirts and running forward. Perhaps the golden-haired woman could explain how in blazes she'd been swept down the shore to Devon in the blink of an eye. "Wait!"

But the woman kept running, her beautiful golden hair flying out behind her like a brilliant beacon as she turned from the beach and began to vault the rough steps cut into the side of the steep cliff.

"Please! Wait for me!" Felicity begged, cursing on an exhaled breath. But the woman continued upward, disappearing at the top.

Felicity approached the steps, ready to follow her ascent, when suddenly her path was blocked. She had not noticed the two roughly dressed men stepping forward out of the shadows—

Until it was too late.

The pathetic bit of thunder and rain drenching Lyme Bay barely made the Sea Hunter blink. After fifteen years of deep water sailing, Will Court had helped ships ride out the worst tempests imaginable. So this little squirt hardly slowed him.

With half-closed eyes, Will simply rowed through the frigid downpour, concerned only that his hands were calloused thickly enough as they pressed again and again into the wooden oar handles.

The *Destiny*'s first mate had been correct. It was unthinkable for a Royal Navy officer to engage in ordinary ship's labor—from rowing a boat to pulling line through block spool—but Will had little choice. When he'd received the solicitor's notice of his brother Thom's death and the summons home, he'd secured a leave from his naval superiors, then hitched a ride on the first vessel he could find.

The voyage from Egypt had been long and difficult, requiring the efforts of all hands, including even a newly titled peer, such as himself. But Will had not minded in the least. In truth, he'd preferred the physical exertion to idleness, and he'd enjoyed acting as an ordinary member of the crew.

With a quarter mile to go, Will paused his rowing to glance behind him toward shore. The rain was subsiding and a low-lying fog lifted from the beach, revealing an ominous sight far above—the imperious stone walls of his childhood home. The seat of Devon's earls since the eleventh century, his family's grand estate topped these ancient cliffs like a tyrannical crown.

"Castle Seabourne," murmured Will as if breathing a wretched curse. He could not help but notice how the warmth from his lungs was instantly iced by the words. Aye, thought Will, the bay's December air was *still* unforgiving—as unforgiving as the terrible memories that awaited him ahead.

Turning away from the sight of his newly inherited home, Will resettled his seat in the rowboat and once again took up the oars in a steady, pulling rhythm.

When he finally reached the fog-shrouded shallows, a high-pitched shriek caught his attention. With more curiosity than alarm, he turned in his seat and spied the little drama playing out just ahead on Seabourne's beach.

It seemed some local doxy had just gotten more than she'd bargained for. Not an uncommon occurrence on the rough port town docks that Will knew so well—but certainly a strange sight to greet him on the Seabourne estate. Perhaps Thom had been allowing a less desirable element to tenant the family lands of late, decided Will.

"Good God, the financials may be far worse than I guessed," Will muttered.

"Someone help me! *Help me!*"

Will did not wish to involve himself in the doxy's anger over her fees—or whatever in hell the tussle was about. Yet he could not allow the light-skirt's pathetic cries to go unheeded. She was, after all, a woman in distress. And, as much as he loathed society's constraints, he was as a gentleman, and trained as an officer.

After beaching the rowboat with a mighty tug, Will casually picked up a long, heavy oar and, without hurry, set off for the group, some yards away.

"Avast your actions, boys!" he shouted, still a little ways off. "Give the female room."

The men looked up at his call. There was a tall one and a fat one, both dressed in roughhewn clothes. They were obviously trying to disrobe the struggling brunette, and both looked less than pleased at the interruption.

"Sir! Please! Help me!" shrieked the woman, twisting and turning in their grip. "They are animals! Help me!"

"Boys?" queried Will. "Shall I repeat my request?"

"Be off with ya!" called the tall man. "This be our little light-skirt. Caught fair and square."

"She's not a fish," said Will, stepping closer. "Just the same, unhook her now, and throw her back."

The men exchanged glances and a few murmured words.

"We've no wish to fight ya," said the tall one with a change of tone. "So we'll let ye join us, then. There's enough here for three. But you'll 'ave to wait yer turn."

Will hesitated a moment as he caught sight of the fat one's long blade. Then he calmly thought through the situation, and finally selected the wisest course of action.

"Aye," Will replied to the two ruffians. "Make some room then for me."

Three

"May the devil damn you, sir!"

In such a situation as this, Felicity had always anticipated a swooning faint would overcome her. But it did not.

When the two ruffians had first lunged for her, she had used all her fury to fight them. Her sturdy half boot had even connected with the fat one's knee, but the tall one's slap came hard to her face, then his silver blade was tight against her throat, stilling further resistance.

Now held down on the cold, rocky ground, Felicity's eyes widened when she saw the third man approach. The physical build on her newest assailant was far more powerful than that of the first two, and there was something about his features that seemed even more dangerous.

The heavy blue coat and rolling gait would have suggested him a sailor, even without the oar he balanced between his two rough hands. Long black hair, capped by a folded piece of canvas, fell past his shoulders. A thick charcoal beard covered his cheeks and chin. And a black patch covered his right eye, leaving the left to stare with a menace darker than thunder.

Felicity was afraid of her first two assailants, but this new black-bearded man absolutely terrified her. For one thing, these two men had seen her disheveled state on the beach and believed her a doxy from the start, but this new one—what sort of man would hear a woman's screams, pretend to help, then decide to join in the vile assault? What sort of dark-hearted demon was this?

"May the devil damn you straight to hell," Felicity cursed again at the approaching sailor.

"She's a bit feisty, eh, boys?" cracked the ruffian sailor in response.

The first two attackers remained wary a moment at the third man's nearing, but when they heard his remark, they burst into their familiar harsh laughter and turned back to their filthy business.

Felicity's cape had been torn off and her plain beige gown ripped at the front, exposing her left shoulder and a good deal of her cream chemise. The men's hands reached to finish the job when the sailor's voice interrupted.

"Pardon me," he stated with a chilling detachment that sent ice through Felicity's spine, "but did I not *advise* you to make room for me?"

The men looked up. And in the next instant the ends of the boat oar had struck first the tall one and then the fat one square on their chins.

Faster than lightning, the sailor leaped forward and struck once more, knocking down her two assailants again and again, until they were rolling on the ground, moaning surrender.

"Be off with you both," snapped the sailor at last. Then he stood fast as Felicity's attackers crawled clear and scurried away. "And do not let me see you again on this beach! Else you'll have the earl himself to answer to!"

Quaking at the violence taking place above her, Felicity had barely rolled clear of the fighting before the sailor turned his eyes back on her.

An injured ankle left Felicity partially lame and prevented anything close to a clean escape. She had only managed to lunge for the bottom of the cliffside's rock staircase before she felt the rough sailor's iron grip fastening around her upper arm.

A horrified shriek was her instant response. "Please!" she cried. "Do not harm me! Please!"

"I do not intend to harm you," said the sailor with surprising tenderness. His grip softened at once. "I never intended to harm you."

"N-no?" stammered Felicity, daring to turn and look the

sailor in the eye—the eye she could *see*, anyway. His un-patched orb was dark green with a slight bluish hue, not unlike the sea on a fine day. And it appeared to be looking upon her without any sign of the malice she'd witnessed in it before his violent assault.

"There were two of them and one of me," he explained simply with a shrug, his speech oddly gruff and genteel at the same time. "Surprise in battle is always a strategic advantage. Can you walk?"

Felicity tried to compose herself. The sailor had saved her from harm, from rape, possibly even from death. And he had done so with the casual ease and valiant modesty of a seasoned Knight Templar.

She drew herself up, fighting the instant admiration for her raven-haired rescuer. The glowing warmth blooming inside her was not at all appropriate to the situation—not to mention the man's obvious low station.

"I can limp, I suppose," she told the sailor, fighting to keep her voice steady.

"Good." The sailor released her and walked a few steps. He gathered up her plain brown cloak and moved back toward her. Then he paused, seeing something else on the rocky sand. He bent down and picked it up.

In silence he returned to gently drape the torn cloak around her shoulders. The caring gesture was close to an embrace, and Felicity felt herself wishing the man's arms would have lingered longer about her. Instead, however, he pulled away and held out the open palm of his large, rough hand, revealing what he had picked up. The flash of gold came again to Felicity's vision.

He'd found her star.

"It must have fallen from my cloak's pocket," whispered Felicity, eyeing the star and then the man holding it. He appeared put off by her words.

"Do you claim this as *yours*, then?" he asked, more than a note of skeptical disgust in his voice. Why, he sounded as if he'd caught a female pickpocket in the act of claiming a man's purse as her own.

An immediate streak of pride whipped through Felicity. "I discovered it on the beach," she stated defiantly. "I was hoping to find its owner."

"Then take it."

Felicity reached out for the heirloom. As her delicate gloved fingers touched his large, rough bare ones, a crack of thunder split the clouds, and rain again began to fall.

"Come," the sailor said simply, and turned toward the staircase. "Shelter's above."

Felicity limped after the man. In agony, she peered up at the steep cliffside steps, wondering how in heaven she would make it to the top under these conditions. The wind was kicking up, and sheets of water lashed the narrow beach.

"Do you need aid from me?" asked the man sincerely, turning to observe her injured state.

Felicity wanted his help, and saw that he was ready to give it; but it was precisely her desire to feel the man's touch again that made her quickly answer. "No. I need no further aid from you."

In truth, Felicity did not wish to incite more glowing responses within her. Feeling this man's hands upon her would surely do nothing but spark additional inappropriate feelings. And anyway, she told herself firmly, she'd be damned before she'd ask for more charity from this ruffian sailor who quite obviously believed she had *stolen* that golden star. It was outrageous that he could not see exhibited in her person or hear inflected in her voice that she was genteel.

"I am quite capable of taking care of myself," she found herself adding, her tone a bit harsher and more superior than she'd meant it to be.

The sailor stared at her a long moment, as if considering what to do. "Very well," he finally said, then he started up the steps without looking back.

Castle Seabourne's gardens had degenerated into a tangled mess of brambles and weeds, but beyond them there was no mistaking the exalted walls of the great house.

To Will Court, the stone structure cast a more daunting shadow than the cliff he'd just scaled. The sprawling mansion had begun with a foundation built well over six centuries before, when his family had employed its own small army. Battlements, long since leveled, once stood on the outer perimeter of the grounds. Now badly kept shrubbery lined them instead, ringing in a haphazard yet still noble-looking house that had been built and rebuilt over time.

Beneath the pouring rain, Will's newly inherited castle stood before him with thirty or so rooms on two wings, three floors, two useless towers, and a main building with a ballroom, formal dining room, and chapel. There were lands, as well. Tenant farms in the area's rich valleys. What state they were in, God only knew—God and Thom's solicitor and bailiff.

After a few moments gazing at his childhood home, Will decided to glance back down at the woman below. He considered descending the steps and hefting her on his shoulder. But, from the fire of pride and streak of mistrust he saw in those surprisingly luminous brown eyes—not to mention her stubborn refusal even to *thank* him for a rescue that had risked his own life—he decided that she'd likely fight any attempt to aid her physically. The result could send them both tumbling to their deaths down the wet cliffside.

No, thank you. Will would let her feel the strain of the climb herself. He'd practiced such methods on the pressed-ganged young seamen under his command and found they often worked better than the prescribed naval floggings. Extreme physical effort always tamed a dangerous temper, and Will wanted hers exhausted before it entered Thom's home and set fire to something.

Thom's home. The earl's home. Now his, of course. For he was the new earl. Will sighed, still adjusting to the idea.

As he waited for the injured doxy to limp herself skyward, he gazed back at the castle, this time with a less critical eye.

I once enjoyed living here, he admitted.

As a boy, the parapets atop the two stone turrets—the only remaining parts of the original castle—had been his favorite place, where loopholes for archers still allowed a bit of medieval fantasizing. Unfortunately, those towers were about as useless as the dozens of empty rooms within. Still, they had cheered him in his long-ago youth.

A dark memory came over him at the thought of that youth, and Will's vision clouded as it always did when he thought of days past. His blood grew cold, his limbs stiffened, and his heart became harder than Seabourne's foundation.

"Hurry it up, woman!" he called, his impatience showing.

Aye, thought Will. *Haste is my friend now. For the quicker I enter Seabourne, the quicker I shall leave it.*

Murder had never crossed the Honorable Felicity Fairchild's mind before. But upon hearing the haughty sailor's command to "hurry it up," Felicity decided the only way to heave her body up the final dozen steps was to think of ways of killing the man who waited atop them.

"Hanging," grunted Felicity, taking a step. "Suffocation," she moaned, taking another. "Strangling. . . ."

"Come now, woman, you can move faster than that!"

"Decapitation . . . poisoning. . . ."

Grimacing, Felicity continued to lift her aching body up those last agonizing steps, until finally, she reached the very last one. Her head felt light, her vision unfocused. Gray stone towers seemed to loom in the distance as the sailor's demonic face swooped down into her view.

"One step to go," he informed her.

Felicity blinked and stared at the black-bearded bastard. With gritting teeth she heaved her pain-wracked body up the last step.

"There, now. You've made it," said the sailor.

Felicity grimaced, then moved her lips. "Arrow through the heart," were the only words she managed before her body crumpled at the sailor's feet, the pain finally sending her mind into oblivion.

"Tactical error," muttered Will to himself an hour later as he stood before Thom's dressing mirror, scraping a straight razor across his cheek.

Haughty women, Will had discovered this day, could not be dealt with the same as impressed seamen. *Lesson learned,* he decided, dipping the razor in the porcelain bowl on the stand beneath him.

The unconscious doxy was now resting comfortably in the room adjoining his. Part of him felt guilty. His examination of her inert—not to mention attractively curvaceous—body revealed no lasting injury, but the pain she must have suffered pricked his conscience.

God. I should have helped her make the climb.

Will decided he would make it up to her. Tonight. He'd

make sure she was fed and given a bed. Then he'd find her a ride to town in the morning.

He chuckled. He had to give Nolan Smith credit. The castle's butler had quickly managed to hide his initial shock when he opened the door to his new lord carrying a light-skirt across the threshold. But then the house staff always had been well trained.

When they were alive, his father and mother had run Castle Seabourne and its surrounding estates with skill and generosity. The staff had been as honorable as their employer. Unfortunately, Nolan Smith and his wife, Clara, the housekeeper, were practically all that remained of what had once been a small army of servants. The state of neglect to which Seabourne had sunk was highly alarming to Will. His late brother had not even managed to keep on a personal valet.

"Hello? . . . Hello? . . . Where am I?"

The muffled feminine voice came from beyond the hidden connecting door. It was the woman, Will realized. Apparently, she had finally awakened.

"Clara!" called Will after splashing cold water on his face. "Clara!"

His brother's fresh linen shirt hanging loose upon him, Will grabbed a towel and moved to the master bedroom's main door. A part of Will wanted to use the secret connecting door and respond to the woman himself. He had been long at sea and would have liked to invite a bit of saucy flirtation. Perhaps the little doxy would even make him an interesting offer.

She appealed to him, he had to admit. And he'd lingered longer than he'd had to when he'd examined her form. The exposed neck and shoulder from the torn gown had shown skin of ivory smoothness. Her features were delicate, excepting her too-wide mouth. Yet it was a generous mouth, thought Will, one that tempted a man's lips. And her breasts were generous, too, beneath the thin chemise. They were full and gently rounded, inviting a man's touch.

Ah, the thought of having that curvaceous female form in his cold bed warmed Will's blood and tightened his loins. But he was an officer. And a gentleman. And such a proposition was out of the question in his family's home and earldom's seat. Will called again for his housekeeper, his impatient roar betraying his own irritation at having to subdue the confounded call of nature burning within his flesh.

"Yes, Master William?" asked the plump woman, hurrying down the hallway, her gray hair covered with a white frilled cap.

"Sleeping Beauty's awakened. See that she's comfortable. Get her a change of clothes and have her join me for dinner. With this weather, she'll need to stay the night."

Clara Smith nodded stiffly, her tight lips telling Will exactly what she thought of harboring the light-skirt.

"I trust Nolan has contacted Thom's bailiff by now?"

"Yes. Charles Jones will be coming by first thing tomorrow morning to discuss the condition of the tenant farms. And . . ."

"Yes, Clara?"

"The . . . the late Lord Devon's solicitor is waiting in the study, to speak with you about the estate's finances and . . . about . . . about . . . a delicate matter."

Will eyed Clara. "What matter?"

Clara's frantic shaking of her head alarmed Will. "I cannot be the one to explain . . . it is not my place . . . not my place—"

"Calm down, old girl, calm down. I'll see the solicitor. Do not worry yourself." After the raging sea battles Will had witnessed in the last decade and a half, the least thing he would be bothered about was news from a damned lawyer.

With a heavy sigh, Clara nodded. "Thank you, Master William."

Will's lips quirked at the housekeeper's manner of addressing him. Informing the staff of his recent knighthood following his actions at the Battle of the Nile seemed a waste in the face of his newly inherited higher rank. "My lord" or "Lord Devon" would now be the appropriate way to address him, even if he should need time to grow used to it.

"Clara, I know you have been with Seabourne since Thom and I were babes, but "Master William" is a bit juvenile, do you not think? I am not one to stand on such things, but have not you an understanding of my new title?"

This question seemed to fluster Clara all the more.

"Oh, never you mind. Tell the solicitor I shall be down directly. And do one thing more for me."

"Of course, Master Will—*sir*—of course."

"The woman in the next room. Find out her name."

Four

An hour later, Felicity Fairchild sat before the mirror in the large bedchamber. With hands still shaking from her ordeal, she picked up a hairbrush and slowly began to smooth out the tangles in her long, chestnut hair.

A short time ago, the castle's housekeeper had come to see to her needs. Felicity had politely asked the plump, gray-haired woman to have Seabourne's groom and coachman prepare one of the closed carriages to take her back to her brother's home. But Clara had frostily replied that since the earl's death, the estate no longer kept any closed carriages, let alone a groom and coachman. Felicity was quite clearly stranded.

"Is there a golden-haired woman with a blue shawl who is part of this household?" Felicity had then asked Clara Smith. But the housekeeper snapped "No" with a stare that implied Felicity had gone daft.

"The gentleman of the house wishes you to dine with him," Clara had informed her dismissively before departing. Felicity did not decline. According to the housekeeper, the "gentleman" was William Court, the brother to the late Earl of Devon, and Felicity well knew that one did not disappoint a relative of such a peer. At least, not when one was a guest in his home.

His home. The very idea of how she'd gotten to Castle Seabourne made her feel as if she'd gone temporarily mad. *Heav-*

ens, and that black-bearded sailor, she thought, shuddering with the memory of her inappropriate reaction to him.

Still . . . she should have at least *thanked* the man. Perhaps her host would know where he could be reached, and she would have her brother send a generous reward. *Yes, that's what I shall do.*

Hearing the rain steadily beating against the window, Felicity considered her brother and sister-in-law. She knew they would worry, and only hoped they would assume her walk had taken her to visit old Mrs. Jennings at the Sea Spray Inn— given the storm, she might simply have stayed the night there.

Putting down the brush, Felicity tried to pin up her locks loosely. But her chestnut waves were too heavy and thick to be tamed and they cascaded down her back in flowing defiance.

Frustrated not to have her lady's maid to secure it, she grabbed a velvet rope from the bed curtains to cinch it at the nape of her neck. She then turned to the dress laid out for her. It was one of the housekeeper's, no doubt. Sturdy enough, but far too big.

Her own filthy, ripped gown, chemise, and cloak had been gathered up and taken away, so Felicity had to resort to limping around the bedchamber for possible alternatives. In the small attached dressing room, she found only the clothes of a young man.

She shrugged. What she decided to wear was far from conventional. But she was sure the late Earl's brother would be gentleman enough to understand her predicament.

When she was finished dressing, she left the room. She had never before been inside Castle Seabourne, though when she'd been young, she recalled her parents had sometimes visited here, especially at Christmastide.

The endless hallway was tiring, given her limp, but Felicity finally found the large staircase and slowly descended, taking care not to put too much weight on her still-sore ankle. As she reached the first floor's great hall and began to search for the formal dining room, she was startled by a shy voice. . . .

"*Bonsoir.* Are you a boy? Or a girl?"

Felicity turned to find a sad little angel peeking curiously at her from a bright doorway.

The boy was no more than six. Big blue eyes stared up with a combination of innocence and wariness. The gold of his curls seemed to light up the darkened hall, though his expression seemed terribly grave for one so young.

"I am a girl," Felicity answered, walking toward the child, who was clearly confused by Felicity's found clothing—a young man's white linen shirt tucked into loose-fitting light-blue silk knee breeches with a long waistcoat to match. "My name is Felicity. Who are you?"

"Jacques."

"Jacques who?"

"Jacques Court."

Felicity's eyebrow rose at the little boy's answer. Thomas Court had never married, not that she had ever heard. A few years ago, before his death, the late earl was rumored to have had a French mistress with family connections to King Louis's court—a tragedy, to be sure, what with all the beheadings and arrests during the revolution's Reign of Terror—but that is all Felicity had ever recalled from the society gossip. Perhaps Jacques was *William* Court's son.

"Would you care to meet my friends?" asked the little boy.

Felicity nodded at the child—his little, fragile voice reminded her of her younger brother, Christopher, who'd been only a little older than this boy when their parents had died.

Little Jacques led Felicity into Seabourne's vast drawing room. Much of the room's furnishings had been covered over with white cloths to keep off the dust, but one corner was cozily set up. A fireplace blazed and the little boy's three toy soldiers were happily standing at attention on the thickly loomed rug.

Stooping down, Felicity gestured to the soldiers. "Are these your friends?"

The little boy shook his head. "*Non!* Those are my *soldats.* There are my friends. . . ."

Felicity followed the boy's pointing finger. The wall was lined with portraits: grand oil paintings of the Court family members through the ages. The little boy took Felicity's hand and pulled her along the wall of austere faces.

"This is Peter, and this is Elizabeth. This is Katherine, and this is James . . ."

Felicity observed the child. "Jacques, do you not have any other friends? Friends your age? Brothers or sisters?"

"No," said Jacques. "Not in *Ang*land. Just Clara and Nolan, since my father has died. . . ."

Felicity's eyebrow rose. So this was Thomas's son, after all? How intriguing. If he was legitimate, then she was now in the presence of the new Earl of Devon.

"My uncle has come to the castle," continued the child. "Perhaps he will also be my friend, but I have not met him yet. He is up here, too. That is him."

They had stopped before a formal portrait of a striking young man of no more than twenty. His green eyes were bright, his hair raven black, and his square jaw attractively dimpled in the center. But it was the expression more than the handsome features that held Felicity's attention.

Unlike the austere faces around him, this one seemed buoyant and bold. There was something alive here—highly noble and proud. Not vain pride, but the pride exhibited by a true gentleman, the kind of man who tries with all his heart to do the right and good thing.

"William Withers Court," whispered Felicity, reading the small brass plaque at the base. Why did his eyes seem so familiar? Felicity did not recall ever meeting Thomas's brother, but she felt struck through the heart at the sight of his face—and the great goodness she saw in it.

"What an impressive man," she found herself whispering aloud, while inside she secretly wished such a man would fancy her.

It was an impossible wish, of course, Felicity knew. She had found such honorable men to marry her sisters but, at Felicity's age, no such man would seek her company. Not now. And yet . . . something in her wish seemed to trigger an odd sensation . . . a strange warmth touched her. . . .

"What's the matter?" asked Jacques, seeing Felicity frown and rub her leg.

"I do not know." Felicity's fingers traced a hard object in her pocket. Reaching inside, she drew out a chunk of very warm metal—it was the golden star.

"Well, I never!" Felicity exclaimed in shock. She had left the star on the dressing table. How in heaven's name had it entered her pocket?

"Look!" exclaimed Jacques, his face brightening for the first time. "It is the Christmas star!"

"The Christmas star? You mean the Star of Bethlehem?"

"No, no! The Magi's Star. Like the song."

Felicity's brow furrowed. "Song?"

"The song of *Noel*!" said Jacques. "About the Magi who brought the gift to the baby Jesus. And the babe gave him a gift in return. I just learned the words in *Ang*lish!"

Felicity gazed at the star. "I recall the carol, little one, but this isn't the star in the song. I found this on the beach—"

"Near a fish?"

"A fishing net, but—"

"That is the one, that is the one! Wish on the star and you will find love!"

"Jacques, that's just a *story*, dear. We call it a *legend*. But it isn't true. This heirloom surely belongs to a gentlewoman, or perhaps a gentleman, who meant to give it as a Christmas gift. I mean to find its owner, and return it."

Jacques shook his head. "*You* are its owner. You found it!"

"But—"

"The shining star up in the sky / Is not the only Christmas light," Jacques began to sing, "the little babe reached out a hand / To bless the Magi who gifted him. . . ."

Felicity marveled at the little boy's sweet singing. The words were familiar to her—like the song of that golden-haired woman on the beach. What had happened to the woman? Felicity wondered yet again. The housekeeper had told her she was not part of this household—but she had ascended the cliff staircase that led directly to Castle Seabourne.

"One star of gold its center blue / Now carries what is brave and true / A love that came as Heaven's gift / Gave love to one who honored him / Star of heaven in the night / Now shines for one who treasures light / And if you find the Magi's star / The peace of love will bless your heart—"

"Jacques!" a voice sharply called, interrupting the child.

Felicity looked up to find plump Clara Smith frowning in the doorway.

Jacques's smile vanished. "*Oui,* Clara?"

"What did I tell you an hour ago?"

"I know, but Felicity found the Magi's Star and—"

"There'll be no singing Christmas songs any longer. And there'll be no mention of Christmas from now on. Do you understand?"

Felicity was dumbfounded at such a statement. But before she could question the housekeeper, Clara waved Jacques to her. Then she grabbed the little boy's hand and her chilly gaze disdainfully swept Felicity's dining costume.

"Jacques has eaten his dinner, Miss *Fairchild*," she snapped as if she did not believe Felicity's own name. "Yours is waiting. Follow me."

"What has this family come to?"

For a long time after the departure of his late brother's solicitor, William Court watched the flickering shadows in Castle Seabourne's grand, utterly empty dining room, and wondered why he had come back to this echo chamber of a home.

"Why?" he muttered to the tapestries hanging high on the wall, depicting the Court tribe's earliest patriarchs. "Do you hear me, old Courts?"

According to his late brother's solicitor, the estate was in terrible debt—a sum that exceeded even the fortune he'd amassed in his years at sea. What in hell was all his work for? he asked himself.

And to top that lovely news came an even more bitter pill. Thomas had a son—a *legitimate* heir.

"It is he who has become the heir, sir, not you," Thom's solicitor had informed Will in a crisp, official tone an hour before. "However, you have been named the boy's guardian, and shall hold the estate in trust until his eighteenth birthday."

"Hold the *debts* in trust, you mean!" Will had exploded.

The shock was still settling within him. The newest earl, apparently sequestered somewhere in this very house, was a young child—a near bastard, no less, made legitimate only by a hasty marriage before his birth. And he was half *French*!

Though Will had yet to meet the boy, years of grueling sea battles had taught him to despise that nation across the Channel, as well as its bloodthirsty occupants. How in hell could he now serve as guardian to a usurper claiming that wretched enemy as half his heritage?

"You wish me to endure, do you?" he barked at the still-life faces weaved into the tapestries now hanging over his head. "For the family honor, eh?" His gaze took in the face of Baldwin Etoile, the first sheriff of Devon. "You wish to remind me of my own Norman heritage? Well, damn your honor . . . and damn your damned heritage.''

Will rose and swallowed the estate burgundy, the last bottle of which sat desolately upon the endless oak table. "Your wine has soured, do you hear!'' he shouted, then hurled the glass into the hearth's dying flames.

The shattering sound echoed sickly through the room, then seemed to land directly in his pounding forehead. *Acceptance might well come to me,* he decided, *but not tonight.*

Tonight, he needed to throw honor on the fire.

Unbidden, an image came to him of the woman—the doxy—he'd carried upstairs. His swift examination of her clothed body had presented enticing curves. And the flash of fire in those gypsy brown eyes had promised barely banked passion.

She appealed. As did the generous shape of her mouth and the way she'd cursed him, then lifted her little chin in defiance. *Aye,* the promise of saucy friction heated Will's skin and coiled his muscles. It was to his taste. What he liked. And what he wanted.

I've been long at sea. Too long.

Seducing a whore in his old bedchamber was not a thought that had entered Captain William Court's mind when he'd first arrived at Seabourne. Acting the part of the gentleman was something he'd been willing to endure—for the respectability of his family name. But now that he knew what had become of the Courts' earldom, such was not his primary concern.

Not tonight.

Tonight he would thwart tradition as it had thwarted him, then perhaps, by morning, he could find enough honor left in him to do the right thing and accept the position of guardian to his nephew, the *legal* Earl of Devon.

As Felicity limped along behind Clara toward the formal dining room, she observed the castle with new eyes. Unlike Maidstone House, this grand place was barren of any garland or trinket. No holly, ivy, pine bough, or ribbon cheered the desolate halls they walked through.

Cobwebs hung in corners, dusty suits of armor seemed ready to swing battle-axes at trespassers, and there was no sign—not one—that Christmas was only eleven days away.

What a wretchedly stark place, thought Felicity. *Doubly so for a child at this time of year.*

At the dining room door, Clara gestured for Felicity to enter alone. She nodded and waved a silent little farewell to Jacques. Her heart went out to the golden-haired child. His wide blue eyes remained fixed upon Felicity with a sad kind of longing, right up to the moment she stepped out of sight.

The dining room she entered was large and richly paneled. A massive, magnificently carved stone fireplace dominated the room and a large table sat at the center, only a small portion at the end covered with a white cloth. At the head of the table sat a dark-haired gentleman, the nearest candelabra a good three feet away from him.

The man, whom she presumed to be William Court, sat so far back in the shadows that Felicity could not see the features of his face nor guess his age. But she could see that his attention was openly directed at her as she limped across the room.

The blatant inspection made Felicity uneasy—and uncharacteristically shy. She did not look hard into his shadowed face. Instead, she kept her own brown eyes cast downward. And since he failed to rise as she neared, she pulled out her own chair and sat at the only open place setting—three feet away, beside the candelabra.

The food had been served already. Stale bread, a small portion of cheese, and a roasted game bird. Shockingly simple, but she was hungry. She had not realized just how hungry until the scent of the food reached her nostrils.

"Eat," was all the man said, and he picked up his knife and fork without ceremony.

Felicity did the same and they ate in near-silence, the only sound an occasional chew, swallow, or clink of fork against china. It was the last sort of dining experience she expected at an estate as grand as Castle Seabourne, but then this day had been all-around strange.

If this truly was William Court, then Felicity had been gravely misled by the portrait in the family gallery. This man was acting nothing close to the role of a good gentleman. On the other hand, to be fair, the only actual contact Felicity had ever made with the Court family had been with Thomas, and then only briefly at a large dinner party in London almost two years before.

The late earl had drunk quite a lot, and seemed generally aloof and dispirited, not at all an easy man with whom to socialize. But he had been active in the House of Lords and respected in the first circles, so Felicity had then maintained her decorum—just as she was attempting to do now.

In silence, her dining companion poured her a glass of red wine and placed it, rather awkwardly, between them. She noticed a signet ring on his right hand when he placed the glass down. A family crest of some kind was likely embedded there, but she was sitting too far away to determine what it was.

Felicity stared at the glass of wine a moment and considered not taking it, but the ache in her ankle prompted her to reach for the glass and drink deeply. Unfortunately, the taste was slightly sour—not entirely unexpected given the state of cuisine in the place—and she had to force herself to finish it.

When their plates were nearly empty, Felicity finally raised her brown eyes to the man's face. His intense gaze was still on her, yet he remained silent. In pure frustration over her host's unorthodox lack of civil introduction—not to mention conversation—Felicity finally attempted a remedy herself.

"Shall I presume you are the late earl's brother?" she asked rather pointedly. "You *are* William Court?"

"What sort of outfit do you call that?"

Felicity tried not to sound apologetic about her appearance. After all, she was quite stranded and without options.

"The gown left for me was far too big," she explained coolly. "It may have fallen off me at any moment, and—" She stopped.

He was laughing.

"What is so amusing?" asked Felicity.

"Nothing. Go on."

"These were the only clothes in the room, and—"

"They're mine, you know. All the rage of 1778."

Felicity leaned closer toward the clean-shaven, short-haired man, trying to better view his shadowed features—perhaps to discover some resemblance to the younger man in the portrait. Then he laughed again, and she suddenly felt a shiver crawl through her. The familiar sound sparked her blood with simmering suspicion. Boldly she rose from her chair, picked up the candelabra, and moved two seats over, to the chair next to him.

When she slammed the candle stand in front of him, she noticed his right eye squint for a moment. Swiftly she took in the illuminated sight before her: The broad-shouldered physique was powerful beneath the tightly cut jacket. The raven-dark hair was *not* cut short after all, as the day's fashionable men preferred, but tied back in a tail. The face was handsome with a dimpled chin and squared-off jaw like the young man on the canvas. But a shallow scar marred the left cheek, as did the weather-worn skin and the hard, chilly expression in the features.

It was only the eyes that still bore the identical bold fire to his younger image. Their intense green was a striking distraction—the orbs even had a bluish hue. Like the eyes of the black-bearded *sailor*, realized Felicity with a jolt. This wasn't just William Withers Court. This was also her rescuer—the ruffian seaman with the eye patch!

With angry boldness, Felicity lifted her hand and covered his right eye.

"What happened to your eye patch?" she demanded, annoyed at being played for a fool. An instant later, Will Court's hand captured hers and held it fast. And in the long silent moments that followed, he studied her.

Felicity's blood raced at the slow, searing raking of her face and form. The raw stare assaulted her modesty, sending wave after wave of heat to the surface of her skin.

"I need it only in daylight," he finally informed her in a voice so low and intimate that it made her insides unsteady. "I am most comfortable in shadow."

Felicity tugged on her hand, but William Court would not release it. The audacious act of possessiveness stole the breath from her lungs.

"Why did you mislead me on the beach?" she asked, struggling to keep her voice steady. She'd die rather than show this brute how powerfully his nearness was affecting her senses. "Why did you not introduce yourself properly? You are not a lowly sailor."

"Indeed, I am not."

"Then why are you set on acting the part at present?"

"Perhaps tonight it better suits me." William Court's chuckle sounded dark and dangerous.

Felicity ignored the warning and tugged once more on her

hand. "What would Lord Thomas think of such behavior in his own home?" she goaded, still held fast.

"Thomas is *dead*," said the man, suddenly no longer amused.

Felicity swallowed. "Yes. And you are his *only* brother?"

"I am."

"Then you are the new Earl?" she pried with unpardonable curiosity. "You have inherited the—"

"I am not. I did not. His *son* assumes the title."

"His son?" So, it was true, realized Felicity. The boy she'd met was the late earl's legitimate son. Jacques Court was England's newest, and perhaps youngest, peer. "But why is this not known—"

"Few knew of the boy's existence, including me, until just before our dinner. The boy had been lately in France and everyone here had assumed that I had been the one to inherit . . ." Will Court's voice trailed off, then his green eyes searched her face. "But that is not your business," he pronounced. "And, speaking of your business . . . now that we have dined, what say we move toward it directly, my dear?"

Felicity blinked. The heat of the nearby fire and the wine, not to mention the day's events and her unhappy attraction to this unconventional—if not dangerous—man left her feeling very strange. The late Earl's brother was still holding fast to her hand and now he was beginning to move his fingers over it in a gentle massage. The sensation was far from unpleasant, but it was *quite* inappropriate.

"I do not understand," she told him. "Toward what?"

"Toward the bedchamber, I should think."

Felicity's sharp intake of breath seemed to amuse the man.

"You blush like a virgin, my dear," said William Court, his eyes shining brightly in the firelight as the tip of one callused finger began to circle her palm in a shockingly intimate caress. "It is quite an attractive device."

"It is no device, I assure you," rasped Felicity, fighting the dangerous responses that grew more heated with every brush of his long finger against the sensitive skin of her palm.

"Come, come, you need not make a game of this," he said. Then very softly, he added, "You forget how I found you."

Felicity's mouth gaped and she pulled on her hand so hard that William Court could no longer hold it. "Mr. Court, did your housekeeper not inform you of my name and connections?''

William's dark eyebrows rose as his torso leaned back into the menacing shadows. "She informed me who you *claim* to be.''

"I do not claim to be anyone but who I am: the Honorable Miss Felicity Fairchild, sister to the baron of—''

"Spare me,'' said William with weariness. "As my housekeeper also informed me, Lord Lyme's sisters, though they were raised nearby, do not reside in this region. They have lived in Bath for well over a decade. Clara says this has been known for years, and I cannot fathom why you are carrying on this silly charade. There is no need—''

"Sir, I—''

"That you were, at one time, mistress to a fine gentleman is suggested by your speech and manner. But set your mind at rest, my dear, you've no need to fear that I shall treat you as anything but a gentle creature within the bedchamber, if that is what this charade is all about—''

"What!'' shrieked Felicity, her cheeks flushing red.

"Be assured, I am no animal as those ruffians were on the beach. Though I am not at liberty to keep a mistress, I am prepared to pay you handsomely for one night of service. You are an appealing creature, and I will love you with gentleness. *There*, that should quell this theatrical show of outrage.''

"It is no show, I assure you, sir. Your assumptions are wretched and not to be borne. I have nothing more to say to you, except perhaps that you have been too long at sea and do not know how properly to act in good society.'' With as much dignity as she could muster, Felicity rose from her chair, threw down her napkin, and began to limp away.

When William Court finally responded, Felicity was almost at the doorway. "Very well, my dear, *honorable* miss,'' he called. "I shall yield to your wish. And, perhaps, in the end, I will take delight in your victory. Off to bed with you, then. I myself shall retire shortly.''

Felicity turned to eye the broad-shouldered man at the far end of the long table. His shadowed face was unreadable, but his tone of voice was far too superior, despite his appeasing words.

Felicity felt a shiver of wariness as she passed the cobwebbed suits of empty armor in the great hall. Resisting the urge to take one of their battle-axes to bed with her, she ascended the castle's daunting staircase.

I must be sure to lock my bedchamber door, she decided, hearing the howl of the freezing winter wind beyond the windows. *And leave as soon as morning comes.*

Five

Back in her bedchamber, Felicity shivered as she removed the long vest and silk stockings she'd donned before dinner. Now, of course, she regretted her choice—not only of clothing, which had clearly fueled the reckless and shocking assumptions of the late Earl's brother, but also the very act of attending dinner in the first place.

What, in heaven's name, had turned William Court, brother of Lord Thomas, into such a barbarian? An intriguing barbarian, she had to admit, but a barbarian nonetheless.

As she removed the borrowed loose-fitting silk knee breeches, she felt the hard points of the golden star inside it. She removed the charm and gazed at it once more, confused as ever at how it had gotten into her pocket. Then she placed it at her bedside.

She now stood naked, except for the oversized linen shirt, which fell nearly to her knees. The shirt would serve as a night rail, she decided, trying hard not to recall what the wretched man had said—that it was once *his own* shirt. The thought of that strong chest once filling the same garment that now brushed against her naked breasts nearly sent her into apoplexy.

"The door," she blurted in instant alarm. Rushing across the room, she tested the lock. It held firm. Still, she needed assurance that she would not be disturbed. She looked around the room for a heavy piece of furniture. A large bookshelf sat in the corner, but it appeared too large to move, so she settled for dragging the wooden dresser across the floor.

"There!" she said as she finished. "Get through *that*, Mr. William Court!"

Then she moved to the bed, blew out the bedside candle, and pulled the covers to her chin. The hearth was cold, of course, a fire being a clear extravagance for a household that appeared vastly lacking in servants and nearly shut down. But despite the icy cold, sleep came quickly to her.

Unsettling dreams came just as swiftly, unfortunately.

Disturbingly inappropriate ideas filled Felicity's head once her guard of propriety had dozed: a pair of brilliant green eyes, a whispering deep voice, and the feel of her hand being caressed. The intimate memories made Felicity toss and turn beneath the bedclothes.

"Are you asleep, Honorable Miss?"

It was the deep voice whispering again, realized Felicity, only it was not in her dream. Groggily she opened her eyes to the dim room. The corner of the room where the large bookshelf had been standing was now glowing with a warm golden light.

The shelf had been swung aside, she realized, like a false door on hinges. And, leaning against the passageway's frame, was a powerful, broad-shouldered physique, backlit by the hearth in the next room. The face remained in shadow, but Felicity knew well who it was.

Having removed his cravat and jacket, her uncouth dinner companion stood before her now in a half-opened linen shirt and skin-tight trousers—all the rage now for men of wealth in London and Bath.

William Withers Court had comfortably assumed the pose of rake.

That he had called her *"Honorable Miss"* implied, of course, that he knew her station as the daughter of a baron. But the act of lingering on the threshold of her bedchamber was an appalling insult to that station. What he was doing was *unthinkable*.

Every proper particle of Felicity's being was outraged. A banquet of bitter condemnation sat upon her tongue, and she parted her lips to serve them up forthwith . . . yet, for some reason, that useless piece of muscle in her mouth refused to offer a crumb.

"Shall I enter, Miss Fairchild?" The deep voice queried as sweetly and politely as if he had asked her to save a dance for him.

Felicity swallowed. She stared at the man in the doorway, knowing she should—she *must*—turn him away. Yet she *still* failed to speak a single syllable.

"They say silence implies consent, you know."

Felicity felt more than saw William Court smile in the shadowy room, and his first step across the threshold pushed her heart to her throat. *I cannot do this,* she railed to herself. *Turn him away. Now!*

But she did not.

There was a dangerous curiosity at work within Felicity, along with a deep-seated anger she barely realized. The rage she'd thought to dispel this morning with a mere walk upon the beach still burned within her—along with the echo of her cousin's overheard bibble-babble: "*And, at her age, you know what else is said . . .*"

Felicity could not help but measure that cold gossip against the warm whispering promise that William Court had made to her just an hour ago: *Set your mind at rest, my dear . . . I will love you with gentleness . . .*

Suddenly the desolation of spouting the label "spinster" on a frigid beach seemed a terrible contrast to the word "mistress" murmured by a worldly man before a roaring fire.

Felicity knew she could never live as a man's mistress. Nor should she ever have to. With her generous inheritance of thirty thousand pounds, she did not require a man's financial protection. But that was not precisely what concerned her now.

What concerned her now was living the rest of her life without knowing the feel of a man's love. . . . What concerned her now was the powerful physique of William Court striding casually across this bedchamber.

Felicity watched the man's back muscles move as he stooped by the cold hearth and worked to light it. The flames reached up to caress the dry kindling and the dark room quickly brightened with a red-gold glow, burnishing the breadth of his powerful torso, the wide shoulders, and broad chest that tapered down to lean hips and strong, long legs.

"Are you very cold?" he asked softly as sheets of rain beat at the window. "I shall find another blanket, if you like."

"I am fine," Felicity managed to whisper, moving to a sitting position. The bedclothes slipped to her lap and she let them stay there.

The earl's brother clearly noticed. His glimmering gaze took in her own form, exposed above the quilt. Her delicate shoulders and full breasts seemed to give him unashamed pleasure. "The gale blows furious tonight," he remarked with glimmering eyes as he started for the bed. Beneath the tight-fitting trousers, the muscles of his strong thighs bunched and relaxed as he moved. "There'd be bloody hell to pay under sail."

"Oh?" Felicity managed uneasily, trying to understand her own mind—and why in heaven's name she was allowing this to happen.

But she knew.

If good society could tread upon her reputation without pause, if it could fester rumor to destroy her chance for a respectable husband, if good society could drive her to feel like an outcast, then why should she bow to that society's rules?

This final streak of rebellion so distracted her that, before she knew it, William had crossed the room, and the weight of his powerful form was depressing the edge of the mattress.

Felicity's brown gaze suddenly caught on the glimpse of the smooth-muscled chest peeking out from the V of his parted linen shirt. She swallowed uneasily as her hands nervously fingered the fold of the blanket. Her palm recalled the tingling feel of this man's teasing touch only an hour before. The action had not been proper, but neither had it been unpleasant, she was forced to admit.

"Relax, my dear," soothed William's deep voice, as the heat of his long fingers came to rest lightly on the blanket above her thigh.

Felicity's response was a shocked gasp.

"I meant what I said belowstairs," insisted William. "I shall be *gentle* with you."

"Gentle," whispered Felicity.

"Aye," he said.

"And you acknowledge who I am?" she asked, her gaze finally meeting his own.

The question seemed to distress the man. He sighed heavily. "Did I not, just moments ago, call you by your *preferred* name?"

"My *what*?"

A tone of impatience entered his voice. "Why do you press me, woman? Is this not the game you wish to play?"

Felicity tried to reason out William Court's response—and behavior. Logic gave her the only answer possible. "You still believe I am pretending to be a genteel woman? You believe that I am some sort of doxy—that I am not truly Felicity Fairchild?"

"What does it matter who I believe you are? You and I both know we shall never see each other again after this night. . . ."

"But there should at least be truth between us . . ."

"I am a willing man, and you are a willing woman. That is truth enough for this bedchamber. If you wish to enhance our encounter by playing the genteel virgin, then by all means, do not let me begrudge you your pleasure."

"But I am not playing—"

"Enough," he said, putting a rough finger to her lips.

No matter what I say, Felicity considered frantically, *he does not believe that I am a Fairchild. When morning comes, he will send me on my way, convinced that his encounter was with an unknown woman. . . .*

William's dark-green eyes again began to measure Felicity's appearance in the flickering firelight.

She grew nervous when she realized this. She knew she was no raving beauty. Her mouth was too wide, her chin too weak, her nose far from perfect. But William Court did not look displeased with his unabashed inspection.

"Your skin is so very soft," he whispered, brushing her cheek, "and your eyes so very luminous. Their depth and warmth greatly appeals . . . And I should say your hair is better left unbound. There are strands of auburn and gold in these waves . . . quite lovely," he murmured, "like the sunset's rays in calm." Then he moved his finger to play with a curling lock.

Felicity watched William Court, amazed at his gentle sentiments.

She weighed them against John Drury's hard rejection of a

few weeks before, still raw in her mind. Words she'd never expected from a man she'd stupidly assumed had thought her dear: *Your honesty, Miss Fairchild, does you credit. However, you must understand that I, like most men, seek a woman who is, without question, capable of bearing him children. Therefore, I regret that our . . . ah . . . friendship cannot continue in any way that might give society—or you, of course—a reason to misconstrue it . . . indeed, I should think our . . . ah . . . acquaintance should, therefore, cease at once. . . .*

William Court seeemed to enjoy playing with one of Felicity's long chestnut curls, twirling it around and around his finger. "So silky . . . and soft . . ." he whispered, the motion mesmerizing her, relaxing her tense limbs, soothing the raw memory of Drury's rejection.

"Is that generous mouth the same, I wonder?" he asked. Then he slowly leaned forward, allowing her ample time to protest, to pull away, to run screaming from the room.

But she did none of those things.

Instead she studied his own mouth, sitting above the strong, dimpled chin. The lips were well formed and invitingly full. She watched them press forward toward hers, until feeling replaced sight, and she was fully occupied with the exquisite sensation of warm, full lips brushing featherlike against her, making Felicity feel as if she had as much to offer as he.

The last was a startling notion—for Drury had left her certain she had nothing whatever to offer a man.

The kiss lasted several moments before William pulled slowly away. "You are sweet to taste," he whispered raggedly. "More so than Seabourne's burgundy, I think. And so, I shall prefer to sample you tonight."

Sweet to taste? thought Felicity, feeling the heat of a blush upon her face. *What did he mean by that?* she wondered, and ran her tongue unsteadily along her lower lip.

She noticed him watching her innocent action. Curiously, the languidness of his dark eyes seemed to take on a growing intensity, as if the flames he'd ignited in the hearth were gradually leaping inside of him.

Then, in one swift move, he leaned in to take her mouth with his once more. This time, however, the kiss was no mere light brushing. The pressure was more forceful, the intensity more passionate. She felt his lips part and the light tickle of his tongue against her closed mouth.

Unsure what to do, Felicity stiffened.

In response, Will Court stiffened.

After a moment, however, a low chuckle issued from deep in his throat.

"You play your part well," he whispered against her mouth, then his tongue pushed forward, urging her lips to part for him.

The spearing was a shockingly intimate sensation, and Felicity's sharp intake of breath seemed to encourage the man's ardor. As his tongue twined and teased her own, the hand resting on the blanket began softly to stroke her thigh, while the other hand reached around to her neck to coax her head first this way and then that, allowing him further access to her mouth.

The passionate kiss was exquisite and Felicity felt a low moan of wonder escape her throat. *If I am to enter the life of chilly celibacy among good society,* she concluded at last, *why should I not at least have an anonymous taste of what I will be missing for the rest of my life? Why should I not, for one secret night, sample more of this forbidden fire between men and women?*

Her intermittent moans of pleasure, combined with the curling of her arms around his neck, seemed to produce yet another reaction from the late earl's brother. His hand became bolder, moving up her thigh on a deliberate course.

The callused fingers slipped beneath the makeshift night rail and traveled to her naked waist, then they brushed along her rib cage. Felicity could feel the cool, smooth metal of his signet ring—an intriguing contrast to the ticklish warmth of his rough skin.

She tried to remain relaxed during this shockingly intimate contact. She was, after all, supposed to be a worldly woman. But maintaining composure was beyond difficult.

When his long fingers reached a naked breast, Felicity's heart nearly stopped. With slow, gentle movements, he cupped the full round of flesh, then used one callused thumb to tease the tip.

The stunning response in Felicity's body was a revelation.

She had no words for what these almost reverent touches made her feel.

"Do you enjoy this?" whispered William against her lips.

"Yes," Felicity answered raggedly, her head tilting backward, her lips parting in ecstasy. "Oh, yes. . . ."

The low throaty chuckle sent more shivers of pleasure through her. Then a hand was at the back of her head and strong, eager lips were at hers again. A warm, soft tongue plunged into her mouth and she moaned as she felt the power of this man's desire for her. It was a heady, incredible gift, making her feel more alive . . . more cherished . . . more *real* than she'd ever felt in her life.

After many more minutes of his passionate kissing, Felicity heard her lover expel a soft moan, then suddenly pull himself away and rise from the mattress.

For a terrible moment, she felt panic. Had she done something wrong? Was he going to reject her?

No, she realized, in the next moment. He had risen to remove his clothing.

You can still turn back, cried one last, respectable part of Felicity as William Court began to disrobe. It was that modest part of her that could not help but blush and look away as he stripped off his shirt and trousers. Within her turbulent spirit, however, there was but one driving desire: to give even more liberties to the man who had so patiently and sweetly revealed the passion inside of her—a passion she had never realized she possessed. A passion that made her feel both joy and power in being a woman.

When William had finished undressing, he slipped beneath the bedclothes and swiftly drew Felicity into his arms. With deft movements, he pulled the night rail from her naked curves and tossed it toward the foot of the bed.

At her age, and with the background he believed of her, Felicity was not surprised to have him desire a coupling without further preamble. Despite this, however, she could not stop herself from stiffening as he swiftly covered her small, soft body with his own hard form, then urged her legs to part for him.

Something went awry on his first eager attempt to enter her, and Felicity's eyes closed with anxiety. For a few moments, there was an awkwardness to his movements as his hand slipped below. Then he thrust forward once more and a low moan escaped his throat as the hard length of him filled her completely.

An instant later two things happened in quick succession: a sharp pain high inside of Felicity made her cry out; then her lover instantly stilled.

Felicity opened her eyes to find a dark-green gaze staring down at her in nothing short of shock.

He knows, she thought in horror. *He knows.*

Felicity waited for him to ask the questions so clearly written on his face. But he said nothing. Instead, he instantly pulled out of her and rolled away.

With the warm weight of his body gone, she was startled at how utterly bereft she now felt.

Is there not more to this act? she almost whispered, but held her tongue as he silently rose from the bed and gathered up his clothes.

The fire had lessened in intensity by now, but enough flames still breathed with life to shed flickering gold on William Court's face as he turned to speak.

"I am sorry I did not believe you," he said softly at the bookshelf passageway. "Truly sorry." Then he turned and left the room, firmly pulling the connecting door closed between them.

Six

What will she demand of me?

It was the first thought that entered William Court's mind when he awakened the next morning, one eye squinting in the sun-washed room. A woman in such a position as Felicity Fairchild's could require one of two things: marriage, or to be kept as his mistress.

She has entrapped me, thought Will unhappily as he reached for his eye patch. Then he instantly cursed himself. He could not blame her for this. The woman had tried to tell him, over and over, that she was a virgin—and sister to a highly respected landowner in the region. It was his own stubborn arrogance that had assumed she was lying.

But why in heaven's name did she not turn me away from her bed?

Again and again, as he washed and dressed, Will Court replayed the events of the night before. He recalled the haughty friction from her in the dining room, but after he'd entered her bedchamber, there'd been no further protests to his advances.

As he descended the castle's staircase, Will tried to drive away the lingering desire she'd ignited within him. . . .

"Do you enjoy this?"

"Yes . . . Oh, yes. . . ."

Her every response had inflamed him! The intoxicating mix

of modest blushes and sultry moans nearly undid him before he'd even disrobed.

Will had stupidly thought her reactions were the masterful tricks of a professional. How could a woman with such a hungry mouth, and such powerful responses to his lightest touch, be inexperienced in such matters?

I still burn for her, he thought miserably.

Indeed, pulling away had been one of the hardest acts of his recent years. But, thank heavens, he *had* pulled away. At least he could be assured that no offspring would be forthcoming—that fact alone was his only leverage with her now.

"Perhaps she will be reasonable," he muttered to himself, "and allow me to set her up as my mistress."

Yes, that will be for the best.

He did not want marriage. Nor children.

Nor the agony he knew so well when things went awry with them.

He would return to the sea, and, on occasions that suited him, return to warm her bed. A slight smile touched his lips at that prospect. Then Will stilled in the great hall, as the horrible memory of the solicitor's visit came back to him.

I cannot set her up, he realized. As the guardian of his brother's son, he was now morally obligated to pay the debts on Castle Seabourne. It would wipe out every farthing of his hard-earned funds. Unless . . .

Unless he *sold* the castle, along with its lands and title.

It was a terrible betrayal of his family's legacy—and honor. But the entailment tangle had been made clear to him the previous evening by the solicitor. Entailment of any estate—and prevention of its sale in whole or in part—was only achieved if a deed of settlement was signed by its owner. Each deed legally covered two generations of inheritance.

William's grandfather had been the last to sign such a deed, which kept the land intact down to Thomas. Thomas should have signed a deed himself, to continue the primogeniture tradition, but he did not, which meant the entailment stopped with Jacques.

Selling Seabourne, as abhorrent as the idea felt to William, was a legal option.

The sale would pay off the accrued debts and leave quite a bit extra to set up his brother's half-French child with a very handsome trust fund and tuition in some respectable English boarding school or other.

It was, in many ways, a heartless and ruthless option to take. But William Court had not been named "Sea Hunter" for being soft. He had spent enough years in naval warfare to know that all practical strategies, even ruthless ones, were options to be seriously weighed—*without* emotion.

So he strode to the drawing room to weigh them.

"Mr. Court, sir?"

William had been standing before the gallery of family portraits for what seemed like hours. He stood now below a single one—it was the face of a twenty-year-old young man. The expression of great good hope stunned him.

He had not seen that face in his dressing mirror for at least fifteen years. It was distressing to him—more deeply than he cared to admit—to realize how much good Will Court had changed.

"Mr. Court?"

Will turned to find his housekeeper panting. "Yes, Clara, what is it?"

"I've heard some news—it's about that woman. You know, the one who *claimed* to be the Honorable Miss Felicity Fairchild. Well, I've just heard—"

"That she *is*."

"Yes, sir! How did you know?"

"Lucky guess," said Will dryly.

"Your bailiff brought the word," Clara continued. "It seems her family put out a search for her last evening. God knows how she ended up here—but I've just been upstairs to check on her and—"

"How is she?"

"Not well, sir."

Will's brow furrowed. "What do you mean?"

"Fever, I'm afraid. Shall I summon the doctor?"

"At once. At *once*!" Will exclaimed as he started for her bedchamber.

"What of your bailiff, sir?" called Clara after him. "Charles Jones is waiting in the kitchen—"

"Send him to her family to set their minds at ease. I will sit with Miss Fairchild until the doctor arrives."

• • •

"Yes, Jacques. The song you sang for me was the French version. When I was a little girl, I learned another version."

"Sing it for me, *s'il vous plaît, mademoiselle*?"

"You may call me Felicity."

"*Oui*, Felicity, sing it, please?"

Will stopped a few feet from the doorway to his old bedchamber. He heard the conversing voices of Miss Fairchild and a small child. *Thom's heir,* he assumed, an arrow of bitterness instantly entering his heart.

"Star, star come from afar / Shining night and day," sang Felicity's light, sweet voice. "Star, star, come where we are / And show us the blessed way...."

Will tensed, as he always did when he encountered Christmas carols—or anything having to do with the Yule holiday. The dark memory of one terrible Christmas Day here at Seabourne came back to him, but he quickly buried it, as he always did—just as he had buried the essence of that good Will in the drawing room portrait, well over fifteen years ago.

"Wait! Let me learn it!" cried the child.

"All right. I'll sing it slowly, so you may join me. 'Star, star come from afar—' "

Stepping up to the doorway, Will quietly surveyed the scene in the bedchamber. Felicity was propped up with pillows—and the sight of her there on the mattress, her lovely chestnut hair still unbound, sent shivers of memory over his flesh and a tightness through his loins.

Taking a breath to compose himself, Will quickly shifted his attention to the other side of the mattress, where a fairhaired child gazed at Felicity adoringly.

Like mother and child, Will thought. He wanted to push that thought away ... but for some reason, he could not. So he simply stood there, watching them. After singing the song, Jacques became so excited he began chattering in French. Felicity joined him. Will's own French was quite good, but he shifted uneasily. He did not care for the enemy's language to be spoken in his own home.

"Oh," Felicity exclaimed, finally catching sight of him. "Mr. Court."

"Yes," said Will softly. "I understand you are not well?"

"It is only a touch of a headache—"

"Clara says fever."

"I am slightly warm, but—"

"Monsieur?" the child interrupted. "Are you *mon oncle?*" asked the boy, staring solemnly up at him.

The child was an angel, with a strong Court chin and his brother's sky-blue eyes. Will's heart naturally began to open to his nephew, but he resisted this. He could not make a proper decision about the boy and the estate if he allowed his emotions to cloud his judgment. And, since Will did not intend to stay long at Seabourne, it would be better for the boy not to form an attachment.

"Speak English," said Will stiffly.

The little boy shrunk back at the chilly rebuke. *"Oui,"* he whispered nervously. "Are you . . . my uncle?"

"I am your father's brother, William. And your legal guardian."

"Then I am pleased to meet you, sir."

William's gaze strayed to Felicity's face. What he saw there distressed him greatly. She was angry. Terribly angry. With him.

"Please leave us, Master Jacques," said William. "We have adult affairs to discuss."

Jacques nodded, then he turned to Felicity and chattered in French for a moment. Finally, he said, "I will go now, but, here, you keep the golden star . . . and you also hold my *soldats* to guard you from—" The little child glanced unhappily back at his imposing uncle and said a few things more in French. "You know," he finally whispered. "To keep you safe."

"Merci," said Felicity, petting the child's head while glaring daggers at William. *"Merci, mon petit Jacques."*

"Do you have no heart?" snapped Felicity the moment the child was gone. William Court stood dumbfounded a moment, then he silently moved to close the door.

Felicity took the opportunity to survey the man. His eye patch was back in place, and his broad-shouldered physique was without a jacket. The flowing linen shirt was casually open at the neck, revealing a glimpse of smooth muscle. The memory of having that hard torso pressed against her naked breasts came back to her—and the resulting trembling nearly undid her.

Quickly she dropped her gaze. But that helped little. His tight-fitting trousers again outlined the movements of his powerful thighs as his polished boots turned from the door and moved across the large room. Felicity tried to distract herself from the overwhelmingly masculine presence—and her annoying reaction to it—by reminding herself of her anger.

"Did you hear me?" she challenged, fighting the ridiculous feminine fluster going on within her.

"Yes."

"And?"

"And the answer is *no*," stated Will Court. "I have no heart. Not any longer . . . which is why I might suggest you consider your present options quite carefully."

"Pardon me, sir . . . my *what*?"

Pulling over a stiff wooden chair, the young earl's rugged uncle sat down and crossed his legs. "Your options," he said calmly. "What happened last night was a mistake, *Miss Fairchild*, we both know that."

Felicity's unsteady hands gripped the edges of the blanket. "So *now* you choose to believe me?"

"You are a virgin, or *were*, before I . . ." The man sighed and rubbed his eyes, then the back of his neck. It appeared this was not as easy for him as he'd first led her to believe.

"Do not worry yourself," said Felicity, suddenly calm. Now that she saw his distress, it was easier for her to feel at ease. "I release you from any obligation."

The stunned look on William Court's face made Felicity break into laughter.

"Excuse me, Miss Fairchild, but what in heaven's name can you possibly find *amusing* about this situation?"

"You," Felicity burst out on a bubbling chuckle.

William moved closer to the bed and put his hand against her forehead. "Are you delirious?"

"I am fine," she said, pulling his hand away. The brush of rough calluses against her smooth skin sparked an intimate memory. Her flustered reaction was impossible to hide.

William Court studied that reaction for a long moment, his hand lingering the slightest bit to maintain contact with her own, then he pulled away and sat back in the chair. "There is a doctor coming,'' he said softly. ''You are warmer than is healthy.''

''I am fine, but I do thank you for your concern.''

''It is quite apparent that you should stay here at Seabourne,'' he said as resolutely as a military commander. ''You must not be transported in this cold weather.''

''I am sound enough to—''

''You shall stay. I insist,'' he fairly barked.

Felicity regarded him. ''Were you, by chance, in the military?''

''I *am* in the Royal Navy.''

''Let me guess, you are a *captain*?''

''Aye, and up for promotion to rear admiral.''

''Why am I not surprised?'' she remarked wryly.

''A ninety-gun man-of-war, Miss Fairchild. Nearly shot to hell at the Battle of the Nile.''

''The Nile?'' Felicity's eyebrows rose. The battle had been a great victory for the British Navy. Napoleon had been resoundly stomped—for the moment, anyway. If the man sitting before her had participated, he was likely a very fine officer, and decorated, as well. ''You were knighted?'' she guessed.

''G. C. O. B.''

Felicity could not help being impressed. Grand Commander of the Order of the Bath was a high distinction of knighthood, conferred for distinguished military service.

''Your eye?'' she asked. ''Did the injury happen at the Nile?''

William nodded. ''It may improve. The ship's surgeon gave no assurances.''

''Were you relieved of duty, then? Is that why you are here?''

''I am here because my brother's death has left me a mound of unhappy responsibilities, of which I am attempting to sort out.''

''I see. And would Jacques be one of them?''

''Yes.''

Felicity considered this news while William Court gazed at her in awkward silence. It seemed to her that there was something else bothering the captain—something that put him in a sort of perplexed agony. Yet he could not seem to get the subject onto his tongue.

"Is there something on your mind, sir?" Felicity finally prompted.

"No . . . yes . . ." He shifted awkwardly then sighed. "Last night. Why did you . . . Why did you let me . . . ?"

Felicity could not blame the man for being curious. "It is my business," she answered quietly. "And, as I say, you are released from any obligation."

"Well . . . ," said William Court, rising to pace the room. "Well . . ."

"That is a deep subject."

William halted and stared at her. "Stop trying to be amusing. This is not an amusing matter."

Felicity shrugged. "You are anxious for no reason, Sir William—"

"Just call me William."

"No."

"Then 'Captain,' if you please."

Felicity exhaled. "Perhaps, *Captain*, you have spent too many years deciphering enemy strategies. And—you may be surprised to hear this—but that is an endeavor with which I am not completely unfamiliar, given the duplicitous state of fashionable society,—not to mention the complexities of courtship. But, I assure you, there is no trick here, if that is what you imagine. No *game*, as you incessantly suspected last night—"

"What if I do not wish to be released," he blurted.

Now it was Felicity's turn to be struck dumb—and perplexed. "But . . . it is not your prerogative!"

"Why not?"

Felicity thought about this a moment. "Society gives you the option to hold land and office. In return, I suppose, it gives me the option to hold you to a moral obligation."

"Damn society."

"Yes." Felicity's eyes brightened. Her mouth twitched. "That is something I tried to do last evening."

William looked surprised. "Is this why you let me . . . ? Were you angry? Or, perhaps, tired with the rules of propriety?"

"Something like that."

William Court seemed to be studying Felicity with new eyes. It was as if he'd discovered something about her that he enjoyed—perhaps even admired. "Miss Fairchild . . . I have a proposition for you—"

"Unlike the one you made at dinner last evening?"

"Please do not shame me."

"You, sir? Shamed? I think not."

William laughed, but there was a sharp edge to it. "You should not attempt to believe you know me so well, Miss Fairchild—it may prove dangerous."

"I am not afraid of you."

"Perhaps you should be."

"I am an independent woman, sir. I have a generous inheritance, and do not seek the protection of any man, if that is what you were going to—"

"Forgive me," said William Court shortly. "I withdraw my offer."

Felicity leaned back against the pillows. Her pride had injured his. With uncertainty she looked into his face. "What *was* your offer?" she asked, her voice softer. "Forgive *me*, Captain, and please tell me."

William Court's hardened expression softened at the apologetic tone of Felicity's voice, but it seemed he could not bring himself to speak.

As she waited for him to make up his mind what, if anything, to say, Felicity absently reached for the tiny toys Jacques had left for her. The little wooden soldiers were clearly a beloved talisman for the child.

The boy had come to her room this morning to see the golden star again—or so he claimed. Then he'd stayed to chatter with her for over an hour.

The child had told Felicity that his mother had died when he was just a baby; and that he'd been moved from family to family across the French countryside for years, until his father had tracked him down.

Nine months ago, Thomas Court had finally brought his son to his rightful home of Seabourne—and just one month after that, the man had died.

Felicity's own heart went out to the child. She knew too well, from raising her own broken-hearted brother and three sisters, how losing both parents so very young would make a child feel helpless and alone—as if there was no one who could ever make the child feel safe and loved again.

"What do you have there?" asked the captain, spying the toy in her hands.

"Jacques's *soldats*," said Felicity, holding one up.

"*French* soldiers," he remarked with slight disgust upon seeing the uniform.

Felicity frowned, her earlier anger returning with lightning speed. "Captain Court, do you have no feelings for your own nephew?"

A menacing cloud of thunder seemed to enter the man's unpatched eye. "I warned you, Miss Fairchild. Do not presume to know me."

"Your treatment of him is cold. The child needs love and acceptance—"

"Luxuries which are hard to come by in this world."

"That is a hard view, sir."

"It is my view."

"Then I am truly sorry for you . . . but not as sorry as I am for Jacques."

The captain folded his arms across his broad chest. "You presume to know what he needs, then? You think he needs a family? A home?"

"Of course. Do you not mean to provide one for him?"

"I know only how to make my living on the sea, not on the land. What if I told you that I intend to sell Seabourne and place Jacques in a boarding school?"

Felicity's heart nearly broke at such words. "But this is your family's home, is it not?"

"Aye, and the seat of the Devon earldom for centuries."

"Is it not entailed?"

"Not at present, miss. A loophole of sorts has opened."

Stunned, Felicity studied the hard face of this hard man. "How can you be so . . . so unfeeling? So lacking in honor!"

"No heart. I warned you at the outset."

"I do not believe you. Every human has a heart. Why would you do such a thing?"

"Debts, my dear. Massive ones. And lately, a mortgage on the entire property. She sinks as a whole, I'm afraid."

Felicity considered his statement for a moment. "How massive are these debts?"

"Twenty-two thousand. Five more than I've amassed in my years of lucrative campaigns."

"But eight less than my dowry," she whispered.

William Court's eyes widened in obvious shock and, it seemed to Felicity, slight embarrassment. "You are indeed an independent woman, Miss Fairchild . . . and so I will leave you—"

"Wait," she called, making an instant decision as he bowed respectfully, then started for the door.

"Why?" he asked, turning back.

"Because, sir, I have a proposition for *you*."

Seven

"Married!"

"Aye, Clara, that is what I said."

"To the *Fairchild* woman?"

"Aye." William Court had to smile at the shocked face of his housekeeper. "Do not you think Jacques could use a mother? And I a wife?"

"Of course, sir, yes, indeed! But it is so . . . so sudden."

"Aye, we've just clapped hands on the bargain up in my old bedchamber— Good heavens, Clara, do not look so shocked. We are both beyond our tender years, she and I. It is a good arrangement and Miss Fairchild has proven herself a very rational and level-headed woman—quite refreshing from my usual encounter with the female mind . . . ah . . . excepting, of course, your practical self, Clara . . ."

"Thank you, sir."

"She says she desires to be a married woman, and she has taken a liking to Jacques. Enough so that she has agreed to sink her dowry into securing Seabourne—"

"Thank God," whispered Clara.

"And thank Miss Fairchild," added Will with a wink. "Her family's expertise in managing tenant farms will be valuable to us all. Her brother, and her father before him, have made the Fairchild lands among the most profitable in the region. She says she will work to see that the Court lands are keenly evaluated by her brother's own bailiff—and brought up to speed on the most modern farming methods. Aye, I should think she will prove herself a great asset to you and Nolan and, of course, our own bailiff, Charles Jones, after I leave—''

"Leave? But, sir, you've only just arrived!''

"My life is on the seas, Clara. Once I've married the new Mrs. Court, I shall apply to my naval superiors for a new ship. Miss Fairchild understands this—indeed, I think it is what induced her to agree to the arrangement. She likes to say that she is an 'independent' sort of woman—one who seems comfortable without a man around.''

"But . . .''

William eyed the old housekeeper. He respected her opinion too highly to leave that "but" hanging over him. "What, Clara? Tell me your mind.''

"It is not my place.''

"For heaven's sake, woman, you've known me longer than anyone living. I'll be relying on you and Nolan to take care of my new wife and Seabourne's new earl—so please, damn propriety a moment and tell me what you *truly* think.''

Clara's eyes widened at her master's blunt invitation. After a moment's deliberation, she finally spoke. "Your wife *will* need you, sir, despite anything she might say. And so will the new earl. And so, if I may say it, will Seabourne. Your brother, Lord Devon, may he rest in peace, was never the same after . . . after the terrible Christmas accident on the cliff—''

"I well remember,'' Will whispered.

"—and then you left for the Royal Navy and your mother, bless her soul, passed on, and Lord Devon lost touch with Seabourne—likely because of the bad memories—letting her suffer under neglect, as I'm afraid all her tenants have, as well. The crops have gone from bad to worse, and this household is in the same condition.''

"My brother had acquired *other* interests, I understand,'' said William coolly. "In France.''

"Yes, sir. And I understand he loved Jacques's mother very much,'' said Clara pointedly. "He told Jacques as much before he himself died.''

"Then why did he not bring his wife to Britain, and make his marriage known?''

"Lady Anna Devon was the daughter of a French Viscount

and, with your brother not being French, she would not agree to marry him until she was with child. By then the terrible events began in Paris to bring down the aristocracy. Lord Devon was frantic by that time to convince her to leave, but she refused, wishing to stay close to her large family, who tried holding tight to their properties. So Lord Devon married her there in Paris and stayed to be near her.''

Will was surprised to hear these details. ''What happened then?''

''It was not long before Lady Devon's father was branded a traitor by those who'd killed King Louis. When he was thrown in prison, your brother raced back to London to secure help. He could not bring his wife, for she was about to give birth to Jacques. But Lord Devon felt the trip was worth the effort. He believed he could persuade the British Crown to intervene and save the lives and property of Lady Devon's family.''

''But, of course, they could not,'' Will provided on a knowing breath.

Clara nodded. ''While Lord Devon was in London, the Viscount's entire household was thrown in the Bastille. Lady Devon might have been all right if she had been strong. But she had just given birth, and was weak. Though she had managed to have Jacques smuggled out of Paris, she herself died of exposure in her prison cell.''

Will was stunned to hear such a heart-wrenching story. He had imagined another scenario entirely. Something much more sordid—and selfish. He was now sorry for his lack of faith in his older brother. ''What did Thomas do?'' he asked. ''I cannot imagine how he must have—''

''He was devastated,'' supplied Clara softly. ''But he never gave up trying to find his son. Hard drinking, I am sorry to tell you, was his only solace. It is a tragedy that he had but one month with his child before his own body gave out.''

''One month? The boy knew his father for only a single month? Why?''

''It took years for Lord Devon's agents to find the boy. He was living with distant relatives in a tiny town one hundred miles from Paris, near his mother's hometown of Rouen—''

''Normandy,'' murmured Will, the irony hitting him hard.

"Where is the child now?" he asked, glancing about the great hall.

"Likely one of the old towers. I've told him a hundred times to stay out of them, but he manages to slip up there despite all I say—like two *other* young gentlemen I remember," she said with a scold in her tone, but a light from happy memories in her pale-blue eyes.

"Thank you for your candor, Clara," said Will softly, then he turned.

"Mr. Court, where are you going? Your bailiff is due to return for your meeting!"

"Tell Jones to come back when Miss Fairchild is feeling better. My future wife is the one with the land sense. It is she and her family who will wish to review all of his practices, and she should be present at the meeting."

"I shall tell him, sir, but where are you off to?"

"Family business," he called, heading toward a courtyard door. "Then I'll be traveling. I must consult with Miss Fairchild's brother in Lyme, then journey directly to London for a special marriage license. Miss Fairchild wishes to wed on Christmas Eve. I shall be back by then."

"Jacques?" called Will.

Atop the old stone tower, the fair-haired boy turned from his pretend sword fighting on the parapet with a look that said he knew that he was in trouble. To the boy's credit, he did not cry or protest, but simply stood awaiting his uncle's sentencing.

"You know you should not be up here, do you not?" scolded Will. "These old towers are a hazard. I'll never understand why my father did not tear them down."

"Oui, monsieur," the boy said loudly, staring Captain William Court down, daring him to challenge again the use of his native tongue.

Will said nothing; instead he strolled closer to the child with the stubborn Court chin and his brother's eyes.

"You know, of course, that I grew up here—along with your father?"

"Oui . . . yes . . ."

"And do you know that this tower you are standing on is hundreds of years old?"

"Hundreds?"

"Aye . . . " Will gazed down at the boy. "Do you see these chinks in the stone? They were likely made by battle-axes."

"Truly?" The boy's small fingers reached up to feel the indentations.

"And, of course, my name—*our* name—Court—is a shortened version of the French town Courtnay."

"It is?"

"Yes, Jacques. The first Earl of Devon, the very first, descended from a man who lived on this spot seven hundred years ago. His name was Baldwin Etoile, and he was Norman—from Normandy." William gave the child a hesitant smile. "Like you."

"He was French, like me?"

"Yes, like you."

"Was *he* allowed to speak French here?"

Will could not help but broaden his smile. The child was both stubborn and clever—a Court to be sure.

"Yes, Jacques," Will told his nephew, "and so may you . . . if you speak equal amounts of English. For you are half English. Never forget that."

"*Oui, monsieur.* I mean . . . yes, I understand."

"Good." William turned to go.

"And what happened here after this French man came, Uncle William?" the boy called, his young voice clearly reaching out to a man cast in his papa's likeness.

Turning back, Will gazed at the child's sky-blue eyes. For a moment—the briefest of moments—it felt as though he was with Thom again, laughing as they pretended to be knights at war on their battlements. The memory touched him like a breath of wind on a dead-still sail—it was a sweet gift, and made him want to give something in return.

"Well, let me see now," said Will, moving back to the boy. "We Courts have a history of being great seamen and traders. It has been in only the last century that we acquired the landed life. In fact, men from this county of Devon led the way to sailing the world's seas. Hawkins, Gilbert, and Grenville were all Devon men. And perhaps the greatest of them all was Drake—"

"Who was Drake?"

"Who was *Drake*?" said Will, hunkering down closer to

the boy. "Only the greatest British sailor who ever sailed! And a Devon man, through and through. Why, he set off to circle the world—"

"And what happened to him?"

"Well, now, you'd better have a seat, my boy, for this is a lengthy tale. . . ."

From her bedchamber, Felicity peered out the window to have a look at the view. Beyond the tangled gardens, the cliff's dramatic drop gave a sweeping vista of Lyme Bay, and the English Channel beyond it.

"The mistress of Castle Seabourne," whispered Felicity. "The wife of Sir William Court."

She could hardly believe the turn of events. But then, life's road was never lacking in turns, in her estimation. She only hoped, given the captain's unpredictable disposition, she could hold on for this ride.

The thought was followed by an encouraging sight on the property. Atop one of the old stone towers, a tall figure with the blackest of hair sat next to a small one with golden curls. The two were talking, Felicity realized. And laughing into the wind.

She watched them for half an hour, the smile of contentment never leaving her face.

"Miss Fairchild?"

Felicity turned to find Clara Smith hovering at her door. "Yes?"

"May I help you with anything more?"

"Yes," said Felicity, her mind working. "When I was a small child, I seem to remember wonderful Christmas Eve parties were held here at Seabourne. I was always too young to go, but I recall my parents did."

Clara nodded at once. "Oh, yes, miss, the late Lord and Lady Devon, William's parents, loved to throw a grand feast for their tenants and the neighbors from miles and miles around."

Felicity turned back toward the window. "And then the parties stopped. Do you know why they stopped?"

The silence in the room unnerved Felicity. "Clara?" she asked, turning.

"It is not my place to discuss it," she said stiffly. "You must ask Mr. Court."

"Yes, of course . . . but, Clara, you know he is a *captain*, do you not?"

Clara's eyes widened. "He did not mention it. But then, Master William was never one to stand on such things. However, I shall remember the distinction from now on."

"Thank you," said Felicity with a warm smile, happy to have done something more for her new husband-to-be—such a man who was willing to take her, even with her full confession that she might never be able to bear him children. Her dowry was, of course, the compelling reason for their bargain—but Felicity knew that if he'd wanted to, a man as accomplished and attractive as Sir William might have applied to the marriage mart for a younger wife with an even greater dowry. In her heart, Felicity hoped that, even in their short acquaintance, some spark of affection had been ignited within him—as it had in her—enough for William to desire their union in more ways than simply financial.

"And Clara, I was thinking . . . since I am to marry Captain Court on Christmas Eve, why not bring back the tradition of the Seabourne Christmas Eve feast? My brother, I know, will be all too pleased to finance it, and lend us some of Maidstone's staff, and I would like to surprise my husband-to-be. What do you think?"

Felicity watched Clara consider the idea for a long minute. "It is perhaps time," she said solemnly. "Yes, perhaps a wedding is just the thing that will bring joy back to Seabourne, and so a party cannot be wrong, then, can it?"

"No, of course not. How could a wedding party ever be wrong?"

But Clara did not elaborate; she merely smiled warmly, then asked what she might do to help Seabourne's new mistress.

Eight

"They marry tonight, Charlie."

"And she'll be runnin' the place tomorrow. What say ya ta that?"

Charles Jones, bailiff to Seabourne for the past ten years, scratched his red head and grimaced at the two men who'd approached him in the nearly empty pub. "I say I should 'ave known better than to leave an important job to you two."

Tall Tim and Fat Tom sat down at the scarred and stained wooden table. The two were only semireliable henchmen, as far as Charles Jones was concerned, likely as not to bungle a task as to pull it off. But they were second cousins and the only ones he'd trust well enough to help handle this.

"Eleven days ago, all I told you to do was keep an eye on the bay for Court's ship," Jones muttered, "then simply set up a little 'accident' on the cliff steps. But you two've got less brains between you than a pair of sheep."

Charles Jones had grown used to years of Lord Thomas's absence. The neglect had allowed him to amass a very nice pocket of graft. The new heir, being no more than a babe, left Jones an even better opportunity to extort from the estate of

Seabourne. William Court's guardianship was his only fear.

Court's showing up on his own beach looking like an ordinary seaman had been an unhappy surprise. Will Court's violent turn on Tim and Tom had been an even greater shock. But his quick connection to a smart wife with land sense was the greatest stunner of all.

"What say ya, then?" asked Tall Tim, bringing a sudsy ale to his lips.

"Aye, what do we do?" echoed Fat Tom.

"We wait," said Charles Jones; then he took a long drink from his own glass, glanced around the nearly empty pub, and lowered his voice. "The right moment will present itself again, boys. I understand the *cap'n* means to return to the navy. When he sails off, we kill the woman."

Fat Tom smiled. "*Just* kill her?"

"I don't give a bloody care what you two do with her before she dies," rasped Jones. "Just as long as she ends up dead."

The coach from London had taken Captain William Court as far as Exeter. But there his luck ran out.

"Damned land travel," he grumbled after the fifteenth mile on horseback. "I'd give anything for a pair of oars."

At least the weather was not as painful as his seat. The air was crisp enough to harden any mud on the roads, yet warm enough to prevent the tips of his ears from falling off.

The sight of Seabourne's lights at sunset was a great relief. In fact, it warmed his heart to know he would soon be seeing Jacques again . . . and, of course, Miss Fairchild. Will smiled at the thought of her. The memory of the woman's luminous eyes, generous mouth, and unbound hair—and even her fiery tongue—had vexed him every night since he'd left Seabourne.

"Felicity," he breathed on the twilight wind, trying the ticklish syllables on his lips in anticipation of the wedding night to come. "Not to worry, my dear one," he whispered, "this time I shall finish what I start."

Will chuckled to himself, despite the saddle travel—until he drew closer to the castle and realized why the great house was so lit up this evening. When he saw the wagons and carriages, the servants and crates, it hit him. Someone had *presumed* to throw a party—a *Christmas* party.

Despite his sore backside, Will urged the horse to a gallop.

His ire rose as he puzzled out this act of cruel bad taste. Of course it was the doing of his bride. It had to be. And what appalling nerve the woman had!

Clara *must* have informed Miss Fairchild why Christmas had not been celebrated at Seabourne for the past fifteen years. Surely his bride-to-be would have guessed his feelings—yet still she chose to overrule any respect to her future husband's wishes in favor of her female vanity, her selfish need for a party!

"Is this the sum of your character, Miss Fairchild?" Will bit out angrily as he pressed the horse forward. He could hardly believe he had misjudged the woman so.

Galloping through the road's sharp turn, he skirted that tragically familiar cliff drop and his body tensed with the terrible memories. He could still see his younger sister's green eyes, so like his own, and the long raven hair. He could still hear her laughter on the winter air, even as she fell from the overturned curricle he had been driving.

But that little light was gone now—extinguished in that wretched accident all those Christmases ago, an accident that *he* should have foreseen. It was Will's own fault that young Eliza Court had been relegated to a chiseled name on a cold gravestone amid the family plots. His fault that she should never open another Christmas present, or laugh again, or grow up and fall in love and stand before a vicar, as he was about to do.

As he approached Seabourne's back drive and heard the festive music, William Court was more resolved than ever to extinguish every light in the place.

"Happy Christmas to you, Miss Fairchild, and a happy wedding day, as well."

"Why, thank you, Mr. Jones." Felicity smiled at the charming, red-haired bailiff. Jones was a thinly built man, no less than forty years old, with pale, hazel eyes and a calm and trusting voice. Though a bit overbearing when he dealt with the farmers, Felicity could not fault him in his manners toward her.

"Do you expect Captain Court soon?" asked Charles Jones.

"Any moment. He sent an express from London asking that we should be prepared for the vows by six. Are you having enough to eat, Mr. Jones?"

"Eat," he said, turning with a laugh to a pretty young woman beside him. "You have not seen a thing to eat in this place, miss, have you?"

The girl giggled and nodded, as it was more than apparent that neither had seen so much food in their lives. The dining room table, which had been moved out to the festively decked great hall, was all but groaning under the weight of the roasted meats, freshly baked pies, sweet cakes and, of course a brandy-soaked, holly-topped Christmas plum pudding.

The large room was filled now with the music of harp and pianoforte, as well as the bubbling laughter of neighbors, tenants, and regional gentry. All ate and drank and danced with gaiety.

Though Felicity's younger sisters and bachelor uncle could not arrange to come down from Bath on such short notice, her beloved brother Christopher and his wife had ridden down from Lyme, and Felicity was very pleased that they had. Their warm good wishes had meant the most to her, for they were now more than her relatives—they were her neighbors.

"You know, Miss Fairchild," remarked Mr. Jones, "if you haven't yet chosen a wedding gift for the captain, I might have a suggestion."

Felicity's eyebrows rose with interest. Mr. Jones had been very helpful during William's absence over the past week. She had already met many of the tenants and surveyed their farms.

Of course, she meant to have her brother's agents do a much more thorough valuation come January, but she wanted a first look herself.

Turning Seabourne around financially would be an overwhelming challenge, but she was more than pleased to take it on—for Jacques's future, for William's pride, and even for her own satisfaction. Her life had a new purpose now, a very worthy purpose. And she was both excited and happy to begin her marriage.

"A wedding gift, you say? One that the captain might enjoy? Do tell me, by all means, Mr. Jones. I would very much like to please my bridegroom."

"I understand there is a lost portrait in the family gallery," he said softly.

"Really?"

"It is likely stored away somewhere in one of those closed-up wings. But if you could find it, I wager the captain would be pleased to see it hung.''

"Who is the subject of this portrait, Mr. Jones?"

"It is a young girl. I believe it was painted just before Christmastide some years ago, when she was but eight years old. She has long, black hair, a sweet face, and bright green eyes."

"She *must* be a Court, with those features," said Felicity with a laugh. "But who is she to William?"

"Ah, that's a surprise, miss. A surprise for the captain—"

"Miss Fairchild, Miss Fairchild—"

Felicity turned from the bailiff to find a young servant girl tearing toward her with a wrinkled brow and frantic eyes.

"My dear, what in heaven's name is amiss?"

"The captain's arrived in the back entrance—"

"But this is good news! Mrs. Smith! Tell the minister the captain has arrived, and we should directly usher the guests into the chapel—"

"Miss Fairchild!" exclaimed the girl, still by her side. "Captain Court wishes to see you at once."

"Yes, of course. He will see me soon enough in the chapel—"

"No, at once! He said to tell you!"

With a swift curtsy, the girl turned and Felicity followed her to the far end of the hallway, stopping at the door of Seabourne's musty library.

"He's in there," whispered the girl, then curtsied again and practically ran back down the hall.

Felicity strode in without a moment's pause. "Captain?"

William Court was furiously pacing, and not yet changed for the wedding. In fact, to Felicity's alarm, he was still wearing his overcoat, hat, and gloves.

"Captain? What is wrong? And what in heaven's name did you say to that poor girl?"

Will Court stopped dead at the sound of Felicity's voice and glared daggers. "I *said*, find Miss Fairchild at once and ask her why my home is lit up like a brothel!"

Felicity stared at her husband-to-be in utter confusion. "Are you *mad*? This is a *wedding* party. *Our* wedding party, in case you've forgotten—"

"It is a party on the eve of Christmas!"

"Yes, of course," Felicity countered, her ire rising. "Which means, sir, it should then be *twice* as festive!"

"You should not have presumed to do such a thing without my permission."

"But, you left so quickly for London and—"

"You should have refrained from the female urge to display your plumage, until you *gained* my permission!"

Felicity was utterly shocked at William Court's barbaric reaction. *Is this the sort of man I am marrying?*

Then Felicity's form stilled. In a searing flash of realization, she knew it was more than the man—it was the institution. This *was* marriage, plain and simple. She was not simply giving up her worldly goods to her husband's complete control, she was giving up *herself*. Felicity had no doubts in wanting to offer up her dowry—for she knew it would mean new life, and new opportunities to the many families that depended on Seabourne, not just the Courts. But she now had every doubt in giving up her freedom.

"So this is the price of becoming *visible*," she murmured.

"What?"

Felicity cleared her throat. "Is this to be how you shall treat me from now on? As though I have no right to make decisions in my own home?"

Will Court's brow furrowed and he looked away. "It is my home, too, Miss Fairchild," he said quietly. "But . . . I am not an unreasonable man . . . just an injured one."

Injured, thought Felicity. Could a grown man's pride be so easily wounded? Simply because she had not asked for his permission to throw a wedding party? "Forgive me then, sir, for the injury," she said coolly.

"I do not think I can."

The two stared at each other in chilly silence for a good long minute. Neither, it seemed, wished to battle—yet neither wished to offer an olive branch.

"Miss Fairchild? Miss Fairchild?"

It was Clara Smith's appearance in the library doorway that finally severed the unhappy staring match.

"The guests are moving toward the chapel," said Clara. "It is time for you to change, Miss Fairchild. And Captain Court, your new clothes arrived from London in fine condition and they are laid out in the master bedchamber. Come, come now you two, it is not polite to keep your guests waiting.''

Felicity stared at Seabourne's loyal housekeeper. If the woman detected the bitter tension in the room—and it seemed she had—then she was doing her best to dispel it with hurried reminders of their dutiful obligations.

And this, realized Felicity, clearly defined what William Court's agreement to marry her was. It was an unemotional act of duty to him—an obligation to his family's legacy. And no more.

There would be no love for her, no romance. To expect those things would be sheer folly. She had obviously deluded herself with impossible daydreams for the past ten days. Daydreams of growing their affections—and relighting the ardor she had felt in his kisses that first night.

Felicity now realized the only possible shield in this marriage would be to harden her heart to feeling, just as he clearly intended to.

''Who told you to address me that way?'' the captain suddenly asked Clara.

''As 'captain,' sir? Why, Miss Fairchild. She said you preferred it to 'Sir William' and she felt strongly that your service had earned you the respectful use of the title in this household—and I certainly do agree. I simply wish you had told me when you first arrived.''

Felicity regarded the captain. ''Do you disapprove?''

''No,'' said William softly. ''I was merely surprised by it.''

''Come quickly now, you two,'' prompted Clara as she turned to go.

Knowing there was really no turning back, Felicity could only follow Clara back down the hall and hope that when she arrived in the chapel, her bridegroom would decide to be there.

''. . . that each may be to the other a strength in need, a counselor in perplexity, a comfort in sorrow, and a companion in joy. . . .''

Will listened to the vicar's words with a sobriety that surprised him. It was not that he did not take this wedding ceremony seriously. But he had begun to think of the arrangement as more of a business transaction than a blessed union. Now, however, standing next to Felicity Fairchild in Seabourne's candlelit chapel, seeing the earnestness of her kind brown eyes, the beauty of her shining spirit, Will's heart began to understand why men and women have been taking such vows for centuries.

"Give them grace, when they hurt each other, to recognize and acknowledge their own fault, and to seek each other's forgiveness," continued the vicar, "and finally, make their life together a sign of Christ's love to this sinful and broken world, that unity may overcome estrangement, forgiveness heal guilt, and joy conquer despair."

"Amen," whispered Will along with the congregation—and his new wife.

My new wife.

She was a vision tonight in her thin, white muslin dress, a white lace veil elegantly draping her curving figure. And around her neck was the golden star she'd found on the beach, its blue sapphire glowing with an almost otherworldly radiance.

Will himself had provided the necklace it now hung from. He'd sent the fine gold chain from London as his wedding gift to her, with a note telling her that since the star seemed to have brought them together, she should wear it on their wedding day. He had wanted to show her that he was ready to begin their arrangement . . . but, given her cold shunning of his feelings of grief for his sister's death, and her insincere apology to him before the ceremony, he now wondered how *she* truly felt about it—and him.

Her smile seemed strained, and far too cautious, but there was hope in her eyes. Hope for what, he could not say.

Perhaps, given time, she would tell him.

Nine

"Shall I enter, *Lady Court*?"

The room glowed golden in the firelight as Felicity settled beneath the bedclothes. At the sound of her new husband's voice, she sat up, surprised. Given all that had happened, she had not expected Captain William Court's presence on the threshold of her bedchamber to make her feel even *more* unsteady tonight than the first night he'd loomed there.

"Lady?" the deep voice prompted again. "Did you not hear my question?"

"Yes," said Felicity, "and I am surprised, Captain, that you would require a response. Why not simply do as you wish? It is your right, is it not?"

Felicity dared to look to the corner of the room, where the hinged bookshelf masked the connecting door. Her new husband was stiffly standing in the black trousers of his wedding suit. The black jacket and waistcoat were gone now and his snow-white shirt draped the impressive width of his shoulders like something out of Roman legend. The shirt was partly unfastened, the black cravat untied and loosely hanging about the open collar. He was, all in all, a most compelling specimen of masculinity. Unfortunately, the look on his rugged face was dark as thunder. Clearly, he had not cared for her cool response.

"Do you think, my good woman, that I am that far removed

from civility?'' he asked, his voice under tight control.

"I think that you are my husband now and, as such, you have a right to''—she looked away—''demand what you wish of me.''

Will Court's voice was tight. "I want nothing that you are not willing to give freely.''

"Oh.''

"Now, shall I enter, Felicity? Or shall I leave you?''

The sound of her Christian name on his lips sent a shiver through her. She hesitated. Felicity *did* desire her husband's company. She had fairly longed for his touch these past dozen nights. Yet given the man's insultingly aloof behavior all evening, she was afraid of what letting him into her bedchamber would do to her heart. She cared for this man, more deeply than was obviously *required* for their arrangement.

"Am I to assume,'' remarked Will, "that silence once again equals consent? Have I married a woman who knows not her own mind? Nor how to express it?''

Felicity's eyes narrowed at her new husband's goading. "Come in, then,'' she snapped.

"Indeed, I shall,'' he said, his arrogance up, "for, as you have pointed out, it is my right.''

Felicity glared at her husband.

"Your are obviously angry,'' said William as he sauntered across the room, stopping to lean upon the hearth's mantel. "Tell me why, if you please.''

"Look to the events of the day, sir, and tell *me*.''

"No, Mrs. Court, if I look to the events of the day, then I am astonished that *you* should bear any right to peevishness.''

Felicity did not wish to battle with her new husband on this, of all nights. Yet her blood was boiling to such a degree that she simply could not hold back the explosion: "Your aloofness at our wedding party was unpardonable! I realize that our union is nothing but a mutual bargain between two practical minds, but I have pride, as well as you, sir. And you have given everyone the impression that our marriage is nothing to you. You would not dance, you would not eat, you would not sing, nor socialize—''

"It is a wonder to me that you should have expected these things of me tonight,'' he cut in sharply. "And a further wonder that my behavior would matter a jot to you. It is more than apparent that your own wishes were of more consequence to you than mine.''

''All this because I did not gain your permission for a party! I have changed my mind, sir. If our marriage is nothing but a financial arrangement, then I would like you to *leave* this bed-chamber.''

Will Court blinked a moment, as if Felicity's sudden rejection of the physical aspect of their marriage was a slap to his face. But this reaction was incredible to her—why then had he acted all evening as though he could not have cared less about their union?

In silence William stared at her.

''Did you not hear me, Captain?'' asked Felicity.

''You know I did. I simply do not believe it is what you desire.''

''It is.''

''It is *not*,'' William firmly insisted. ''For why else would you tremble whenever I approach you?''

''I . . .'' Felicity's mouth gaped as William Court moved across the room. He seemed to loom larger with every step. His jaw was freshly shaved and he'd had his hair cut while in London. But the dark locks were not neatly combed. They fell rakishly across his forehead, shining darkly in the firelight.

''You tremble,'' he said harshly. ''Do not deny it.''

Stopping at her bedside, Will Court unashamedly ravaged her with his eyes. Like a touch, she could feel the response in her body to the hard sweep of his bright green gaze from her unbound hair, to her flaming cheeks, down to her bared arms and low neckline, where the golden star necklace still hung from the chain he'd given her, its lowest point dipping between the ivory mounds of her breasts.

His breathing seemed to quicken as his gaze discovered this, then his vision dropped lower, to take in the curve of her sheer white night rail—a gift from her sisters in Bath. When his gaze reached her lap, where her hands were indeed trembling as they worried the bedclothes, he turned his attention back to her wide brown eyes and upturned face.

''You have vexed me every night I have been apart from you,'' he told her. ''Every night, I have seen your wide-eyed gaze; your soft, white skin; the strands of fire in your unbound hair. And every night I have wanted you.'' With a sense of gentle possessiveness, his large hand reached out to cup her cheek.

Felicity scarcely stopped breathing.

"Look at your flushed face, your quivering lower lip" he murmured, his callused thumb brushing across its fullness. "You want me with you in this bed. More than you can say. More than your pride will *let* you say."

"No," she whispered, more afraid than ever of her heart falling victim to this man's mesmerizing effect on her senses.

"No?"

The spark of challenge had entered his eyes, as if she had pointed her cannons at his broadside. For a moment he hesitated. Felicity could hear the winter wind outside their window, the crackle of the fire. But her gaze never left his as he slowly and resolutely bent toward her.

His lips were soft—and as warm and gentle as they'd been the first time he'd brushed them featherlike across her own. But the response in her body was far more powerful, for now she knew what he could do to her, what passion he could unleash with a mere flick of his callused thumb.

"Felicity," he whispered against her mouth. "I promised myself from the moment you proposed our marriage, that I would, come our wedding night, *finish* what I started."

He looked into her eyes and waited.

What else could she do but give in to what she desired—with all her mind, with all her body—and, unfortunately for her happiness, with all her heart.

"Yes," she finally whispered. "I desire it, too. . . ."

The kiss was ravenous. His tongue was eager to taste every particle of her, his hands hungry to bare every inch of her curves to his gaze and then his touch.

Her husband's lovemaking was every bit as sweet as she'd anticipated. His every caress, his every whisper implied his affection for her. So much so that she began to be persuaded that he *did* care for her, despite her age, despite her lack of raving beauty and, most of all, despite any assurances that they would ever conceive children.

When the time came for their coupling, he stilled above her.

"Do you truly want me?" he whispered.

"I do," she told him for the second time that evening and, for the second time, she meant it.

• • •

Will could not fathom the depth of feeling that washed over him as he settled between his wife's warm thighs and eased himself into her: Knowing that he had taken her virginity already did not dissuade his anticipation a jot. In fact, he burned so hotly for her, he could barely hold himself in check as he stroked and kissed and finally disrobed her.

Her body was a treasure to him. Knowing she had married him, that she had taken on the burdens of the Court legacy with him, the responsibility for raising a new Devon earl . . . it moved him, more than he had ever been moved.

The velvet-smooth skin, the creamy, rose-tipped mounds of her breasts, the soft, generous mouth—all were becoming more precious to him with each new touch and kiss. Her own tentative touches inflamed his passions even more, and now as he set a slow and sensuous rhythm of strokes within her, he marveled at her sweet responses. It felt as though she'd been made just for him, a perfect fit.

"William," she whispered on a moan, "it is wonderful."

The words undid him. He could no longer hold back. She stayed with him as he increased the pace of his ardent thrusts, amazed that his usual control had escaped him to such a degree.

This new wife of his was weaving her magic around his mind and spirit; it was a honey-sweet tangle he would have to make a great effort not to become caught in.

"Felicity," he growled as his final possessive strokes brought cries of his own name from her lips. And then he was undone—his body could no longer hold back the natural culmination of his desire for her.

Spent and damp, he finally collapsed upon her.

A moment later, concerned for her comfort, he rolled to his side and lifted his weight upon his elbow so that he might continue to gaze down into her lovely face. He marveled that his new wife's eyes and mouth held as much passion as intelligence, as much wit as warmth.

"What is wrong?" whispered Felicity, her limbs languid as he casually fondled the tender curve of her breast. "Why do you stare at me?"

"Nothing is wrong, my dear," he murmured. "I merely wish to look upon my new wife."

The caress of his eyes seemed to disturb something within Felicity, and a slip of a tear dampened her cheek. The sight of it brought an instant frown of anxiety from him.

"Felicity? Why do you cry? Did you not enjoy—"

"Of course I enjoyed it, William—it was more wonderful than I ever imagined."

"Then . . . are you having second thoughts about our bargain?"

"Oh, please," she whispered, "do not use that *hateful* word."

"But it is *you* who used it. Is that not what you wanted—as an independent woman—an arrangement to suit your wish for freedom? You said as much when we first discussed our union. Did you not strike a bargain for a husband bound to leave you for the sea?"

Felicity looked away, toward the dark of the chill winter's night. William suspected she was thinking that her bed would be cold without him. He well knew his own bed would be ice without her—but he was a man who had learned not to dwell on unhappy outcomes. When it came to an assault of unpleasant emotions, retreating inside an unyielding tower of stone was the Court way, and he had learned it well.

"Felicity? Did you not purchase what you wanted?" The irony did not escape Will. For just eleven days previously, their positions had been entirely reversed.

"I wanted a husband," Felicity whispered, still looking away.

"And so you have one, if you'd care to tip a glance to your side."

"But . . . you are resolute to leave Seabourne, are you not?" She searched his eyes in such a way that moved him. Yet he was resigned to his course.

"My living, and so my life, is elsewhere," he told her gently. "You know this, my dear. But . . . let me give you something for your reassurance."

"What?"

Shifting upon the mattress, William removed the signet ring on his little finger and slipped it on the third finger of her left hand. The silver sparkled in the firelight against the gold of her wedding band.

"Your signet ring?" she asked softly, noting the starburst at the center.

"It has been passed down for many generations. From Court ancestors, Normans by the name of Etoile." He smiled. "As you see, we take our family crest from its French meaning of the name."

"Star," whispered Felicity.

"Aye," said Will. "We seafarers stake our lives on following those radiant lights, Felicity. They are what guide us home."

"And so? Why have you given this to me, William?"

"Because, my dear, I want to assure you that I will follow *my* star," he said, softly touching the ring, "and yours," he added, touching the golden star at her neck, "back to Seabourne again. I will come back home to you and Jacques again, Felicity. You can be sure of it."

Will watched his wife gaze at him a long moment. It seemed as though she wanted more from him, but if she did, she would not say it. And, he suspected, he could not give it.

"Thank you, William," she finally murmured. "I will treasure the ring, and keep it safe."

And I will treasure you and Jacques, thought William as he stroked her cheek, though, knowing he would soon leave her, he felt it was better left unsaid.

Ten

"Where can you be?"

Hunting for a needle in a haystack may have been easier than searching for one portrait in a castle with twenty unused rooms. This could take days, decided Felicity, but she was determined to try.

"She must be hidden somewhere. . . ."

It was mid-afternoon on Christmas day, and Felicity was searching for the portrait of the little girl that Charles Jones had described to her.

All morning she'd found herself gazing at the star ring that her husband had given her, and she wanted to give him something in return. The portrait would be the perfect gift.

The day had started out so lovely, with William's passionate kiss, followed by a slow and gentle reprise of their lovemaking the previous night.

It was, without doubt, the most wonderful Christmas gift of her life. And she was sure she'd ask for more of the same by this evening.

Next came a happy holiday breakfast with Jacques and then a cheerful few hours by the fire in the drawing room, where they gave the boy his presents. Felicity laughed when she saw William's gift—an entire army of British soldiers, likely pressed into service by a stop at every last toy shop in London.

Jacques was so thrilled to see so many toys that he jumped into his uncle's arms with sheer delight.

He was almost as happy with her own gifts—a wooden rocking horse and a little drum—the latter which he played as he sang every Christmas song he knew for them both.

For some reason, William became sullen during the singing, and Felicity wondered why. But he would say only that he was tired, then withdrew into the library to read.

A part of Felicity feared that the cozy family setting had somehow been depressing to her new husband. Perhaps he was concerned that she would try to tie him down, to stop his intention to return to the Royal Navy, but she vowed to herself that she would not.

It was now more clear than ever to Felicity why he was content with a wife who would likely not conceive his children. William wanted little ties to the land. For this she could not fault him. The salt was in his blood—he'd said as much about Devon men, and she would not try to change what was in a man's blood.

Their marriage could only be what each of them tried to make of it. She could not force him to try, nor could she demand that he be happy in a settled life if his heart was set on returning to the Navy.

So she would let him go. For his own happiness. And that would be her Christmas gift to him. That, and the portrait of the little girl—

"Oh, my goodness, there you are!"

Felicity found her in a cluttered room, filled with cobwebs and dust, old dolls and childish furniture. The portrait was dirty but in good condition. And true to Charles Jones's word, the girl was a pretty little raven-haired, green-eyed Court.

"Elizabeth Mary Court," whispered Felicity, reading the plaque. "Well, little Miss Court, I shall clean you off and place you at the foot of William's bed. Tonight, my husband will be only too surprised to see your pretty little face!"

"Clara! My God, Clara!"

From halfway down the castle's lengthy second-floor hallway, Felicity heard her husband's roar of agony. She had just kissed Jacques goodnight and was about to join William for bed when she heard his awful call and remembered that she'd placed the painting of the little girl in his bedroom hours ago.

But why was William's cry not one of joyful surprise? It sounded, instead, as if someone had pierced him through the heart.

"Lady Court? What is wrong?" called Clara Smith from the staircase.

"Clara!" roared William again.

"I do not know," said Felicity, rushing toward the master bedroom.

The two women arrived together to find William Court holding the portrait of little Eliza Court, a look of raw pain twisting his features.

"What is the meaning of this?" he rasped, lifting his eyes to the elderly housekeeper.

"My word," whispered Clara, her eyes wide.

"Why did you dig out this portrait?" he demanded of his housekeeper, unshed tears glistening in his green eyes. "Why?"

"Captain, I swear I did not."

"Then who?"

"It was a surprise," said Felicity. "What is the matter, in heaven's name? Are you not pleased that I found it?"

"Pleased!" roared William. "And I thought *I* had no heart—"

"William!" Felicity could not believe the look of hurt and rage upon her husband's face.

"Clara," he said, turning to his trusted housekeeper, "I have married a heartless woman, to be sure. But there is nothing to be done about it. So please, take this painting from my sight. . . . No! Better still, I shall remove myself from the sight of it."

"William! What is the matter? What have I done wrong? Tell me!"

But there was nothing more that he would say. He had swept from the room with long, powerful strides. Felicity lunged to follow him, but Clara swiftly moved to hold her back.

"Let him go, Lady Court. He will return."

"But—"

"The Court men are all the same. Their tempers rage like the wind but eventually blow over."

Hearing the echo of doors slamming below, Felicity followed Clara back into the room. The lovely little green-eyed, black-haired girl was there waiting for her, just as serene as when she'd first found her. "Who is the child, Clara?"

"Did he not tell you?" asked Clara.

"No."

Looking more tired than she'd ever seen her, Clara shook her head. "Forgive me, ma'am, forgive me for not telling you . . . but I felt it was the captain's place."

"Tell me what? Please, tell me now. Who is the child?"

"William's sister."

"But why should he be so unhappy about my finding her—"

"Because he killed her, ma'am. On Christmas Day."

Felicity felt as though she'd been struck in the face by a wooden board. She stumbled backward until she found a chair to sink into slowly.

"When?"

"Fifteen years ago."

"Tell me . . . tell me all of it. How it happened."

"You have to understand, ma'am, that the brothers were like two fathers to that child. Her own father died when she was but two, and for six years the brothers doted on her. Thomas had inherited the earldom and he lavished the family with gifts. When William turned twenty-one he asked for a curricle, and Thomas took pleasure in purchasing the fastest two-wheeler in the region. He unveiled it on Christmas Day."

"It was the curricle? An accident?"

"Yes, ma'am. The roads were ice that Yule, but the little girl wanted her ride, and Will and Thomas could not deny that sweet child a thing. They both took her out. First Thomas and then William. But when Will took the treacherous turn by the cliff drop, he lost control. . . ."

"And she was killed."

"Yes, ma'am. It was a terrible day. Terrible."

"And that's why the Christmas parties stopped."

"Yes, ma'am. Thomas and William blamed themselves for her death—and then they blamed each other. It was a wretched, wretched fight those brothers had the day they laid little Liza in the cold ground. The next day, William cursed the land and living any more of his life on it, then he packed up his things, and left for the Royal Navy. As far as I know, the brothers never spoke again.''

"What can I do for him?'' asked Felicity, devastated.

Clara regarded her with kind eyes. "His mother, God rest her soul, asked the same question to me, ma'am. And, I am so very sorry, but if there is a good answer, I don't know it.''

For hours Felicity waited in her husband's bedroom. She read by the light of the fire, then paced and, when all the kindling was used up, she wrapped herself in a blanket and sat in the large upholstered chair, facing the door.

"Lady Court?''

For a moment she thought she was dreaming and William was finally standing over her, his warm, strong hand on her shoulder.

"Felicity?''

She opened her eyes to the man she loved. She knew it, without doubt, the moment she saw those green eyes with the bluish hue. He had come to her rescue, and she had failed to come to his.

But she refused to give up so soon.

"William, I've been waiting for you. . . .''

"So I see.''

"Please forgive me. I did not know what had happened. . . .''

"Yes, Clara told me. . . .'' He turned from her to spy the cold, dead hearth. "It is freezing in here, come, let's use the fireplace in your room.''

Still wrapped in the blanket, Felicity followed her husband to the room they had made love in three times. Three precious, wonderful times. A fear that there would never be a fourth gripped her heart as she watched his defeated-looking shoulders move to start and stoke the fire.

"William, please, tell me that you forgive me. I did not mean to hurt you. I would never wish to hurt you—''

"I know that. And I know what is in your heart. Truly, I do. Goodness, pure goodness . . . seeing you with Jacques, knowing how you feel about helping Seabourne's tenants. You said I was aloof on our wedding day, but my eyes were on you the entire evening—your little kindnesses, your care and concerns for your guests, these things did not escape me, Lady

Felicity Court. You are a remarkable woman. . . ."

"But . . . ?" she whispered, seeing the word in his eyes.

"But . . . I am not a remarkable man."

"You are wrong," said Felicity.

"I am a flawed man, my lady, a very flawed man. And I do not believe I can ever truly be a happy one—"

"No. Please do not say that. . . ." Despite the cold, Felicity threw off the blanket and went to her husband, cradling his cheeks in her hands. "Has Jacques not made you happy? Have I not? What of our intimacies together in this very bed?"

A sound like agony came from William's throat. "Do you not understand? The pain is too great—when I am happy, I think of her—of the life she could have had—"

"But William, her life is over now. And Jacques's is just beginning. And your life with me is just beginning. Do you not understand? He needs you . . . and I need you—"

"Do *you* not understand, Felicity, I have killed a child. How can I allow myself happiness?"

Felicity's hands dropped. The words were stark and plain and cold. A stone tower that he stood within. A tower with walls so thick he could not hear anything she said to him—or would not. Yet still, she had to try. "It was an accident," she whispered. "One in which you also could have lost your life."

"But I did not. She did. And someone must pay for that—"

"William, my God, William." Felicity felt dizzy and sick. "I am losing you, I am losing you, and I do not know how to stop it—"

"Then do not try."

"No! You must listen to me. You must try to hear. I did not think that I would ever need anyone quite so much as I need you. But what I speak of now, in the privacy of our bedchamber, is not titles or properties or legacies. It is not propriety or ceremony or appearances. It is the need to be near you so much that my life feels empty without you. It is everything the vicar said last evening: 'that each may be to the other a strength in need, a counselor in perplexity, a comfort in sorrow, and a companion in joy—' "

"Do you not hear your own plea, Felicity? The things you wish from me cannot be! How can I provide those things to you? I cannot . . . which means I cannot be true to our vows."

"Please, William, do not say such a thing!"

"I leave in the morning for Portsmouth. I have decided."

The light left her eyes in an instant. The decision was made—in his tone; in his gaze; in his tense, aloof stance. And in one moment it carved a chasm deeper than any valley on earth.

"So I see," she whispered.

Then he turned away, and she let him. For deep in her heart, she knew there was nothing more that could be said.

Eleven

"*Bonjour*, Aunt Felicity."

"Good morning, my little one." Felicity pet the golden curls of Jacques's head with the saddest of smiles. "You must get up, for we are going on a trip today."

"Where?"

"You and I are going to my Uncle Claudius's town house in Bath, to celebrate the new year."

"A trip! A trip! Hooray! Is Uncle William coming, too?"

"No, Jacques . . . Uncle William has gone away."

The life in the little boy's sky-blue eyes instantly vanished. "Where has he gone?"

"Back to the sea."

"When will he be back?"

Felicity hid her emotions. "He will be back someday," she said, trying with all her heart to believe it, but knowing that the last time William Court's guilt and grief had driven him from Seabourne, he had not returned for fifteen years.

"They say that is what my father told my mother," said Jacques, looking away angrily. "But when he came back, it was too late."

Felicity frowned at the little boy. "You must not give up hope, Jacques."

"What is hope? *Je ne comprend pas.*"

"It is like a star—*l'etoile*—that never goes out," Felicity said softly. "Like a Christmas star that guides us to things we cannot quite see until we're over the hill where it shines."

"Like the Magi's star?" said Jacques, pointing at the charm Felicity wore around her neck. "The star the wise men followed?"

"Yes, Jacques . . . like the Magi's star."

Gazing at the little boy, Felicity fingered the signet ring William had given her on Christmas Eve, then she silently touched the golden star charm at her neck. She knew then that she would not take either off until William returned. Even if it took another damned decade and a half, she would be here waiting. For he was the one man who had rescued her; who had believed in her; and who had showed her what passion lived inside of her.

And he was the one man on earth she loved with all her heart.

"He will be back, Jacques. He said he would, and so I will not give up hope that he will."

"*Oui, l'etoile.* Then neither will I."

The star at her neck seemed to agree. For the first time since the day she'd found it, the charm began to grow very warm. The strangest warmth she'd ever felt, as if her flesh was being touched by a calming hand.

"They've left for Bath this morning," Charles Jones told the two men sitting with him at the back of the Devon pub.

"What's yer plan then, Charlie?" Tall Tim asked.

"The new scullery maid told me the woman's uncle's givin' a party on New Year's Eve. Lots o' gentry, lots o' dandy sort of men. An' I'm thinking, where there's gentry at a party, there's jewels and half crowns. An' where there's dandies, there'll be no resistance."

"So?" asked Fat Tom.

"So, we pretend like we're just the hired help. We get into the house and we rob 'em, then take the Court wife as a hostage. We slit her throat outside o' town, dump her in the road, and ye've put me back in business."

"Right," said Tall Tim, "the business of losing a fortune on the London tables."

"Shut your hole, you. What I do with what I earn is my own business—"

"What ya steal, ya mean."

"I'll not tell you again to shut it."

"All right, all right . . . just tell us when we leave."

Will Court was numb by the time he boarded the coach to Portsmouth.

He felt as if everything he cared about was lost to him—and there was nothing to be done about it. The sea called out to him again, and he was going, as he had before, without looking back.

Only this time it was different. This time, it was almost impossible *not* to look back. All the way to Exeter on horseback, he could not forget the courageous last stand she'd made the night before. The woman's heartfelt words were stunning—but his time in the Navy had only reinforced what he'd come to practice after little Eliza's death. Emotions were no good to him and, in his mind, the only way to survive beyond their reach was to run with the wind when they tailed you. And yet, even as he boarded the coach to Portsmouth, it took every effort not to turn back.

The coach was crowded as he settled into it, and Will found himself dozing an hour into the trip. Restless dreams filled his head—of Jacques and Felicity. But mostly Felicity—of her dancing eyes, her clever tongue, and the way she looked at him when he made love to her.

Will's dozing dreams of her ended abruptly with the rumble of coach wheels and the rough bump of the seat beneath him. Rubbing his eyes, he looked up to find that a new passenger had taken the seat across from him—though he had not recalled the coach stopping to take any new fares.

Instead of an older gentleman with a black hat and gray coat, there now sat a lovely young woman with golden hair, aristocratic features, and eyes as blue as those of Jacques.

"Are you staring at me?" asked the woman, her words laced with a strong French accent.

"Pardon me, miss," Will said. "I was dozing, and I didn't see when you boarded—"

"I am not a miss. I am married."

"Oh. Again, pardon, Madam." Will tried to glance away, but there was something about the woman that disturbed him. Her dress and beautifully embroidered blue shawl for one thing

—the garments were far too elegant for a ride on a public coach. Who was this woman?

"My husband is with me now," said the woman abruptly. "And we are very happy. But there was a day when he made a mistake in judgment. He left me at a time when I needed him most."

Will shifted uncomfortably in his seat. This was an exceedingly odd conversation for the woman to be having with a perfect stranger. Will looked around the coach to see what the other passengers thought, but they were not listening. They seemed caught up in their own conversations.

"Do you wish to know my husband's name?" asked the golden-haired woman pointedly.

Will felt his mouth grow dry, his palms dampen. "I—I do not know you, do I?"

"It was Thomas," said the woman. "Thomas Court, Earl of Devon."

Will stared at the woman as if she was insane. But she merely smiled serenely at him and said, "Take care if you choose to leave those who need you. Those who love you. Or you, too, may lose them forever. . . ."

In the next instant, the golden-haired woman was gone, her image dissolving as if it were sea mist. Behind her was the passenger who had been sitting in the seat opposite him since the ride began—the older man with the black hat and gray coat.

Will rubbed his unpatched eye, but he was certain he had not been asleep—or at least he was *almost* certain. Which would mean only one thing. He had just seen a ghost, or an angel—or both!

"My God," he rasped. "Felicity and Jacques . . ."

They were in trouble. He knew, unequivocally, from the depths of his soul. *They need me.*

"Driver! Stop the coach!" he roared, seeing a farmstead up ahead. "At once, do you hear!"

Twelve

Felicity's bachelor uncle lived in Upper Town on Queen's Square. It was a fashionable address within a brisk walking distance of the gilded bronze head of Minerva—the first hint to the people of this West Country spa town that ancient Roman ruins still lay beneath their cobblestone streets.

Uncle Claudius, as he preferred to be called—in honor of his favorite Roman emperor—was really named Clyde Oscar Fairchild, younger brother of Felicity's father, and avid lover of all things Roman, which was why, at the age of eighteen, he'd left Lyme for Bath and never returned.

It had been Uncle Claudius who had started the Annals of Tacitus Club, of which Felicity's previous suitor, Mr. Drury, had been a part, along with two dozen other gentry and four titled peers. Nearly all of them had assembled this evening with escorts in tow for Uncle Claudius's "End-of-the-Eighteenth" Saturnalia soiree.

"Saturnalia is the feast Romans celebrated to mark their new year," Uncle Claudius informed little Jacques as Felicity put him down to bed. "For Saturn was their symbol for time, and Saturnalia put forth the mythic idea that old reigns must give way to new ones."

Jacques stared for a moment at the incomprehensible words of his scholarly great-uncle. "But why can I not stay at the *party*!"

Felicity smiled up at her uncle. They were old hands at this. For, after her own parents had died, he had helped her raise all four of her younger siblings. A new whelp, it seemed, was no bother to Uncle Claudius—in fact, the man said he was pleased once again to have a young peer sleeping under his roof.

"Well, Uncle?" asked Felicity. "What say you?"

Uncle Claudius loudly cleared his throat and then used the same story on Jacques that he had used countless times on Felicity's younger brother Christopher. "You are not Roman," he said very studiously to the boy. "Which means you must get to sleep before midnight or the mystical ruins of the ancient world will rise up and transmute your golden curls into slithering snakes."

"Snakes?" asked the little boy, his eyes wide.

"Uncle Claudius—" began Felicity in protest.

Jacques interrupted in French, asking whether Felicity believed this.

She shook her head. *"Non."*

"But I must still go to sleep, eh?" Jacques asked his uncle in English.

"That's right."

"All right, then," said Jacques with a yawn. "Good night, Aunt Felicity. Good night, Great-Uncle."

"Good night, young earl," said Uncle Claudius as Felicity kissed Jacques's forehead.

"Yes, and Happy New Century," she whispered. *"Bonsoir, mon petit."*

Felicity smiled at her uncle as they descended the stairs and entered the drawing room, which was quickly filling up with elegantly dressed ladies and gentlemen. Felicity herself was looking quite attractive in an emerald green muslin gown— she'd tried not to think of William's eyes when she'd selected it earlier in the evening, but she'd failed.

"I see Drury has arrived," remarked Uncle Claudius.

Felicity glanced across the room. "With his fiancée," she added absently, seeing the fair-haired duo drolly laughing with another couple, likely over some cruel piece of gossip over-heard at an earlier soiree.

"I am sorry he is here, Felicity," her uncle said softly. "I did not know you would be coming—"

"It is of no consequence to me," she said honestly. "Truly." Without thinking, her hand went to the golden star around her neck, and the memories attached to it gave her comfort. "I am a married woman now."

"So you say," murmured her uncle, concern evident in his eyes.

Felicity knew well her uncle's meaning. Her unexpected arrival in Bath without her husband—and during what should have been the honeymoon period—had sparked instant whis-perings. Reports had already begun about her hasty marriage, and her new husband's lack of joviality at their wedding feast. To all around her, Felicity Fairchild—matchmaker extraordi-naire for all her younger siblings—had concocted a too-hasty marriage on the rebound of a public rejection and reaped a pitiably disastrous union.

Still, she loved her husband, and could not help but answer her uncle with faithful confidence in that feeling. "As you see, I wear his rings," she told him, proudly showing off William's wedding and signet bands.

"Yes, yes . . . and you know, of course, why the wedding ring is worn on the third finger of the left hand?" he asked pointedly.

Felicity laughed. "Let's see . . . I do believe Romans were the ones who started the tradition, after having discovered that a single nerve traveled from that particular finger, connecting it directly to the heart."

"Excellent scholarship, my dear—just make sure you un-derstand what such a connection can wrought."

"I do understand, Uncle. And I have accepted it."

Uncle Claudius nodded, then bent closer to look at the star charm around her neck. "That piece you say you found is quite old, you know . . . yes," he said, leaning even closer, "*quite*. Appears classical in origin. Perhaps you should remove it and I'll have Fitzwilliam over there bring it down to his brother-in-law the antiquarian for valuation."

"Thank you, but I'm not taking it off."

"What do you mean? Never?"

"It's brought me luck."

"Has it?"

"And hope."

Her uncle's bushy gray eyebrows rose. "I see. Well, then, my dear girl, by all means, keep wearing it."

"I intend to."

Outskirts of Bath, 11:01 P.M.

"Giddiyaaaw!"

William Court had never ridden so long, nor so well, in his life.

After arriving back at Seabourne and learning of his wife's destination, he'd secured a fresh mount and set off at once. He could not be bothered with coaches or carriages now. Hell-bent for leather, he knew he would ride a saddle until his blasted skin was rubbed away.

He needed to reach her—and Jacques—and make certain they were safe. Safe from what, he did not yet know; but with every hard mile between Devon and Mendip Hills, he keenly felt as though his own life depended on keeping them well. And, as he neared the glimmering lights of Bath, shining like beacons to guide in the New Century, Will realized his life *did* depend on it. For without Felicity and Jacques alive and well, he cared neither to enter the New Century, nor to stay in the old one—not any longer.

"Giddyaaaw!" he cried again to his mount. These past days of riding had finally fortified his hide. For the first time in fifteen years Will Court could spur a beast on as he had in his youth—for, he found, when he put his true heart into it, riding was as easy as lifting a sail on a trade wind.

"Fly on, horse," he roared, "and get me to my wife!"

The Fairchild Town house, 11:31 P.M.

"It cannot be them," Felicity whispered on a horrified breath.

But her realization had come too late. The silver dagger was already poised at her throat, and three loaded blunderbusses pointed at the shocked, impeccably dressed crowd.

To be sure, violent robbery was a novel experience for the Annals of Tacitus Club. And the sudden appearance in her uncle's town house of the two men who'd attacked her on the beach two weeks before was a perplexing nightmare to Felicity, one that sent her into a dizzy confusion.

How can this be? her mind screamed again, still reeling from the very idea. *The tall one and fat one who'd nearly raped me, now dressed as one of the extra hired servants at my uncle's party! Am I going insane?*

"Release my niece!" demanded an outraged Uncle Claudius. "At once, do you hear!"

"Uncle, no!" cried Felicity, seeing him advance on the barrel of the firearm. "Please, no!"

"That's right," purred the tall one. "Do not induce me to cut 'er throat. Jus' do as I say an' no one'll have any great gaping holes in their finery tonight. . . ."

It *appeared* to be a house robbery—plain and horrifyingly simple. But Felicity knew there was more to this than met the eye; there had to be. Why else would these men have followed her all this way—after all this time?

She soon discovered the answer. After the fat robber had finished grabbing every jewel from every lady's neck and stuffing every man's plump purse into his bulging canvas bag, the tall one pulled her roughly toward the back stairway.

"If any o' you follows," he warned the crowd, "I'll cut 'er throat. Jus' stay put and she'll be released unharmed on the edge o' town."

To the crowd inside, it would appear as if Felicity had been taken as a random hostage in a terrible robbery. But when she was dragged down to the alley, she saw her capture had indeed been far from random. For there, on the walk, was the man who'd engineered the entire ghastly affair.

"Charles Jones," murmured Felicity on a stunned breath.

"At yer service, m'lady," said Jones with a smooth smile.

"Why? Why are you doing this?"

But Felicity's desperate question went unanswered. To prevent any screams, a scarf was secured tightly around her mouth and her hands roped behind her back. Her eyes widened in fear as she saw the knife blade swiftly descend. The sound of ripping came next and Felicity struggled as she realized the

blade was slicing her gown's skirt straight between her legs.
For a heart-stopping moment, she thought they were about to
rape her right in the alley, but she instantly saw they'd simply
wished to force her to ride astride. At gunpoint, she was lifted
upon the horse's back and the tall one mounted behind her,
his lewd comments polluting her ears as his hateful hand
snaked forward to squeeze a breast painfully.

"You can sample that later," barked Jones. "Stick to the
plan. Get her out, now!"

In seconds they were galloping along the alley and then
down Charles Street and heading for the Avon River. They
clearly wished to take her out of town to assault her and then
dispose of her.

But Felicity Fairchild Court was far from swooning.

She was already violently manipulating her jaw, working
the scarf free of her mouth, and plotting her strategy of escape.
After reading of Roman battles all her life, she was not a
woman willing to go down without a fight!

Midland Bridge Road, 11:50 P.M.

With midnight almost upon the city, the streets were blanketed
for the briefest of minutes with silent anticipation as heads all
over town turned toward the skies to watch for the display of
fireworks that would signal both the New Year and New Century.

It was out of these silent minutes that Captain William Court
saw the three horses galloping full speed toward him on the
Midland Bridge and heard the ringing out of one woman's
voice.

"Help me! *Help me!*"

The familiar sound of his wife's voice shocked Will into
drawing hard upon his horse's rein. The rearing up was inevitable and nearly threw him, but he held on for dear life.
And when the hoofs slammed to the ground, he did not hesitate
to wheel his mount and pursue that entreaty for all he was
worth.

To hear her distress, to know she was in danger, unleashed
a tempest in Will's spirit the likes of which he'd never felt

before, even in the thick of battle, even in the most turbulent of seas.

"Felicity! Hold on! Hold on, my love!"

For she was his love. The love of his life. Now that he could lose her forever, he knew she meant everything to him. Everything that was good and true and worth living for.

"Please, God in Heaven," he prayed aloud. "Do not take her from me. Give me one more chance. I beg you, one more chance!"

Felicity had thought she was in control of her senses, but the shout of her husband's voice made her doubt it completely now. Whoever the man was coming to her aid, though, she thanked the angels for his bravery.

"Felicity, I'm coming!"

"My God," she rasped, it *was* her husband. It was *Will*!

"My husband is following!" she screamed to her captors. "Release me now, my husband is on your heels!"

But the men around her refused to slow, the gallop of horse hooves continued to pound like thunder in her ears. Then Charles Jones glanced back and saw that Felicity was not bluffing.

"What in hell is *he* doing here!" screamed Jones in fury.

Will was gaining and his shouts of "Robbers!" to a passing carriage had raised a general alarm. Now the very escape of Jones and his henchmen was compromised. And they knew it.

"What'll we do?" cried the tall one from behind Felicity.

"Cut 'er throat and dump 'er!" instructed Jones, then he spurred his mount and raced ahead.

In desperation, Felicity tried to make herself fall from the horse, but she had not the strength. The tall one's iron grip held her tightly against him and, in the next moment, she felt him shift the reins into the hand below her breasts and unsheath his knife with the freed one. "Sorry, pretty one," he purred. "Would 'ave liked to sample ya, but—"

"Felicity!"

It was done in one quicksilver flash, the knife's slicing motion had begun, and, with her hands tightly bound, there was nothing she could do to prevent it.

Felicity was stunned that she felt no pain. Had he severed an artery? she wondered in a flashing instant. Would she now

bleed to death on this dark, dark road? Was this to be the sum
of her life? Who would take care of little Jacques—who would
keep the lights burning for William?

She waited for the black to close in. But it did not.

Nor was there any blood.

Then she realized: She had not been cut in the least!

The tall one cursed and raised his knife again. And this time
Felicity realized what was happening. *It was the star!* The
golden star about her neck, the one she'd refused to remove,
was moving by itself to shield every new assault of the blade.

"What in bloody hell!" cursed the vile ruffian behind her.

"Felicity!"

Will Court's voice was stronger than ever now as his horse
gained on the man trying to kill his wife.

When the knife came a third time, Felicity was ready. As
the golden star leaped up from her neck, she threw her weight
sideways with all her strength. The confounded attacker was
confused enough that he finally lost his grip—and she fell hard
from the horse to the cold, hard road.

Felicity was bruised and battered as she rolled to a stop. But
she was alive. As the first fireworks resounded in the distance,
Felicity knew she had made it to the new year—and the New
Century!

"My God! My God!" her husband cried in torment as he
reined in his horse and bolted to her side.

Despite the aches and pains and pounding of her head and
heart, Felicity smiled at William, overjoyed at the sight of
those sea-green eyes that were so filled with unguarded love
that she could barely believe it.

"What took you so long?" she whispered through her
pained smile, then she fell back into his strong, warm arms,
relieved beyond measure.

"By Jove, everyone! Felicity is returned to us!"

Felicity smiled as her uncle led the way into his town house.
Despite the kidnappers' claim that they would release her, Uncle Claudius and a few of the men from the party had instantly
called for horses after she'd been spirited away.

Late, but well meaning, the little posse had galloped upon
William just as he was returning her safely to Queen's Square.
Now William carried Felicity into the town house and placed

her gently on a damask settee just inside the entryway.

The crowd from the party was still as thick as ever—and abuzz with the robbery that had taken place, a drama good for a few hundred tellings and retellings at a dozen new parties.

At Felicity's dramatic entrance in the arms of a rugged-looking, caped rescuer, a dozen jaded guests wandered into the anteroom, a dozen more looking on with uncharacteristic curiosity from the drawing room arch.

"Oh, look," someone remarked. "She has been returned."

"Yes, but will the gentleman who returned her stay around longer than her new husband?"

"I should think the time to consume a cup of tea should suffice for that!"

Cleverness was everything to this crowd, whether at the expense of others or not. But Felicity had been too long exposed to such unkind wit to be overly disturbed by it.

Not so for William Court.

Amid the tittering whispers, she watched the whirlwind enter her husband's eyes and the cannon within him load for firing. "I am her husband!" William suddenly roared to the stunned crowd. "And I love her!"

The entire party gasped, along with Felicity. Such declarations of sincere feeling were simply *not* the fashion. And yet, it appeared to Felicity that every woman present seemed to turn the color of envy when her rugged sea captain and knight of the realm went down on one knee. "Will you take me as your husband, fair lady?"

It was a show of affection clearly meant to erase any public doubt of his feelings at their union—and Felicity's heart filled to bursting at the gesture.

"William, you are sweet beyond measure," she said softly. "But you know I have already married you."

His intense gaze caressed her face, and then he whispered: "But would you take me again, if you could?"

In his eyes, Felicity saw the sincerity. This was much more than a show, she realized—this was an honest, heartfelt plea for a second chance to uphold their vows.

"Yes, William," she said without hesitation. "Let us try again."

And so, under a starlit sky, in the first hour of the new century, William Withers Court kissed his newly wed wife;

and this time, it affirmed not a union of convenience, but a marriage of love.

"Where is Jacques?" William asked Felicity as the buzzing crowd dispersed behind them.

"Upstairs. Help me up and let us see him together."

At the top of the staircase, William lit a candle, and they quietly entered the child's bedroom together.

The boy was not deeply asleep. "Is it the new year yet?" he asked with a yawn.

Felicity smiled. "It is, little one, and look what the turn of the century has brought you."

"Uncle William!" cried the child with joy. He was out of his bed in an instant, his arms wrapped around his uncle's strong neck with open affection. "Have you come back to stay?"

"Aye, child," Will murmured, his gaze straying to meet Felicity's. "I'll not leave either of you again. And that I do promise."

After a few minutes listening to Jacques's excited chattering, Felicity settled the boy back into his bed.

"Your star," Jacques said abruptly, pointing up at his aunt.

Felicity's brow furrowed as she remembered the charm— the golden pendant that had changed, then saved, her life. Her hand moved to her neck and she found the gold chain that William had given to her, but the star was gone!

"I must have lost it," she said in sad disappointment. She looked at William. "Back on the road."

"It's all right," said her husband, drawing her back into his strong, loving arms. "I will have another made for you. . . ."

"Then what is this?" asked the tiny voice below them.

Felicity looked to see Jacques pulling something shiny from beneath his pillow.

"You did not lose it, Aunt Felicity," said the child. "The Star of the Magi must have been with me."

Felicity looked at William and somehow they both knew it had been.

In truth, the star had been with each of them all along.

Epilogue

"The first star of evening," murmured William's deep voice in her ear.

At the ship's rail, Felicity felt the warmth of her husband's strong body coming up behind her to enjoy the last coppery rays of sunset. Wrapping a possessive arm around her waist, he applied a light pressure, urging her to lean back into him. She was only too happy to oblige.

Felicity sighed at the warmth of William's wool coat, its breadth outlined by the powerful chest beneath it. For the last seven years she had come to know every part of him—and love him more than she dreamed any person could ever love another.

"Do you see it, sweet one?" he asked her. "Near the horizon."

"Oh, yes. It is quite beautiful."

"Lucky. To have such a star on this last night of sail. Virginia's shores will be visible by dawn."

"Wonderful, Captain." Felicity smiled. "You should consider the maiden voyage of your *Sea Star* blessed, I think."

"You think?"

"I *know*."

William chuckled. "Then it is true, to be sure. For my wife *knows* far too much to be disputed."

Felicity laughed. She turned her happy gaze up to her husband. His eye patch was gone, for good now. His sight had been restored two years before, just after the Battle of Trafalgar, when the Royal Navy's defeat of Napoleon's naval power secured Britain as mistress of the seas.

Another plentiful crop was sown for all of Seabourne's tenants, and the Court coffers were now overflowing so much that Felicity's brother readily agreed to partner with William in building three merchant vessels. The little fleet was on its way to the American states, an exciting voyage to meet William's new associates in importing and exporting goods between the two countries.

"Where is Jacques and little Eliza?" asked William.

"Eliza is napping below in her nanny's stateroom. And Jacques, I believe, is once again being captivated by cook's tales of mermaids and sirens."

William laughed. "The boy had better be careful; too many fanciful stories is liable to lead him to searching the seas for love."

"Oh, well, my dear," remarked Felicity, "you know what they say—there are plenty to catch out there."

"I've caught my limit," Will murmured, his lips at her temple.

Felicity gazed up at her husband. His eyes were burning with a familiar need. She smiled with mischief. "Well, I hope you're ready for one more."

Will's eyebrows rose. "One more . . . *what*?"

"Little fish."

"Little—"

"Or perhaps I should say little Court."

The captain's jaw slackened as the news struck him. "We are going to . . . going to . . . *No* . . ."

"Yes. We are going to have another child, William. Yes."

"Yes? Truly?"

"Truly!"

"Huzzah!" he shouted suddenly, planting a happy kiss on Felicity's mouth, then turning her in his arms and swinging her around. "Another Court! Huzzah!"

Felicity laughed with pure joy as he twirled her about the deck. It was a surprise to them both when the swift movement caused the chain she always wore to break. With gaping mouths they watched the golden star suddenly fly out beyond the rail.

"Your star!" cried Will, lunging for it. But he was too late. The shimmering chunk of light was already arcing downward, toward the choppy seawater below.

"Look at that," whispered Felicity, more surprised than upset. "Did you see that?"

"Appears a large fish has just consumed your most precious piece of jewelry. My dear . . . oh, my dear, I am so sorry—"

"Do not be."

"But, you loved that star. It brought us together. It saved your life. . . ."

"And now it is right to be returned to the place from where it came, I think."

"You think?"

"I *know*. Someone else will find it someday, William. I am sure of it. Someone else who has the faith and courage to believe that a Christmas wish can come true."

"And you are not upset? Truly?"

"How can I be?" she asked him, her small hand touching his rough cheek. "When I now have *everything* I could ever wish for."

William smiled, his eyes glistening with unwavering love. "Then turn your gaze forever more to this *Etoile*, Felicity— for this is one star that will never stop shining for you."

Last Kiss at the
Loving Cup Saloon

✳✳✳

TESS FARRADAY

One

"So long, cowboy."

Joe turned in time to see a sad smile on the whore's scarlet lips as she swung the iron skillet. Pain jangled from his head through his teeth and dropped him to his knees.

That had happened at about noontime, right after he'd discovered the saloon he'd won at cards stood smack in the center of a ghost town.

At least it stood. Trotting down a main street empty of everything except one bounding tumbleweed, he'd cursed the prospect that the Loving Cup Saloon resembled the other gray buildings leaning shoulder to shoulder against the bitter wind.

Now, cheek down on the saloon's splintered floor, Joe raised one eyelid. Past the clouded glass window, a pale December sun dropped behind the mountains.

That floozy Lucy had a good head start, but it was ten miles in any direction to a real town or ranch and the mare he'd seen tied out front was short-legged as a sheep. She wouldn't make it far in this snow.

If he set out before nightfall, he could bring her back to face her duty.

Joe Nelson planted his hands just out from his shoulders and raised his face a couple of inches off the floor. Only a little woozy, he pushed himself up to a sitting position, then let his face fall forward into his palms. *Jehoshaphat*. He had a headache fit for a horse. He touched the black hair in dire need of barbering, and found a sticky little mess of blood and a lump the size of his fist.

He kept his lids clamped shut against the light, though he might have shaken the feeling that the old chandelier overhead was spinning if he'd only opened his eyes.

"Told you he wasn't dead."

"Just said he *looked* dead, 's all."

"Nuh-uh. You said only dead men drooled thataway."

Joe backhanded his knuckles over his mouth and remembered all too fast why he couldn't give Lucy, Soaring Peak premiere soiled dove, a chance to fly the coop.

She'd left him with a passel of brats.

Joe looked up. Three pairs of owlish eyes peered at him over the back of a mangy red velvet settee.

Shaking his head in disgust would only make his brain spin again. But damn, when he'd won the Loving Cup Saloon in an all-night poker game, Colin Stark had lied that the establishment was flourishing. He'd also failed to mention it had occupants. Then again, maybe he hadn't known.

Lucy's hennaed ringlets had bobbed as she swore Christian charity had made her take the kids from town when a fever had killed their hurdy-girl mothers. She figured the kids might survive, out in this godforsaken shack.

"Hey, mister?" One of two identical faces spoke and Joe blinked, making sure he wasn't seeing double. They were twins, all right, with skin the color of an old maid's milky coffee. "Mister, can you cook?"

"Mind your manners, boys." The tallest child scooted off the settee and sashayed around front. A towheaded girl of about ten, she moved like a lady in spite of her too-short dress, burned at the hem. "Let me get a cool cloth for your head."

"Thank you." The rumble of his own voice sent sparks dancing across Joe's vision, but not so bad he couldn't see she held something against her hip.

It mewed and thrashed. Joe prayed it was a kitten, a vicious wild panther—anything except a baby—but he'd caught the Lord napping.

Four. That trollop had saddled him with *four* orphaned children, one of them a babe.

"That Lucy, is she mama to any of you?" Joe took the cloth from the towhead and dabbed it against his wound.

"No." The girl hefted the baby higher on her hip. "Lucy is an actress. She plays the Purple Swami in the medicine show. Lucy's *sister* was Sal's mother—" She nodded down at the baby.

He didn't want to know the brats' names. Once that started, they'd want to know his, and then they'd be begging him to stay. Joe Nelson was a gambler, not a nursemaid, and he wasn't staying anywhere with any kids, especially two days before Christmas.

"—but the fever took her. Lucy said her own heart ran away with her head or she wouldn't have had any part of us. And then Mr. Stark scared Lucy off."

"They was yellin'," said one of the boys.

"I bet they were." Joe's mind thumbed through the rumors about Colin Stark.

The British gentleman was notorious for more than ranching fancy Hereford cattle. He'd been mentioned when squatters on his land turned up dead. And this bunch sure qualified as squatters.

Money silenced most gossip, and now that Stark had started talking about running for Congress, he was spreading gold coins all over. Joe figured the voters would never hear of this saloon full of misbegotten children. Still, why hadn't Stark made it clear Lucy should take the kids with her when she skedaddled?

"They was yellin' really loud and Lucy cried." It was the other twin, this time.

Joe nodded so the kid would know he'd been heard, but not enough to keep him going. This talkative twin was slightly smaller. Not that Joe'd be around long enough to need to tell them apart.

Pattering at the window told Joe the snow had started up again. It was probably just as well these young ones had been left behind.

All at once, the baby screamed. Her legs drew up and her face turned red. She twisted in the girl's arms and uttered little trembling bleats as if her heart would break.

"What's wrong with her?" Joe didn't really want to know. He sure didn't care, but that shaky sound levered the words right out of him.

"Colic." The girl rushed to put the baby back in the half barrel serving as a cradle.

It seemed kind of cold-blooded, but lord, she was a kid playing house—only the baby was real.

Wind-driven snow thumped the window harder. His chance to ride was slipping away.

"It's the cow's milk makes her feel like this." The towhead gave a resigned shrug. "It's not good for her. What she needs is mother's milk."

His self-conscious nod must have come across as dim-witted, because the girl added, "From her mother's breast."

Joe held out his hand for her to halt. Every minute he sat here, he heard more than he wanted to know. He stood up.

And caught the two little boys staring.

Joe wondered how long it had been since he'd gazed at another soul with such hope.

He'd probably been five or six, about their age, when his parents left him at the fort. He'd survived on pity, then grown up doing odd jobs for food and blankets. He'd stayed at the fort until he was twelve, when Dan the blacksmith had whaled the living daylights out of him for stealing.

Joe still had the scars to remind him of Dan and his bellow-ing. "You're smart enough to be anything you want—a doc-tor, a rich man, even a preacher—but I won't take the blame for letting you grow . . . up . . . a thief."

He'd punctuated the sentence with blows from a harness with metal rings. And though Joe had grown up to be a lot of things, mostly a saddle tramp and gambler, he'd never been a thief. Never again trusted anyone pretending to do him a good turn, either.

These children would learn.

"I'm Gussie." The little towhead bobbed a curtsy, so set on making introductions it wasn't worth the painful shaking of his head. "The baby is Sal." The infant took a shuddering breath as if trying to master her emotions for the occasion. "And these two are Rack and Ruin."

The shorter boy slipped his thumbs beneath his suspenders

and raised his voice over the wind screaming around the corners of the house. "We can read."

Gussie gave Joe a sidelong glance which said she couldn't. *Rack and Ruin.* What kind of ma named her kids so? Or taught her daughter to curtsy when she was born to such a life?

Someone at the fort had cared enough to teach him pretty manners. He'd "pleased" and "thank-youed" folks half to death. Which just went to prove where courtesy took a fellow.

In the end, Joe's memory, not all those begging brown eyes, convinced him to stay and feed them.

"I've got cornmeal and coffee and a hunk of bacon in my pack." He pointed toward Blacky, tied at the hitching rail out front. "If you're not too awful particular"—he smiled, wishing for a crack in their sober anticipation—"I could probably put together supper."

Joe sipped coffee and watched the kids sop their flat, eggless corn bread in molasses.

He could ride off, now that he'd filled their bellies. The girl, Gussie, could tend them. On the low shelves behind the bar, he found a few dry goods, including oats and crackers, but no whiskey. Lucy must've provisioned the place at the same time she'd swept it free of mice and cobwebs.

They'd have milk from the cow, too, which was docile enough to share its shack with Blacky. A big patchwork-quilted bed stood in a back room. For warmth, he figured they could all cuddle up together, like a tangle of pups.

Chewing quick as an October chipmunk, Gussie watched him. Her expression made Joe consider shaving his black beard, until good sense reminded him why he'd grown it. A man had fewer fights if he looked bad.

"This is good, mister." Ruin held his plate up. He licked off the last of the molasses. "Gussie can only make mush."

"But it's good mush." Rack darted a look at Gussie, whose freckles shone against her blush.

They needed a female to watch over them. Any female. A mother who could take a few more chicks under her wing, a widow woman, even an old-maid schoolteacher.

Once the brood knew other meals would follow each one

they gobbled down, they'd brighten up. Once he left, they'd quit worrying over his intentions.

"D'you shoot people with that gun?" Ruin should have wilted under the glares of his brother and Gussie, but he didn't.

"Naw." Joe touched his revolver. His answer was pretty much the truth.

The brood waited for a further explanation, but Joe only moved a step away from the stove.

"Tell you what. You all put yourselves to bed. I'll put my bedroll down on that bench. I won't be here when you get up, because I'm going to find you a—" Joe stopped. He couldn't offer them a *mother*.

In the silence, he heard Rack and Ruin swallow. Gussie turned away to straighten the blanket over baby Sal.

"A lady to . . ." That knock in the head had made Joe forget he had no idea what ladies did. All the females he'd known had skills of a lusty, temporary variety.

"Fix my clothes." Ruin poked his finger through a hole in his flannel shirt and Joe felt gooseflesh rise on his arms.

"A lady to tell us stories?" Rack slipped his thumb into the corner of his mouth and leaned against his twin.

"She could curl my hair for Christmas." As Gussie sighed, Joe realized he'd been smelling burnt hair since he walked into the Loving Cup Saloon.

He hadn't seen a curling iron work, but he imagined Gussie could get into trouble heating one in the stove. That might explain the scorched edge of her skirt.

"I'll go out and get you a lady, tomorrow morning." *And light out before Christmas Eve grays the sky.* "I figure it won't be much tougher than tying down a bobcat with a piece of string."

Ruin gave a short humph of laughter and Rack smiled around his thumb. Gussie stared at the front door as if she wanted to erase it from the wall.

Hell's bells. He'd done tougher things. He just couldn't remember when. At daybreak, he'd search for a female with hard hands and a soft heart. One with no notion that living at the Loving Cup Saloon in Soaring Peak, Nevada, was no life for a lady.

Two

Wakened by the train's uphill chugging, the gypsy snorted and rubbed her hennaed head on Katherine's shoulder. Afraid the woman would drop the crystal ball balanced in her lap, Katherine didn't scoot away, even when the gypsy exhaled breath that smelled like cod.

At dawn, two days before the last Christmas of the century, Katherine Victoria Stark felt bilious. She knew her father would have said she'd gotten just what she deserved.

Katherine should have been dining from china and crystal dishes in the private car her new husband-by-proxy had reserved for her. She would have been, if she'd obeyed Father who had, after all, arranged this splendid marriage.

Katherine twisted her gold ring. She blocked visions of bracing tea, of crisp toast with marmalade. Stewards did not come to the back of the train. Neither did respectable ladies.

The gypsy, for instance. After midnight, while men with snow shovels labored at clearing the tracks, the gypsy had come slinking in. Her demeanor convinced Katherine she had not paid her passage.

Katherine felt a warm muzzle snuggle across her instep. She owed her seat *here*, in the last car before the caboose, to Mistress Molly of Muroc.

Father had insisted one did not bring dogs on the train west, especially if one was a lady and the dog a blue-blooded basset hound accustomed to better accommodations. Father predicted Katherine's stubbornness would doom her marriage before it began.

Katherine speculated that a man who married a spinster of twenty-eight would expect an eccentric bride. The Leland Pacific Railway Company understood no such thing. Women with pets were banished to this last row of seats before the caboose.

Molly snuffled Katherine's carpetbag, then raised doleful eyes which described, quite eloquently, how much Molly needed the two petit fours wrapped in a lace hanky inside it.

"No," Katherine whispered. Her voice lured Molly to her feet. The dog swayed from side to side in the narrow space, tail striking Katherine's skirts hard enough to make her wince.

Ah, me. Katherine assured herself Mr. Colin Stark would appreciate a lady with the daring to come west. She possessed other qualities vital to a lady, as well. Foremost was her practicality.

Her presence on this train proved as much. The day Father had returned from the Nevada territories to their new home in Boston, he'd brought Katherine an offer of marriage. After London, Boston had seemed raw and rugged, but Father had been forced to travel to the Wild West to find a proper Englishman eager to have an English lady with knowledge of Hereford cattle as his bride.

After considering her parents' hopeful faces and the prospects for adventure on this new continent, she'd forsaken her dreams of a real wedding.

Her November nuptials had no flower girl dressed as Cupid, no fairylike maids in white organdy, no gown of Duchess satin or bouquet of ivy and white roses. There'd been a recitation of vows—Mr. Stark's part read by her cousin Noel—the signing of the certificate, and a sherry toast before boarding the train.

She'd donned her "going-away" attire last night, in case the train arrived ahead of schedule. Katherine looked down at the rose wool gown, at gloves trimmed in pearls. The ensemble should please Mr. Stark as much as the rest of her trousseau, which waited in a trunk in the private car.

Molly's acute sense of smell made her less than patient. As Katherine took note of the stirring of her gypsy seatmate, the dog began a most unseemly rooting accompanied by a frantic whine.

"All right, you beast." Katherine gave the gypsy an apologetic smile. "Excuse me." She reached into the carpetbag, moved aside her drawstring moneybag and her pocket pistol, and rummaged for the sweets.

As Katherine unwrapped the iced cakes, the gypsy made a sound much like Molly's whine.

"Ma'am, I would be more than happy to swap you a reading of your future," she said, raising the crystal ball from the folds of her skirt, "for that cake."

A faint twang of the American South tinged the woman's voice. That accent, the ill-fitting paisley gown, and non-Romany hair color made Katherine wonder if the woman had stolen the costume from a real gypsy.

Molly's tongue lolled in impatience. Her black and tan brow furrowed as she glanced between the two women, then snapped the nearest cake off the handkerchief and gulped it down.

"Oh, dear." Katherine sighed. "I don't suppose you'd still care to have this one?"

"Don't give it a thought." The gypsy took the cake without bothering to dust it off. She popped it in her mouth, chewed, and nodded toward Molly. "The mutt looks cleaner than most men I . . ."

The gypsy smoothed the scarf over her ringlets. "Well, *you know.*" She knotted the scarf above a gold hoop earring.

Katherine did not know.

"Are you a duchess?" the gypsy asked.

"No, of course not."

"A baroness? The way you talk—not a princess, maybe?"

"No, no. Just British."

The gypsy licked frosting from her top lip, caressed the glass ball, and chuckled as if they had a secret. Well, the crystal ball was a pretty trinket and the train wasn't scheduled to reach Soaring Peak for an hour.

"May I hold it?" Katherine asked.

Katherine cradled the crystal ball, feeling more fascination with its base than the orb filled with a fizz of bubbles. Her thumbs slid over the bauble's copper base. It was fretted with an intricate pattern so tarnished, the pattern was obscure.

"I will need your name, for the reading."

"Katherine—uh, Stark."

The woman's eyes widened and her hand covered the metal cross on her exposed breadth of chest.

"And you're going to San Francisco?" The gypsy blanched ghostly white.

"It makes two stops before San Francisco," Katherine explained. "I'm going to Soaring Peak."

The gypsy closed her eyes, then drew her fingertip over the ball. "He's an evil man, Colin Stark."

Katherine gripped the crystal ball, and set her teeth in her lower lip, trying to convince herself she *had* mentioned Mr. Stark's first name. She knew she had not.

"Don't get off the train in Soaring Peak."

"I most certainly will. I've yet to meet Mr. Stark and, regardless of your opinion, my father thought him a fine match."

The gypsy stared. By the time the woman looked away, Katherine felt certain each strand of her chignoned hair and each ray from the dark centers of her eyes had been memorized.

Hands shaking, the gypsy stared into the ball as if she really saw something. "If you go with him, look at what you'll have: enemies." She tapped the glass. "Burning children. A great mausoleum of a house with windows dark as eyeless sockets." The gypsy slipped off her scarf and scratched the scalp beneath her ringlets. She uttered a hollow laugh as if she'd frightened herself. "And he's cruel. In bed."

"Well." Katherine wet her lips and sought to swallow. "I— well, I surely don't mean to talk of conjugal matters."

Cruel in bed. Sweet Lord, what could that mean?

The gypsy grabbed Katherine's hand, pulling it free of the orb's base. As she did, Molly sat up.

"I'm going to tell you something, and I never meant it more sincere," said the gypsy. "Are you listening?"

Molly pawed at Katherine's skirt and made a moaning demand that threatened to build into a howl, but the gypsy's eyes held Katherine's with such intensity, she couldn't tell Molly to hush.

"Of course I'm listening," Katherine managed. "But you must release my hand."

"It's him I'm runnin' from. Stark."

Chills rained down Katherine's nape.

"I found a man to tend my . . . my responsibilities," the gypsy said. "And then I come upon this train flounderin' in the snow. Tell me that's not a sign," she sniffed.

She's peculiar, Katherine scolded herself, but not mad. No gypsy and no true fortune-teller, either. In fact, Katherine might have found her quaint if she hadn't spoken of Colin Stark.

"And just in case he comes lookin'," the gypsy continued, "I'll be hiding in the necessary room of this train when we pull into Soaring Peak Station."

The gypsy released Katherine as Molly nudged her skirt. The dog obviously required a trip to the train's open-air back platform, but not until the gypsy sighed and slumped back against the seat with closed eyes did Katherine gather Molly's leash and stand. It would be a good time to creep away and leave the gypsy—charlatan or not—to nap.

As she followed her right arm while Molly towed her down the aisle, Katherine realized she hadn't been exactly gracious.

"I do thank you for the reading," she called over her shoulder. "I'll return shortly."

Only for an instant did Katherine puzzle over her impression that the gypsy's one open eye had looked watchful, not drowsy.

She should have brought her cloak. Once out on the platform at the rear of the car, she was surrounded by snowy fields pierced with ink-green pine trees. Tree limbs lashed in the December wind. She would have anticipated the cold if she hadn't been so eager to escape.

"Another false alarm, is it?" Katherine looked down at Molly.

Eyes half-closed, ears streaming back, Molly ignored her mistress. Her toenails overlapped the edge of the platform. Her nostrils spread, lips rippled as she drank in the winter scents like chilled champagne.

Katherine wished she could be so carefree.

To the continuous rumbling of wheels on tracks, she decided Molly was happy because Katherine met all her needs.

Katherine ran her hand down the dog's long, sleek back. Other women depended on husbands to meet their needs, but

Katherine couldn't picture herself as any man's pet.

She leaned her gloved hands against the platform's low railing and wondered if Mr. Stark had an opinion on women's suffrage.

At the horizon, wisps of smoke curled toward the blank white sky. Soaring Peak lay just ahead.

The gypsy might be a gifted thespian, but not a fortune-teller. *Evil,* the woman had said as she read crystal ball visions of burning children and enemies and that other . . . thing.

Nonsense. It took little imagination to understand the "gypsy" was a disgruntled household servant or somesuch. Colin Stark was a gentleman, but that female was surely no lady.

With her mind settled and spirit serene, Katherine petted Molly's long, white throat and stared at the landscape. A clutter of abandoned wooden buildings flanked the tracks, but up ahead the town looked almost hospitable.

Three

He wouldn't call it kidnapping. Or abduction.

Joe made his way through the crowded train station. Most days, you could empty your six-gun through the place without hitting a soul, but the holiday had created a stampede of folks so cussed jolly, he thought about unholstering his gun just the same.

Today's search was more of a treasure hunt. Any respectable woman would bend to a good cause. And she'd see it as a good cause as soon as she laid eyes on the children.

Joe had trimmed his beard and dressed proper, in fresh denims, a white store-bought shirt with fold lines still showing, and a black leather vest. He didn't want to scare her off before he'd had a chance to open his mouth and lie.

Joe scanned the crowd. Everywhere he looked, folks held armloads of silver- and gold-wrapped presents.

Gussie, with timid persistence, had suggested he look for a wet nurse for Sal. He'd lacked the courage to ask how in hell he could tell such a thing by looking.

Then he spotted a hefty gal with tomato-plump cheeks. She smiled down at a babe too small to have stopped suckling. But the woman was hemmed in by a bull of a husband on one side and a gray-whiskered gent on the other.

Joe startled at a low screech, thinking at first of Blacky. But he'd tied his horse behind the ticket office. For a donation, the preacher Crazy Jack had promised to keep his eyes peeled for horse thieves.

No, the awful moan had come from the brakes of the train, confirming it was one contraption he wanted to stay clear of.

Joe's sudden stop to stare earned him a parasol in the ribs and a luggage cart pushed by a uniformed porter about to run over his bootheels.

"Sorry, Joe. Ha, ha." The man's nervous laugh said he might have been among the gawkers who'd watched Joe spar with a welsher in Gert's Card Parlor last week. There'd been a fair amount of blood, and that made some folks nervous. "No harm done, right? Ha, ha."

"No harm done." Joe nodded the porter on his way.

In fact, Joe had about decided to throw in his hand and quit this place, when a tyke in short pants grabbed him around the thigh. The boy looked up with a grin, pointed a spit-slick finger, and crowed, "Da!" Then he burst into tears at his error.

The mite was scooped up soon enough, and cuddled. That cuddling sharpened Joe's perseverance. How hard could it be to lasso a nuzzler for that brood back at his saloon?

He narrowed his eyes on each female who passed. Mostly they wore horse-colored dresses—brown, black, with the occasional gray or dun—and each respectable woman, every danged one, had a man at her elbow.

The brood hadn't asked for much. Any female could curl hair and sew, but Rack wanted a woman who could read.

He needed to set the spurs to himself. These folks would vanish once they'd loaded up their luggage or found their way to a boarding house.

One girl caught his eye, but not before he had caught hers. Joe squirmed under her scrutiny. Her outfit looked proper enough—black skirt, a silly hat with streamers hanging down, and an inviting smile. Too inviting. She wouldn't stay with the children.

Some fool with a squeeze box huffed Christmas carols as snowflakes spun down from the wintry sky. Only fear of laming himself kept Joe from taking a running kick at that fool and all the other sentimental idiots whose brains, all weighed up together, wouldn't amount to an ounce. Couldn't they see there were more important things to be worrying about than Christmas?

Joe strode back toward the ticket office. His last hope was finding a female so dim-witted she'd gotten herself stranded.

"Come on, Boss." Joe looked up into the dizzying flakes spinning down from the skies. "All I want is a woman, and to get out of town. Now."

And there she was.

Joe touched the brim of his Stetson in a salute to Heaven. He sidestepped a slick spot, trying to keep from walking over the top of her.

She dipped down, pink skirts pooling on the snow. Her back was to him, and her face was hidden by a fussy hat and the glossy wing of hair across her brow. But Joe could see all that mattered. The lady was alone and she held a baby bottle.

"Molly, don't be such a scold." She spoke like the most prim and proper sort of foreigner. The cry yodeling up from the other side of her didn't sound exactly human.

Turned out, it wasn't.

"Oh, no you don't." The lady kept an admirable grip on a hound struggling to avoid the bottle. "You've caused me quite enough trouble already, miss. I won't have you howling and carrying on and making him cross."

The lady's voice faded to a murmur as she stroked her gloved knuckles along the dog's throat. It gave in. Joe thought he might've done the same.

Then the snowy breeze shifted and he got a whiff of the stuff flowing from that baby bottle. Brandy. He'd bet his saddle on it.

Joe hesitated. It was a pretty queer thing, feeding hard liquor to a dog, but her whispered words cinched his decision: "We want him to like you, *assuming* he ever gets here."

It took Joe one stride to land in front of her.

"Miss?"

"Yes?" Straightened to her full height, the lady's head only reached the top button on his vest. She backed off a step and looked up. *"Yes?"*

Her impatience convinced him to play at being hollow-headed. "I come to get you," he said.

"Is that so?" Her tone came smooth and cool as cream.

For a minute, Joe despaired. Such a queen would never surrender to a clutch of ragamuffin brats. Then he smiled. Joe Nelson had schooled himself to spot a bluff. This lady was good. If he'd blinked, he would've missed the unguarded movement that gave her away. In the space of a heartbeat, her fingers rose to shield her lips, then lowered to rest against her skirts, and a faint flush crept up the curve of her temple.

Joe wanted to horsewhip the man who'd left her stranded and prey to one such as him. Instead, he answered, "Yes'm."

The dog shot to the end of its leash, nose twitching, tail wagging. When Joe squatted down to scratch behind its brown ears, the lady yanked it back.

"Who sent you, exactly?"

"Why, the foreman." Joe snatched off his hat and turned it in his hands. "He said to look for a lady with an outlandish way of talkin'."

"But surely your 'foreman' speaks with the same accent."

It wasn't polite to look a lady in the eye. When Joe did, he saw hers were brandy brown with just as much bite as that potion she'd poured into the dog.

"What was his name, did you say?" She raised one eyebrow and tapped the leash on the palm of her glove.

In for a dime, in for a dollar.

There was only one Englishman in Soaring Peak, but Joe hoped like hell his answer was wrong.

"Stark." He waited for her to spin away, undeceived.

"And *Mr.* Stark was unable to meet me himself." She tugged her gloves up tighter, giving them her wounded attention.

That son of a bitch Stark had gone and paid for a mail-order bride and left her standing out in a snowstorm.

"That's so." Joe wondered if he should change his plan. He'd follow the same trail whether he was going to the Loving Cup or the Stark mansion. Only difference was, he'd turn south at the woods to deliver this lady.

He *might* do that.

Blacky might take it into his equine head to start singin' opera, too. But it wasn't likely.

Even though Joe felt downright mean taking advantage of her, after everything else—the whore with the strong skillet arm, the abandoned brats, and a saloon roof that had commenced leaking as he'd left this morning—the notion of stealing Stark's betrothed tasted sweet as pie.

Smothering his satisfaction, he set off to fetch her trunk. He

had no intention of hauling it past the ticket office, but the
delay would give her time to hide her hurt feelings. It might
even give him time to figure how he'd get all three of them
onto Blacky, through the brewing snowstorm, and home to the
Loving Cup Saloon.

Katherine looked after the cowboy and released her fingers
one by one from their grip on her skirt. She'd never encountered such a man. Not in England, and certainly not in Boston.
His height was emphasized by his habit of standing too near.
He spoke with ill-mannered brevity, and yet his stare was an-
alytical.

Some might think him a handsome brute.

Katherine bit the inside of her cheek against an unseemly
smile. It was all very well to appreciate his appearance, she
told herself, but his fine looks didn't guarantee an aversion to
ravishment.

But she was too practical to be frightened. If he hadn't been
sent by Colin Stark, would he have recognized her? Of course
not.

And didn't the cowboy display the rough gallantry she'd
read about in accounts written by ladies who'd come west? Of
course he did.

Besides, Father had told her that unprovoked attentions toward ladies were savagely and swiftly punished by hanging.
This cowboy looked too bright to risk death over an old maid.

Katherine checked her carpetbag's clasp. Even though she
knew how to use the Sears and Roebuck Company's pocket
pistol which was tucked inside her bag, she'd welcome a
man's protection. All her valuables were hidden inside, too.

Colin's hired hand would do nicely as her escort home.

Just then, bells jingled across the station yard. A fine gray
horse plodded through the crowd, pulling a sleigh that was
piled high with fur throws. Warming in anticipation, Katherine
felt her worry fall away.

Profanity alerted Katherine to back away from two men jug-
gling a nail-studded trunk far larger than hers. Struggling past,
they gawked with open curiosity.

"What the hell's he doin' with a decent woman like that?"
puffed one in a porter's livery.

"Don't plan on askin'." The second man wore clerical garb and hair like a work-worried broom.

Katherine fixed her gaze on the landscape beyond the rugged village. White mountains jutted against a blinding blue sky while snow lashed her cheeks.

The two men released their burden with a crash and stood talking so loudly, she couldn't call it eavesdropping to listen.

"Joe Nelson don't say nothing much, but it ain't safe to ask him questions. If you plan on crossin' him over a woman, I'll just start plannin' your funeral."

Katherine clinched her hands on Molly's leash. They were talking about her. And the cowboy.

"He's sure got guts," said the porter. "Why, I heard he played a couple hands of stud with Stark and when they finished up, that slick son of a gun didn't have a tailfeather left to waggle."

"Better pick up your end, Preacher. And get your ass back out there to watch his horse."

Still laughing, the two moved off, leaving Katherine convinced the cowboy must be trustworthy if a gentleman like Colin Stark played him at cards.

A faint chiming made Katherine turn. The cowboy wore spurs. It seemed barbaric and in perfect keeping with the rough beauty of this place that something that inflicted pain could ring with fairylike music.

He strode right past her, caught the discomfited porter's elbow, and gave orders. He acted like no man's underling. In fact, he seemed little different from Father or any man who knew what he was about.

His face wore the same authority as he turned toward her.

"I'm afraid your things will have to be brought on after us, miss."

Katherine prepared to correct him about her designation—she was a legally married woman, no "miss"—but then she noticed the gun he wore strapped in plain view. The dull gray gleam of the weapon drew her stare and she knew why other men skirted him with respect.

"Miss?"

She forced her gaze up from the weapon. "I'll trust you to know what's appropriate in this uncommon situation, Mr . . . ?"

He missed her gentle nudge toward introduction. When she glanced up, his expression was a protest. "Sir?"

He made a dismissing motion and muttered what might have been a curse before he snatched the black hat from his head and trapped it under one elbow. Then he scooped her gloved palm into his. Katherine braced for a raucous pumping like those she'd seen in greetings all around her, but it didn't come.

Their hands seemed suspended, bridging the space between them as if balanced on a cushion of air.

"Joe Nelson, miss." He pressed her hand gently. "Nice to make your acquaintance."

Tongue-tied at his chivalry, at manners more precious because they were obviously not in daily use, Katherine nodded and turned her attention to Molly.

Through no fault of her own, Molly drowsed in drunken slumber. A Boston physician—a friend of the family who was acquainted with Molly's loud bouts of nerves—had prescribed brandy for its sedative properties. He insisted Katherine could more safely administer it than ether.

"Poor Molly, I'm sorry." Katherine gave a gentle tug on the leash. If Molly could just walk as far as the carriage . . . Molly sighed, thumped her tail once, and nestled into the snow as if it were a feather bed.

Katherine didn't look up at the cowboy's sound of disapproval, but she tried to explain. "Molly howls a good deal when frightened. Napping, she's easier to manage and I thought this might be best for the journey."

Wordless, he jammed bare hands into the snow beneath the basset's body and hefted her. Molly's freckled paws made a brief scrabbling against his vest, then one ear flopped over her eyes and her lips lifted in an expression awfully like a smile.

With a curt motion of his head, Joe Nelson indicated Katherine should follow him. And she did.

Four

Only her nimbleness in high-buttoned kid boots allowed Katherine to miss the snow-covered horse droppings.

Joe Nelson probably thought his irritation was justified, but she wished he'd maintain a dignified pace. With the holiday crowd thinning to a few souls, many of an unsavory sort, she required an escort. Unless he shortened his stride, he'd leave her behind.

When the cowboy rounded the corner of a building, Katherine lifted her skirt an inch and sprinted after him. *Don't slip,* she begged her slick-soled boots. As she entered a sort of alley with hitching rails and he looked back at her, Katherine resumed her sedate walk.

The scruffy preacher she'd seen before stood near a black stallion of outstanding beauty. She could not guess its bloodlines. Though its fine head and high-flung tail bespoke English Barbs, the animal's shoulders and haunches were muscled enough to carry an armored knight.

While Katherine studied the horse, the preacher tattled on some wrongdoers in a nearby gambling den.

"I am a soldier of the cross." The preacher sidestepped the eye-rolling stallion, "And they're by God gonna run these games fair and quiet if I have to kill every bastard and bullwhacker in town!"

A unique approach to ministry, Katherine thought as the preacher swaggered away.

She glanced at Joe Nelson and he looked down. "I could go wallop him for you. Or wash his mouth out with soap—"

When Katherine tried to protest, the cowboy talked over her.

"—but Preacher Jack is the local sin-buster and devil wrassler. To tell you true, he's pretty much a law unto himself."

"I took him for a local eccentric, Mr. Nelson. Don't trouble yourself."

Silence hung over the alley. Then, shifting Molly to one side, Joe Nelson dug into a pocket. He gave a shrill, summoning whistle.

"Hey, Jack!" he shouted. "Y' left with an empty collection plate."

The preacher turned, sighted the tossed gold piece, and snagged it from the air.

"Blessed be, Joe Nelson!" The preacher cawed the benediction and shambled toward a back door through which a staggering man had been ejected.

The cowboy cleared his throat. "Now. I figure you can ride."

His refusal to look at her face when he spoke made Katherine suspicious.

"Definitely," she said, and still he regarded the horse.

Only once, as she'd tested him to assure he'd been sent by Colin Stark, had the cowboy met her eyes.

"Get on up, then."

"I beg your pardon? You can't intend for me to *ride* to the Stark estate."

"It's too far to walk."

"But what about that sleigh?" Katherine pointed without an ounce of regret for the unladylike gesture.

"Not ours."

"All right." Disappointment didn't stop her. "Mr. Nelson, I assumed a carriage or wagon, some sort of conveyance would be waiting."

"No ma'am, but that storm is and I don't think we oughta test its patience." He nodded toward the mountains. No longer clear-cut against the sky, the peaks were blurred by a lowering shroud of snow.

"You expect me to ride this horse." Katherine spoke

slowly. It would be indelicate to point out that she wasn't dressed for riding.

She scanned the alley. With the ruckus outside the back door ended, no other living thing moved. Then, a worse thought bobbed to the surface of her mind.

"Where is *your* mount?"

Joe Nelson expelled a breath.

"Oh, no," she warned.

The cowboy shook his head and stayed silent.

"No. Absolutely not. You are not asking me to share this horse with you."

"He's strong."

"That is beside the point. *Quite* beside the point, isn't it?" Katherine stifled a disbelieving laugh as he remained mute. "I'm not disputing the animal's strength, of all things, but you have not provided a sidesaddle."

Katherine looked pointedly at her gored skirt, but the cowboy did not take the hint. "Dumb as a bucket of bolts," her father had once called his discharged valet, and Joe Nelson was worse. Still, she tried to explain.

"Clearly you've never worn a bustle and corset, Mr. Nelson. Yes, you *may* blush, but I tell you the very idea of riding is ludicrous. Outrageous. No, I'll say it straight out: to dream of me assuming such a position is positively dim-witted."

That last struck a cold spark from Joe Nelson's eye and Katherine caught her breath. Drat. This man was apparently all that stood between her and these *prairies* full of wolves and vipers. She gathered her humility and tried one time more.

"And then there's Molly."

"We won't be exactly comfy," he said, looking down.

Katherine's instincts sharpened. Joe Nelson wasn't hurt by her insults. Quite the contrary. That tremor in his voice said he was amused by her predicament.

"Miss, this is how it is: it's nearly Christmas. The livery stable is closed, so I can't get another horse. The boarding house is full up, so you can't stay the night. In an hour, they're dousing the stove and lowering the bar on the train station's door. The town will be closed up and a storm's moving in.

"Now, you can ride in the saddle, holding the dog, with me behind, or vice versa. That's it."

When Father had come west, had he been treated with such discourtesy? Impossible.

Katherine twisted her hands, then halted. The gesture might be taken for desperation, and she was merely angry. Her eyes followed the dangling end of Molly's leash. It blew in a gust of frigid wind, swinging like a pendulum.

The cowboy waited, holding her dog and her immediate future in his power.

"Very well. I'll sit in the saddle holding Molly. I *will* ride sidesaddle."

"And fall on top of the dog when you both go sliding off."

Red bolts of anger swam behind Katherine's eyelids, but when she opened them, she presented the blackguard with a mild countenance. "You drive a hard bargain, Mr. Nelson."

Expressionless, he moved to hold the horse's head. "I don't see that you have much choice."

A gentleman would have apologized, but she didn't say so. Instead, she reached up for the reins, faced the horse's midsection, and addressed her request to the saddle.

"If you could avert your eyes while I mount."

"Yes'm."

Curse his insolent, audacious, western soul! Her boot slipped in the snow-slicked stirrup. She hopped, unbalanced by the weight of the carpetbag slung on her arm, made a grab for the saddle skirt, and mounted. She sat with one leg on each side of the horse. She reached for Molly and stared into the intricate meshing of the dog's fur, while the cowboy climbed on. Katherine felt his care, reaching wide around her for the reins, trying not to offend.

Just the same, the way his arms encompassed her upper body, an onlooker might have mistaken it for an embrace.

"Almost there."

They were the first words the cowboy had spoken in an hour. Or a month. Perhaps longer.

Katherine only knew her arms were crippled from holding Molly and her lower limbs, exposed to the driving snow because her skirts had hiked up as she rode astride, had frozen.

Her cloak's warmth waned as the wind picked up. When she shivered, the cowboy drew his arms around hers. When she still shuddered with cold, he leaned forward, forming his chest against her back.

Neither of them spoke. Though the position made a travesty of the master-workman bond and a mockery of her rage, Katherine welcomed his warmth.

She blessed the brandy for Molly's steady snoring, and extracted a stiff arm from beneath the dog to push hair back under her hat. Given a chance, she would have traded her useless pink bonnet for a child's stocking cap.

As they moved into a pine grove, Joe Nelson slowed the horse. Another trail led away from the one they rode and he seemed to consider taking it, before urging the stallion into a faster, bumpier jog.

She couldn't guess the time, but violet shadows gathered in the odd casket-shaped track ahead of them.

"What do you suppose it is?" Her words sounded mushy as the wind snatched them away.

He leaned closer. With his cheek's warmth nearly touching her, Katherine wondered if cowboys came for dinner at the Stark mansion.

"That track?" As she shouted, the wind slackened and her voice echoed.

"Shh." He pointed.

Just ahead, mounted men clustered around two laboring horses. Curses and clots of snow spewed into the air as the animals lurched forward, fought for footing, and tried to drag a huge box through the deepening drifts.

"Lay on the lash." The man's voice sounded like home, in spite of his cruelty.

"Is that . . . ?" As Katherine twisted in the saddle, her lips grazed Joe's cheek. Before her apology, he lay a finger across her lips.

Dear Lord. Did that count as a kiss? Did he think her a hussy? And that man just ahead, speaking in a voice so like Father's . . . was he her husband? Above the hammering of her thoughts, Katherine hoped not.

"They're doin' their best, sir, it's—"

"Lay on or get down and pull for them."

The whip cracked, a horse screamed, and the stallion beneath them gave a low rumble.

Joe reined his stallion behind a stand of trees, slid to the snow, and held his arms up as if she should jump into them.

She handed him Molly, then floundered down, hitting her ribs against the bulging carpetbag as she landed in a tangle of skirt. Snow clumps stuck in her hair as she struggled to sit. Though dignity was impossible, when Joe offered his hand, she ignored it.

He hardly noticed. Instead, he glared over his shoulder at the men and contrived a concealing stance to hide her from them.

"Is that . . . ?" Wind-deafened, Katherine all but shouted. "Is that my . . . ?"

He moved behind her. "Shut up." In one grab, he clamped his hand over her mouth and pinned her tight against him.

Realization stabbed through her mind. Joe Nelson was no savior, no hireling of Colin Stark's. She was trapped in the arms of a kidnapper.

Katherine stomped her heel onto his boot. As he recoiled, she jabbed him with her elbow and screamed against his glove.

"Lady, stop." He lifted her off her feet. The indignity of her boots pedaling above the snow made Katherine obey. Slowly he lowered her. "Now, look. *Look.*"

He forced her to watch. As she did, the man in a tan duster whose face shone an unnatural maroon snatched the whip from an underling and beat the horses himself.

"That," said the cowboy, "is Colin Stark."

A strangled neigh came as one horse fell and dragged the other to its knees.

Joe kept his hand over her mouth, but the pressure eased as if he knew she'd lost the urge to scream.

Still, she refused to be bullied, even if . . . *the pistol.* That would even their positions. Her eyes scanned the snow at her feet until she saw the carpetbag.

Her hands were so cold, she wasn't certain she could open the bag. But she had to. Joe Nelson had a gun and so did she. The weapon would end this desperado's commands and open negotiations between equals.

Katherine pretended to relax in his grip. One lunge and she could have it.

"That's better," he said.

Face-first, she flung herself at the bag. Snow slapped her bodice as she stretched and dug inside the bag. *There.* Her numbed fingers struck metal. It could be nothing except her pistol. She gripped it as he tackled her flat.

She couldn't breathe. His body slanted across hers, printing her deep into the snow, until she rolled, pulling the gun from her bag, tipping him so they lay facing one another as she raised her weapon.

"Not on the head." Joe grabbed her wrist and it was there, over his right shoulder, that Katherine saw her mistake.

She held the gypsy's crystal ball.

Not her gun. She dropped it into the snow, struggled to her knees, and dug in the carpetbag once again.

"She stole my gun." Katherine littered the snow with a blue crepe blouse, a mirror, a silver-backed brush, and a daguerreotype of Colin Stark, but the pistol wasn't there.

"That's a shame." Standing, he pulled a knife from his boot sheath and slipped it, bare-bladed, into his holster. "Now, lady, I won't gag you. Can I trust you to stay put and stay quiet?"

She shook the rest of the bag's contents onto the snow. A candy cane rested next to a pair of pearl earbobs. "And my money. She took my money." Katherine struggled to her feet and adjusted her sodden skirts. "I suppose it doesn't matter to you that I'm penniless and defenseless."

"Truth to tell, sugar, you're right."

Sugar?

He snatched up his horse's reins. "I'm gonna ride over to stop that." He nodded toward the team, the wooden box, and the whip.

Katherine counted. There were five men.

"And it bein' nearly Christmas, you might say a little prayer Stark don't shoot me in the back. When this is over, if you still want to be Stark's bride, I'll give you to him."

The black horse bolted into a snow-spattering gait and Katherine watched him go. Joe rocked in the saddle. Loose, relaxed, *foolhardy.*

"Please God," Katherine began, but then she didn't know what to ask for.

Five

Blacky knew how to play the game. The stallion answered Joe's bid for a casual lope, even as his ears swiveled at the draft team's distress.

Joe tensed, spoiling for a fight. He'd ridden miles with the lady's fussy hat in his face, her wet cloak slapping his legs and her dog drooling on his saddle. That wasn't the worst of it, either. The worst—and best—had been the rhythmic rising and sinking away of her back against his front.

Nonetheless, he'd kidnapped her as a nursemaid and that's just what she'd be. He needed to move on. He wanted no part of a fine lady who'd never ridden astride a horse or kissed a cowboy. She certainly hadn't meant those soft, pink lips to part when he touched his finger there to hush her.

His brain knew all that. His body didn't.

The whip's crack might've shattered the cold air. Joe was close enough to see the ranch hands all but licking Stark's boots.

"Sir, I just don't know how . . ."

"The team's game to do it, sir, but . . ."

Except for one.

"Leave it, man." Mounted on a wildly spotted Indian paint, Dingo Collins lit a smoke and leaned back to enjoy it.

Stark had been smart enough to hire the shrewd Australian

as foreman, but the rich Englishman bristled at Dingo's lack of deference.

"Come back when things've iced up. Then she'll slide."

The men nodded in agreement. All except Stark.

"That piano's for my bride. It and the provisions for her wedding supper must be arranged in the parlor for her arrival."

Joe considered the hump of supplies tied on the mule at the same time the beast's hellish braying alerted them all to Joe's approach.

In the instant of Stark's surprise, Joe spurred Blacky through the midst of them. With the men scattered, Joe's knife slashed the traces holding the horses to their burden. No sense makin' a feeble entrance when a man meant business.

Three guns were out when he wheeled Blacky to face them. Joe ignored the nervous cowboys. As he listened to the draft horses' labored escape, it was Dingo Collins he watched. Dingo kept his hand ready beside his holster.

Joe pulled Blacky to a head-shaking halt and faced Stark's silent rage. "Gonna shoot me for it, or thank me for savin' good horses you might've ruined in a temper?"

"I'll thank you for nothing, except getting on your way." Stark's face had swollen with anger.

"Stark, you might've mentioned that Loving Cup Saloon was out of business and infested."

Because Stark had sheltered the brats, he'd leave the man some dignity. Besides, every man at this end of the state knew Stark had lost the saloon gambling. Joe didn't rub in the loss.

Stark ignored him until he'd ordered a man to recapture the draft horses and another to silence the mule.

Stark reined his big bay onto its heels and spurred a few yards off. Though it galled him, Joe followed.

Stark regarded Joe with disdain. "I assumed you'd send them packing. It's your saloon and your chore to dispose of them."

An edginess lurked beneath Stark's brusque statement and his breath came in harsh gasps.

Joe tested him with the truth. "There's four children there. The woman's gone. Next to no food's in the place, and there's precious little wood for the stove."

While Stark shifted in his saddle, swearing, Joe glanced

back at the pines. Katherine could come bursting out at any minute. He'd best get what he could and go.

"Hand over that mule loaded with provisions and I'll be on my way."

"Of all the bloody nerve." Stark wiped at the sweat ringing his lips. "Run off my horses, ruin the piano, and . . ." Stark swayed in his saddle and only righted himself by grabbing the saddle horn. "I tell you, they're for my bride."

Stark didn't seem drunk. He looked like he had sunstroke.

"If she knew there were hungry children . . ."

"My bride could not conceive of hungry children." Stark sneered. "You can't imagine the life of privilege she has led. Coming here will be trial enough, but she will stay."

Stark set his jaw and focused on a distant dream. Was Stark musing over his papered Herefords, a breed so delicate they'd die calving if Stark didn't keep them penned for human help? Did he imagine the same life for Katherine?

"She'll be a princess in my castle," Stark insisted.

"And the voters?" Joe shifted his attack. "I hear you're running for Congress, Stark. Voters might take a dim view of throwin' babies out into the snow."

Stark tightened his grip on the saddle horn. "Ride away and don't look back." Sweat sheened his face and he roared like a monarch. "Do not think of returning to that saloon." Stark's eyes burned like coals with wind howling over them. "Forget what was there. I'll take care of it."

Joe felt his scalp contract with caution. The man was worse than drunk.

Overbalanced by his rider's weight sagging off to one side, the bay stumbled. Stark raised his riding crop and tried to strike the horse, but even that action seemed beyond him.

Fighting the bit, the bay moved back to the other horses.

Katherine should have made her choice by now, but Joe decided to force her hand.

"Stark," he called. "That train your bride's on? It's long since come in." If Katherine aimed to be Stark's woman, she'd best come running. "They're closing down the station, 'bout now. Seems to me, you might think about goin' after her."

"Damn your eyes. You couldn't have said so before now!" Stark gestured at the oldest ranch hand. "You . . ." Clearly, he couldn't recall the man's name. "See the animals are taken

back to the ranch and tell Lenox I want tea in the parlor and
a three-log fire in the grate. The rest of you''—Stark gestured
like a commander gathering troops—''come with me.''

As Stark rode out, Joe hazarded a look back, then chastised
himself. It meant nothing to him that no skirted figure slogged
over the snow.

Joe turned to the old man with drooping gray moustache
and eyes. ''Ornery cuss, that Stark.''

''Got him a reserved seat in Hell.'' The old man joined Joe
in staring at the loaded pack mule.

The food Stark had ordered for Katherine could fill out the
hollow cheeks on Rack and Ruin, and yank a smile onto Gussie's face. If this hoard belonged to Katherine, maybe she'd
share.

Again, he looked toward the pines and though his own smile
made his cheeks ache in the cold, warmth spread out from his
center.

''Set here a minute, if you can,'' he told the old man.

''Don't be tryin' anything fancy with that knife.'' The old
man raised a revolver big and black as a calf's leg. ''I take
the man's money. I owe him somethin'.''

''Fair enough. Let's just see if I can't up the ante.''

The old man took a flask from inside his coat, took a long
draw from it. ''I figure you got ten minutes before me and this
mule start to feel the nip in the air and head home.''

Joe touched his hat brim and trotted back to Katherine.

Her lips were blue.

It was the first thing Joe noticed as he drew rein inside the
cluster of pines. What the hell was he supposed to do about
it, when she sat on a boulder, cloak gathered around her with
the dog underneath? Maybe the cold would keep her quiet.
He'd never seen such sass over riding a horse.

She'd pulled her arms inside the cloak, too. The fact that
he couldn't see her hands made Joe a mite nervous. She
rocked, humming like an angel, but the hard resolve in her
glare said she'd found her gun.

He dismounted without taking his eyes off her. She'd made
up her mind against Stark, but she had a yen to make Joe
Nelson squirm. He'd oblige her, as long as she took over the
brats and set him free.

Katherine sniffed and wrapped her arms tighter around the

dog. She watched him as carefully as he watched her.

"Mr. Stark appeared annoyed."

"Being made a fool does that to a man."

"I daresay." She closed her jaws until her teeth's chattering stopped. "And will he catch his horses?"

Joe shrugged. He tried to think of the quickest way to tell what had to be said before the old man rode off with the mule.

"It started before. Playin' poker, I won a saloon from him."

"Yes."

"He didn't say the saloon was full of kids."

"I beg your pardon?" Katherine's eyes came wide open.

Joe told himself to play this real careful. "See, a woman was running sort of an orphanage. When I got there, she left."

"She abandoned them? Left . . . children alone?"

"Well, with me."

Katherine's dismissing motion made him want to brag he'd filled their bellies with a hot dinner, but that didn't suit his purpose.

"There's two twin boys, a babe in arms, and a little girl Gussie, who's doing her best to care for the lot of them."

"Oh, dear."

Joe pressed his advantage. "Gussie has freckles, about a million of them, all over her nose and cheeks."

"Very *well*." Her tight smile wasn't superior this time. It only said he'd oversold that particular bill of goods.

She stood, slowed by the effort of hefting the dog. He figured she couldn't be holding the gun, too. She nodded toward the old cowhand. "I trust you didn't say I'd return with him."

"Not exactly."

"And yet he still sits there."

"Stark told him to take that mule back to the ranch and have some servant lady set up—"

"I heard as much." She bit her lip. "And I suppose you think I'm the sort of woman who'd go have a merry Christmas celebration while children starve in the cold?"

Her tone turned shrill, as if something rode on this.

"There's a fine stove at the saloon," he said. "They're warm enough."

"You didn't answer my question. Do you think I'm a mean-spirited woman?"

It quaked between them.

Lord, how had they skipped courtin' and jumped straight to this? Not passion, but a thick yearning that simmered on the edge of it. She'd asked him what he thought of her. His answer would determine what she thought of him.

It'd be easier to pluck off her silly hat, pull the pins from her hair, and kiss her till she knew what he thought. But she'd asked for words.

"Lady, I don't know—"

"Of course you don't." Disappointed, her face turned fragile.

He stepped close enough to lift her chin. "My gut says you'll help me think of a way to take that food and get out of here before Stark comes back."

"Your 'guts' are right." A smile broke over her face. She nodded toward the ranch hand. "I suppose we could rob him."

Her considering gaze made his skin prickle with gooseflesh. "He's a pretty old fella."

"That *is* troublesome." She tapped the toe of her boot, thinking. "I fear we'll have to use my second plan. Could you please hold Molly for just a moment more, and turn your back?"

"Not before hearin' what you've got in mind." He might want Katherine in his arms, but he sure didn't trust her.

"Bribery," she said. "I have a few dollars sewn into a pocket in my petticoat."

He took the blasted hound and turned away. She couldn't know that the rustle of her petticoat made him see silk and lace against creamy skin.

"You may turn back," she said, but at once she snatched the money beyond his reach. "Oh no. I'm going with you. A lady may convince a gentleman to abandon his scruples, even when another man cannot."

"After you." He bowed her ahead, trying not to think how convincing Katherine could be to a man like him, who had no scruples whatsoever.

Six

Excitement charged through Katherine like a sip of wine. Each time she snuck a glance from the corner of her eye, she caught Joe Nelson regarding her with confused pride.

They trudged through the drifts with Molly gamboling between them. Awake and refreshed, the basset shoveled her nose through the fresh snow, then turned and gave a bossy woof at Blacky.

Even with skirts soaked and legs shaky, Katherine delighted at the way the old cowboy—he'd introduced himself as Teddy—had taken her money and handed her the mule's rope. His expression had said he didn't mind losing to a stronger player.

When she claimed control, a truce had opened between her and Joe Nelson. Could it be that a lifetime of stored female strength, improper in the East, was welcomed in the West? Her conscience cautioned her not to move past truce to attraction, to . . .

"Y'all right?" As Joe caught her elbow, Katherine avoided his eyes. Had she made an audible rejection of that ugly word?

"I'm fine, thank you."

She'd admit their situation was immodest, but it was not immoral. It could not be wrong to bring food and music to orphans.

"Do you think Blacky minds?" Katherine looked over her

shoulder. The piano slid behind the sleek animal she'd pressed into draft work.

"I don't suppose he has many expectations from life," Joe said. "Besides, you had a good idea, striking off the box and making the planks into runners. You can serenade him while he munches his hay."

"And the piano *is* mine. Didn't Mr. Stark say so?" Formality clamped between them at the mention of her husband.

"Yes, miss, he did."

Those mistakes again. First the designation as an unmarried woman, and then Joe's smile of admiration. She wanted both but she couldn't have them *and* the legal title to this piano. If she had the right to enjoy this walk with Joe, taking the piano was robbery.

She looked toward the piano again. The exertion of walking through deep snow had enabled her to shed her cloak and drape it over the cherrywood spinet, so it wouldn't spot from moisture.

Her husband had given it to her. Before he'd made a vile stamp on her mind—red-faced and furious, cruel and conceited—he'd purchased this gift.

Legally she was bound to Colin Stark for a lifetime. That sleigh at the train station had surely been his. If not for the gypsy's warning, she might have resisted Joe's order to mount Blacky at the train station. She might have approached the sleigh driver and be, at this very instant, traveling to Stark's mansion, ignorant of his temper, until the first blow fell.

Molly stopped, nearly pulling Katherine off her feet.

"Just a moment," Katherine said. She noticed Joe waited with a tolerant expression, even though Molly was dawdling again.

For fear of wolves or coyotes, Katherine kept Molly leashed. The dog flopped on her back and wriggled in the snow, eyes closed in contentment. Molly was a nuisance, but Katherine loved her. Remembering Stark's directive to beat the bleeding horse, she realized his wrath could have struck Molly, too.

Katherine felt the weight of the gypsy's crystal ball in her carpetbag. Did it have power? Or did magic dwell within the gypsy? At the first opportunity, Katherine planned to examine the globe, clean it, polish its fretted metal base, and learn why her instinct debated with logic, telling her it was more than just a bauble.

Blacky broke into a trot, surging past, nearly bowling Katherine over.

"There it is," Joe said.

As they rode closer, the door of a deserted general store creaked on rusty hinges. Cobweb-fine curtains streamed from the broken window of a milliner's shop and a set of front steps rocked in the wind, working loose from an empty sheriff's office.

"It's what they call a ghost town, isn't it?" Katherine felt a thrill of anticipation and wondered how much Joe Nelson had to do with her lack of fear.

"Just a little place folks left behind," Joe said. "The saloon lasted longest. Hands riding from Soaring Peak to Cold Creek got thirsty and probably some of Stark's—"

"Indeed." She cut him off as they reached the saloon. Mother would weep at the pleasure Katherine felt at seeing the decrepit Loving Cup Saloon. Beards of ice clung to its rafters and a sign suspended on rusty chains. Upon closer examination, she saw the sign showed a double-handled goblet, one side gripped by a manly fist, the other by a pale, ringed hand.

Because Joe crouched to release Blacky from his burden, he didn't see Katherine rub the redness beneath her own jeweled band.

The Loving Cup Saloon looked like a one-story log house except for the false front jutting skyward and the poster glued to its wall. She heard small feet pounding about inside and waited, giving them time to look her over.

She read the advertisement for Limerick's Great Southern Liniment, which claimed to cure ailments from boils to scald-head. She winced at the gruesome name, then smoothed the expression from her face, lest the children take fear of her and—

What in Heaven's name was she about? Katherine's hands shook, though her mind tried to discipline them.

She, the youngest in a family of six, knew nothing of children. She, an old maid at twenty-eight, knew less than nothing about men. What enchantment had compelled her to come here?

No enchantment, she decided. She'd responded with compassion, with Christmas spirit, with charity.

"Ready?" Joe tucked her gloved hand through his arm.

Oh, and with fondness, for the most unlikely man to lead her across a threshold.

If Joe had exceeded Katherine's expectations of things western, the Loving Cup Saloon did not.

Without lit lamps, the saloon was awfully dim. No garish roulette wheels spun in a corner. No bottles clinked in raucous toasts. However, the walls were decorated with small American flags and a number of taxidermied beasts. And it did have a crystal chandelier overhead and the portrait of a naked nymph smirked from above the mahogany bar.

"He brought us a lady." The incredulous voice came from the far end of the room, where a small figure warmed itself before a potbellied stove. Once she found him, Katherine saw others ranged close together for warmth.

When Joe introduced the boys, Katherine didn't question the names Rack and Ruin. She only wondered if their mother had been joking, or reflecting on a dreadful life.

"Can you read?"

"She ain't got no books."

"Or tell stories without readin' books?"

"Yes, of course," Katherine said. At least that skill could cheer them. But pleasure faded as they shrank away from her.

"She talks like a queen." Ruin wheeled on Joe as if he might return her to a shop.

"No queen, I assure you." Katherine tugged at Molly's leash. She'd counted on the dog to make friends, but Molly remained in the doorway. "However, I grew up in England, where they have queens. And I know stories about them."

"I'm called Gussie, ma'am, but I'd rather be Augusta, if you please." The child wore the freckles Joe had described and a too-short brown-and-white plaid Mother Hubbard gown. She'd crisped her blond hair into stiff pipe curls that cocked off at odd angles.

Gussie extended her hand in a fragile handshake and the others followed suit, clearly eager to touch her.

"I am pleased to make the acquaintance of you all."

"You haven't," one of the twins said.

"There's Sal, too, but she's sleepin'." A small hand pulled her toward the makeshift cradle.

The bundle resembled a loaf of bread, but it smelled more like ammonia. Katherine awaited a twinge of tenderness, but she only felt a need to get Sal fresh nappies.

As quiet lapped in around them, Katherine remembered the gypsy's crystal-ball vision and checked that nothing sat near enough the stove to catch fire.

Joe had gone to the rear of the saloon, where a small room served as a sleeping alcove. He leaned against the doorframe, alone. Then the twins began pointing.

One shouted, "She gots a dog!" As they descended on Molly, the basset moaned, tugged, then threw back her head and howled. Next, Sal began to cry.

"She's really not used to children!" Katherine nearly lost her grip as Molly backed under a table and the baby sobbed. "Give her a little while to . . ."

She wished Joe would rescue the weeping Sal, but the coward only retreated behind the mahogany bar to remove the immodest painting.

"We used to have a dog, but he was fluffy." The shorter twin—Ruin, she thought—squatted, then rolled onto his back and angled his face up for Molly's kiss.

The gesture of trust worked.

Shivering and crawling forward on her belly, Molly licked his face. Ruin's giggles drew his twin down, too. Molly slathered them both while Gussie ran a fingertip down the dog's backbone.

"I'm sorry I don't look nicer. I need a mirror." Gussie risked a glance at Katherine. "My mama had one."

Though the baby's plea was louder, Gussie's quiet need seemed greater.

"And so do I." Katherine made a no-nonsense gesture toward her carpetbag. "You may use it, if you like."

Eyes wide, one finger twisting in her skirt, Gussie whispered, "I might break it."

"I doubt that."

Had the girl been beaten for breaking a mirror? Katherine wondered as she crossed to her carpetbag. She was still rummaging when Joe came through the front door.

She didn't know when he'd skulked away, but now he balanced parcels from the mule's load and she forgave his desertion.

Once she found the mirror and matching brush, Katherine offered them to Gussie. The child backed away and rushed to retrieve the squalling baby. At last, Katherine lay the brush and mirror on the table Molly and the boys had taken as their playhouse.

"Besides, Augusta," Katherine feigned interest in the goods Joe was unloading, "mirrors are made in factories by the hundreds. Breaking one is no tragedy."

Katherine thought she'd done well, until she heard Gussie's sigh over Sal's weeping and went to help her. Gingerly, Gussie folded back the diaper.

"Oh, merciful heavens." Katherine wheeled toward Joe.

He presented the delicacies before him with a wide gesture. "Anyone for supper?"

He still had time to get out before Christmas.

Joe had planned to leave once the mule was stabled with Blacky and the cow, and once the piano had been brought inside.

He'd laid more runners to move the instrument and now it sat across the room, facing the bar. Though the boys had done their best to help, it had been Katherine who'd set her shoulder to the burden. She'd shoved with a ladylike grunt and a pandemonium of petticoats.

After they shifted it into place, she'd stood, puffing and wiping her palms on her rose-colored skirts. When she ran one finger in a tinkling waterfall of notes down the entire keyboard and crowed, "That's got it, now!" he thought for sure the children would laugh.

They didn't. They watched Katherine as they might a fascinating beast, as if she might turn on them at any time. Thinking of his childhood at the fort, on the many hands which ruffled his hair in pity, then went away, Joe understood.

As she sorted through the collection of exotic food, Katherine was more excited than the brood. Rack and Ruin kept glancing at Joe. He sat by the stove, whittled, and waited. The kids had to crack smiles sometime. He wouldn't mind seeing it before he left.

"Champagne!" Katherine held two heavy green bottles aloft and waggled them.

Joe smiled, thinking she looked like a proper schoolmarm about to go on a tear. When Gussie crossed her arms to hug herself tight, Joe wanted to tell her that Katherine was harmless, but he knew better. If the brood started believing Katherine was here for good, she'd break their hearts.

"I'll tell you what we'll do. We'll lay out this white tablecloth." Katherine tossed one end of the linen toward Rack and he caught it. "Spread it and smooth it so there are no wrinkles. Lovely." The children clustered on the benches facing the table. "Now, let's see what we have here, shall we?"

They had tinned oysters, artichoke hearts, and canned milk for Sal. They had bags of white sugar, potatoes, buckwheat flour, pretzels, and hard little red apples. Folded, oiled paper held sticks of elk jerky flavored with burgundy wine. The labels on one jar read "Jugged Hare" and two others held canned peaches. Yards of tissue paper wrapped a full dozen fresh eggs.

But if Stark had meant to dazzle her with his wealth, he'd failed.

"Hundreds of cattle on this range and practically no vegetables." Katherine removed her pink hat and set it aside to inspect a wilted stalk of celery. "Children need vegetables."

Joe had never heard such a notion. Folks needed meat and potatoes. But he didn't contradict her. Since he'd lighted the brass wall sconces behind the bar, the light flickered on her hair, making it glow a rich brown.

Tomorrow maybe he'd climb up and see about that crystal chandelier. Except he wouldn't be here tomorrow.

"Oh, my." Katherine displayed a wax-coated wheel of cheddar cheese. "Augusta, can you guess how delicious this will be with those crackers? And maybe a bit of that hard, peppery sausage?"

Gussie could, until Joe interrupted. "You don't want to be eating it all at once."

He'd caused the brood's haunted expressions to return, but damn, who'd be around to hunt fresh game? That howling banshee of a dog?

"Make the meat and cheese last a while."

"And how would one do that?" A hairpin fell pinging on

the bar as Katherine's head tilted to one side. The children turned toward him, doing precisely the same thing.

"By . . . well, shoot. What do I look like, a—?"

When Gussie flinched, Joe bit back his irritation and lowered his voice. "You might do it by mixing sausage with eggs and flour into fritters." If Katherine was testing him, she was a mighty fine actress, because she looked purely mystified. "By chopping up some jerky and frying it with potatoes and wild onions," he continued.

"Fritters." As if he'd spoken a foreign language, Katherine seized on the one word she understood.

It was then Joe knew she wasn't teasing. It looked like he'd kidnapped the only woman on the continent who didn't know how to cook.

Seven

They'd eaten enough fritters and red apples to make them all sick. Now, Katherine wanted them to dance. Little as Joe knew about youngsters, he still figured this was a bad idea. It was just as well he'd stowed his gear and bedroll out in the cowshed. While they frolicked, he'd step out the back window.

In the meantime, he stood behind the bar, watching.

The twins and Gussie jammed in more dinner and Katherine tried to entertain them.

"I've got something rather special in my carpetbag." She hauled the bag up from beneath a grunting Molly. The children's chewing slowed. "I'm not saying it's magical, exactly, but since it's Christmas, it very well could be."

"No such thing as magic." Rack swallowed the last of a cracker. "Mama says it's a sin against Heaven to say so."

Joe watched Katherine mull that over.

"I expect she's right, but mightn't there be things which only seem magical to us, but are really gifts from Heaven? Like rainbows. And snowflakes."

"I want to see what you got," Ruin insisted. Clearly, religion wasn't his main concern.

"Faces, first." Katherine produced the clean cloth she'd heated in snow melt on the stove. Before they could protest, she wiped the children's mouths and cheeks clear of dinner and a week's accumulation of grime. And transformed them.

They looked healthier. Not a one had yet parted with a smile, but with their faces pink, it seemed possible.

As she withdrew the globe from her bag, Katherine beamed, but the children turned back to dinner.

Gussie's long sigh came first. "That's Lucy's."

Suspicion renewed the ache in Joe's skull. How in hell had Katherine come to have something belonging to the floozy who'd bashed him?

"Remember, I told you." Gussie ducked her head toward Joe. "In the medicine show, she played the purple Swami. She used that to see visions. It's only pretend."

Ruin stabbed his finger into a canned peach. It slid across his plate. Again, Joe recognized the gloom. Christmas always promised magic, but when the gaiety ended, nothing had changed.

"That may be." A dozen questions rained over Katherine's face, but she didn't ask one—only bustled within inches of him, behind the bar. "But I have enough curiosity, that I want to see this crystal ball cleaned up and sparkling."

He'd never imagined he'd share the backside of a bar with a lady. But the experience had his pulse jittering. Come-hither waves of warmth flowed off Katherine, though she spared him little attention. With an elbow grazing his, she dabbed at the crystal ball's base with polish that smelled of turpentine and ash.

The dog's head lifted, nose testing the air, then she commented with a single whimper.

"What's wrong with her?" Gussie bit her lip.

"Molly doesn't like the smell, she's a very particular dog," Katherine said.

"It's nasty," Ruin agreed.

"Perhaps you could help her think of something else."

When the children abandoned their seats to sprawl beside the dog, Katherine opened her lips to protest. Then, though the floor was far from clean, she gave a half shrug and returned to her task.

Sap popped in the potbellied stove and the children babbled to the dog, but Joe felt the silence build between him and Katherine. The crook of his elbow remembered the warm pressure of her hand as she'd trusted him to lead her inside this old saloon. And though they hadn't spoken for hours, except through the young ones, this was no frigid silence, but the scalding stillness that came before a violent boil.

It was time for him to go.

"All right, Mr. Nelson." As she plucked at his sleeve, the space behind the bar contracted. In the wide world, nothing existed except his body and hers. "It's left to you to appreciate this bauble."

Joe tried to retreat. Hard-learned manners enforced with backhand smacks told him even a lady couldn't protest if he excused himself to the privy. Once outside, he'd ride away. It's what he should do, but Katherine beckoned.

"Never heard of a saloon with no whiskey," Joe grumbled, but he followed her all the same.

She stood directly beneath the chandelier and lifted the globe. It caught the light and shot off spangles of silver.

"Mighty nice." He watched her thumbs smooth over a raised pattern on the globe's base. "What's that? Fish?"

"Yes. . . ." Her voice had a wondering sound. "Dozens of overlapping fish swimming in all directions. Look at their long tails, draping like scarves and— Why, they have long whiskers."

"Like catfish." As Joe turned the base to catch the light, he felt its weight and then his hand touched hers. Bare of its glove, her hand was white as sugar and soft.

"Really?" She sounded dubious, and if she noticed their hands touched, she showed nothing. "Don't they look rather Oriental?"

"Wouldn't know about that." He could be out the back window in two minutes and her hands would become one more Christmas memory.

"It's an odd design. I believe it's quite old."

He could be on Blacky in five minutes.

"I truly should try to get it back to her."

"To Lucy?" He gave a snort that must've revolted Katherine. Lord knew she'd have nothing to do with him if he hadn't abducted her. "You'd have a better chance catching a snowflake." He gathered the brats' plates in a stack.

"You know her well, then?"

His hands stopped as if a spell had hardened them. He recognized her tone. He thought of Lucy, painted-cat pretty and sultry in a way Katherine wouldn't recognize as practiced.

Jealousy glinted in Katherine's words and it worked on him like a match on kerosene.

"No, ma'am." Joe glanced down at the kids. They didn't appear to be listening. "Only thing I know, she packs a wallop with a skillet."

"He looked dead." Rack glanced up from stroking the dog's belly.

Katherine held the globe against the front of her dress. "That gypsy struck you unconscious?"

Her lips stayed open in a shocked "O." Joe imagined hurdling the bar and kids to kiss her.

"He drooled on the floor." Ruin experimented with a scratch that made Molly's hind leg twitch.

"I can take a look at the wound for you," Katherine said. "I have some skill in nursing."

If he wanted this closeness to turn the corner, that would do it.

He didn't look at her small, capable hands. They'd wiped the children's cheeks clean and rosy. They'd polished the crystal ball into something fine. He wondered what would happen if her hands tended him.

"It's nothing." He knew she couldn't hear his swallow, but it echoed in his head like a downpour.

"All right, then, we'll have a Christmas promenade."

"Like a dance?" Gussie's hands plucked at her corkscrew curls.

"Like a fancy dress ball." Katherine nodded. "And I have things in my bag. You'll all have something special to wear while I play the piano."

"It's not a player piano." Gussie warned. "And there's no music in the bench. I peeked."

"I remember the notes to a few tunes." Katherine cut her eyes toward Joe in a confiding, between-adults look. "And I daresay Mr. Nelson can lead us in some carols he knows by heart."

By heart. Joe remembered his Mama singing, "Joy to the World." Each year, music and laughter had charmed him. Ladies' hands had petted his hair. Cider-soaked men had slapped his back and bellowed, *"You're a good boy, Joe."* But his mama had never come back to sing to him again.

"I don't know a one," Joe said and Katherine looked more disappointed than the kids.

On the saloon's blank windows, Joe saw reflections of old Christmases. Back then, his hopes had vaulted up, fueled by games, good food, and praise.

But each year, midnight came. Fiddles screeched to silence and were latched into their cases. Candles were snuffed out. Cuddling and holding hands, folks shuffled to tents just big enough to shelter a family.

Celebrations always ended and Joe always returned to his shed and straw pallet. There, he felt circled by a bottomless trough of darkness, too wide to jump.

During his ruminations, Katherine slipped away. There was only one place she could've gone. The back room held a bed big enough for all three children. Its compromising presence should have made Joe stop.

By the light streaming from the main room, he watched and caught her primping. Back turned, she held the mirror with one hand, trying to pin up her hair with the other.

"Need some help?"

The mirror bobbed, but she didn't turn.

"No. This will do." Her tone asked, *Won't it?*

When he kept quiet, she did turn, looking up into his face, waiting.

But how could he tell this well-bred lady he admired her grit? She'd be snapping and snorting all over again and here in the darkness—he liked her soft.

"This gown isn't exactly fresh." Katherine smoothed her skirts. "But I don't suppose neighbors are likely to drop in."

"Not likely." Joe shifted his jaw from side to side. He owed her more truth before leaving. "Word says Stark's having a shindig after the new year. That's the only place you'd likely meet neighbors." He rubbed the back of his neck. "January sixth, I'm thinking."

"And are you invited to this 'shindig'?"

Joe shook his head. "Guess there's no harm telling you. I know some folks who mean to break it up."

"Break it up? Overrun the party, do you mean?"

"That's about right. Stark and some other gents are brewin' plans to string barbed wire and run off folks on the small ranches."

Her eyes challenged him and Joe thought of how he'd tackled her in the snow and wrestled her for the crystal ball. Even though she'd known she was overmatched, even as the fragile bones had shifted in the wrists he'd pinned, he'd felt her indignant pulse and daring.

"Some small ranchers think he means to burn them out."

Katherine closed her eyes and shook her head. When she met his gaze again, Katherine's expression had turned mild.

"I'll reflect on what to do about that." With a small smile, she laced her fingers together. "And about Mr. Stark. I don't see how I can go to him."

Before he could get the right words off his tongue, Katherine cleared her throat and used the baby as a distraction.

"Doesn't she look like a little sunflower?"

Bolstered on two sides with blankets, baby Sal slept on the bed. Her thumb rested an inch from her mouth. Her lips sucked at nothing. Joe hadn't noticed the auburn fuzz on her head before. Now he did, and her tender looks surrounded Joe's heart like the roots of something poisonous.

"Sunflowers don't have red hair, do they, now?"

"Your imagination is sadly out of practice, Mr. Nelson." Her eyes rolled in exasperation.

But when Katherine wheeled away, her little bustle twitched temptation and Joe's imagination raced. Warm, sleepy children with full bellies; close conversation in a half-dark room, and a piano played by a lady who loved him. Damn Katherine for dangling more Christmas promises.

This time, he'd be the one who left before midnight.

Sitting in the darkness by Sal, Joe waited for his chance.

Katherine had positioned the crystal ball in front of a lantern. There it glittered, and she declared it would serve as a decoration until they could bring in pine boughs tomorrow. She'd also dressed each child in a woolen muffler, but she didn't call them that.

"Fine cummerbunds for you gentlemen." She double-knotted the scarves—one ivory, one green—around the twins' middles. "And for m'lady"—she draped a violet square over Gussie's shoulders—"an evening stole of incomparable beauty."

When the children didn't twirl or preen, but simply stroked

the soft knit with quizzical looks, Katherine sat down at the piano.

She began with something unfamiliar, and though the brood stood and swayed then clapped dutifully, it was not the response she wanted.

Joe fancied he could almost hear Katherine think as he covered the baby with another thickness of blanket. He didn't close the back window he'd left ajar for his getaway. As soon as he saw what Katherine tried next, he'd leave.

She shifted to a saloon favorite, "I'm Only a Bird in a Gilded Cage," and Joe's amazement grew when Gussie sang along. Her small, white throat and piping voice sent gooseflesh down his arms. It was only fitting he stay until the last note hung trembling in the prisms of the chandelier.

Katherine clapped and slid from the piano bench. She drew the shawl together at Gussie's breastbone and kissed her cheek. "You, my dear, have an absolute gift for singing."

"Gift?" Gussie's eyes widened. Then she blushed. "I didn't mean—"

"Gifts?" the twins chorused.

"A sweet singing voice is a gift from God," Katherine explained. "And the other sort of gifts come on Christmas morning."

Katherine gave a playful tug to Gussie's burned dress and turned away, pretending to adjust the position of the crystal ball next to a lantern. Joe had noticed her looking and he'd noted the charred cloth himself. Katherine fought for a light tone. "So tell me, Augusta, how did you scorch your hem?"

"It looks terrible." Gussie stared down. The glow faded from her cheeks.

"Nothing we can't mend in a minute." Katherine waved a hand. "I only wondered."

"I had an accident with the curling irons."

"Beauty is simply not worth that sort of trouble, is it?" Katherine returned to the piano bench, but her precise movements showed she was still listening.

"People go away when you're not pretty." Gussie's chin jerked high with her declaration.

Rack and Ruin watched Katherine. She smiled, and Joe wondered how she could, when all those abandoned children fixed her with the burden of their eyes.

"No, Gussie, you're wrong."

"They do." Gussie folded her arms hard, as if holding her heart in.

Enough. The baby didn't stir as Joe stood to go.

"Only the lowest sort leave," Katherine said. "People who love you only go away when they must."

Joe shrank further into the shadows. *Damn Katherine.* He snatched his hat from the floor, adjusted his gunbelt, and faced the open back window.

"Do you know 'Oh, Susannah!'?"

Joe could still hear her petticoats rustling as he stepped into the chill night. Ice-crusted snow crunched beneath his boots. He lowered the window as cold pierced his jacket.

Blacky nickered with sleepy incredulity before Joe slipped the bit into the horse's mouth. The bass notes of Katherine's playing throbbed into the shed, but the cow and mule dozed on. Blacky mouthed the bit, as if it were an insult. His ears flicked at the muffled barking inside the saloon. Standing next to all that animal warmth, Joe clucked and tugged at the reins. Blacky stomped one hoof and refused to back away from shelter.

"Damned independent cayuse, why'd you think I left you saddled?" Joe chafed his hands together, wishing he'd taken gloves from his pack. No time to do it now.

He had to leave before that new sound—a stomp-slap, stomp-slap—which shuddered through the saloon wall lured him back inside.

Still, he might risk a look through the front window, while Blacky got used to the idea of moving on.

Joe stepped onto the porch so that not a board creaked. He advanced a step, pretending someone inside would pull the trigger if he didn't move as stealthy as a cougar.

Rack and Ruin were smiling.

Stomp! Eyes fixed on each other, the boys slammed their right heels down, then slap! they clapped in unison. Katherine played faster and faster. How they kept time without tipping over, he couldn't tell. How Katherine kept playing, laughing so hard she was hunched over the keyboard, he didn't know.

Arms locked around the dog, Gussie swayed and shouted, "Oh, Susannah, don't you cry for me!"

Gussie'd strangle that hound if she didn't loosen her grip.

"Oh, Susannah" flowed into "Buffalo Gals." The children held hands and spun in giddier and wilder circles.

"Come out tonight, come out tonight!" Around and around they whirled, unsteady as a broken-spoked wheel, legs wobbling with dizziness.

Joe pressed his hands against the windowpane. Cold burned. The pain felt good.

The window shivered from their shouting and the pounding piano, and then a link in their ring broke. Children stumbled and lurched. Joe heard a crash and breaking glass. *Just the lantern. Go now. They're fine. Go. They'll never hear the hooves now. Go!* But his eyes remained on the scene inside and the tongue of flame on Katherine's skirt.

Eight

The saloon floor was less forgiving than snow.

This time when Joe tackled her, Katherine's head struck wood and he slapped at her with hands colder than ice.

"Fire's out!" he shouted into her face. "It's out! Why are you screaming?"

"I'm not screaming." Only in the moment she saw his eyes of vivid blue did Katherine realize her eyelids had been closed.

"You were," Rack said.

"Like a teakettle," Ruin added.

To her further humiliation, Katherine looked up and saw the children surrounding them in a sheepish half circle.

She addressed them in a composed manner. "Mr. Nelson saw that the fire had caught my skirts and he was . . . well, his hands were quite chilled, and . . ."

Helpless to finish, Katherine used the concealment of their bodies to thump her fist against Joe's chest. His belly sucked inward in surprise and his gun struck a painful collision with her hipbone.

Standing, swatting dust from her skirts, Katherine lowered her voice in a grumble intended for his ears only. "If you mean to make a habit of this improper and compromising behavior, sir, think better of it."

"I'm sorry." His rogue's smile said he was no such thing, but Gussie's moan distracted them all.

"I didn't do it!" Ruin backed away from the shattered crystal ball with hands hidden behind his back. Rack also hid his hands.

Well, drat. Katherine considered the sparkling pieces. The children had further proof they deserved no magic, no fancy or frivolity. Their dancing had caused a disaster. Drat upon drat. At least they wore shoes to prevent bloodshed.

"Oh, lady, look." Gussie sunk toward the floor, disappearing into the center of her skirt. Her rapt expression drew Katherine.

Only a few links of chain lapped outside the fish-fretted base of the crystal ball, but the pendant—a glorious sapphire in the heart of a golden star—had escaped its hiding place.

Katherine worked the necklace free and held the pendant in the palm of her hand. "Oh, my."

"Treasure," Ruin sighed.

"No. Nuh-uh. *I* know what it is." Gussie knelt and gazed into the sapphire. "My mama told me the story."

"It does look . . ." Katherine resisted the enchantment. It resembled the fabled Star of the Magi, but the ancient jewel was the stuff of myth. "Surely it's only a replica."

The sacred power didn't exist, except as a parable to inspire faith that the world would not end with the century.

"But it has the fishes and everything." Gussie pulled the violet shawl close against shivers of delight. "Oh, lady, make a wish."

"It doesn't work that way, Augusta. It's not a wishing well. Besides, this is all just a pretty coincidence—"

"One of you tell me what in Sam Hill is going on." Joe moved near enough to touch her and he radiated curiosity.

Glass grated beneath Katherine's boots. She held the necklace by its chain and let light catch on its star center. If nothing else, the jewel held Joe mesmerized.

Minutes ago, he'd meant to desert her. She'd heard him slip out and she'd pounded disappointment and fear into the piano keys. Fear stirred by Joe's speculation that Stark might "burn out" small settlers had recalled the gypsy's prophecy. But fear and disappointment had vanished and joy tempted her to tease him.

"I regret I can't tell you the story now, Mr. Nelson." Katherine touched a finger to the tip of his nose and scuttled backward, out of reach. "Decorations, sweets, and stories must wait for the morrow." He took a long, menacing step closer. "I can't help it. They're Christmas Eve traditions."

Katherine gathered the children before her without daring to raise her eyes to Joe. "Now, you three, off to bed."

"Hey mister, want to see our dance?" Ruin stalled.

"I saw it."

"Want to see it again?" Even sleepy, Rack tried to divert Joe's irritation.

"I want the story. Now." Joe's rough voice reminded her of his beard against her chin as he'd borne her to the floor. "I'm not one of them." When he jerked his thumb toward the children, Rack and Ruin smiled and turned for Katherine's rejoinder.

"Of course not, Mr. Nelson. You may certainly stay up as late as you wish."

The sound in Joe's throat warned Katherine that she'd pushed him far enough. Holding her skirts on each side, she shooed the children toward the other room. On the instant, she decided she'd be safest in their bed. With a hip-swinging, tail-wagging walk, Molly walked ahead of them all.

Inspired by her dog's insolence, Katherine smiled back over her shoulder before letting the blanket-door drop.

Safe on the other side, she called back to him, "Would you mind tidying up that broken glass?" Then she added, "Pleasant dreams, Joe."

Katherine slept on one edge of the feather bed, Gussie slept on the other edge, and the twins sandwiched in between. Sal, tummy warmed by a bedtime bottle, nestled in her cradle within Katherine's reach.

Katherine stared into the darkness long after the children had nodded off. If they noticed she wore the necklace underneath her white night rail, they didn't say a word.

At the end of her prayers, Katherine told herself the pendant had no magic. The warm currents surrounding this bed and mismatched brood were imaginary. But two things of note did occur: Katherine slid Colin Stark's wedding ring from her finger and stowed it in her petticoat pocket, and Joe Nelson stayed the night.

• • •

In the darkness before dawn, a twin intent on using the chamber pot crawled over Katherine. As she waited for the child to resettle, Katherine listened for some sound from the other room. She heard only stillness.

After the storm had passed and left a dazzling blue-and-white day behind, Katherine woke again. Her search of the saloon and the shed behind it verified her guess. The cow and mule had licked their mangers empty of an early feeding and Blacky was missing. Joe had gone.

When Gussie shuffled out of the back room and stood staring through the front window, Katherine stopped burning bread for toast long enough to watch the child.

"He'll be back." Katherine touched the star sapphire hidden beneath her gown, but snatched her hand away before Gussie noticed. "I'm sure of it. Who doesn't want to be someplace cozy on Christmas Eve?"

Gussie fogged the cold window with her breath. "Don't worry." She used her fingertip to draw a star on the pane. "I won't get the little ones pining."

By the time the twins tumbled out of bed, Katherine had confided her goal to Gussie, and they'd already melted seven bucketsful of snow.

"By sunset, I'll have bathed every one of us." Katherine perched her hands on hips swathed with a bar-towel apron. "And since the pump's frozen, we must melt loads of—"

"Even Joe?" Gussie fixed Katherine with a look that was adult and entirely incomprehensible.

"Of course not, Augusta." Katherine busied herself scraping charcoal from another slice of bread. "I believe Mr. Nelson can scrub his own back."

Rack and Ruin chortled. "You're funny, lady—whoa! Watch out!" The two made a game of baiting Molly to sit up. She obeyed, but spat out each reward of scorched bread. And that was even more amusing than the prospect of Joe's bath.

"You *may* call me Katherine," she offered, but the children only shook their heads and kept laughing.

After breakfast, she sent them outside and performed her toilette with what care she could. She bathed in water dotted with miniature icebergs, twisted her wet hair into a rope, and pinned it sternly at her crown before returning to the porch.

Molly and the children galloped across acres of snow,

breaking through the crust into blue-shadowed caves.

"Don't lose anyone," Katherine called from the porch.

Gussie waved as Molly and the twins thrashed out of snowy confinement to begin the game all over again.

Katherine hoped they'd be chilled through and eager for baths. If not, she wouldn't be deterred by complaints. They'd all get scrubbed before she shared their bed again. And yet . . .

Katherine searched her conscience and found more concern for their comfort than for her fastidiousness. How in heaven's name had this happened?

With lashes half closed, she raised her face to the sky's brilliance and fingered the pendant, savoring the winter sun because its warmth was so unexpected.

What explained her warm satisfaction in children who were strangers? How had she fallen into longing for Joe, and why did her heart feel certain he'd appear on the horizon, riding back to her?

She should have no trouble dispelling thoughts of Colin Stark, and yet, in odd moments, she did think of him. While she searched through cupboards and into crannies for tin to cut out as ornaments, Katherine remembered Joe's mention of Colin Stark's Twelfth Night gala.

While she combed and curled Gussie's hair with her own ivory-handled iron, Katherine half listened to the child's theory that prettiness could hold loved ones, and worried over the idea that Stark meant to burn out squatters.

While the twins helped her stir up cinnamon syrup to pour over baked apples, she ignored her mind's insistence that she admit her proxy marriage. Would it make any difference to Joe? Did she care if he cared?

All day, she planned gifts. She found Joe's when the twins finished their washtub bath and cavorted like naked imps in the warmth of the potbellied stove, while Gussie used both hands to pencil a Christmas message on a scrap of brown paper.

The bottle was ornate and wore a parchment label. "Rose wine," it read, "gathered while dew." Though the rest was blurred with moisture, Katherine recalled Joe's lamentation over the saloon's lack of whiskey and thought he'd be pleased.

She turned the bottle in her hands. The heavy glass was cut into beveled diamonds. Of course, she'd have to offer this gift after the children slept. She wouldn't have them make too much of her affection for Joe. He wouldn't, surely. The wine would make a lighthearted gift with no touch of romance.

Romance was the last thing she wanted. Katherine nodded to herself as she balanced on tiptoes atop the table, skirts tucked up so she wouldn't trip while she stretched for the chandelier.

"Stand on the bench, Augusta, and please take these last crystals as I hand them down to you."

The walls already shimmered with rainbows from prisms hung to catch the sunlight streaming through the windows, but she wanted just two more.

Later, Katherine blamed her greed on the fact that she was poised like a shameless ballerina, ankles exposed, when Joe dragged a Christmas tree into the Loving Cup Saloon.

Moonlight had glimmered over the snow as Blacky moved at a swinging lope down the path left by the piano. Joe had headed for Colin Stark's ranch, determined to force the stuck-up Englishman to face his responsibilities.

Joe Nelson didn't plan on playing white knight to anyone. Still, he worried about giving the brood over to Stark's care. And Katherine . . .

Katherine could make up her own mind. About everything.

Riding toward the crest above the saloon, Joe faced a million stars glimmering through the pine forest ahead.

He drew rein. "Don't they look like a buncha candles on a bunch of Christmas trees." He sorted Blacky's mane all to one side and swore. What kind of mush-minded sissy had Katherine turned him into?

He owed nothing to those kids, but last night, watching them romp to Katherine's music, he'd wondered how his life would've changed if someone had dabbed at his face, tied a little sash around his tummy, and promised him a future. Even if that future was no more than a story, to be told on the very next day.

"Decent women are a curse, Blacky." Joe narrowed his eyes until the forest faded into a greenish cloud flecked with gold. "Got me thinking we're going to ride back to that orphan asylum."

It would cost him nothing to give those brats one real Christmas. Cutting a tree was the hard part, but he could haul it back to the saloon and he was a fair hand at whittling, so he could make some simple toys. He might bake a Christmas pie with the cinnamon and apples. Maybe Katherine would play Christmas tunes and he'd swing little Gussie around, make her smile at his tangle-foot dancing, before Katherine's story.

And maybe Katherine would think him so kind, she'd kiss him. Or more.

"That's the only reason I'm doin' it," he said out loud. He scanned the trees, looking for one that'd fit inside the saloon. "Just want to hear that petticoat rustle for me," he mumbled. Up ahead, silhouetted by the rising sun, he saw the perfect tree.

The December sun was about to drop behind the mountains by the time he got the cussed tree dragged back as far as the crest above the saloon. He and Blacky had sweated up something fierce, so Joe let the horse rest while he took a snow bath.

The cold nearly killed him, but by the time he'd donned his gambling duds from his saddlebags and looked once more at the viney piece of mistletoe, he felt fine.

One thing even an orphan knew about Christmas: If you caught a pretty girl under mistletoe, she had to give you a kiss.

Nine

One sorrel-colored curl hung to the small of Katherine's back. Arms over her head, she stood shoeless, legs flexed so tight Joe could see a flowery pattern in the knit of her cream-colored stockings.

"Oh!" She leaped from the table to the floor. The star pendant swung like a berserk pendulum as she yanked her skirts down and folded her hands at her waist. "I do beg your pardon."

Frosty wind outlined Joe in the doorway. He should close the door against the cold. And he would, as soon as he gathered his wits.

"It's all right." He squatted and hefted the tree trunk—which had escaped his grip and crashed to the floor at the sight of her legs—back onto his shoulder.

He almost lost it a second time as she tucked the sapphire down the neck of her gown. Then Ruin tugged at his vest. "Is that for us?"

"Naw, it's just . . ." Joe's sarcasm fled before the doubt in Ruin's eyes. " 'Course, it's for you. Think I brought it in for Miss Molly the dog?"

The dog's tail thumped the floor. Gussie appeared in front of him with a cup of coffee. Joe sighed. The brew smelled strong enough to haul a wagon, but at least it'd keep him from watching Katherine as she sat at the table, relacing her boots.

"What smells so good?" He nodded toward the stove, convinced Katherine had beat him to baking a Christmas pie. Maybe she wasn't so hopeless in the kitchen, after all.

"Drat!" Katherine shouted, stood, and the pendant swung free again, winking blue as she bolted past and jerked open the oven door.

"I'd thought to make them a proper nursery tea, with graham crackers and chocolate soup. . . ." She used a fold of skirt to protect her hand from the hot pan. "Perhaps pumpkin buns and bread pudding, too."

She slapped the pan on the table. "But I haven't the foggiest notion how to cook any of those, so Gussie and I baked apples."

The pan did have apples in it. And sugar and cinnamon, probably. But it sure wasn't any sort of sweet he recognized.

"Well." Joe folded his arms across his gunbelt buckle. He rocked back on his heels and considered the windows going dark instead of listening to Katherine's knife hack the hardened syrup to chip the apples loose.

"Yessir, you baked 'em." He figured that was a safe comment, especially when he followed up with an offer to decorate.

They hung the tree with tin stars and bows. The white satin ribbons were narrower than his small fingers and Joe would wager they'd spent time on a lady's drawers. As he reached for boughs beyond the children's reach, he wished he were untying the ribbons, not knotting them up in clumsy bows.

There was some justice in using one of them to hang the mistletoe. Not that Katherine took notice.

When Rack's stomach growled, Joe figured he'd better make dinner. Katherine had let them turn sticky-faced from sucking chunks of the hard syrup which Gussie had generously christened "apple candy."

As they quarreled over the last bits of it, Katherine's lips hovered so near his ear that Joe shivered.

"We must talk about their gifts," she whispered.

When he turned to answer, her brows arched, her lips parted, and her whole being hummed with secrets.

Words skittered out of reach as he imagined sweeping her off to bed, feeling the vibration of his bootheel kicking the door closed behind them.

When Katherine glanced guiltily toward the children, he thought she'd read his mind. "Have you been thinking of gifts for them, too?"

"Yes." He sucked the thumb he'd stuck with a ragged-edged ornament. "Just now, though, I'm going to turn out some dinner."

Joe traveled with dried chile peppers in his saddlebags because they made the rankest meat edible, but tonight he used them to transform the jugged hare into chili. He stirred up soda biscuits while the meat browned, and sorted out the best parts of an aged onion while he watched Katherine feed baby Sal.

They seemed to be warming up to each other. After the bottle was empty, Katherine still held the baby close. They looked so sweet together, he should've been shamed by his bedroom thoughts.

He nearly chopped off his thumb thinking of that hidden pendant nestled warm between her breasts. It was wicked, thinking that since she'd be angry when he left, anyway, he might just give her something to be mad about.

Distraction made him put one pepper too many in the pot. At the first bite, the little ones fanned their mouths. Katherine's eyes teared at the spicy stew, but they all kept eating, even while Gussie scolded Ruin.

"One biscuit at a time."

"They was stuck together."

"Heavenly days, Ruin." Gussie pointed with her fork. "That chunk is as big as your head!"

Joe smothered a laugh, then a curse. If this is what it might've felt like to have a family, he was glad he missed it. All this cozy chatter rubbed him the wrong way.

"A tasty dish." Katherine smiled indulgently at the brats.

"Somebody had to cook," he grumbled. "If we had to depend on you . . ."

The twins' eyes rounded. Gussie braced both palms on the table and stared into her lap.

"What?" he demanded.

"He's simply joking." Katherine laughed toward the children, dismissing Joe with a wave of her hand. Then she turned so only Joe could see her face. "The children thought you were *cross*, Mr. Nelson."

"I'm sorry," Gussie whispered.

Katherine drilled Joe with schoolmarm's eyes, requiring an excuse for his bad behavior. He'd be damned if he'd walk on eggshells just because—

"Don't fight," Gussie uttered the words as if someone would strike her for them. "You don't have to leave. We'll be good."

He'd scared the good times out of every soul seated around him. *One good Christmas memory.* That's all he'd planned to give them, and he couldn't even manage that.

He looked to Katherine for help. Her cheeks flamed red and it occurred to Joe that men who thought proper females had ice water in their veins should take a gander at this one.

"I'm not *cross*," he said. "In fact, the only thing that riles me is people—me, especially—gettin' hurt." Joe noticed Rack's thumb stealing into his mouth. "Why, if you was to come up and kick me in the shin, I'd probably—"

"Leave and never come back," Gussie finished.

Joe swallowed, twice, and then Katherine's boot nudged him under the table.

"What I meant was, if you kicked me in the shin, I'd scream like a chicken."

"Cock-a-doodle-*dooooo*!" Ruin's screech woke baby Sal and set Molly barking.

"While chaos reigns, Mr. Nelson, perhaps you might clear away dinner while I tell stories and ready these children for bed."

Though he was no one's hired hand, Joe gave in. As he worked, he listened to Katherine's tale of a star, a babe, and a stable. It reminded him to feed the livestock, but the story baffled him. No folks had ever admired him for being reared in a barn.

Outside, he poured heated water over the pump handle. As it thawed, he listened to Katherine pound out what must be a suffragist tune, since she sang about "women leading the way."

Half frozen, he stormed back inside and couldn't believe she was playing the notes with fussy Sal balanced in the crook of one arm. The older children listened, picking up a few more words with every verse, and it turned out to be a Christmas song after all. Just when Joe had started learning it, Katherine held a shushing finger to her lips and eased Sal into her cradle. Then she gathered the brood onto a blanket before the pot-bellied stove and sat down among them.

"Mr. Nelson, won't you join us?" Katherine coaxed him as her arms circled her skirt-covered legs like a girl. "Please?"

"I'm fine where I am." He stood behind the bar.

"Scoot in," Katherine urged, and the twins claimed the spaces next to her. When Gussie drew apart, Joe winced. "And I'll tell you a story of what happened to Melchior, one of the Christmas kings, just before he traveled home from Bethlehem.

"It all began when Melchior leaned down to peer into the manger. The baby Jesus gazed up at the pretty pendant swinging and shining above him. With fingers tinier than Sal's, he caught the necklace, cooed"—Katherine took a long breath—"and it was transformed.

"Now, it had been lovely before—fine enough for a king—with a beautiful sapphire nestled in a compass rose of gold. But when He touched it, the magical star which led the kings over mountains and snowy fields appeared in its center. And, even better—it shimmered with the powers of love, peace, and hope."

"It could *do* stuff?" Rack asked.

"Oh, yes, it could do wonderful stuff," Katherine said. "Being a generous soul, Melchior reached to lift the necklace off, to give it to Jesus, but the baby's mother wouldn't let him. 'No, you have a little girl at home who needs that necklace very much,' she said. And so he took it home to her."

Gussie rocked back and forth, arms around her own thin body, nodding.

"You know the story, don't you, Gussie?" Katherine yawned. "I'd be ever so grateful if you could help me finish it."

"Me? I can't remember."

"It's a very old story, Gussie. I hardly think the details matter, as long as it has a happy ending."

Reassured, Gussie began her recitation. "His daughter was not so little. Older than me, but younger than Lady. And she wanted very much to get married."

Joe watched Katherine's face, but it gave nothing away. *Do you?* he wondered. *Do you want to marry that rich scoundrel Stark?*

"But Melchior's daughter . . . was her name Mimi?" She paused for Katherine's nod. "Mimi had been scarred in a fire." Gussie tucked the burned hem of her skirt beneath her. "She knew she'd never meet a man who could love her, because she was ugly. . . ." Gussie's voice dwindled, then came back so strong, Joe fancied he heard an echo of the mother who'd told Gussie the tale.

"The necklace healed Mimi's hopeless heart. She met a man who loved her and all their children. Then," Gussie yawned and the twins sagged closer to Katherine, "somehow, the necklace was lost at the seashore and swallowed by a fish. Right, lady? Oh, do take it out for us, please."

"She's been hiding it all day." Ruin looked up at Joe.

"Not hiding it, exactly." Katherine tumbled half her hair as she lifted the chain from around her neck and held the pendant in her lap.

"Finish the story," Rack whined. He barely sat upright now, and his thumb was firmly lodged in his mouth.

"*You,*" Gussie said to Katherine.

"Well, the necklace has lasted through hundreds of years. And though it reappears wherever it's needed, it has a habit of cropping up at the end of centuries, and always, *always* finds its way to a lady who must right the wrongs done by men."

That last bit was meant for him, Joe figured.

"And a magical fish always brings it back, lady." Gussie tugged at Katherine's sleeve. "Like on the bottom of the crystal ball."

While Gussie hummed the carol about a "woman leading the way," Katherine slipped the necklace back over her head, and tried to ease the sleeping boys toward bed.

"No! Not until we look at the stars," Gussie insisted. "And sing the song. We have to, now that you've really, truly got the necklace." Gussie's energy drained away. "We just have to."

"If that's how your mother did it," she checked for Gussie's nod, "we will." Katherine took her cloak from a hook. "Stay close and I'll keep you warm."

Joe told himself it was to hurry them along that he followed and stood near Katherine and the children as they gazed up into the night sky.

"Star, star, come from afar, shining night and day . . ."

Suddenly awake, Ruin wheeled on him and broke off singing. "Are you going to be here in the morning?"

By reflex, Joe almost hedged. For hours, he hadn't thought of leaving. " 'Course I'll be here," he said. "Think I'd miss the lady's Christmas breakfast?"

The twins looked at him with sleepy uncertainty and Gussie's giggle was cut by Katherine's rising voice.

"Star, star, come where we are . . ."

This was where he wanted to be, Joe thought. Only closer, gathered with Gussie and the boys under the wings of Katherine's cloak.

"So a woman can light the way."

She didn't leave him. Once the little ones bedded down, he'd figured she would, but she seemed determined to stay beside him, tempting him. First, she showed him a brooch shaped like a bluebird which she had in mind to give Gussie as a gift.

"I ordered it from Sears, Roebuck and Company's catalog to disguise the purchase of my double-action police pocket pistol."

She shook her head and Joe chuckled at the way she still fussed over losing that gun. Magic or not, that crystal ball had kept him from getting his ear shot off.

In turn, Joe showed her the pine horses he'd carved for Rack and Ruin. He didn't show her the start he'd made on a wooden dog that ought to end up looking like Molly.

"How did you make them so quickly?" Katherine turned one of the toys in her hands, while Joe took out his knife and began to smooth the splintery spots on the other one.

"You didn't think it took me all day to cut that tree, did you?" He held it up, pretending to squint at his work, while he watched her.

"I didn't know how high you had to climb for the mistletoe." She blushed and set the toy aside. "I thought it might have taken a while." She fidgeted, embarrassed by the way she'd cranked up the tension between them.

He liked it, that feeling like the instant before you bet on a good hand, or bluffed on a poor one.

"It was a trial to get," he sighed. "And it hanging over there all alone," he said. "Just going to waste."

Katherine fumbled with the brooch and abandoned the conversation she'd begun. "What a shame we have no wrapping paper."

"A shame."

"I have an idea, though it means going back outside"— through that doorway, under the mistletoe. He tried not to grin—"and filling the washtub with some of that sawdust from the barn. It's called a Christmas pie. You needn't look so skittish, Mr. Nelson. We fill the tub with toys and sawdust and tie on a piece of cloth and it looks rather like a pie."

They did it, but Katherine moved through the doorway so quickly, Joe almost lost hold of his side of the tub. Inside, he yanked a chair over in front of the potbellied stove.

He might as well carve the jump-rope handles he'd been picturing, since he sure wasn't going to get any sleep, listening to her move around in bed again tonight, all silky.

He turned his knife blade in the firelight, checking its edge and watching her.

What was she thinking, pacing with downcast lashes, and what was keeping her up? He supposed she might not want to walk past him to the bedroom.

"I have a gift for you," she said, "but it's rather . . . I didn't want to give it to you in front of the children. It's on the second shelf, over there. Behind where you were standing all night." She gestured and bolted away.

Last chance.

Joe stood. Before she slipped past, he gently caught her wrist.

"Katherine." He felt her arm tremble. "Aren't you ever called 'Kate'?"

She looked almost angry, but her voice stayed mild. "I could be," she said, then pushed past him for the bedroom.

It was shameful. She'd slipped into the white silk night rail meant for her wedding night. Shameful, lying in this child-crowded bed, when she considered all the "lady rules" she'd listed for Gussie today.

Katherine had explained that a lady always made a decent appearance, never spoke loudly even when provoked, and did not scorn the use of a needle. Reciting rules had passed the time as they waited for bathwater to warm. Now her mind counted down the tiers of being a lady. Not one rule told a lady what to do if she fell in love with one man when she was legally wed to another.

Katherine stretched a sheltering arm over all three children. They were cuddled that close together. In her cradle, Sal slept.

Outside, snow whipped the saloon windows, but inside, Katherine only heard Joe remove the cork from his bottle of rose-dew wine. When wind squeezed through the walls' cracks with long, harmonica moans, she heard Molly's tail thump the saloon floor.

"You're the sorriest mutt I ever did see and you will, by golly, share the heat. Now, get over."

Katherine smiled into the darkness. Joe even liked her dog.

In Katherine's dream, she stood barefoot in a ballroom. Satin gowns, champagne punch, and hard heels striking waltz steps on the marble floor were mere background to the man descending a broad staircase.

Hatless in black and white, Joe came to her slowly and the violin's song deepened into the throb of a lone guitar.

In her dream, a flicker of warmth touched her face and shoulders. As he took another slow and serious step, sparks fizzed from her fingertips, braceleted her wrists, and rushed up her arms.

No dream dancers noticed when Joe smiled and moved one step lower, but Katherine felt tiny flames nibble the threads of her dress until it fell away completely. Naked and unashamed in the ballroom, one knee grazed the other as she moved through the crowd and extended her arms, inviting Joe closer.

When he came to her, a flag of flame wrapped around them. Katherine, dreaming, tried to peer past, tried to ignore the summons of a voice.

Fire. Toes tangling in her hem, in the blankets, she tried to understand. Had he said "fire"? Awake, she swung out of bed.

"Kate?" Joe called low. To keep from frightening the children?

She ducked out of the bedroom, into the light, with her mind still spinning.

The saloon smelled of roses, not smoke and burning rafters.

Joe leaned back, both elbows propped on the bar. He held a squarish glass and cocked his bootheel at an angle. Katherine fought to make sense of it, but Joe didn't look like a man who'd sounded an alarm just before midnight on Christmas Eve.

A dream, she realized. A brazen dream of adultery, lit by flames of desire, not smoldering rafters.

"Well, now. You heard me." His wolfish smile started her retreat. "Don't go. I don't want anything indecent, just"—he sighed—"company. Swear to God, Katie, I won't touch you."

Unless you want me to, he might have shouted.

Katherine's bare toes gripped the floor. Her mind lingered in that fantasy ballroom where she'd met Joe more than half-way.

"I want t' thank you." He raised his glass in a toast.

"As gifts go, I fear it's rather poor."

There. That sounded quite sensible.

"It's the first one I've ever had." He winked, the gesture at odds with his grim, set lips.

"I'm not that gullible, sir. You must be near thirty."

He drank off the rest of the wine. "You've got that right."

His confiding tone had vanished. Low-lidded, his eyes held her transfixed. Here was a rough man who wanted something equally rough.

"I hauled you back out here to break in the mistletoe."

He'd confirmed her prediction, and she knew a lady would defy him. Katherine knew she would have, if something vulnerable hadn't hidden behind that harsh proposal.

"Very well." She raised her voice. "I've been thinking that, myself."

The purring insistence of the pendant kept her in thrall. It could not be her own wildness clamoring to hold him and be held.

Joe took her hand. London lords had led her onto ballroom floors with less delicacy. As if she could keep him from drifting away like that dream, she clasped his hand tighter.

He positioned her beneath mistletoe that dangled from her bloomers' satin lace. His fingers curved under her jaw, *there,* beneath her ear.

He lifted her face and in the moments he took bending down, she thought, *How can I be doing this?* When his lips finally reached hers, *how* changed to *how wonderful, how warm, how perfect, how awful if I'd missed this.*

Her eyes opened as his lips drew away.

"I do believe I like mistletoe," she said, and then she knew it was no magic. Her own recklessness told her to touch his face, to sway against him as his hands fell like hinges over the bared skin between her neck and the tops of her shoulders.

Desire streaked through sweetness. Heat soaked through the silk night rail. She pressed her cheek against his chest, hiding her face, denying herself another kiss until she told him a secret that would end the wonder.

This was more intimate than the kiss. Why, in her old-maid daydreams, hadn't she imagined hearing a man's heartbeat? The familiarity of pressing her ear to his shirtfront made her understand swooning.

"If this is your first Christmas present," she said, convinced by no more than his kiss, "why?"

No one would have noticed the slight catch in his indrawn breath. No one except a shameless wench pressing her face against him, wishing she hadn't asked because she'd hurt him. Katherine willed the moment away. If only time could reverse a single minute. But it didn't.

"It's common enough for brats to be orphaned out here, like them." He jerked his head toward the bedroom.

"You were orphaned?"

"Most likely."

"I don't understand." When she tried to lift her head and meet his eyes, his arm trapped her.

"When I was five or six years old, my parents stopped at Fort Benton and left me, before heading wherever they were bound."

Her mind raced for a way to save him from saying more. "They fell ill, then. Was it an epidemic, like . . ." Now Katherine indicated the sleeping children, as if they'd become a code between them.

"No. They slept with me in an empty stall in the smithy, I'm told. In the morning they were gone, and so was the smith's big dappled mare, but my folks left a note. 'We traded you the boy for Nell.' That's what the note said."

This time he let her pull away, but his mocking expression cut her. "My name, *Nelson* . . ." He gave a short laugh. "I didn't know what I was called, beyond 'Joe.' Referring to me as 'Nell's son' was the blacksmith's joke."

Thumbs slung from his gunbelt, Joe strode to the window.

"So, there you go." Face close to the glass, he peered out.

Katherine considered his fine linen shirt and silver cuff links, his black vest soft as glove leather. All the trappings of a successful gambler contradicted the story.

Knowing only the most foolhardy woman would press him, Katherine tugged at his sleeve. He turned, hand still close to his gun, and his expression reminded her he was a stranger. Heartache gave her no ability to predict what he would do, but she didn't stop.

"Someone lied, Joe." She rubbed her hand up his sleeve, studying his raven hair and blue, blue eyes. She drew her hand down to his wrist. He would have been a beautiful child. "Parents do not trade their children for animals."

"Maybe they won't in this new century, but in this last one? They surely did."

Battling his sneer, Katherine pressed against him. Her arms wrapped him and her lips claimed his, insisting she could make up for all those bleak years without kisses.

"If that's outta pity," he spoke between kisses, "don't bother tellin' me. I'll take 'em every one. Whatever you've got for me, I'll take it, Katie girl, and more."

His arms pulled her hard against him and when she gasped, his tongue teased her lips to stay open. She'd never dreamed of such an invasion, but she wanted it.

Murmuring as if he'd quiet her rapid breaths, Joe smoothed the small of her back.

"Stay with me, Katie." He tugged her hair, baring her whole throat and she offered it, wanting more. "I know I've got nothing to give you."

Don't talk, don't talk, oh, please. Guilt fused with passion. She twined closer, pressing her very center to his, wishing the heat between them could consume her secret.

"You're a well-off woman. And every penny I ever made was earned doing something shady."

"Joe, no." *It doesn't matter,* she wanted to say. *This is all that counts. What is a brittle piece of parchment compared to this?*

"I don't know how." His hand stroked the length of her unbound hair. "But we could take care of this brood together. Please, say you'll stay with me."

Katherine fought the tears choking her. This feeling would

crack her chest wide if she didn't speak, and break her heart if she did.

"I can't stay with you," she told him.

In the silence, Molly scratched her ear with a hind paw and rearranged her length in front of the potbellied stove.

He stiffened, released Katherine, and stepped back.

"Well hell, of course you can't." He scorned himself for giving in. "S'pose it was the rose wine that made me think so? Or maybe this trinket?" Joe hooked a finger through the pendant's chain and jerked it from the cover of her night rail. He stared at the star shimmering on the surface of the sapphire, then dropped it. "Something sure muddled up my mind."

"Joe." She swallowed, throat burning. "I want to. More than anything I ever, *ever* wanted, but I . . ."

Too cowardly to say the words, Katherine crossed the room, dug into her carpetbag, and pulled out the wedding certificate. Though his hands were raised in an order to keep back, she thrust it at him. He took the document, then shook it in the space between them.

"Damn it, woman, do you really think a kid raised in a barn can read?"

Katherine pressed her face into her hands, broken by her own cruelty. And now she'd make his humiliation complete.

"I'm married to Colin Stark. By proxy. A ceremony in Boston. I've never met him."

He crushed the certificate and it cracked like flame inside his hand. "And it's good as a church wedding?"

"It's . . . binding, yes."

"Well, whip me to tears!" His self-mocking laugh brought Molly to her feet, growling. "If this don't beat all the Christmases I ever had. Hell, Katie, unless somebody dies, I don't see how I can top it . . ."

The contemplation that darkened his eyes so suddenly needed no interpreter. Katherine stared at his gun even before he touched it.

"No," she said, but if Stark died, she'd be a widow.

Sweet Heaven, she should be struck down where she stood for allowing such a thought. She closed her eyes and clutched the pendant in both hands. "You can't do murder on Christmas."

She didn't hear him open the door, but a blast of wind wrapped her night rail around her legs.

"It's just another day to me, sugar," he said. "Another god-awful day."

Joe didn't think about the brats. He didn't think about carols, presents, or Katie's kiss. As he rode toward the black outline of Stark's mansion, Joe thought about revenge.

Keeping his stallion at a walk, he surveyed the grounds. Dingo should be wheeling out from behind a rock, wielding a Sharps buffalo rifle. That old codger Teddy should be hobbling toward the house, hollering for help from whoever sat outlined by candlelight at that upstairs window.

Joe considered the dark bunkhouse. It was possible even Stark had the humanity to give his men Christmas off.

For a couple of hours on Christmas Eve, Joe might have applauded such generosity. Not now. The celebration had ended when Katherine had told him the truth. Even that dizzy moment when he'd held the sapphire and felt it speak a silent language of hope, had been nothing. This time, Christmas was over for good.

He left Blacky and advanced up the front porch stairs, too aware of his spurs' ringing in the frosty dawn. He didn't knock. If the butler, maids, or the cook Stark called Lenox were sleeping in, he'd let them. He wasn't much in the mood for conversation.

Joe opened the heavy front door, stepped inside, and stood there. The door wasn't cut out of pine. Oak, maybe. It was thicker than his hand was from wrist to fingertips. To a man who'd spent his life in tents and boomtown hotels with walls so thin you could hear your neighbor part his hair, this sort of door was a wonder.

What he wouldn't give to put those kids behind a door like this.

Sconces lit a room big enough that he could have galloped Blacky inside and ridden laps. The stone fireplace was deep enough to hold four men standing and the ceiling—crossed with beams that still looked like tree trunks—went up forever. Thick draperies covered windows that should have been open to the sky.

Joe followed a blue and red carpet runner up the center of

stairs flanked by flickering candles stuck in copper sconces. No one stopped him as he followed the sound of bull-deep breathing.

In the doorway of the first room on the left, he let his eyes grow accustomed to the darkness. First, he smelled a broth that made his mouth water. His eyes found the bowl an instant before he spotted Stark. The Englishman sat straight up against an ornate headboard, fixing Joe with a stare.

Joe got off the first words. "You've got debts to pay, Stark."

The bull-breath snort startled Joe into grabbing for his gun, but Stark made no move to escape.

"I'm not talking about money. I'm talking about Katherine and that brood of children whose nursemaid you ran off."

Stark's stillness made Joe glance back over his shoulder. Maybe Dingo had hidden someplace in the house and Stark was biding his time.

"No sense talkin' to him, there isn't."

Joe's gun cleared leather before he realized a woman hunched in a chair in the corner.

"Jehoshaphat, ma'am!" Joe jammed the revolver back into the holster. He shook his hand free of the jitters. He'd never come so near shooting a female.

"Didn't mean to give you such a start. And I'm no ma'am. I'm Lenox, cook to Mr.—him that was Mr. Stark."

Out of respect to her, not Stark, Joe removed his hat. The woman was smaller than Gussie and her white hair stood out as if she'd seen a ghost. When she blew her nose into a hankie, she revealed surprising strength and the source of the bull breaths Joe had taken for Stark's.

"He died of an apoplexy not an hour since. Came home raging about his bride, his piano, his gambling losses and"— she lowered her voice to a whisper—"whelps born on the wrong side of the blanket, *if* you get my meaning."

Joe nodded. "Yes, ma'am."

"No ma'aming for me." Another snort rocked her frame. "Mrs. Lenox."

"Miss." She patted her hair with both hands. "The names he called that poor lady, it's a mercy she didn't come here. And didn't he give me the dickens over his tea not being spread in the parlor, before the fire, and me having none of the dainties he babbled about? Not that I'd speak ill of the dead, you understand, but his face turned purpler by the second, and who was I to call?"

"Sorry for your—" He moved to replace his hat and escape.

"Sent him to bed, I did, and do you think he thanked me?"

"—trouble, ma'am." Joe bowed and backed away, still holding his hat and wishing his mind would stop spinning, wondering what this meant to Katherine and whether she'd return to Boston. "I'll be leaving, now."

"Then, wasn't he just a mess? Foamin' at the mouth, calling for Dingo and poor old Teddy to sleep in the hall outside his room in case"—she squinted through the dimness—"some gambler, which I imagine is you, sneaked up on him.

"He called them in with such bellows it woke me and I been here ever since." She tsked and shook her head. "Sent them off on some bad business. I could tell by the droop of Teddy's mustache. Never could hide anything from me." She blew her nose in a daintier honk. "Kind of sweet on me, Teddy is, and look"—she waved the sodden hankie at the bed—"they needn't have ridden off into the cold at all."

Joe had backed as far as the doorway. He didn't want to stay long enough that she'd ask him to help bury the villain. He wanted to ride home to Katherine, tell her she was a widow, and tumble her on a blanket in front of the potbellied stove before the brood rose to open their presents.

"You go along, young man." Lenox flicked the hankie in his direction. "Dingo can dig the hole, while Teddy rides in to send a telegram to the bride."

"I'll do that, ma'am. And if I run across those two, I'll send them with shovels." Joe considered Colin Stark's only mourner. "You know, that broth smells so good, if anything could've revived him, that would've done the trick."

"Well," she gave a weary chuckle. "Aren't you a dear?"

"Yes, ma'am. Merry Christmas."

Dressed and dozing by the stove, Katherine dreamed giant rats gnawed off a corner of the Loving Cup Saloon. She jerked awake to Molly's growl, to the crunching of boots on snow, and to the smell of kerosene.

Not Joe, not the children, and certainly not Colin Stark come for his runaway bride. Molly's head jutted out low and stiff. Her lip curled away from her teeth.

"Molly?" Katherine whispered, but the dog ignored her to sniff at the bottom of the door.

Wondering how she'd come to such a pass, Katherine lifted down the Winchester rifle Joe had left hanging on hooks and stood, feet braced apart, waiting.

Kerosene. All at once, Katherine remembered the gypsy's prediction of fire and burning children. She raced to the door and before she shouted a warning to the two men slopping kerosene around the base of the saloon, Molly attacked.

Katherine recognized Stark's henchman, the cowboy with the Australian accent, just as Molly hit his knee with her jaws agape. When he fell, Teddy, who'd sold her the muleload of food, reached to strike Molly and got a savaged hand for his trouble.

Katherine shifted the rifle from side to side, following the battle. As the men kicked and shouted to escape, Molly lost interest. Katherine clutched the rifle. The warm pulsing of the sapphire signified something. On this last Christmas of the century, it counseled kindness. Dear heaven, she hoped it was right.

"Molly!" Katherine leaned the rifle against the saloon's outside wall. "Molly! Will you please come to heel?"

The basset lifted her head, wrinkled her brow with intense concentration, and sneezed a snoutful of snow before meandering away from the men, past Katherine to the three children huddled in the doorway.

"She's just not used to visitors." Katherine wondered if she spoke too loudly over the pounding of her pulse. She'd decided not to mention the stench of kerosene. "But I am. Please come in, gentlemen. Teddy, isn't it? And sir, I'm afraid we didn't meet, before."

The Australian rocked back on his heels. Then, in a demonstration of unimaginably poor judgment with all of the kerosene fumes wafting about, he lit a cigarette.

"Back inside, everyone." Katherine used her skirts to shoo the children. "It's awfully cold." She hoped there'd be no explosion before they reached safety.

"Colder 'n a dead snake," said Teddy, rubbing his hands together. "Beggin' your pardon, ma'am."

"Not at all," she said, but she watched the other man, who squinted through his cigarette smoke, watching her.

At last, he walked a few steps away from the saloon and doused the cigarette. When he returned, he extended a gloved hand.

"Dingo Collins."

"I'm Katherine," she swallowed, and told the truth. "Katherine Stark."

"The mail-order bride."

"Close enough, sir." She shook his hand, met his eyes, and sighed. "And if you come inside for a bite of breakfast, I trust we can work through this beastly coil of events."

Dingo Collins always rode an unmistakable Indian paint. When Joe saw the paint horse and a stocky bay tied a quarter mile from the saloon, dread claimed him.

He'd left Katherine and the children alone—and Stark had sent Dingo and Teddy out on some dirty business.

Joe untied the horses and sent them trotting for home, then he spurred Blacky into a run. No sense in sneaking up. Whatever had to be done would have to be done fast.

Joe smelled the kerosene as he came over the ridge. But he saw no fire. He drew two calm breaths before spotting the Winchester leaning next to the front door.

It was loaded, and when Joe kicked in the front door of the Loving Cup Saloon, he was ready to drill a new socket in Dingo Collins's skull.

Barking, Molly planted herself between Rack, Ruin, Gussie, and the door. In a single slow instant, Joe raised his hand, telling the children to stay back. Then he faced Teddy and Dingo. They'd already jumped to their feet and leveled their revolvers across the breakfast table.

It was a standoff now, but Katherine had already bribed these two hard cases with burned coffee and fruitcake reeking of rum. The woman had some nerve.

With the star sapphire shining against the bodice of her rose-colored gown, Katherine stood.

"Joe," her voice quavered a little. "You're just in time for breakfast."

"Katherine." He matched her level tone. "You're a

widow." He heard her gasp, but he kept his eyes fixed on Stark's men.

"Y' kill him?" Dingo asked.

"No. He was dead when I got there. According to Lenox, he died in a 'vengeful apoplexy,' right after he told you to set the fire."

"He didn't say there were kids," Teddy insisted.

"Or his mail-order bride."

"He didn't know." Katie blushed pinker than her gown, and none of the three men could keep from staring. She didn't fold under their stares. "At first, I was hiding from him because I was afraid," she admitted. When she lifted her chin, Joe recognized the expression of a woman going for broke. "And then I *couldn't* go to Colin Stark, because I fell in love with Joe."

Joe had never heard the ocean's roar, but he imagined it sounded like the rushing in his ears. He could see the brats' lips moving and Teddy slamming a fist into his palm as he smiled. He could feel Katherine pressing against him, too, and that lit a fire in his belly that would probably never burn out.

But beneath the passion, beneath the pride that this woman wanted to be his, there was more. For the first time ever, Joe Nelson felt the peace of coming home.

Epilogue

This time Katherine stood at the top of the staircase and this time, it was no dream. In minutes, her wedding would begin, but Rack and Ruin had disappeared.

Cinnamon and woodsmoke, fresh pine and imported perfumes wafted up from the great room filled with wedding guests. Swags of red satin draped the windows and glittered with gold tinsel tiebacks. Candles blazed in copper sconces and hand-buffed wood glowed everywhere, making her new home solid, permanent, and real.

Katherine smoothed the sash at her gown's waist. High-necked and white, the gown was plain except for the shimmering Star of the Magi.

Although she hadn't quite decided how to notify her parents of her second nuptials, this wedding had given her few worries—until now.

Each day leading up to this Twelfth Night celebration had run smoothly. Word had spread through Soaring Peak that Stark's ugly summit of rich ranchers had turned into a celebration. The hasty wedding and mismatched brood of adopted children insured lots of gossip. Not a soul refused an invitation.

Though Katherine wondered where the twins were, and what they were about, she smiled at her mingling guests. Around the table graced with Lenox's tiered cake—iced with white and studded with golden raisins—guests in calico skirts gossiped with guests fluttering ivory fans. Scandal made a good mixer.

Joe had no trouble persuading Preacher Jack that Katherine should skip the traditional mourning period. Out West traditions were less stern. Besides, the preacher dismissed Katherine's late husband as "lower than a polecat," and agreed to play the fiddle as well as preach.

Of course, she'd had to convince Joe that he was no gold digger. She'd pointed out that while she might bring a ranch and money to their marriage, he had all the expertise. Without his knowledge of this land, its weather, and people, she'd retreat to Boston by springtime. It was a partnership, she insisted—and then, of course, there was love.

Mother had spoken of wedded bliss and Katherine supposed that serene state would come. But these few days with Joe had burned with passion. Joe had little interest in a chaste courtship and even less in an engagement that lasted thirteen days. Finally, the wait was ending.

Katherine looked down the staircase, feeling proud that she needed no parent to "give her away." She'd given her heart to Joe. Now he stood waiting at the foot of the stairs, waiting for another surrender.

He looked quite proper in his white shirt and black trousers. But his smile made her flush with anticipation. If any guests lingered overlong, she'd toss them out into the snow herself.

Only Gussie worried her. Since Christmas, she'd grown as glum as the twins had giddy. Gussie appreciated the red-and-green plaid taffeta dress she wore today. She agreed to bring Molly to the wedding on a green ribbon leash and she seemed pleased when Katherine suggested the star carol be sung as the bride and groom walked down the aisle. But Gussie considered every word before she spoke, made every motion deliberate. She was so very careful to do nothing wrong.

Katherine and Joe tried to understand and they searched for ways to mend Gussie's wary heart.

"Star, star, come from afar . . ."

Katherine caught her breath. It was really happening. At last.

Preacher Jack, dressed in a black frock coat and collar, sawed at his fiddle and the guests began to sing. Katherine stopped searching for the twins, certain they'd pop up at any minute.

As she took her first step toward Joe, his smile sobered into
awe. When she reached his side, he took her hand to his lips
and kissed it.

"None of that!" Preacher Jack yelled from his place near
the mantel. Laughing, guests rushed back to their chairs.

Katherine whispered, "Merry Christmas."

"I think you said that before."

"I can't stop celebrating." Katherine trembled as Joe's hand
rested on the small of her back.

"Just you wait." It was the friendliest of threats, or maybe
a lusty promise. Katherine beamed as they walked, hand in
hand, toward Preacher Jack.

Suddenly Gussie and Molly stood in the aisle. Freckles
bright against her flushed cheeks, Gussie gave them no time
to wonder.

With a rustle of taffeta, Gussie drew back her polished black
shoe and kicked Joe in the shin. Molly pulled on her ribbon
leash, and if the guests noticed anything, it was the excited
basset hound.

"For the . . . !" Joe sucked in a breath and stared at Gussie.
"Why'd you do that?"

"Did I ruin your wedding?" Gussie's lips trembled. "Are
you going to leave?"

Gussie had thrown down a dare.

Katherine squeezed Joe's arm. In time, he'd pass Gussie's
test, because he'd never leave. But right this minute, Katherine
was at a loss. How should he answer the child's challenge?

"I'm never leaving. And you'd better stay, too." Then Joe
whispered into Gussie's ear, just loud enough for Katherine to
hear, "See, you're the only gal I got with freckles." He flashed
Katherine a pitying look. "And, far as I'm concerned, a girl
with no freckles is like a summer night with no stars in the
sky."

Gussie's sigh heralded the first smile Katherine had ever
seen her wear. And then, beyond the voices raised in song, a
loud ruckus started.

Up ahead, Preacher Jack was flanked by Rack and Ruin.

"Oh, my." Katherine watched the twins cavort in the same
stomp-clap dance they'd created two days before Christmas.

"All rise," bellowed Preacher Jack. "Time for these folks

to get hitched. I got a bride blushing and a groom who's mighty impatient.''

''Star, star, come where we are . . .''

The words poured over them like golden streamers unfurling. Katherine linked arms with Gussie and Joe.

As they walked, it seemed to Katherine that the ancient pendant resting on her bodice hummed in a celebration all its own.

Joy to the World

✳✳✳

KATE FREIMAN

Christmas card. Sympathy card. Sympathy card. Christmas card. Sympathy card.

"Joy to the—"

I jumped up, dislodging Laurel and Hardy, my Yorkshire terriers, from my lap. Jabbing the mute button of the dining room intercom speaker silenced the voices pouring out the Christmas carol. The ring of triumph in music was cruel torture. There was no joy in my world this Christmas. I wanted no singing. No celebration. My world was filled with the unwanted dull ache of mourning, the stunned disbelief of loss. And the endless influx of solemn sympathy cards mixed in with brightly illustrated Christmas cards.

Still, I didn't have the heart to ask the housekeeper to turn off the music everywhere in the house. Olive was trying so hard to keep her Christmas spirit through all our shared misery. Not the commercial spirit of Santa Claus, but the spirituality expressed in the carols she loved to hum along with as she worked. I owed her too much to deprive her of that small joy. Reluctantly, I sat again.

Irritated at having their comfortable nap disturbed, the little Yorkies curled up together under the table, grumbling softly until they fell asleep again. I turned my attention back to my task.

Several sympathy cards were simply addressed to "The

McMichaels Family Charitable Foundation,'' as if an organization could feel grief, could be comforted. The personal ones didn't make me feel any better. How could any preprinted or handwritten card console me for Matthew's death? My big brother, my only brother, gone forever, ripped out of my life, out of all the lives he's touched with his kindness, his compassion, his humor. How could painted sprays of flowers and gilded images of cherubs and the words ''in sympathy'' stop the stinging flow of my tears, or staunch the bleeding of my heart?

Some of the card senders were long-time friends of our family. I understood their helplessness in dealing with Matthew's death, because I wasn't dealing so well with it. Many cards were from supporters of the charitable work done by our family ''firm,'' the McMichaels Foundation. Other senders were recipients of aid from the foundation, including relatives of children in hospices and group homes—terminally ill and abandoned children Matthew and I had probably held and hugged at some fund-raiser or celebration for their benefit. Those were the ones that, without exception, reduced me to silent tears.

I knew none of them intended to make the pain worse with their solemn expressions of sympathy, their now inappropriately cheerful wishes for a Merry Christmas and Happy New Year. But none of them could make the pain lessen, either. Matthew was gone, and I was too angry to think about celebrating Christmas or the birth of a new millennium. All I could think of was, *Why?*

Why did Matthew have to die now, so young, so full of life? Why so suddenly, and why in a place, in a manner, that made finding him impossible? The unanswerable questions had replayed in my head since I'd gotten the awful news on Sunday. That was just five days ago, with Christmas Eve tomorrow, Friday night.

It was no consolation, as several people had suggested with well-intentioned tactlessness, that our parents were no longer alive to mourn their firstborn, or comfort their remaining child. But at least our parents' illnesses had given them time to say good-bye, time to prepare us and themselves. Our parents had married late in life, and we'd come along after they'd despaired of having a family. They'd both died peacefully in their bed, here in the familiar surroundings of their own home—our father three years ago, our mother only two. At the age of twenty-eight, I was an orphan with no other close family, but I felt as lost as if I were only five.

As I continued numbly sorting the newest batch of cards, the mellow tones of the front doorbell echoed softly outside the half-open dining room door. The dogs, typical terriers, scrambled up and raced out of the room to investigate the intrusion. I froze at the thought of having to deal with anyone right then. Surely the housekeeper would send whoever it was away without having to be told. After forty-odd years of working for the McMichaels family, Olive knew us— *Oh, God! There was no us anymore! I was the only one left!*—so well. Olive knew I couldn't bear another pitying face, another smothering hug, another babble of sincere but ineffective sympathy.

When several minutes passed with no sign of Olive or the dogs, I relaxed slightly. The stacks of cards to be sorted, and the sorted ones to be acknowledged, still had me on edge, like a child waiting to be bullied. So far this morning, I was keeping my chin up, but it wouldn't take much to make me cry . . . again.

"I thought you could use some company."

The unexpected voice startled me badly, but I quickly managed to muffle my involuntary yelp. My heart leaped and started to race. Resentful of the intrusion yet rather glad to see this particular intruder, I dropped my handful of unsorted cards onto the dining table.

"Joshua, honestly! You scared the daylights out of me, sneaking up like that."

I tried to muster my dignity, but the truth was, I was too glad to see Matthew's friend, my friend, Joshua Davidson leaning against the doorjamb to try very hard. He had a small package tucked between his left elbow and his ribs, and was cradling a frenzied Yorkie in each hand. The gentle concern in his slate blue eyes made me want to run to him for comfort.

Joshua frowned. As stressed as I was, I couldn't help noticing the way his furrowed brow made him look both intense and vulnerable. His ruggedly masculine looks always startled me; I was accustomed to the polished and pretty looks of wealthy young men whose idea of working with their hands usually involved sports. Joshua had the kind of roughly sculpted sex appeal that could sell jeans, boots, cigarettes, whiskey, and pickup trucks. Wherever he went he turned heads, not just because of his looks, but because of his quiet aura of power, of strength. But there was a modesty about him that made me wonder if he ever looked in a mirror, or into the eyes of the women who openly admired him.

"Sorry." Joshua was one of the few people these days who said that simple word as if he truly meant it. "Olive asked me to bring this to you." He tipped his head to indicate the carton. "I thought you saw me standing here." Some of my own grief seemed reflected in his eyes. "I . . . I didn't like thinking you were here alone."

His few thoughtful words, punctuated by a wistful smile, made me feel just a tiny bit less raw. Joshua's voice had an intimate, smoky rasp, like a singer's voice. He once explained that his voice was really just rusty, because he spent so many hours working alone, speaking to no one. Whatever the cause, the confidential timbre of his low, evenly modulated voice held a quiet charisma that drew people to him. I doubted he was any more aware of this quality than he was of his compelling appearance.

Another thing Joshua never seemed to take for granted was our relationship. He never displayed macho possessiveness, never assumed he had tacit permission to embrace me, to kiss me, simply because he had before. The *feminist* in me appreciated his respect for me, but the *female* in me occasionally yearned for him to lose a few layers of civility.

The one time I'd hesitantly discussed my frustration with Matthew, he'd explained that Joshua was acutely conscious of the differences in our upbringing and wealth, and had too much pride to risk appearing to be a fortune hunter. So, while I hungered for him to set down the package and the dogs and stride over to engulf me in a comforting embrace, he continued to lean on the doorjamb, keeping his respectful distance. I envied my pets, contentedly curled in his big palms.

Now, looking steadily into my eyes, he lifted an eyebrow. "How are you doing?"

I tried to smile, but I couldn't. "Terrible would be an improvement." My voice came out like a croak, the result of intermittent crying for five days.

He straightened. "What can I do?"

"Make it all be a dream." It wasn't a fair answer, but it was honest.

Poor Joshua recoiled as if I'd slapped at him. "I'm a *wood*-worker, Angela, not a miracle worker."

It was the first time I'd ever heard him snap at anyone; the grief and anger in his tone filled me with guilt. My first impulse was to run into his arms, to apologize, to be forgiven. I stood too quickly, almost overturning the delicate Sheraton dining chair. Joshua took a step toward me as I steadied the chair, then halted.

"Oh, Angela, honey . . . I'm sorry."

He'd misinterpreted my action. I shook my head. "Christmas is supposed to be a time of miracles, Joshua." My wavering voice made me sound like a disillusioned child. It was how I felt, but this wasn't about discovering that Santa Claus isn't real.

"It's Christmas. All I want is world peace and Matthew home, safe and sound." I was practically wailing. I strove for some self-control. "Think I'll get my wish?"

"Isn't that what faith is for?" He spoke gently.

"I'm running low on faith. A miracle would be a nice sign that the world isn't going to Hell in a handbasket, don't you think? A miracle or two to mark the new millennium would go a long way to restoring a lot of lost faith and shutting up all those Apocalypse prophets."

Joshua's forehead creased again, and he started toward me. Because I was afraid I'd fall apart completely if he offered me comfort right then, I moved in the opposite direction. Wrapping my arms around myself, as if I could hold myself together, I began to pace the width of the dining room, blind to the beautiful things around me.

I heard a soft thud behind me, and then Joshua was suddenly holding my shoulders, stopping me in my tracks. Perversely, because I needed his touch so much, I stiffened against the temptation of his warm, gentle hands. True to character, he silently waited me out, until my resistance began to soften. Then, he moved just close enough for me to feel the heat of his chest on my back, as if some electrical force field could defy the layers of clothing between us. The dogs yelped and pawed at our legs for attention.

"Hey." With that whispered syllable, I felt the warmth of his breath near my temple. "You don't have to go through this alone. I'm here, honey. Lean on me. Okay?"

Joshua's intimate tone, his gentle words, seemed to weave a mantle of peace and safety around me. I couldn't speak, but I relaxed until I was literally leaning on the solid wall of his chest. I wanted him to take advantage of our situation to embrace me. But he only stood quietly, with his strong hands still clasping my shoulders. After a while, I felt less desperate. For the first time since a pair of somber FBI agents had broken the news of Matthew's plane crash, I felt a tiny easing of the twisting agony of grief.

I was grateful—but still, it felt somehow wrong to let myself lean freely on Joshua. I was the one who usually reached out to help others; I was a professional fund-raiser, an expert at finding solutions to the needs of others. Until now, I hadn't ever thought of myself as someone who could have a crisis, who could be needy. Matthew and I had grown up in the rarefied world of hereditary wealth, social privilege, and servants, but our parents had raised us to be independent, self-reliant, and strong for others. Seeking and accepting help for myself felt like wearing my shoes on the wrong feet.

Perhaps I had learned those lessons too well.

Joshua's fingers tightened on my shoulders. "You don't always have to be the strongest one, Angela. You'll wear yourself out. The people who love you, who love Matthew, want to help you get through this."

His quiet words echoed my thoughts. From our first meeting, our minds had been uncannily in harmony about so many diverse things. Too practical to believe in love at first sight or fated lovers, I always gave the credit to Joshua for being unusually perceptive. He read people well, he was incredibly sensitive to mood and motivations, but never seemed manipulative. Joshua's ability to establish a rapport with several troubled youths the foundation was sponsoring had impressed Matthew. People trusted Joshua implicitly, myself included. Matthew, who trusted with more than a pinch of realistic cynicism, had once confided that he would trust Joshua not just with his own life, but with mine. Right now, it felt as if Matthew's judgment might be tested.

"I miss Matthew." I spoke past the sudden lump in my

throat. "It's so awful thinking of him dying alone, so far away. I can't help wondering if he knew what was happening, or if it was so sudden that he didn't know. Was he in pain? Why can't they find him?" My voice broke.

"Don't, Angela." Joshua's head pressed gently against mine. I felt his lips on my temple, a touch, not a kiss, somehow more intimate than a kiss. "Don't torture yourself. It would break Matthew's heart if he could hear you."

That nearly undid me. "I can't help it!" I squeezed my hands into fists. "He's my brother. I want to know! I need to know!"

Joshua gently but firmly turned me to face him. He gathered me into his arms, but my fisted hands on his chest kept some distance between us. Although I longed to lean my head on his broad chest, to feel the strength of his arms around me, I held myself too stiffly. I really was afraid that once I accepted his support, I wouldn't be able to stand alone, and we were too new for me to be sure he would be there whenever I needed him. But Joshua didn't try to force me to give in. He just rubbed my back and neck with a patient tenderness that melted my inhibitions.

"It's not fair!" The childish words burst from me before I realized I was speaking. I lifted my head to look into Joshua's eyes, but tears clouded my vision. "I can't even say good-bye to him. All I can do is hold a memorial service over an empty grave. Why can't they find him?"

Joshua's hands slid down my arms until he caught my clenched hands in his. His fingers were warm, calloused, strong like steel, yet incredibly gentle as he pried my fists open. I allowed him to unclench and massage my fingers. Then, one after the other, he drew each hand to his lips for a brief kiss on my knuckles, then to his shoulders. The gesture was incredibly sweet and undemanding, but the soft warmth of his lips on my skin sent tiny chills of awareness racing up my back.

The primal impulse that gripped me, the selfish urge to make love with Joshua in order to forget my sorrow, in order to dull the pain in my heart, made me feel off-balance. And guilty. We'd come very close to making love, probably already would have become lovers, if Matthew hadn't . . . No, I wasn't blaming my brother for interrupting my love life with his death.

My guilt came from my impulse to use Joshua to make myself
feel better. He deserved better than that.

So I kept myself very still, fighting temptation. My hands
rested on the solidly muscled flesh and bone beneath his soft
flannel shirt. I could feel his heart beating, racing a little, like
mine was doing. He placed his hands over mine. I let myself
relax a bit more, glad neither of us had done anything rash.
When my unshed tears cleared a bit, I looked up into his face.
The half smile he gave me was both sober and reassuring. I
almost managed an answering smile.

I sought a topic that would distract us both from the tripping
of our hearts. "Thank God Matthew finished processing all
the donations and grants before . . ." My voice trailed off.

My brother, along with Lucian Drake, the sole paid em-
ployee of the foundation, directed the complicated finances
that enabled us to do so much for people in need. I didn't have
a clue about that end of our work. I was the director of fund-
raising and community awareness, which Matthew and I pri-
vately called "party planning." Usually, Matthew distributed
the Christmas funds earlier in the fall so they could be in time
for the holiday. This year, some computer problem had caused
a delay.

A distressing thought occurred to me. "Oh, God. I'm going
to have to take over the financial planning from Matthew." I
gave Joshua a slightly panicked look. "What I know about
investing this kind of money wouldn't fill a matchbook."

"What about Lucian?"

Ah. What about Lucian? I almost smiled at Joshua's question. Lucian was a studious, rather shy man of about my own
age of twenty-eight, who performed his many duties meticu-
lously and quietly. Without his black-framed glasses, Lucian
had the almost unworldly beauty of a male model, but he was
the most self-effacing person I'd ever known. Sometimes, I
had the impression that if he could have become invisible, he
would have.

Lucian had worked for the foundation for nine years, starting as a part-time volunteer while he finished his college
degree. His dedication to the foundation, which tended to op-
erate behind the scenes, had estranged him from his wealthy,
flamboyant California family, but endeared him to my parents.

"Matthew had a genius for investing. I doubt that Lucian

and I could step into his shoes. Besides, I don't know anything about the computer system they use. It's totally different from the PC I use for my event planning."

"Get Lucian to teach you."

A rational suggestion, but easier said than done, and not for obvious reasons. It wasn't fear of an alien computer that kept me out of the basement offices of the foundation. But Joshua wouldn't know that, and I hesitated to explain the real reason. Joshua had seen me weeping and raging quite a lot in the past few days. I didn't want to risk slipping even further in his estimation by sharing a full-blown phobia with him now. Other than our parents, our housekeeper Olive, and Matthew, few people knew, which was my choice. I'd always believed that kind of personal information should be revealed on a need-to-know basis only, and really, no one else needed to know.

I offered Joshua what I hoped was a plausible excuse. "There are so many sensitive bits of data in the foundation's computers I'd be petrified I'd erase it all."

Joshua's half smile deepened the sun lines around his mouth and eyes. "I doubt that, but you don't have to solve that problem now."

His soothing tone drew the closest thing to a smile that I'd given in days. I tipped my head back, a little breathless at the tantalizing contact between our bodies. I wanted the kiss I could see in his piercing gaze.

"Excuse me, Miss Angela."

Olive spoke from the open doorway. Her odd tone made me suddenly self-conscious of standing in Joshua's embrace. I tried to step away. After a brief tightening of his arms, Joshua released me. I caught a glimpse of his quickly erased frown as I was turning to face Olive. Guilt sent a blush to my cheeks; he probably thought I was embarrassed to have Olive see me in his arms because of the differences between us. If so, he was only half right. I was disconcerted at Olive, who had diapered me and taught me how to make mud pies and arranged my hair for my first formal dance, seeing me in the arms of any man.

I cleared my throat. "Yes, Olive?"

"I hope whatever is in that package isn't breakable." At Olive's pointed comment, Joshua's cheeks reddened. Before either of us could scoop up the package, Olive spoke again.

"Lucian is in the library. He says it's urgent that he speak with you." Olive's eyes darted a glance at Joshua, then returned to me. "Shall I bring him in?"

Puzzled but curious, I shook my head. "Thank you, Olive, no. I'll go into the library."

With a nod, Olive slipped away from the doorway. I turned to Joshua. "Do you mind . . . ?"

His expression hardened. "Yes."

His answer took me by surprise. I opened my mouth to protest that he had no reason to object, but Joshua's sudden smile silenced me.

"You asked, I answered. That's all." He shrugged. "Why the formalities? I thought Drake pretty much had the run of this place."

I shook my head. "Not the house. Only the computer lab and conference rooms downstairs. He has everything he wants there."

"Not everything."

It was difficult to believe Joshua was jealous of Lucian. The notion of anything romantic between Lucian and me was totally implausible to anyone who knew us. But when I searched Joshua's face for an answer, splashes of red appeared in his cheeks.

Before I could say or do anything, he bent toward me and touched his lips to my forehead. The contact lasted mere seconds, and then he was turning me to face the doorway. Confused by his behavior, I took the easy way out and left the dining room, feeling Joshua's gaze follow me like a reassuring touch.

Lucian Drake stood by the fireplace, his back toward me. With his head bowed, his lanky frame looked dejected. His corduroy slacks and tweed jacket looked slept-in and his sandy hair was mussed. I suddenly felt terribly guilty for not remembering that Lucian would be terribly upset at Matthew's loss. He'd always been so open in his admiration for his mentor.

I crossed the room, my steps muffled by one of the thick Oriental carpets that had been trod on by dignitaries, nobility, and many recipients of foundation grants, and stopped beside Lucian. When he didn't move, I touched his sleeve with my fingertips. He jumped as if a snake had bitten him, which made me start. He turned toward me, his boyish face beet red behind the thick black frames of his glasses.

"I'm so sorry, Lucian. We're all on edge these days."

"It's okay. I mean . . . I'm okay." He swallowed audibly. "Angela, we have a . . . a serious problem. That is, the foundation has a serious problem."

My stomach felt as if it were falling down an elevator shaft. Before I could ask Lucian to explain, he grabbed my hands in his, the wintry cold of his skin burning into mine. I stifled the impulse to rub his hands to warm them, as I would a child's, and gazed at him, silently encouraging him to speak.

"All the checks Matthew wrote . . . every single one would have bounced. All the funds had been transferred out. Nothing left to cover any of the Christmas checks to the charities. I . . . I transferred it all back in time, but . . ."

I stared without comprehension at Lucian. He swallowed hard and spoke again, his voice almost raspy.

"I don't want to think Matthew . . . I don't know who else could have done it . . . The trail was pretty complicated, but when I finally found the money . . . Matthew was flying to the Cayman Islands when he went down, Angela." Transfixed by the intense light in Lucian's pale blue eyes, I could barely make myself nod. "Five . . . Over five hundred million dollars . . . of foundation money somehow ended up . . . in accounts in a Cayman bank."

I began trembling uncontrollably. Lucian's frigid fingers tightened around my hands, but he was shaking also, and offered no steadying support. Despite my own shock, I felt sorry for him.

"Angela, all the trans-transactions were made un-under Matthew's log-on pass code. I don't want to believe it, but . . . It looks like—"

"No!" The word burst from me with enough force to wrench my hands from Lucian's. Horrified by the implication of his words, I stepped back. *"No! That's impossible! What are you saying?"*

Lucian looked into my eyes. "I'm saying Matthew had been stealing funds from the foundation's accounts, and was flying to the Cayman Islands to get the money when his plane went down." Then, as if sharing the shame of his accusation, he lowered his head.

My hands came up in front of my face, as if I could protect myself from Lucian's horrifying condemnation of Matthew.

"It gets worse, Angela." Lucian's voice dropped to a hoarse whisper, pursuing me even as I took a half step backward. "We spent a year making sure the computer system was Y2K compliant, but Matthew did something . . . If I hadn't caught the transfer in time, the system would have crashed at midnight on January first, as if the millennium bug was still there. All traces of his activities would have been erased."

Y2K? The millennium bug? All traces erased? What did any of that have to do with Matthew's death? I took another step backward and slammed into Joshua's chest; my surprised gasp came out like a croak. This time Joshua's arms wrapped around me, holding me steady while I shook like a wet kitten. Briefly, I allowed myself the luxury of closing my eyes. When I opened them again, Lucian was glaring over my head, at Joshua.

"What the hell is he doing here?"

I flinched at the anger behind Lucian's unexpected, totally uncharacteristic bellow, but Joshua stood firm.

"What are you doing, Drake? Don't you think Angela's got enough to deal with right now?"

Joshua didn't raise his voice, but I could feel the anger inside him vibrating through me. Or maybe it was my own anger, but at whom, I didn't know yet. Or didn't want to know. I was still struggling with the information Lucian had imparted.

"I've got proof, damn it!" Lucian's answer was a muffled shout. "I'm trying to protect Angela, which is a hell of a lot more than you can say. If the media or the cops get a hold of the facts, what *they* do to her will be *more* than she can deal with."

"What proof?"

Something in Joshua's tone made me uneasy. I took advantage of his divided attention to wrench myself away from him.

"There *is no such proof*!" My voice rose in a shriek that startled both men.

Suddenly overwhelmed by everything, I knew I had to escape the intensity of that confrontation. I ran across the hallway to the dining room. Call me a coward, but there I felt temporarily safe from the ugly accusations Lucian had made.

I was furious, too furious to cry. *How* dare *he? Why?* I pounded the dining table with my fist, ignoring the pain that shot up my arm to my elbow.

One of the Yorkies barked at the noise I'd made, which drew my attention to the two little dogs. They were under the dining table wrestling fiercely with something. It was the package Joshua had dropped on the carpet. The dogs had already torn several corners of the box and were starting to peel off strips of the manila wrapping paper with their sharp little teeth. I bent to rescue the package, but the instant I looked closer, I thought my heart had stopped. I know my breathing did stop.

It was a small box, maybe eight inches on all sides, covered with brown shipping paper, an unremarkable thing at Christmas. But the address label—and the return address label—the dogs hadn't destroyed them. I could never mistake that handwriting, bold, so even, like Matthew himself. The package was addressed to me. The return address was our own. It was from Matthew . . . a Christmas present, postmarked from New York City the day before he disappeared into the Caribbean Sea. He'd sent it a mere hour before he'd taxied his plane down the runway. He was supposed to be returning home tomorrow so we could go to the midnight service and exchange presents on Christmas Eve, according to family tradition.

I had an idea what his present was. Several generations of McMichaels family members had maintained a tradition of giving the children their own special ornaments. Since our parents' deaths, Matthew and I had continued the tradition, exchanging whimsical ornaments between us. Except for this year.

When Matthew had announced that he intended to spend a few days diving in the Cayman Islands before Christmas, we put up the tree early. I gave him the ornament I'd made for him, a small but functional kaleidoscope. It was hanging from the end of one of the upper boughs of the potted live Christmas tree we'd set up in the family parlor.

Poor Matthew had been distressed that I'd been so efficient, while he still hadn't found a suitable ornament to give me. I'd assured him that it didn't matter, that one less decoration wouldn't ruin the effect of the tree, which was so laden with dangling things that it was virtually impossible to see the tree itself. But he'd insisted, promising to get an ornament for me before he went away, so I could hang it before Christmas Eve, when he planned to return.

But now he'd never return, and having some last token of him suddenly did matter, more than I expected.

My hands were shaking as I lifted the package and completed the Yorkies' earlier efforts to open the wrapping. Would there be a note inside? Perhaps his conscience had rebeled, prompting him to explain the unexplainable. One part of me—the logical part—balked at condemning him without proof. The other part of me—the emotional part—was afraid to learn that Matthew indeed had a hidden dark side.

After a steadying breath, I burrowed into the nest of red tissue paper under the box lid. The object I found made me smile even as tears welled into my eyes. Matthew had sent me a gaudily painted, fat papier-mâché fish-shaped tree ornament. It was oddly heavy, a silly, oddly appealing object. There was no note, not even a gift-enclosure card. No confession, no last thoughts.

Trembling, I stared at the ornament through unshed tears until my chest ached and the blood pounded in my temples. The ragged breath I finally drew ended in a cry of anguish I couldn't have muffled if my life had depended on it. My stomach clenched so painfully I was afraid I'd be ill, but I couldn't move. All I could do was bury my face in my hands. The sobs that shuddered silently out of me shook me and twisted me, but gave me no relief.

Dimly, I heard Laurel and Hardy whining for my attention, felt their tiny paws on my legs, but all I wanted to do now was hang Matthew's gift from the tree, where it belonged. Shaking off my paralysis, I hurried to the family parlor with the little dogs dashing back and forth around me, as I cradled Matthew's last gift to me in my cupped palms. I found a waist-level bough on which to hang the gaudy little fish, which was heavy enough to bend it.

Carefully, I steadied the ornament. And without knowing why, I felt my pain at Lucian's accusations, at Matthew's death beginning to fade. A sweet peace was trying to take its place, warming me gently. I longed to let that serenity surround and engulf me, longed for the strength it would surely bring me.

But then the Yorkies barked sharply and raced ahead of me down the hall, reminding me that I wasn't alone. As I went from the family parlor to the dining room, I could hear Lucian and Joshua speaking in the library; their voices were just low murmurings, their words indistinguishable. Wishing they would leave, I resigned myself to finish sorting the cards after I picked up the shredded wrapping paper the dogs had scattered under the table.

A moment later I sensed, rather than heard or saw, Joshua enter the room. I prayed he was alone. I couldn't face Lucian's accusations again. To my relief, when I lifted my head, Joshua was indeed alone. He knelt on the carpet beside me. The strain in his eyes mirrored the distress in my heart. Neither of us could spare a glance, a smile, for the Yorkies trying to climb into our laps.

With gentle, steady fingers, he brushed the tears from my cheeks, then cupped my face in his hand. I let myself absorb his warmth, his gentle strength, his support. It felt right.

"Joshua, I don't know what to do." I blinked rapidly to shut off the tears that threatened to spill over, and strands of my tangled hair caught on my lashes. "Oh, God, I don't know if doing anything even matters anymore. Matthew was a good and honest man. He was the soul of generosity and compassion. Why would Lucian accuse him like that?"

"Oh, Angela." With his free hand, Joshua brushed my hair out of my eyes. "I don't know what to tell you. After you walked away, I could have taken Drake's head off, but . . ."

I waited until I couldn't stand the silent suspense. "But *what*? Don't tell me you believe him?"

Joshua drew me toward him. Part of me wanted to pull away, hurt that he could doubt Matthew. But part of me couldn't help noticing, when he gathered me close, the way I fit into the strong circle of his arms, the hard contours of his chest and thighs.

"Angela, some of what Lucian said makes sense." I stiffened against Joshua, but he held me tighter. "Hear me out. I don't want to believe it any more than you do, but the way Lucian explained things, it sounds possible."

"*Possible?* How could you think Matthew was capable of *stealing* from the foundation? From the charities and the people our family has been supporting for generations?" My voice rose shrilly. I tried to calm myself, but the rage inside me kept trying to burst out again.

"How can you think he would do all that and lie to me as well? We couldn't have been closer if we'd been twins. I would have known if he was planning something dishonest. I would have sensed that he was lying. Even if Matthew intended to defraud the foundation, he would have known he could never get away with anything so devious and underhanded and . . . and *evil*, without my knowing somehow. You *know* that about us, damn you!"

Joshua kept hushing me, and when I finally wound down, he bent his head and kissed me. For the briefest second, I softened at the feel of his lips on mine. His kiss, his embrace, felt so right: this was the man I was falling in love with.

Suddenly, it occurred to me that Joshua wasn't comforting me over Matthew's betrayal. He was trying to distract me from *his* betrayal, of Matthew and of me. With more strength than I suspected I could muster, I pushed away from Joshua and sprang up and away. My right ankle turned as I got to my feet, but I ignored the pain to stand my ground and face that seductive traitor.

He rose slowly and stood still, his blue eyes full of regret. "Angela, are you hurt?" I shook my head. "I saw your ankle turn. Let me see it."

Before I could tell him to go to Hell, Lucian burst into the room. His sudden appearance startled the Yorkies out of the dining room in a frenzy of yaps and growls.

"Angela? What did he do to you?"

"I thought you were leaving." Joshua's words and the chill in his tone echoed my own thoughts and feelings.

"And leave her alone with you? No way. I work for the foundation. I'm looking out for Angela. You're the one who should be leaving."

I turned my incredulous gaze from Joshua to Lucian. "You can both get out. Do you honestly think I want either of you hovering over me while you play Judas to Matthew?"

"But Angela, I . . . I care about you."

After his declaration, Lucian turned red. Any other time, it might have been endearing. Any other time, I would have thought him rather courageous to declare his feelings in front of another man. Now, all I wanted was his unconditional loyalty to Matthew.

"If you care about me, Lucian, you'll do everything you

can to prove your suspicions about Matthew are wrong.''

"But I already told you, I covered the checks and transferred the money back. No one was shortchanged, so no one needs to know. As far as anyone outside the three of us is concerned, Matthew died on his way to Grand Cayman for a few days of diving before Christmas."

"*I'll* know!" I glared at Lucian and saw him glance at Joshua as if the two of them had been conspiring. "What about the auditors? If you could find a trail, couldn't they?" Lucian went pale. Obviously, he'd forgotten about the foundation's routine audits. "I'll call them in right after Christmas."

"Wait, Angela. If Lucian is right about Matthew, it will be worse to do an audit now, won't it?" Joshua's gaze went from my face to Lucian's and back to mine. "If auditors find something wrong, aren't they obliged to say so? At that point, the media would have a feeding frenzy, and you'd be on the menu." His voice gentled. "Haven't those vultures put you through enough over Matthew's death?"

Joshua's touching concern for me couldn't distract me from my determination to clear Matthew of Lucian's accusation.

"They won't find anything wrong," I told him with far more conviction than I actually felt. "They'll prove Matthew has never been anything but honest. You'll see."

"What if they don't?" Joshua's eyes darkened like storm clouds. "Angela, from what Lucian explained to me in the library, Matthew didn't bother covering his tracks. He didn't expect to die before his phony millennium bug could crash the system and cover them for him."

Joshua's accusatory words came at me like blows, but I refused to duck. Instead, I turned toward Lucian, my hands clenched into fists. He must have noticed, because he took a half step backward.

"Lucian, do you really believe Matthew intended to steal from the foundation?"

Even in my desperate, devastated emotional state, I had to give Lucian credit for the way he drew himself up and returned my gaze squarely.

"I don't want to believe it, Angela. Matthew is—was—a hero to me, more than even a mentor. I want to believe he just made a few simple mistakes in transferring his personal funds to the Cayman Island bank."

Joshua gave a slight shake of his head, but I was willing to grasp at any straw, even a flimsy one. "Is that possible?"

Did Lucian hesitate a second too long before answering? "It's possible," he said slowly. His quick nod gave me more hope. "Matthew was under incredible pressure to process everything early, to avoid any potential hassles from the Y2K bug. His personal financial records are on the main computer, and it's easy to confuse files with similar names."

Joshua snorted. "*Five hundred million bucks*' worth of *confusion?*"

The sarcasm in his voice made me feel his betrayal even more sharply. Where was his respect and affection for Matthew? Where was his sense of fairness? Had he always been so quick to judge harshly, hiding it from me until now? Or had I simply not noticed whatever I didn't want to notice? That habit, Matthew had often pointed out to me, was one of my talents . . . as well as one of my flaws. Well, I was noticing now, and I didn't like what I saw.

"Lucian, I need your help. Would you do something for me?"

He glanced quickly at Joshua, then straightened his shoulders in his rumpled tweed sport coat. "Anything, Angela. I'd crawl through barbed wire for you."

I managed a feeble smile. "This may be more painful. I need to understand what . . . what happened. I'd like you to show me on my computer how you traced this supposed trial of Matthew's."

Lucian frowned. Taking off his black-framed glassed and bowing his head, he rubbed the bridge of his nose, then sighed. When he looked at me, he looked very young, very hopeless. My heart sank as he began to speak.

"It's not the same. The computer you use is, well"—his cheeks reddened slightly—"it's sort of a toy compared to the system Matthew and I use. Different operating system, different software. It would take days just to explain the basics."

Dread coiled around my disappointment, because I knew the most logical solution was for Lucian to demonstrate on the system in the basement computer room. Logical but, for me, impossible.

Even after working for us for so long, Lucian probably didn't know about my phobia. Matthew always respected my privacy, and would joke about Lucian and himself being mad scientists, not fit for polite company when they worked. Besides, I had a ready excuse for not working downstairs: I had my own desktop computer in my office, where I could meet with patrons and prospective donors to the foundation. Originally a parlor on the main floor, near the library, it retained the feel of a social setting rather than a place of business, which made people feel comfortable.

Would Matthew have taken advantage of my phobia to commit a crime, any crime, let alone one of this magnitude?

Joshua cleared his throat. "I'd like to see this proof you've got, too."

He couldn't know he was making things worse, but his challenge was likely to prompt Lucian to want to demonstrate his expertise. And, as Lucian had just pointed out, the best place for that was the basement, but it was the absolute worst place for me. I prayed for inspiration, something, anything, that would divert the two men from heading for the stairway to the nightmarish place below the ground.

"How about a diagram?" Lucian offered his suggestion hesitantly, but I could have kissed him for it. "I can do a sort of flowchart of how Matthew moved the money between accounts." He must have caught the sudden and sharp anger that came over me at his accusation, because he coughed and amended his words. "I mean, how the money appeared to move between accounts."

The reprieve from the ordeal of the basement renewed my energy. Thinking quickly, I opened the sideboard and drew out a roll of paper towels. "Will this do?"

Lucian nodded and reached for the roll. Joshua and I, maintaining an uncomfortable distance from each other, stood on either side of him. Lucian withdrew a mechanical pencil from the pocket protector in the breast pocket of his sport coat. With a quick glance at me, he bent over the paper and began to sketch boxes and lines connecting them.

For the next few minutes, I was acutely aware of breathing: mine, Lucian's, Joshua's. I stared at the diagram growing under Lucian's nimble fingers as if I could comprehend it simply by absorbing the sight of it. On the opposite side of the table, Joshua stood studying the symbols with a similar intensity. Twice our eyes met, and twice he looked away so quickly that

I knew he was still considering Matthew guilty as charged.

Which was the worse pain? Matthew's possible betrayal of all that our family had stood for over generations of philanthropic works? Or Joshua's unwillingness to give Matthew the benefit of the doubt, his condemnation of my brother a betrayal of the budding relationship between us? It was all part of the same pain that gripped my heart.

I desperately didn't want Lucian to prove Matthew had committed such an awful crime; I couldn't bear to know that about my brother. But if Lucian failed to prove his allegations, could I bear to face Joshua again, knowing how easily he'd believed the worst of his friend and my brother?

Lucian interrupted my agonized thoughts by tapping his pencil on one of the boxes he'd drawn on the paper towels. He began explaining his diagram, and the flow of data each line represented. Although he seemed to be trying to speak in plain English, and paused often to see if I was following him, I don't think I understood more than a quarter of what he said. Joshua grunted occasionally, as if to confirm that he understood, but I saw how his brow furrowed in concentration.

Eventually, I couldn't tell if I was beginning to understand or becoming completely confused. Lucian soon seemed to forget he had a novice audience. He began drawing additional lines to indicate how he'd retraced Matthew's tracks and replaced the transferred funds, confusing me with jargon that flowed easily from his lips. Joshua finally saved me from admitting my ignorance by whistling and declaring that he was now totally mystified by Lucian's explanation.

In addition to confused, I was also apologetic toward Lucian. "I always assumed Matthew was the only computer expert. I guess I underestimated how much you know about them."

Lucian caught my eye and his cheeks turned pink. "Matthew was a good teacher."

Joshua arched a brow. "Are you still thinking of calling in an auditor?"

I pondered his question, uncomfortably aware of his and Lucian's gazes fixed on my face. What was I going to do? What *should* I do? I looked down at the paper towels Lucian had covered with diagrams, boxes, and lines and arrows representing either a perfectly human and understandable error, or a shameful crime: Was the answer there? I didn't know.

"I'm still thinking about it, yes." It was the most honest answer I could offer, as indecisive as it sounded.

Joshua straightened. The expression on his face was so guarded that I instinctively braced myself. From the corner of my eye, I could see Lucian glancing from one to the other of us, but this was between Joshua and me, and tacitly we all knew it.

"If it was me, I wouldn't. Drake's diagram here seems pretty clear. Bring in auditors and they'll have to tell the truth, Angela. And the truth doesn't look good, does it? As soon as the media gets hold of it, Matthew's name and the foundation's reputation will be toast."

Joshua's conviction that Matthew was guilty no longer surprised me, but it still angered me. Never mind what we could have had together. What about their friendship?

"Aren't you being a little quick to judge?"

He shook his head. "I don't think so. Hell, Angela, you might even find yourself under investigation as an accomplice."

I gasped, stunned by that possibility. "But I haven't done anything. I never touch the computer in the basement." I turned to Lucian for corroboration. "You can vouch for that."

He avoided my gaze, and shrugged. "The Trojan horse set to create a phony Y2K bug could just as easily have been sent from your PC's modem as it could have been set up directly on the system downstairs."

"Trojan horse?" I looked from Joshua, who also shrugged, to Lucian, who met my gaze only briefly, then removed his glasses to rub them with his handkerchief. "What is a Trojan horse?"

In the silence following my question, I wracked my memory for something about Trojan horses, but only the ancient myth came to mind. What did hiding warriors in the belly of a giant gift horse have to do with computer crime? I repeated the question, looking directly at Lucian until he met my eyes.

Lucian cleared his throat, replaced his glasses, then took them off again. "A Trojan horse, in computer terms, is a program that a hacker hides inside an operating system until . . ."

He paused and put his glasses back on. I restrained myself from prompting him.

With his gaze fixed on the table, Lucian continued in a voice so low I had to lean toward him to hear. "A Trojan horse waits until a prearranged time or event in a computer, and then it acts. Some of them just let hackers get past security checks, and some of them . . . Some of them . . ." Again, Lucian paused. I knew I wasn't going to like what he had to tell me. I just wanted to get it over with, so I could sort myself out.

He swallowed hard. "The one Matthew hid is designed to crash the foundation's whole system on the dot of midnight, New Year's Eve, to make it look like the year two thousand bug took it out. Before it crashes the foundation's system, it, uh . . . it's set up to erase all the data that could lead to Matthew."

It was too much for me to comprehend. Not just the technical details, but the criminal ones. How could the brother I adored, the man who had earned respect and love around the world, the son who had gone days without sleep to remain at our parents' bedsides when they were dying—how could this man also be the heartless demon behind a scheme to defraud and betray? I felt as if the breath . . . no, the blood . . . had been drained from me. All I could do at that moment was weakly shake my head, determined to deny even the tiniest grain of truth in Lucian's evidence.

No, Matthew had to be innocent!

While my confused thoughts whirled, I felt the gazes of both Lucian and Joshua. They were waiting for my response. Well, so was I. I didn't know what to do. All I knew was that I couldn't let Lucian's accusations go unanswered—I owed that much to the nine generations of the McMichaels family who had created and nurtured the foundation, as well as to the generous donors and the thousands of needy recipients who benefited every year. I owed that much to Matthew's memory, too.

But what if my attempt to disprove Lucian's charges only served to prove them? What if Matthew wasn't innocent? It would nearly kill me to discover his guilt. But didn't I owe that truth to the McMichaels family, and the foundation's beneficiaries, also?

"Angela?" Joshua's voice drew me out of my thoughts. "If it were my decision, I'd forget about calling the auditors in early, and let the rest of Matthew's plan go ahead. Lucian already saved the funds, and he says that Trojan horse will erase all the evidence before the normal annual audit, anyway."

Joshua's words sapped the remaining strength from me. I had to grip the edge of the table to stay on my feet, but I faced him with as much defiance as I could summon from the depths of my soul. Why couldn't he betray me by being just another fortune hunter? That would have hurt less.

"You truly believe Matthew was guilty of trying to defraud the foundation, of stealing from the poor and disadvantaged who depend on us? Why would he do that? He has access to more family money than he could spend in two lifetimes."

Joshua shrugged. "Who knows why people do things like that? *Someone* drained the account, right? Everything Lucian found points to Matthew, and you can't prove otherwise, can you?" His eyes held my gaze steadily. After a few seconds, during which I suppose he was waiting for my reply, he added quietly, "Lucian's taken care of the first wave of damage control. No one but Matthew got hurt. I think you should leave it at that."

"Get out." I didn't raise my voice, but I was screaming inside. "Both of you. Get out."

Joshua reached his hand toward me. I pulled away, praying shaking knees would hold me up until they were gone.

"Angela—"

"Go away. I can't talk to you now. I don't want to see you. Please. That's all I ask."

Lucian's cool fingers touched the back of my clenched hand. I jerked my head around to meet his eyes. His expression reflected the misery I imagined he felt, first at losing his mentor, then at discovering his idol had feet of clay.

"Angela, I would do anything to make this go away." His impassioned tone was more intense than any I'd ever heard from him. "I don't want to believe it, either. If there's anything I can do to help you . . . Please don't shut me out. I . . . I loved Matthew, too." He swallowed. "And I . . . I care about you."

Lucian's plea touched me. Both of us had been suffering

alone, each in a private solitude. We didn't need to mourn alone, though. I couldn't manage a smile, but I nodded and let my grip on the table edge relax slightly. Then Joshua cleared his throat softly, and my gaze shifted to his face. His own gaze was focused on my hand, the one Lucian was now covering with his. The muscle at the corner of his jaw jumped as if he were clenching his teeth. Before I could look away, Joshua lifted his gaze to mine, and his unguarded expression of hurt baffled me.

I felt trapped between the two men, and I had no emotional energy to deal with them. I thought I was too strung out even to know if I wanted their moral support, or if I wanted the safety of isolation. But as soon as I posed the question to myself, the answer presented itself: I wanted—no, I *needed*— to be alone for now. The idea simmering at the back of my mind was too important, too frightening, for me to face without preparing myself. And to do that, I couldn't have Joshua and Lucian distracting me.

"Thank you, Lucian. I . . . I appreciate your concern. But I need some time alone to think things through and decide on a course of action. Would you both please see yourselves out?"

If I hadn't been so upset, I probably would have laughed aloud—for the first time since Sunday—at the way Joshua and Lucian jockeyed with each other to be the last to leave. Lucian was terribly awkward, trying valiantly to retain contact with my hand while he waited for Joshua to exit first. It was sweet of him to want to remain to comfort me, and touching that he was trying to step into the protective brother role Matthew had played so well. But eventually he must have discerned that Joshua and I needed to speak alone, and he released my hand.

With a dry, brotherly peck on my cheek, and a disapproving scowl at Joshua, Lucian left my office. I heard Olive wish him and his family a Merry Christmas and Happy New Year in subdued tones, and my heart constricted. Looking away from Joshua, I lost myself in thought.

Christmas. Matthew and I had always loved Christmas for its spiritual as well as social messages of hope, love, peace, and rebirth. Our family Christmas tradition included private prayers of thanks that we were able, for another year, to help others less fortunate, less healthy, less safe, and the humble request that we be allowed to continue to do so into the future.

How could I celebrate a holiday of hope and love and rebirth when I had lost my faith in them?

If I could prove that Lucian was wrong about Matthew . . . But how could I? I didn't know—

"Hey." Joshua spoke gently, but the sound of his voice still startled me. Embarrassed that I'd practically forgotten him, I felt my face grow hot and looked down at the floor as if the pattern of the parquet were fascinating. "You look very far away." There was a trace of amusement in his voice, which embarrassed me even more.

Joshua placed one finger under my chin, but exerted no pressure for me to look up at him. When I didn't, however, he slid his hand along my jaw and worked his fingers up into my hair, which by now was a complete mess. His tenderness tempted me to lower my guard, but I steeled myself with the memory of how Joshua had so easily believed the worst of Matthew. Without irrefutable proof, I wasn't willing to lose my faith in Matthew's honesty, nor was I willing to tolerate anyone else voicing doubt.

"I'm sorry, Joshua. I'm not especially good company now."

"If I wanted good company, I'd get a golden retriever. I want to be with you, Angela. I want to help you get through this."

Oh, he sounded so sincere! And his eyes met mine with such an expression of concern that for a moment, I thought I must be nuts to want to send him away now. But only for a moment.

"How can you help me? You believe what Lucian said about Matthew committing fraud."

He must have tried to look hurt, but I saw the color rise in his cheeks. Still, he shook his head, and his thumb traced the curve of my cheekbone in a gentle caress.

"No, honey, I said Lucian has some compelling explanations for his theory. Right now I'm as unbalanced about this as you are." When I arched a brow skeptically, he smiled ruefully. "Okay, almost as much as you are."

"All the more reason for us to spend some time apart." I was trying to be brave enough to believe in my own resolve. "We both need to think, and if we try thinking together, I'm afraid we'll get distracted."

With his warm hand on my face, his eyes gazing into mine, I might not be thinking about thinking for long. It would require far more effort than I could manage now to resist being distracted by Joshua.

He took a half step closer, so we were standing mere inches apart. I had to look farther up to maintain eye contact, which exposed my throat. Realizing I'd assumed a position of surrender, I braced to duck away but, without signaling his intent in any way, Joshua slid his hand down to circle my neck before I could escape. His touch sent shivers up my spine, but I fought to ignore my susceptibility to him. Something in his eyes warned me he was aware of my every little reaction, and was just biding his time.

"Sometimes, distraction helps put things into perspective."

I resisted the lure of his intimate tone. "Not this time."

The smile faded from his eyes. "Angela, it just about kills me to see you so alone. Please, let me help you."

"Okay. Help me trace Matthew's computer trail the way Lucian said he did."

Joshua lowered his hand and stepped back a half step, his eyes reflecting a hurt I refused to believe. He crossed his arms in front of his chest. "It would take years to learn enough to trace Matthew's trail the way Lucian did." He cocked his head to the side and regarded me gravely. "Or *says* he did."

His frustration, which reflected my own, brought the ever-ready tears to my eyes. Not trusting my voice just then, I blinked, then shook my head.

"Okay. I'll leave you alone tonight, but I'll be back tomorrow the way we planned. I owe it to Matthew not to let you spend Christmas alone."

I opened my mouth to argue that he owed *me* the solitude I wanted, but Joshua was too quick. He ducked and placed a soft kiss on my half-parted lips, then strode away before I could protest that, too. Determined not to let him in tomorrow or the next day, I straightened the papers Lucian had used and, the now-awake Yorkies frisking around my ankles, went in search of Olive.

It took several attempts over the course of that afternoon to persuade Olive that she could go to her family for Christmas with a clear conscience. Her daughter, son-in-law, and two sets of twin grandchildren were expecting her to spend the holiday with them in East Hartford, as she had done since Doreen had married and moved away. I wouldn't have asked her to give that up for me under any circumstances, but especially tonight, I needed to be alone.

Olive, being the motherly woman she is, then tried to convince me to join her family celebration. She reminded me that my parents had always included her and her daughter in our celebrations, and my father's parents before them, when she'd been a destitute, newly widowed single mother, but I assured her that any debt she thought she owed had long since been paid. Finally, she let me help her to the hired car, and departed after repeated instructions to take care of myself. Then, with all the day staff gone for Christmas as well, I was completely alone in the echoing halls of the huge McMichaels family home.

Except that there was no family anymore.

Feeling morose and lost, I wandered into the living room to gaze at the Christmas tree. As usual, it was a live potted tree that would be planted on the grounds in the spring, so it gave off a lovely cool scent of pine as I fingered the branches. Most of the decorations were heirlooms, or would be someday.

I lowered my gaze, then my fingers, to the silly ornament Matthew had given me, my last tangible connection to him. Once again, I felt that sweet peace I'd felt earlier, when I'd placed the ornament on the tree. My anger at Lucian, at Joshua, even at Matthew, began once more to ebb, to fade, to ease its grip on my heart.

Stubbornly, I grabbed at my anger and drew it back inside me. Peace would do me no good! I needed the fierce energy of anger to help me do what I had to do: find the truth about what Matthew had done . . . before someone else did.

Unfortunately, my seething emotions showed themselves in my actions, and I accidentally dislodged the bright fish ornament with the sudden movement of my hand. To my dismay, the fish fell to the marble surrounding the hearth. It split into two pieces, disgorging a red velvet jewelry pouch.

For a moment, all I could do was stare. Then, with trembling fingers, I reached for the pouch. As soon as I picked it up, with its contents hard and angular under my fingertips, I understood why the ornament itself had felt strangely heavy. Knowing Matthew as I did, I guessed that he would have pretended not to have a present for me, until he produced the object hidden inside the ornament. Last year, he'd presented me with a large box, beautifully wrapped, containing only an address and a time; a short drive had brought me to the Yorkshire terrier breeder who was holding Laurel and Hardy, Matthew's Christmas present for me.

I was curious about the contents of the velvet pouch. But I reminded myself that, even if Matthew were home as usual, we didn't open presents until Christmas Eve. So I set the bag under the tree with the other packages that had been arriving over the past weeks. Anyway, what did *things* matter now? I would trade everything material for proof of Matthew's innocence.

Somehow, I resolved, I would find that proof.

I knew what I had to do, but the thought made me ill with fear. Fear of the ordeal I would have to face, and fear of the possibility that, instead of proving Lucian's accusations false, I would be proving them true. And fear that I was on the brink of the end of the world as I knew it.

After delaying the inevitable for as many hours as I could, I changed into jeans and a sweater and made my way to the door I'd never opened. If the doorknob had been a snake, I might have grasped it more eagerly, more firmly. Once the knob sat in the curve of my palm, I was shaking so hard that I couldn't turn it. How much more time passed, I don't know, but eventually my trembling eased enough for me to twist the doorknob open.

More time slipped away as I stood before the narrow opening, gathering what little courage I had, and fighting the fear. An inch at a time, I drew the door back, until it stood yawning open, like the wide jaws of a monster preparing to devour me. The dark stairwell was the gullet leading to the even blacker darkness of the basement, like the belly of Jonah's whale.

When I was an adventurous four-year-old, I'd wandered off our property to explore the forbidden mysteries of a neighboring estate. I fell through the rotted flooring of a cabin that had all but disappeared through neglect, and had been trapped in the depths of the dank, dark root cellar. My parents had, along with the police and the media, assumed I'd been kidnapped for ransom. They'd waited in agony for a call until the second day, when my father, walking off his tension, noticed his dogs whining around what appeared to be a grassy mound.

I'd believed utterly in my parents' ability to find me. But this time, I had lost my faith in miracles even before I faced the unknown. This time, I had only myself to depend upon, which made my fears more painfully acute.

What if I failed to disprove Lucian's accusations? What if I failed to rescue myself from the cavern at the base of the stairs?

I don't know how long I stood clinging to the doorknob of the door to the basement; eventually, I became aware of being very cold and very tired. Telling myself a deliberate lie, hoping it would thereby become true, I declared out loud that as soon as I'd rested a bit, I would have the strength—moral as well as physical—to make my way down the stairs. Then I released the doorknob and sank to the floor to sit and gather my courage.

At some point, hugging myself for warmth, I fell asleep on the marble floor at the top of the stairs. My dreams were fevered fantasies of dragons, bright lights, swords, and a palace of crystalline ice. A dragon of uncommon beauty gloatingly held me prisoner, defending its frozen castle with fierce blasts of cold flames. As knight after knight fell in defeat, I pleaded with the beast to release me before I froze to death, but, in the terrible frustration of dreams, my words came out unintelligible, even to my own ears.

Suddenly the dragon lashed at me with its strong tail, and crippling pain tangled my limbs. Ice and fire burned me with equal cruelty. Struggling uselessly, I wailed in protest, but the beast's tail only wrapped more tightly around me, holding me immobilized. A searing heat began to surround me, relentlessly pulling the breath from my lungs. With the last shred of strength I could draw from the deepest part of me, I struck out wildly.

And awoke to find myself in the library. I was bundled in Joshua's arms, wrapped in blankets and huddled in front of a roaring hearth with Laurel and Hardy dancing and whimpering in excitement nearby. Despite the warmth around me, I was shivering uncontrollably, and too groggy and disoriented to know where I was or what the time of day was.

All I knew was that the residual fears from my nightmare

were evaporating in the heat of Joshua's embrace. I tipped my head back so I could see his face, and the heat I felt washing over me then had nothing to do with the fire.

I blinked to clear my vision. "Wha—what happened?"

"I should be asking you that." He sounded half angry, half relieved. "What were you doing sleeping on the floor in the middle of a blizzard?"

I blinked again, as if that could clear my hearing. "Blizzard?" I echoed, totally puzzled.

"Blizzard," he repeated firmly. "Almost two feet of snow, and the ice and wind knocked out the power all around. There's no electricity, no phones, and this place is freezing."

I freed one hand to push my hair away from my face, and touched Joshua's shoulder in the process. His *bare* shoulder! And yes, the air out of the direct line of the fire was as cold as a deep freeze.

"Where's your shirt?"

He gave me a crooked grin. "Around you. You were so cold when I found you, and I knew it would take me a few minutes to find blankets and start the fire."

Something in his answer struck me as out of place, but my brain was as frozen as the rest of me. I mulled over his words until it came to me.

"How did you get in here? Did I leave the door unlocked?" I frowned, trying to recall my actions before I faced the ordeal of the stairs. "I thought I'd locked up after Olive left."

"Matthew gave me a passkey. He asked me to look after you while he was away." I think I gasped in surprise. Joshua gazed deeply into my eyes, his own glowing with sincerity. "Damn good thing, under the circumstances, too. Dumb me, I thought you had enough sense to listen to a weather report, maybe get some candles together and pile a few logs on the fire. What the hell were you doing?"

His indignation sparked some of my own. "I fell. . . ." My indignation dissolved when I realized how silly my reason for lying on the cold marble floor would sound. Oh, and then I'd have to tell Joshua about my basement problem. No, this was enough embarrassment for one night, or morning, or whenever it was. I shut my mouth, but the glint in Joshua's eyes warned me it was too late to backtrack.

"You *fell*? Were you sick? Did you get hurt? Damn! I

shouldn't have moved you. Did you hit your head?''

"I fell *asleep*."

He gave me another one of those long, searching looks. "You were trying to go downstairs."

The way he phrased the comment told me that I'd been hiding my basement phobia in vain. Matthew must have mentioned it, no doubt in connection with his request that Joshua take care of me in his absence. Feeling incredibly foolish, I looked away from Joshua's piercing gaze, but I nodded in silent confirmation. The crackle and hiss of the fire were the only sounds for a while. Then Joshua growled under his breath like a tiger issuing a warning of potential danger. The Yorkies growled in response, but I was in no mood to find them amusing.

"Angela, what did you expect to find, a blueprint for fraud? I've seen the computer installation down there. It's not some friendly desktop any eleven-year-old could figure out. That's why guys like Matthew—and Lucian—study for years."

His tone was scolding, but his arms stayed comfortably secure around me. It was similar to the many times in my childhood when one of my parents had held me and simultaneously chastised me for whatever trouble I'd gotten into . . . but different. Very different. My parents had transmitted a feeling of security that was the absolute opposite of the tremulous uncertainty, the subliminal excitement of anticipation, that emanated from Joshua. Before answering, I had to duck my head to avoid revealing my response, and my confusion at my response.

"Maybe you're right, but I needed to try . . . I don't know what I might have found, but I owe it to Matthew to try."

With typical patience, Joshua said nothing, giving me a waiting silence in which to think. And soon, I came to the inevitable, disappointing conclusion.

"I guess you're right. There's nothing I can do except hope no one ever discovers what . . ." I couldn't accuse Matthew. "What happened to the money." A sigh whooshed out of me. "But that's so wrong, too. I have to be sure nothing else has been done to threaten the foundation's financial security. As soon as the holidays are over, I'll arrange an audit, and if restitution has to be made, I'll cover the deficit personally."

Joshua's warm, callused fingertips traced over my brow, my

cheeks, my chin, and finally, my lips. The slight trembling in
his touch surprised me. Lifting my head to peer over the edge
of the blankets bundled around me, I met his black-lashed blue
eyes and became transfixed by their light, their depth. Without
conscious intent, I worked my hand out of the fold of the
blanket and once again touched his bare shoulder.

Unlike the first, accidental, time I'd touched him like this,
the smooth heat of his skin, the hard curve of bone and muscle
didn't surprise me. But the swift-as-lightning, sharp-as-a-razor
sensations that arced along my own skin startled a gasp from
me. Something changed in Joshua's eyes, telling me that he'd
read my reaction correctly, and then he bent his head toward
me slowly. Always a gentleman, he was giving me time to
react, time to stop him. Stopping, however, wasn't an option
I wanted.

My eyelids drifted closed under the intensity of his gaze,
and I trembled with anticipation, eager for, afraid of, the feel
of his kiss. His lips were smooth, warm, undemanding. I let
myself simply accept the contact as I breathed in his scent, a
fresh and wholly masculine combination of piney fresh air,
wood, and the subtle spice of male skin and aftershave.

Then, as if my body had a will of its own, my hand tightened on the hard contour of his shoulder. I heard his indrawn
breath, and then felt myself being lifted, rocked, and tumbled,
as the pressure of his lips increased. Dizzily I fumbled to bring
my other arm outside the blankets cocooning me, seeking the
stability of Joshua's broad shoulders with both hands. The
movement somehow led to me parting my lips under his, and
he moaned softly. That pent-up sound sent a wave of desire
washing over me, and I heard myself answering with a purring
sound from the back of my throat.

And still, Joshua kissed me softly, sweetly, as if his patience
was limitless. The heat of the snapping, roaring fire beside us
increased the heat rising from the blankets between us. I didn't
want blankets. I didn't want anything between us, not cloth,
not fear, not suspicion, not sadness. The strength of the ache
to feel Joshua's body intimately holding mine amazed me, dazzled me, took control of me. I'd never felt anything like this
before. It was both frightening and wonderful, and my sense
of wonder was far stronger than my sense of caution.

With more courage than experience to guide me, I began

exploring the living marble of Joshua's sculpted arms. As my fingers traced the dips and swells of hard muscle, he quivered in gratifying response. With a low groan echoing in his chest, he drew me closer and deepened the kiss. I opened my lips to the hot probing of his tongue and another groan, more urgent than the last, reverberated through him.

Finally! Finally, I was breaking through that incredible reserve of his! Now, with my hands sliding over the warm contours of Joshua's naked back, with his mouth devouring mine, the only wonder I felt was for the restraint making him tremble.

When he lifted his head, he gave me a heavy-lidded half smile. I think I smiled back, but I was too dazed to know my own name right then.

Joshua lowered his head, but instead of meeting my lips with his, he covered my face with tiny kisses. By the time his mouth reached mine, I was starving for the taste of him and greeted his kiss eagerly. While we kissed, he began unwrapping the blankets that had warmed my chilled body, and now held me prisoner, overheated by desire even more than by fire. Impatiently, I wriggled against the blankets, trying to help him free me, probably impeding his progress instead. Briefly, he broke the sweet contact between our mouths, and when our eyes met, we both laughed softly at our predicament.

Then the last layer of blanket between us gave way, and Joshua lifted the edge of my sweater, exposing my midriff. Our gazes stayed locked on each other. At the first touch of his hand on my skin, I sucked in a gasp and anticipation silenced our laughter. Only a few inches separated our bodies, his partially bare, mine quivering to be naked and feel him against me.

I expected him to slide his hand up my ribs to my breast, but he apparently intended to make me wait. Instead, he returned to kissing me with slow, sweet, deep thoroughness as if he had no other need, no other interests, as if he had all the time in the world to tease me with tenderness. Soon, my impatience dissolved into a haze of appreciation for the art of kissing as if kisses were the sweetest, thickest port, the most intoxicating champagne, the most warming cognac.

Joshua's kisses were all that, and more.

Eventually, though, the haze of sweetness surrounding me

once again gave way to an impatience to feel more than his
lips on mine. I wanted Joshua's hunger, not his patience, not
his restraint. I'd had enough of those.

But bold and impulsive as I could be about many things,
lovemaking was something that made me feel just the opposite.
How could I convince him I was ready for a new level of
intimacy? I couldn't just blurt out what I wanted!

But I could *show* him, couldn't I? Oh, yes!

I worked my hand between us, and hesitantly touched his
ribs. Joshua inhaled sharply but his lips stayed on mine, so I
slowly flattened my hand on the ridged muscles of his stomach. At that, he began to tremble almost imperceptibly, which
I decided was an encouraging sign. Inching my hand upward,
I absorbed his heat, the wild surges of his pulse, the quivering
of his skin. It was like being the first to stroke the satiny hide
of an untamed stallion who has agreed, for the moment, for
his own reasons, to trust a stranger's touch.

When my fingers brushed the silky hairs of his chest,
Joshua's whole body jerked. I felt his nipple harden under my
gently probing fingertips, heard him inhale shakily, so I did
the same caressing stroke on the other side, seeking and finding the same reaction. With a self-satisfied sort of smile forming on my lips, I slid my palm back across his chest and held
it firmly over his pounding heart.

Joshua's moan vibrated through both of us, but just as I was
beginning to think I knew what I was doing, he moved too
quickly for me to anticipate. Less than a heartbeat later, I was
lying flat under him, my arms above my head, my wrists man-
acled in one of his strong hands. Amazingly, our mouths still
clung; when I gasped in surprise, Joshua simply thrust his
tongue deeper. With his free hand, he pushed the lower edge
of my sweater up and eased his fingers under, lightly tickling
my ribs.

And then his warm hand covered my breast. The most wonderful sensations rippled through me, like the first waves of a
rising tide. But even as I arched reflexively into his palm, even
as I absorbed the honey of his kisses, even as I felt the tingling
of arousal, the swelling of sexual need, I felt something more.
I felt *healing*, sharp, painful, soothing healing, as if some
power flowed through Joshua's hand and into my heart.

Breathlessly, I savored the taste of his kisses and tried to draw him closer. As the blankets unwound under our combined movements, I felt Joshua's long legs tangling with mine. Instinct prompted me to bend my knees and guide him to me. In the first instant of contact, the magnitude of his arousal was almost frightening. In the next instant, with the hard length of him nestled firmly between my thighs, his arousal became mine.

Suddenly, he pulled away and sat just beyond my reach, his breathing ragged and labored. The flickering light of the fire gilded his torso. His face, turned away from me, remained in shadows. I waited, but he didn't look at me, didn't speak. The only sounds were the crackling of the fire and the gasping breaths he drew.

I lay quietly a moment, feeling stunned, confused, hurt. And—after several minutes passed without a word or a movement from Joshua—angry. Despite the heat of the fire and the body warmth still rising from my cocoon of blankets, the chill in the surrounding air was the sensation I felt most acutely.

"Oh, God, I'm sorry." His hoarse words were barely audible.

"Sorry for starting or sorry for stopping?" My voice was hoarse as well, but sharp with indignation. Under any other circumstances, I would have winced at my shrewish tone.

Joshua turned to face me, his expression so tormented that I couldn't hold back a soft cry of dismay. It didn't seem possible, but at the sound, he looked even more troubled.

"I shouldn't have allowed that to happen. I promised Matthew I would take care of you, not seduce you."

Men! Why did they think they were responsible for everything—good or bad—that occurred in the world?

"Allow . . . ? That certainly seemed mutual to me! In case you haven't noticed, I'm an adult, well over the age of consent. Since when are taking care of me—assuming I let you—and making love to me mutually exclusive, anyway? If you had doubts about my complicity, you could have asked me, instead of making a unilateral decision."

We stared at each other for a long moment, and then, for the first time in our acquaintance, Joshua looked away from my eyes. That unsettled me more than being dropped like a hot potato. My pulse began racing uncomfortably, and my stomach churned.

Joshua finally met my eyes. "I . . . I got carried away. You're vulnerable, Angela, even if you don't think you are. It would be wrong for me to take advantage of you now."

If I hadn't been raised to behave in a ladylike manner at all times, I would have kicked him!

"Fine," I responded breezily, while gathering my blankets around me. Rising, thankfully without tripping, I aimed my most haughty look down at his unhappy face. "You'll be sure to let me know when it's right for you to take advantage of me, won't you?"

His confused expression was most gratifying. I smiled frostily and turned to walk away. After a night sleeping on a marble floor, I could use some freshening up. And I was desperate to put as much space between us as possible. There was a hearth in my bedroom, and a small store of logs. Once a fire was going, I'd gather candles and flashlights, find the old transistor radio Father kept for emergencies like this, and make myself breakfast. Then I'd find so many things to do that I wouldn't have a second to ruminate on this humiliating incident.

"Uh, Angela?" Joshua slowly got to his feet. With his bare torso, he was a lean, bronze Colossus in jeans.

Now that he was standing, I had to look up, but I still managed a cool lift of one eyebrow in what I hoped was an expression of regal patience.

"Yes?"

"Could I have my shirts back?"

All the training I'd endured to become an unflappable, gracious-under-fire lady—all those hours I considered unfairly wasted with a tutor while Matthew played sports with his friends—preserved my dignity. After a hasty, silent prayer of gratitude to my mother, who'd been right and wise after all— how many times had she predicted that someday, I would thank her for those lessons in etiquette and deportment and social graces?—I gave Joshua another frosty smile.

"Of course. They're hardly anything I'd care to keep."

Letting the blankets pool around my feet in a deliberately careless gesture, I slid Joshua's shirts off one at a time. A faint trace of his scent drifted around me as the fabric billowed. First the soft, navy plaid flannel shirt, then a red waffle-knit thermal shirt, warm from our bodies and carrying our mingled scents. I felt rather proud of myself for handing the shirts to

Joshua without betraying my sense of rejection. The chill in the air was an appropriate dose of reality.

"Thank you for lending them to me. You can see yourself out, I'm sure."

With a curtseylike dip, I caught up the still-warm blankets and wrapped them around my shoulders. My intention was to dismiss Joshua, then stalk upstairs to my own rooms, where I could cry my heart out undisturbed. But when Joshua began slipping into his shirts, I couldn't make myself look away, let alone walk away. The thermal shirt slid up his muscular arms and across his bare back, a poor surrogate for the heated embrace we'd been sharing. Before buttoning the thermal shirt, he shrugged into the plaid one, giving me extra time to stare at his broad chest.

Once, while buttoning his shirts, Joshua glanced at me, then turned his attention back to his task. Before I realized what was happening, his beautifully strong hands were going to the belt of his jeans. With a belatedly smothered gasp, I tugged my blankets more firmly around me and executed a half-pirouette toward the doorway. Two steps into my grand exit, the scrape of a zipper reached me, and I tripped over a trailing edge of the blankets. A blush I had absolutely no control over singed my ears and my cheeks, but I kept my chin high, and continued as if nothing were wrong. As if I weren't even the slightest bit tempted to help Joshua tuck his shirts into his jeans—or, preferably, to help him untuck them.

I almost succeeded.

"Angela, where are you going?"

His voice was gentle, but his tone conveyed the message that if I didn't answer, he'd pursue the subject. And at that moment, he was the last person I wanted to see or hear. Recalling the unfortunate fate of Lot's wife, I paused without looking back.

"Upstairs."

"You'll freeze up there. Stay here by the fire for a while."

"There are two hearths in my rooms. I'll be perfectly fine, thank you." I took another step toward my escape route—

"Do you want to go to bed?"

—and tripped over a corner of the blanket, setting the overloaded Christmas tree swaying dangerously before landing awkwardly in one of a pair of tapestry-covered Queen Anne wingback chairs.

Joshua was all over me before I could catch a breath. Not that catching my breath would have helped, since his touches made inhaling and exhaling nearly impossible. Pride just couldn't resist a fall.

"Are you all right?"

Unable to look at him, I kept my head turned away but nodded. And I would have been fine if Joshua hadn't gently brushed my hair back from my face. His light touch undid me. I felt the sting of tears and tried biting my lip to control them, but I'd never been very good at that. If Joshua had simply risen then, he might not have known I was trying not to cry. But the man seemed determined to torment me, to make every situation as uncomfortable as possible. This wasn't, I was sure, what Matthew had had in mind when he'd asked Joshua to look after me in his absence.

"Angela, baby, don't cry. I'm not worth it."

Of course, he was probably right, but that knowledge didn't do me the slightest bit of good. Instead, his contrite confession undid the last vestiges of my control. A sob hiccupped out of me, and the next thing I knew, Joshua was gathering me into his arms again.

"I'm not crying over you! I'm crying over . . . everything!" I wiped at my eyes with a corner of blanket. "Except you."

"Ah. Good, then. Do you want me to take you up to bed?"

Unable to meet his eyes, I emphatically shook my head, an unspoken lie, because, of course, that was exactly what I wanted him to do.

"No. I'll be fine here. Thank you for checking on me, but Olive has everything prepared for an emergency. You may leave now." Hearing the imperious snub in my own voice made me wince inwardly in embarrassment. I'd never acted the spoiled princess, even when given the role. Now, my behavior had passed spoiled and gone all the way to rotten, and I was ashamed of myself for it. On the other hand, I don't know how I could have done anything differently.

I could *feel* Joshua's searching look, even though I refused to meet his eyes. After a long, silent, and dreadfully awkward moment, he patted my knee and stood. Despite the muffling effect: of layers of blankets, I felt the touch of his hand as clearly as if my skin had been bare. Awareness sent a shiver along my spine; pride required me to suppress it.

"I do have to leave now," he told me. "But I'll be back later to check on you."

"No need, thank you all the same. I'm sure you'd prefer to spend Christmas with your family."

"Angela, I said I'll be back."

He spoke with an insistent finality that fueled a fading spark of hope that Joshua did care, more than a little, in a special way. Curious to see the expression in his eyes, I began to lift my head.

"I gave Matthew my word."

His qualifying comment halted me before I could disgrace myself further by gazing up at him like a lovesick puppy.

"On Matthew's behalf, I thank you," I responded haughtily. "And on my own behalf, now that Matthew is gone, I release you from your promise." Then, feeling a little more in control of my reactions, I tipped my head up and gave Joshua a cheery, utterly phony smile. "Merry Christmas, Joshua. Don't forget to shut the door on your way out."

He stood there scowling down at me for a good thirty seconds, then muttered some words I'd never heard from him before and strode out of the room. A moment later, I heard the front door slam shut, but I couldn't release my breath until I heard the thud of his Explorer's door and the roar of the starting engine.

I let the dogs out to their sheltered run behind the house and refilled their dishes for breakfast. By then, the grumbling of my stomach sent me hunting for something for my own breakfast. The interior of the house, usually well lit, was filled with an almost palpable grayness that the dim light from outside seemed to highlight, not penetrate. Peeking out a kitchen window, I saw a stark and bleak landscape. Our property stretched for several wooded acres around the house, so none of the neighboring homes were visible. Ice and snow coated everything in sight, but this was no winter wonderland. The thin, pale daylight cast no sparkles on the ice-encrusted branches of trees, as a bright sun would have. There was no sense of magic about this view. This, I imagined, was a vision of Hell frozen over.

Before filling my stomach, I gathered several hurricane
lamps and as many thick emergency candles as I could find in
Olive's well-stocked pantry. The flickering yellow flames
helped dispel some of the gloom in the house, but I couldn't
help being uncomfortably aware of the darkness hovering just
at the edge of the light. After munching some crackers and
cheese, accompanied by a glass of cranberry juice, I filled
Olive's old-fashioned kettle with bottled water and found an
antique cast-iron trivet. Back in the living room, I set the trivet
near the brightly burning fire, and set the kettle on top. In
theory, the water would soon be hot enough for tea. Laurel
and Hardy, having devoured their kibble, curled up in front of
the hearth to paw lazily at each other.

The phone lines were down, as well as the power lines. By
cell phone, I reached coordinators of most of the nearest shelters and soup kitchens. Although I offered my services, as well
as any supplies they might need, everyone assured me that
they had enough food and blankets, and enough volunteers to
hold the planned Christmas dinners and parties for the children. It was gratifying to know the blizzard hadn't stolen the
holiday from these beneficiaries of the McMichael Foundation.

That thought fetched another, less pleasant, thought: I'd
never finished sorting those Christmas and sympathy cards
piled on the dining room table. With tea steeping in the hot
kettle, I made my way to fetch the cards, my blankets trailing
after me. I decided to crown myself the Queen of Gloom. By
the light of several oil lamps, I sat on the thickly carpeted floor
in front of the hearth and resumed sorting the cards into two
baskets, to be answered when my assistant returned from holiday leave.

I turned over an envelope addressed personally to me, and
Matthew's bold writing shocked me breathless. Despite the
heat from the fire and the coziness of my blankets, a terrible
chill gripped me. For a long moment, I simply sat staring at
the card in my trembling hand, until the letters blurred and the
lines fragmented into many, like the images inside the kaleidoscope I'd made for Matthew. The hot splash of a tear on
the back of my hand broke my trance.

Slipping the card from the envelope, I saw the bright colors
of a boldly painted Nativity scene, showing the three Wise
Men near the manger, in which the haloed infant Jesus lay.

The closest of the three men stood bent over the manger, his face focused on the child. A pendant dangling from a chain around his neck had swung forward, and in a touchingly babylike gesture, Jesus had closed a chubby infant fist around it. Mary, smiling at the Mage, had a hand raised, as if to assure the man that all was well. The tableau was so sweet, so natural yet so spiritual, that I found myself smiling as well.

Trust Matthew to find a card this special.

But why had my brother sent me a Christmas card through the mail? Had he simply forgotten to send one with the fish ornament?

With unsteady fingers, I opened the card. Matthew's bold writing, tamed to conserve space, covered the inside surfaces of the heavy cream paper. Tears blurred my vision several times as I read his message, but eventually I made my way to the end. Then, still blinking away tears, I reread the card several times, trying to assimilate the meaning of his words.

Angela:

Remember how your nanny Bridget used to tell you all those old stories about heroic women? You loved hearing your favorites over and over again. I used to think you did that just to irritate me, when I was acting like the obnoxious big brother. Mother always claimed that revenge wasn't in your nature, but if it was, it probably served me right. And, as Father used to say, Mother was seldom wrong.

Revenge never was in your nature, but I hope to heaven that heroism is.

At Christmas, Bridget used to tell a story about one of the Wise Men and a pendant like the Star of Bethlehem. She claimed it was based on an ancient Christmas carol almost no one knows anymore, based on a legend about Jesus endowing this pendant with magical properties. The star pendant could avert a major disaster, like a war, and bring true lovers together.

The catch was, the magic only worked for a woman, a special woman who loved wisely, and only on the Christmas at the end of a century. Between centuries, it disappeared mysteriously. At the right time, it would just as mysteriously be found, by that special woman, inside a large fish.

Remember how, every Christmas, you'd tell anyone who'd listen—and anyone who didn't want to listen— that you wanted to be that woman? You said you would use the pendant's power to save the world and find a true love to marry. That always made me laugh; in my childish wisdom, I thought females were helpless, and love was an illusion that made men do foolish things.

The Christmas after your accident, Dad took me aside and asked me not to tease you again about your ambitions. It wasn't easy at first, because you played the role of the little princess so well: a guilelessly charming beauty with perfect manners, who almost always did as she was told. It pains me to admit I was often jealous, even though, like everyone who ever met you, I also adored you.

Now I know you are a mix of Father's intellect and Mother's heart. Your compassion, your faith in your fellow man, your ambitions to help those less fortunate than ourselves, are genuine. So is your intelligence.

Eventually, I understood Father's primary concern: how difficult it was going to be for you to find a man who would love you for yourself, not for your beauty, your social graces, and especially, not for your portion of the family fortune. And that's where Bridget's Christmas legend comes in:

> *Break open the papier-mâché fish ornament when you receive it. The star sapphire pendant inside came from an antique shop called "Pisces." I'd like to believe it's the real Star of the Magi, the star of wonder of Bridget's legend. Maybe it is. This old world of ours could use some powerful magic right about now.*

Hold on to your faith, Angela. Love wisely, and maybe, in the gateway between the second millennium and the third, you can save the world.

> *Your loving brother, Matthew.*

I made my way through the letter several times. Each reading left me with more questions and fewer answers. Was I holding a suicide note? A veiled confession of wrongdoing? Evidence that my brother fancied himself a prophet, or was just plain paranoid?

Ah, but Bridget's wonderful Christmas tale of the *other* Star of the Magi, the one worn as a pendant by Melchior! Matthew recalled correctly that I loved that tale more than any other. And yes, for many years, I firmly—and vocally—believed that I was destined to be the next woman to find the pendant and use its special powers to save the world. Of course, back then, I had no idea what the world might need saving from, nor had I any clue what would be needed to save it. Now, unfortunately, the papers and the news carried story after story about how, in the most technologically advanced era of the world's history, humans were going to Hell in the proverbial handbasket.

How on earth could *I* save even a small part of the world, even with a magical pendant?

A magical pendant? Matthew had to be teasing me about that. Perhaps he'd hidden some additional notes inside the velvet pouch that held the pendant. The logical thing to do was open it and see for myself. Wrapped in my blankets, the Yorkies pouncing on the trailing corners, I made my way through the gloomy house to the family parlor and the Christmas tree where the velvet pouch lay. The air, once I got a rather short distance from the blazing hearth in the living room, was bitingly cold. I could see my breath on the air. My teeth chattered uncontrollably, making me feel terribly clumsy.

When I picked up Matthew's gift, I noticed a dull gold point now protruded from the drawstring opening of the bag. I untied the silken strings and worked the pouch open. Impossible as it sounds, the object inside seemed to leap into my hand.

It was, as Matthew's letter had described, an antique gold pendant shaped like a Christmas star, set with a star sapphire about the size of a quail egg. The ageless beauty of the piece transfixed me even more than the astounding size of the stone, easily a twin of the legendary Star of India. The smooth dome of the sapphire seemed to twinkle and wink at me with some hidden inner light. I realized I no longer felt cold. In astonishment, I sat down on the carpet, the blankets around me, the Yorkies chasing each other across the room.

I stared at the gem lying in my palm. *Love wisely and save the world*—Matthew's advice whispered to me from the depth of my heart. But what did that mean?

I continued to gaze at the star sapphire, hoping it was indeed magical enough to provide answers to the questions circling my mind. All that happened was my vision blurred until I had to blink to clear it. Turning the piece over in my fingers, I saw a small gold ring fastened to the back, where a cord or a necklace could be threaded through. Perhaps if I wore the gem now as a pendant, it would somehow suggest what I needed to do. I had nothing to lose by trying. Perhaps, as Joshua had said yesterday, that was what faith was for.

A quick look around me yielded a package neatly wrapped and tied with a length of gold cord. Still holding the pendant in my left hand, I fumbled with the cord until it came free of the present it bound. Then I slid the cord through the small gold ring and tied a knot in it. When I slipped the cord over my head, the pendant lay against my chest with its lower point just between my breasts.

None of the answers to my questions flashed into my mind, but a sense of having done the right thing filled me with that sense of peace that was becoming oddly familiar. I wondered if the ancient pendant truly had the power to influence people and their environments, or whether that was just wishful thinking.

Now that I'd satisfied my curiosity about Matthew's gift, there were some basic survival issues to tackle. I gathered up my blankets and shivered and stumbled my way upstairs to my rooms. I needed warm clothing that would allow me to abandon the trailing blankets Joshua had wrapped around me. Ski clothes would do, if they were layered enough. The air felt cold enough to chip like ice, yet I felt warm inside as I removed the clothes I'd been wearing. I piled on insulating layers of fresh clothes, then shooed the Yorkies back downstairs.

Finally, bundled into a parka and my heaviest boots, I stomped through the kitchen and the mud room to bring in more wood. The dogs scampered and tumbled outside in the snow, but today their antics failed to make me smile. The sky seemed a dull, rusty yellow, and except for the noises the Yorkies made, the entire world was eerily silent. No birds. No traffic. No voices. If I didn't know better, I might believe I was the only person in the world.

Giving myself a hard mental shake, I set to work bringing in the wood. On my third trip to the woodpile, I thought I saw movement, a brief glimpse of something dark disappearing around the front corner of the house. I'd already sent the dogs inside so they wouldn't get too cold, so there was no one to confirm my impression. Ax in hand, I trudged a little way through the dense snow, but saw no one, so I trudged back to finish hauling armloads of split logs.

Back inside and fairly steamy from exertion, I hurried to peel off some of my layers. Sudden pounding on the front door caught me with a sweater over my head. With my heart pounding in counterpoint, I hurried to the door, then, on impulse, stopped to peer through the peephole. My early-morning caller could have been someone from the security company that monitors our alarms, checking up on me because of the power failure. But instead of some uniformed stranger, Lucian's pale, worried face filled my view, distorted by the convex lens.

Relieved to see him, grateful for his concern, I swung the door open wide and greeted him with a hug. After a brief hesitation, his arms came around me, as much as possible since he wore a heavy parka, and he returned my hug, adding a quick kiss to the top of my head. When we parted, he bent to remove his snow-crusted galoshes, then unwound the scarf around his neck.

He gave me a close, serious look. "Are you all right?"

"Snug as a bug." I smiled more cheerily than I felt, because Lucian looked more worried than I warranted. "I've got some hot tea by the fireplace. Come in and get warm before you take off your jacket." I headed toward the living room. Over my shoulder, I asked, "Is your aunt all right?"

"Uh, yeah. I was awake when the power went, so I got a fire going before the house got too cold. Aunt Agatha is fine." He looked past me. "Thanks."

My very British ancestors would no doubt be tumbling in their graves at my desecration of the tea steeping by the fire. It was strong enough to climb out of the pot by then, so I added more water, and then fortified our mugs with enough sugar to stand a spoon. Lucian crouched near the hearth with his pale hands cupping his mug. The Yorkies, oddly subdued, snuggled next to me and watched him curiously with their huge, dark eyes. It occurred to me that I'd never actually seen the dogs approach Lucian, or seen him make any friendly overtures toward the dogs. I wondered whether he disliked dogs or had a fear of them. But how could anyone not love those two little imps, let alone be afraid of them?

Love wisely and save the world. Unexpectedly, Matthew's words swirled around my memory. Was the pendant telling me I should love Lucian, not Joshua?

With strangely inappropriate, almost boyish enthusiasm, Lucian described the utter chaos the overnight storm had caused.

"This is nothing compared to what will happen on the dot of midnight, New Year's Eve. Between the utilities going down and the world's financial institutions losing most of their records, it's going to be ugly." He sounded excited about the prospect.

I was puzzled. "But I thought almost everyone was prepared now. All the experts, except for the inflammatory fringe, say the only glitches will be minor."

Lucian shook his head, his expression rather fierce. "It's not true, you know. They want to keep people from panicking, but things are worse than the official versions claim." He set down his mug and picked up my gloved hand, his gaze locked on mine. "We don't have much time, Angela, but I've been preparing as much as I can in advance. I'll take care of you."

Another one! Matthew must have lined up potential caretakers for me all over southern Connecticut. Had he anticipated not returning? Did he really believe, after knowing me all my life, that I was in need of a protector? I tried to withdraw my hand, but Lucian tightened his fingers.

"The basement is fortified now," he continued. "People may start rioting. There's food, water, medicines, clothing, fuel for heaters, a CB radio, and a generator. Even . . ." His pale cheeks turned ruddy. "Even a camp toilet, and . . . and everything. It's all the best money could buy, so you'll be safe and comfortable."

The basement?

I'd rather take my chances with rioters.

But I didn't want to hurt Lucian's feelings, so I smiled. "Thank you, Lucian. I'm sure it won't be necessary, but I appreciate all your preparations. And I'm certain that Matthew . . . If Matthew could know, he would be grateful."

Lucian's pale eyes narrowed. "Matthew didn't believe in the 'End-of-the-World-As-We-Know-It' scenario, either. Or maybe he finally believed me, and that was why he had a contingency plan."

Exerting a little extra effort, I succeeded in pulling my hand out of his. "Contingency plan?" I didn't like the sound of that. "Matthew died en route to a diving vacation. I refuse to believe he could do anything criminal."

"I feel the same way, Angela. He took me seriously when everyone in my family considered me a misfit."

At his wistful tone, I felt myself soften toward Lucian again. I recalled how miserable he'd been as an adolescent, unable to fulfill expectations of taking his place in his family's dynasty. Matthew had persuaded Lucian's parents to allow him to live with a widowed sister of his mother, his Aunt Agatha, in the next town to ours. If not for that aunt, our parents would have taken Lucian into our own family, but Lucian himself declined their offers.

"But the proof is irrefutable." He spoke stubbornly.

Just as stubbornly, I clung to my disbelief and vehemently shook my head.

He set his jaw. "The experts are advising people to stock up on cash, Angela, because the bank computers won't work, so the ATMs won't work. But there are some of us who believe cash will be worthless without the banks behind it. I'm positive Matthew was on his way to buy gold, the only truly universal currency."

Again, I shook my head. Lucian scowled.

"We discussed it many times, Angela. Matthew agreed it was a prudent idea. A person could buy a lot of gold for five hundred million in cash."

I couldn't bear to hear any more. "Lucian, stop it, please! Unless you can show me and the auditors proof, I won't tolerate any further slander of Matthew, by anyone, even you!"

Agitated, I jumped to my feet. At that precise instant, all the lights flashed on in the house, and the alarm system began to shriek. The Yorkies awoke and started yapping at some imagined enemy. Crying out in surprise, I ran to the keypad to silence the noise. A second later, the phone rang. It was the security company, checking on me, assuring me they'd send a technician to test the system before evening. When I returned to the hearth, Lucian was standing, his expression sheepish.

"I'm sorry, Angela. I ... I didn't mean to upset you. I ... I better be going, but I'd like to come back later?" He flashed a boyish smile that lit the angelic beauty he hid behind those thick glasses. "I have a present for you."

Relieved that he wasn't pursuing his accusations further, I nodded. "I have something for you, too. Call first, please—"

His smile faded but he nodded. "Thanks for the tea. I have to check on the computers. I'll let myself out from downstairs." He crossed the room toward the doors to the hall, then turned back. "Don't forget. I'll be taking care of you when the world falls apart on New Year's Eve. You won't have to do anything. I'll take care of everything. I promise."

Lucian's earnestness left me dumbfounded, and just a tiny bit uneasy. He was taking a "worst-case scenario" caused by the so-called "millennium bug" so very seriously. Emergency supplies in the basement. Gold. It seemed he was envisioning the world of next week as the setting of a futuristic doomsday movie, like *The Terminator* or *Mad Max*. Briefly, I wondered if he'd gone so far as to hide a gun in the basement, then dismissed the notion as totally out of character. Lucian was too gentle to swat a fly; it was one of the qualities that had made his father despair of ever turning his only son into a properly macho heir.

I spent the next few hours on the phone assuring worried callers I was fine, negotiating with various service providers to minimize the interruption in daily life. There were shut-ins who depended on us to ensure delivery of hot meals, and others who needed assistance with clearing snow from their walkways and doing their own errands. These were only some of the things the foundation did locally; with Matthew gone, it was my responsibility to see that these activities continued as usual.

Even though the heating system was now working, I decided to maintain the fire in the living room hearth. In a New England winter, it was always prudent to be ready for the worst.

Which brought my thoughts back around to Lucian's unexpected bunker mentality. The urge to see his survival preparations in the basement refused to stop nagging at me. Several times during the course of the day, I found myself standing at the basement door, peering into the deep well of the stairs. Each time, I failed to summon the courage necessary to overcome my phobia.

Finally, with the sun tinting the low gray sky faintly pink, I made up my mind I had to go downstairs because of Matthew. I had to do whatever I could to reassure myself that he had died with his soul untarnished by the fraud, the deception, Lucian was so certain he could prove. How I would do this, I didn't know. How else the sum of five hundred million dollars could have been diverted to an account in Matthew's name in the Cayman Islands, I also didn't know. Nor did I have a clue what I would do with whatever truth I might find.

Wistfully I thought of Joshua, but after our argument this morning, whatever we'd had between us was likely over. I didn't really expect him to return. That was just something he'd said to sound in control of the situation. A guy thing—like "I'll call you."

But all of that was immaterial. At some point during the course of that mostly silent, bleak day preceding Christmas Eve, my need to find the truth overcame my abject fear of being in a basement.

It was a blessing in disguise that I'd forgotten to eat all day. Taking the first step left me shaking violently and fighting nausea. Sweat beaded on my face and trickled down my back. My hands, even my knees, trembled uncontrollably. I lost track of how long it took me to take the next step down, then the next, resting between each, clutching my roiling stomach and gulping for air.

A quarter of the way down the flight of stairs, I heard a muffled thump and started so badly that I nearly slid down the rest of the way. My heart hammered wildly, and tension tightened my throat, choking my air supply, threatening to render me light-headed. Hardy, followed closely by Laurel, dashed past me and scampered into the basement. I must not have shut them into the library before embarking on this adventure. A sigh of relief whooshed out of me. Sitting on a carpeted step, I reminded myself that this basement was brightly lit, perfectly safe. No one was here, and no one had any reason to harm me, to prevent me from moving freely about my own home.

"Perfectly safe. This is for Matthew," became my mantra, bracing me for the ordeal of each succeeding step. When standing became too difficult for my wobbly knees, I borrowed a trick of toddlers and negotiated the stairs on my rear. Halfway down, however, I stuck, hunched and shaking, with my arms wrapped tightly around my knees, my head bowed, my eyes squeezed shut.

And there I sat, listening to the humming of the furnace, the occasional creaks houses make when all else is silent, and from somewhere in the basement, playful growls and yaps of my two silly dogs. I sat so still, I imagined hearing the sun setting behind the gray blanket of clouds, imagined feeling the world going dark around me. The basement seemed to vibrate, to pulse like something alive, something waiting to swallow me whole the instant I let down my guard. So I waited as well, daring the monsters to attack.

Nothing happened, but that wasn't enough to ease my fears. The thought of simply rising, squaring my shoulders, preparing to proceed with my stated mission, were more than sufficient to make me tremble and perspire. Phobias that are irrational are bad enough to suffer with; mine was based on fears that were totally rational, based on an experience that, two dozen years later, held me in an iron grip. But I might not have another chance, and it was too profoundly important to me to clear Matthew's memory of any taint of crime to let my personal demon defeat me.

In my mind, I pictured the layout of the basement. The entrance to the computer lab was through a small reception area, and the offices housing the foundation's archives and the desks at which Matthew and Lucian did their noncomputer work. The only ways to enter the basement were by the stairs that led down from the hallway between the kitchen and the servants' stairs to the other floors of the house, and the sole external door into the basement itself. The latter was the door Lucian nearly always used to come and go since, as I'd told Joshua, he didn't have free access to the rest of the house. Matthew and I had agreed to honor our parents' philosophy about keeping our home private, so Lucian had never been given a passkey or alarm combination.

Odd, I mused, that Matthew would give a passkey to Joshua, but not to Lucian.

Or . . . maybe he hadn't. Joshua could have taken a key without Matthew, not normally a detail man, noticing. Matthew's absentmindedness was a standard family joke. One Christmas I gave him one of those gizmos that locate misplaced keys; to the amusement of the whole family, he lost it before New Year's Day.

From the architect's plans, I knew there were no windows, not even the typical shallow basement ones near the tops of the walls. It was a security feature, but also one of the obstacles that had kept me above stairs only for over two decades. I knew too much already about dark basements from which there was no escape.

I couldn't make myself move down another step.

Some investigator I was turning out to be! Even if I'd had the first clue what I was seeking, I couldn't overcome this damn phobia to look for it.

"Angela?"

The muffled call startled me badly. Joshua! Upstairs? My pulse surged, and my heart lodged in my throat. Laurel and Hardy barked happily and pelted up the stairs as if I wasn't there. I stood so quickly that I nearly tripped over my own feet, then sat on the stairs again. Why was I so agitated? Was I embarrassed to be caught trying to snoop into Matthew's business? Or was I mortified to be so obviously stuck halfway down the stairs? Was I pleased—more than pleased!—that Joshua really had returned? Or a combination of those, and other, less easily defined, reasons?

He called my name again, nearer to the open basement stairwell this time.

"Joshua?" I called back, my voice rusty from hours of tension and disuse. "I'm here. In the basement."

With those words, the crushing, sick helplessness of claustrophobia engulfed me. Memories of that dreadful experience came rushing back, so vivid that it was like reliving it, tasting again the metallic fear, the sour helplessness. It didn't matter that the lights in *this* basement blazed brightly, that I was in

fact still on the stairs, that there were phones within sight and
Joshua was calling me.

What mattered was the *basement*.

And then, with my fingers caressing the warm gold and the
domed gem of the ancient pendant, I thought, *So what?*

So what that I was in a basement?

I felt the layers of fear, of panic, lifting off me like layers
of heavy blankets, until my soul felt free of the tyranny of my
phobia. I stood up, feeling stiff in the knees and hips from
sitting in the cold, on the hard steps, for so long. But no longer
feeling *scared* stiff.

Feeling rather pleased with myself, I began climbing up the
stairs. Seconds later, Joshua appeared in the open doorway
with the Yorkies dancing and yelping in joy around his ankles.
The look on his face was priceless. For the first time since I'd
been told Matthew was gone, I felt a laugh—a very tiny one—
bubbling inside me. With a subdued whoop of triumph, I raced
up the stairs and into Joshua's arms.

He caught me and drew me firmly up and into his embrace.
Panting a little from my sprint, I leaned against him and absorbed his scent, his strength, his warmth. Just as I was getting
comfortable, he pushed me away and glared into my eyes.

"Angela, are you nuts? What were you doing down there?"

Before I could respond, Joshua scooped me up as if I were
an errant child and strode toward the main hallway, the Yorkies dashing excitedly around us. I wrapped my arms around
his neck and buried my face in the crook of his neck. The
temptation to start kissing his neck required considerable effort
to quell.

He stopped abruptly and tipped me back so he could glare
at me again. I got the impression he was more than a little
angry with me, but for some reason, I didn't feel at all defen-
sive about it. "Well?" His question came out almost like a
bark. Even the Yorkies halted their silliness to sit and stare up
at him.

I shrugged. "I wanted to do what Lucian said he did. Retrace the path of the funds on the big computer."

Joshua lowered me a bit more, but so suddenly I thought
he was going to drop me. Instinctively I laced my fingers together behind his neck, but he held me fast as he looked into
my eyes. I stared right back. The blue of his eyes was riveting,

mesmerizing, compelling. . . . I recognized the fierce expression in them as worry . . . about me. A warmth spread through me.

"And did you?" His voice jolted me out of my reverie.

"Did I . . . what?" I felt my eyes widen in confusion.

Joshua's eyes narrowed. "Did you retrace the money on the computer?"

"Oh!" I was feeling slightly giddy, but the scowl on Joshua's face didn't invite mirth. "Hardly." I didn't want to admit I hadn't made it to the basement, because then I'd have to explain that embarrassing phobia.

Joshua's laugh astonished me almost as much as the hard kiss he pressed on my lips. "Brave, beautiful Angela! Matthew would be very proud of you."

After another quick kiss, he hoisted me a little higher and closer to his body, and I took advantage of our respective positions to cling tighter. For a timeless moment, I forgot about everything except Joshua. His scent filled my head. His taste teased my lips. My breasts were crushed against the hard wall of his chest, sending tingles of awareness tripping along my nerves.

I felt the pendant, caught between our bodies, pressing into me, and could have sworn a pulsing heat emanated from it to fuel the warmth rising inside me. The silkiness of his dark hair brushed my skin where I'd wrapped my arms around his neck. The sound of his breathing growing harsher, more shallow, echoed my own erratic breathing; it was powerfully suggestive, powerfully erotic.

All my ambivalence, all my vacillations suddenly coalesced into the certainty that I really did love Joshua.

"Don't stop here." I nodded toward the stairs to the second floor.

Joshua hesitated, and for a long moment I feared he would indeed set me down in the hall, and walk away the way he had this morning.

"Are you sure?" His question went straight to the heart of the matter.

My answer came straight from the heart. "Yes."

Without another word, Joshua carried me upstairs to my bedroom, only pausing several times to kiss my lips. By the time he was carefully lowering me to the bed, I felt thoroughly dizzy, drunk on the taste of him, intoxicated by anticipation. Unwilling to release him, I kept my fingers laced behind his neck, pulling him down with me.

With a muffled grunt, Joshua reared back and glanced down at the pendant lying on my chest, then met my eyes with a question in his. I knew what he was asking; I hoped he would understand my answer when I only had unfathomable instincts to follow myself.

"It's from Matthew."

Solemnly, Joshua nodded. Our gazes held a moment longer, and then his lips curved into a smile just before he lowered his head. Perhaps I wanted to believe in miracles; the pendant seemed to grow warmer against my skin.

His hands skimmed over my body as his mouth took possession of mine. Instinctively I arched into his touch, parting my lips for the slow, hot slide of his tongue, clutching at his broad shoulders as my only source of stability. Heat rushed through me, molten honey flowed in my veins and pooled between my thighs. The first touch of Joshua's fingers on my bare skin sent shock waves over every inch of me, erotic lightning searing me inside and out.

No words passed between us, but I understood the sudden storm of his desire perfectly; the same overwhelming urges raged within me as well. There was no patience between us now. No slow savoring of caresses. No experimenting of the sort new lovers do. Instead, we tore at each other's clothes in a fever of need. Whimpers escaped my throat, groans shook his chest. The pendant felt inexplicably hot against my skin, but somehow, I didn't think to question the sensation. Matthew had said it was magical, so it seemed right to hold it between our hearts, kept in place by making love.

We came together, flesh on flesh, both of us trembling. When Joshua halted long enough to fumble with a condom, it seemed to take him forever to return to me.

His lean hips pressed between my thighs until I was welcoming him into my body. Pleasure and pain swirled together in a kaleidoscope of sensations that wrung a surprised gasp from me. Joshua froze, although the vibrations running through his frame testified to the effort it cost him. Before I could urge him on, he lifted his head and gazed down into my eyes.

"Angela?"

"Hush." I cupped his face between my hands and drew him down for a long kiss. "I told you, Joshua, I'm sure."

Still, he hesitated, so I gave in to the impulse to let my hips move, pleasuring us both until his restraint snapped. With a rumbling groan, Joshua pulled me close and thrust fiercely in counterpoint to my movements. I felt as light as a cloud, as sensitive as a butterfly wing, as resilient as elastic, as solidly eternal as the earth itself. And when I could take no more bliss, I clung blindly to Joshua and let the lightning crackle around us until the storm was over.

Time swirled and slowed while we held each other and waited for our hearts' pounding to subside. I gulped for air, trembling with a surplus of sensations still rippling over me, through me. The solid warmth of Joshua's body cradling mine stirred a feeling of utter security, total safety, yet paradoxically, tingling excitement such as I'd never imagined possible.

And, lying there in his arms, I understood why I felt the way I did. I'd fallen in love with Joshua Davidson, and when we made love, I *felt* loved.

Not that we actually said the word then or throughout that night. Truly, we were beyond words! Every look, every touch, every smile, spoke volumes in the instinctive, private language of new lovers. I felt as if something that had been imprisoned deep inside me had finally been set free; if only Matthew could be here with us, Christmas 1999 would have been the most perfect moment of the century for me.

Christmas Day dawned hazily, my own sleepiness reflecting the diffused light of sunrise. We'd made love several times during the night, and between times, we'd shared choice morsels of our lives, our thoughts, along with treats raided from Olive's pantry. When it seemed officially morning, I made coffee and heated sweet rolls while Joshua set a roaring blaze in my bedroom fireplace. And somehow, while feeding each other bits of the sticky rolls, we found the energy to rekindle our own private blaze.

Then, sitting on the living room carpet beside the tree, we exchanged Christmas presents. I'd knitted a heavy sweater for Joshua, from a tweedy deep-blue–colored yarn the color of his eyes. Our parents had taught Matthew and me that when money is no object, gifts given from the heart and hand mean more than the most expensive trinkets and toys. When Joshua pulled that sweater over his head and pronounced it a perfect fit, and the best present he'd ever received, I felt that I had wrapped him in a tangible sign of my love.

Then he gave me his present.

With trembling fingers, I untied the ribbons on a medium-sized box covered in red and gold foil. Joshua seemed to hold himself terribly still, as if waiting for my approval of his gift. He needn't have worried. Nestled inside crisp white tissue paper sat an exquisitely wrought wooden box. The smooth finish gleamed, showing off the delicate inlay design of flowers and leaves.

"Did you make this?"

He nodded. "Do you like it?"

I nodded, too, and managed to keep my tears under control until I opened the hinged lid to find a modest diamond solitaire set in a gold ring.

"Oh, Joshua!"

"I love you, Angela. I want to marry you. I didn't want you to think I was just another fortune hunter and turn me down, so I wasn't going to ask. Matthew convinced me that I should at least give you a chance to say no. So . . ."

My trickle of tears turned into a hurricane, but they were tears of joy. Laughing and crying at the same time, I threw myself into his arms and kissed him.

"Oh, Joshua! I love you, too. And I hate to disappoint you, but I don't feel inclined to refuse your proposal."

He flashed a very cocky grin. "I think I can get over that kind of disappointment."

Then, with his hands folded around mine, the ring tucked into my palm, Joshua's expression turned serious.

"I don't want to rush you, but I don't want to wait, either. Matthew suggested we have a relatively small, private ceremony soon, then do a big reception for all the obligatory-type guests later. That would give you time to plan it the way you think it should be. But if you want a big wedding . . . Well, I'd understand. I mean, that's a female thing, a big, fancy wedding, isn't it?"

As he spoke, the pendant pulsed against me, a phenomenon I was now willing to accept as more than my imagination. I would have had to be deaf and blind not to notice how brave Joshua was trying to be. Love and gratitude enabled me to suppress a smile at his expense. I understood his impatience very well.

"That sounds like a perfect plan to me. Especially now, it would be wrong to have a big, formal wedding without Matthew." It struck me that Matthew's advice eerily presaged his death, but I couldn't say the words to express my disturbing thought. "Our friends and associates will understand. What about your family?"

The truth was, I knew very little about Joshua's personal life, his history. Mother had always discouraged us from outright prying, and somehow Joshua hadn't volunteered much information. Now, after accepting his proposal of marriage, I felt no little bit foolish at the prospect of having to ask him such basic questions.

"My parents will understand, Angela. So will my sisters. They know about Matthew, and wouldn't expect us to have a fancy wedding while you're in mourning." He gave me a little half smile. "In fact, they'd probably be more comfortable with a relatively simple ceremony and dinner, just immediate family and a few close friends. None of us are exactly from the black-tie set."

"Good." Something he'd said caught my attention. "Tell me about your sisters. You never really mentioned them before."

He got that indulgent expression in his eyes that Matthew often wore when trying to deal with me. "Chelsea is older than me, married, with a girl fifteen and a boy thirteen. And Gloria is two years younger, single and too career-oriented to consider domestic bliss. You'll like them. They'll like you, too."

My curiosity wasn't quite satisfied. "What does Gloria do?"

"My parents will love you." Joshua's comment spilled out over my question. Politely, I waited for him to continue. I would learn about his sisters in due time, I was sure.

"Mom is a bookkeeper and Dad is a mechanic. They're simple people, but from what you and Matthew have said about your parents, they would have had a lot in common. Family is important to them. Integrity. Honesty. Loyalty. Like you and Matthew, they're your basic golden rule types.''

This was offered proudly, which pleased me. I didn't want Joshua to spend our married life feeling caught between the world of the haves and the have-nots.

Bending to press a quick kiss on the back of his large, strong hand, into which mine curled in quite a nice fit, I smiled up into Joshua's bluer-than-blue eyes. ''I'm looking forward to meeting them all soon.''

''You will.''

Joshua freed one hand, which he used to cup the back of my head and draw me toward him for a long, sweetly clinging kiss on my already well-kissed lips.

''Speaking of soon . . .'' Another kiss. ''Angela . . .'' And another kiss. ''We have a lot of details to hash out in the next few days, if you're up to it.''

''Details? I thought we were going to keep the wedding itself simple. If you'd like, I can ask our minister to perform the ceremony in church, and Olive can plan a family dinner here.''

He smiled, but his brow furrowed as if something bothered him. ''That sounds great to me. Just name the day. But . . .'' His smile faded, but the furrows in his brow remained.

''Before we finalize anything, you'll have to talk to your family attorney.'' My eyes widened. Joshua's cheeks flushed. ''A prenuptial agreement, Angela. Matthew would approve of that. I don't ever want you to think I want anything from you but your love.''

Joshua's features blurred through the tears that filled my eyes. For a second, I thought the pendant actually grew cold. With the hand that wasn't clutching the ring, I stroked his face, then placed my fingertips over his lips.

''No prenuptial agreement, Joshua.''

Behind my fingers, his lips parted, but I shook my head to silence any argument, and the pendant pulsed warmly as if in agreement.

''The foundation is protected, and I don't need to be. Not from you. Matthew thought the world of you. That's guarantee enough for me.'' Releasing his lips, I leaned back a little to look straight into his eyes. ''I love you, and I trust you. Completely. I wouldn't marry a man I don't trust, and I won't insult you by implying that I can't trust you.''

Then I gave him a saucy smile. ''I'd much rather the details we discuss be how many children we'd like to have.''

He exhaled so forcefully that I realized he'd been holding his breath, and I was glad I'd reassured him of my love and my trust. With fingers that shook a little, he opened my left hand and took the ring from my palm, then turned my hand over and slid the ring onto the third finger. It fit perfectly; as I held my hand out for Joshua to see, the diamond caught the firelight in its prisms and sent out sparks of light, like a star. The star sapphire pendant seemed to leap against my skin, as if greeting a kindred gem. Silly thought, but I figured I was entitled.

With his gaze on the ring, Joshua raised my hand to his lips, drawing me toward him at the same time. ''It's not as impressive as you deserve. Matthew convinced me to look for quality, not quantity.''

''It's perfect. I'm not the crown jewels type, despite the silver spoons I was allegedly dining from at birth.''

We were inches apart when our eyes met; when our lips met, we were smiling.

A loud bell chimed, startling us apart. The dogs set up a racket, yelping and yapping, somewhere on the first floor. My heart began to race at the sudden interruption, and I looked at Joshua in confusion, not immediately recognizing the sound of the doorbell. Once I did, I felt reluctant to answer the summons. I didn't want to visit with anyone. There would be time enough for sharing ourselves with others later. For the first magical hours of our engagement, I wanted Joshua all to myself.

But the doorbell rang again, each peal sounding increasingly impatient, and sending the Yorkies into increasingly urgent fits of barking. Whoever was on the porch obviously wasn't considering the possibility that I was otherwise occupied on Christmas morning. Otherwise *engaged*, in fact.

Sighing, I rose to make my way to the foyer, to open the door. A blast of bitingly cold air swirled around me, making me blink and step back. I opened my eyes to find myself face-to-face with Lucian.

His glasses became fogged in the seconds it took me to shut the door and turn around. The frigid outside air clung to him even as he was unwinding his scarf and shrugging out of his heavy black parka. The wind had painted his pale cheeks a raw red, as well as the tip of his nose and his ears. I shivered in sympathy.

"Merry Christmas, Lucian. Come in and get warmed up. I'll get you some coffee ... Or would you prefer hot chocolate? It won't take a—"

"No, nothing." He caught my hand before I could dash into the kitchen. Startled, I found myself stumbling to within a few inches of him. "Angela, I ... I came to wish you a Merry Christmas, and to ... to ask you ..." Behind his fogged glasses, I thought he was blinking, and wondered what was making him so awkward.

Movement behind Lucian caught my eye. Joshua appeared silently in the hallway. He leaned on the doorjamb to the living room, his powerful arms crossed over his chest, a friendly, curious expression on his face. Just seeing him there made me feel a little warmer, made the hall seem a little brighter. He winked at me. Blushing, I smiled back, then focused on Lucian again.

"Lucian, congratulate us! You're the first to know Joshua and I are engaged."

I expected a moment of surprise, perhaps a moment of awkwardness as a bachelor assimilated the news that one more single man was biting the dust; and then, a hearty hug for me, a gruffly sincere handshake for Joshua.

Lucian's reaction stunned me: He tore his fogged glasses off his face and scowled fiercely at Joshua, then turned a wild-eyed gaze at me.

"No!" His voice cracked on that shouted syllable. *"No-o-o!"* His voice rose in a howl that sent the dogs running for cover and prompted me to back away. But Lucian still held my wrist, and his fingers tightened like a vise, preventing my escape. "You ... you *Judas!* How dare you betray Matthew like this?"

Astonished and confused, I tried to determine if he was speaking to me or to Joshua. Finally, I realized he was accusing us both of betraying my brother. Why? How could he think we were somehow violating Matthew's trust by planning to marry? Lucian had to know the two men had become good friends. This was very disturbing and a little frightening. I jerked my captured arm hard, and when I finally succeeded in freeing my wrist, I knew I'd have bruises matching Lucian's grip. Rubbing my sore flesh gently, I glanced at Joshua to find him staring at Lucian with a dark intent I'd never seen in him.

"Touch her again, Drake, and you'll find yourself kissing the floor." Joshua's softly uttered threat sent a shiver up my spine. There was no doubt in my mind he meant what he said, and when I gaped at him I realized with sudden clarity that he was more than capable of following through.

Lucian's snarl twisted his normally choir-boy beautiful features into a startling mask of anger. He glared from Joshua to me, his rage vibrating visibly within him. Frankly I was more than a little irritated with Lucian's display of inexplicable— and truly inappropriate—disapproval. He had no right to spoil this precious bit of happiness in the shadow of Matthew's death.

"Lucian, whatever is wrong with you?"

"How could you do this to me?"

I gawked at Lucian, too astonished to demand an explanation. Lucian apparently intended to continue without any prompting.

"I love you, Angela! I intend to marry you!"

My heart sank as Lucian's voice rose in a hoarse shout. Shaking with his rage, he jerked his head toward Joshua, who was still impassively leaning against the wall. But there was a new light in Joshua's eyes, something very alert, like the gleam in a cat's eyes when it's finished sizing up its prey.

"This . . ." Lucian gestured toward Joshua as if he were pointing out something loathsome. "This *Judas* is the one responsible for Matthew's death, damn it! He's no carpenter, Angela. He's investigating the foundation, and Matthew. That's why Matthew took off in such a big hurry. This guy's the reason Matthew died."

Lucian's accusations were so ludicrous that I couldn't restrain the little laugh that bubbled up inside me. It was such an absurd notion. Joshua Davidson, master carpenter, who despised ATMs and grumbled at the menus on Touch-Tone phones, some kind of high-finance investigator? Another laugh escaped my lips.

Lucian's expression grew even more fierce. "He used you, Angela. The bastard used Matthew to get close to you, then used you to stay close to Matthew. When he gets what he wants, he won't care what happens to you!" Lucian's lip curled. ''That ring is probably from some evidence room somewhere, on loan to make him look genuine.''

Now he'd gone too far. I glanced past Lucian's shoulder at Joshua. He'd straightened, his arms still crossed in front of him. He was scowling at Lucian, a hard, forbidding expression turning him into a stranger. A feeling of unreality engulfed me. I blinked, but Joshua didn't alter his expression.

Suddenly he looked like a stranger, not the man I loved.

''Joshua?''

He didn't look away from Lucian, didn't answer the questions implicit in my barely articulate appeal. My throat constricted so that I couldn't swallow, could hardly breathe. Tremors shook me repeatedly. Tiny dancing spots of light sparkled in the darkness that was closing in around my vision, until all I could see was the face of my false lover. It struck me then that he was furious with Lucian for revealing his duplicity, but seemed unaffected by the knowledge that he'd just devastated me.

I realized that I was completely, irrevocably *alone* in this, and whatever was going on, I was going to have to get myself out of.

Joshua stepped toward me. The expression on his face looked so cold, so guardedly assessing, that I saw nothing of the man I'd come to love beneath that stranger's mask.

Oh, God! Lucian was right!

A cry of pain and disbelief rose from my heart as I threw myself at Joshua and beat his chest with my fists. It seemed to me that Joshua was allowing me to pummel him, but then, he must have lost patience. He caught my wrists in his strong hands, and tightened his grip when I began to twist away.

I was dimly aware of the Yorkies yelping hysterically nearby, and of Lucian shouting at Joshua.

''Angela, stop fighting me and I'll release you.''

Joshua's low growl cut through the noise. I must have paused in my struggles and my tirade long enough to satisfy him, because he slowly unwrapped his fingers from around my wrists. Lucian continued to rail against Joshua, threatening to kill him if he touched me again. Joshua and I faced each other, our breathing labored from our efforts, our gazes locked together.

''Joshua?''

My whispered question silenced Lucian. For a long, uncomfortable moment, all I could hear was the whimpering of the Yorkies, the crackling of the fire, and the uneven rhythms of three agitated people breathing. Time seemed to stand still as I waited.

"He's partly right, Angela." Joshua spoke quietly. It had been what I'd dreaded hearing, but a strange serenity seemed to insulate me from the pain I'd expected to tear me apart. Somehow I found the ability to hold myself still and wait for Joshua to explain exactly how Lucian's accusations were right. "Yes, I'm with the FBI computer crimes division. And yes, I'm investigating the foundation for banking irregularities."

"I told you he's using you!" Lucian's shout rang in triumph.

"No." Joshua held my gaze. "No, never that. Angela, I love you."

"He's lying, Angela!" Lucian appeared at my side, his fingers suddenly closing on my shoulder, tightening, digging into my flesh with bruising pressure. "Don't believe him, Angela. *I* love you—he doesn't."

Still looking into Joshua's eyes, I became aware of the now-familiar warmth emanating from the pendant. It wasn't simply absorbing the heat of my body, as gold does. It was projecting a softly pulsing warmth that steadily flowed into my heart. Everything felt very, very still, like a gentle snowfall late at night.

Both men wanted me . . . or, at least, wanted something from me. Both claimed to love me. Perhaps they both did. But Lucian remained loyal to me, to Matthew, while Joshua, by his own admission, was playing the role of Judas. If I chose to believe Joshua's love was real, would that mean I also believed Matthew had been stealing from the foundation's charity funds? If I chose to believe Lucian's was the love that was true, would that still condemn Matthew?

Deep inside me, that strange sense of serenity allowed me to see my choices lined up with all their attendant doubts and fears, hopes and joys. Time passed, but I had no sense of how long we three sat there waiting for me to make up my mind.

Finally I realized that there was only one choice that my heart would allow.

The star pendant lay warmly against my chest, pulsing its

message of love into my heart. I reached up and placed one hand over Lucian's cold, stiff fingers as they dug into my shoulder. Something hot, like an electrical shock, zipped from my hand to his. We both started. Then his grip on my shoulder relaxed, and he leaned toward me until his head touched mine. I closed my eyes, unable to risk seeing Joshua's expression just then.

"Oh, Angela! I knew you'd choose me!"

My heart sank at having to hurt him. "I'm so sorry, Lucian. I love Joshua. I believe him when he says he wasn't using me to get close to Matthew. I believe he loves me. I intend to marry him."

Lucian pushed away from me with an enraged howl. The force of the blow knocked the breath out of me and shoved me into Joshua's arms. By the time I'd caught my breath and lifted my head, Lucian was backing toward the foyer and the front door, shouting as he retreated.

"You'll be sorry, damn you! You'll see you should have picked me. When the world goes to Hell on New Year's Eve, you'll wish you were with me! I would have taken care of you. Everything is going to stop like a dead watch. No lights, no water, no food, no heat. Looters, rapists, murderers everywhere. No cops, no gas for cars, fires and no fire trucks. No ambulances, no hospitals. Only a few of us will survive. I'm one of them. I could have protected you from all that."

Lucian paused in the foyer, his eyes lit with a fierce passion. "I could have protected you!" He swung his arm to the side and one of Mother's Baccarat bowls crashed to the marble floor with a noise that made me jump, made Joshua flinch, and sent the Yorkies scrambling for safety. For a moment, he stood glaring defiantly at us. Then he wrenched open the door and bolted, slamming it behind himself.

Silence echoed through the house.

Shaking like a frightened kitten, I clung hard to Joshua, the pendant pressed between us. My emotions were too wrung out to let me cry. Joshua didn't say a word as he held me and stroked my hair. His warmth slowly calmed me, until I was able to look up into his now-sad eyes.

"I love you, Angela. No matter what else happens, I love you."

"I believe you, Joshua." Somehow, I managed a weak

smile. "You have a lot of explaining to do, but I do believe you love me."

The sheen of unshed tears in his eyes shocked me, touched me. I hastened to reassure him. "I'm still angry that you lied to me about who you are and what you've been doing, but I *don't* believe you would ever betray Matthew or me."

Joshua exhaled slowly, then offered me a rueful smile. "I'm sorry. I wanted to tell you, but I wasn't authorized to. There was concern that you might inadvertently tip Lucian off before we were ready to show our hand."

"Matthew knew?"

Joshua nodded.

"How did Lucian find out?"

"We let him think he was hacking into Bureau files so he could stay one step ahead of us. He kept cool about it for so long, I was beginning to think he smelled a rat."

The Yorkies trotted back to sit near us. "No, these two clowns smelled a rat. They never liked Lucian." I smiled. "Terriers are natural-born ratters."

Joshua grinned. "We could use them at the Bureau." Then his grin faded and he tipped his head toward the foyer, where shards of crystal sparkled all over the floor. "I'll clean that mess up later. Right now, let's get more comfortable, and I'll tell you what you need to know."

With the somewhat subdued Yorkies following us, we went into the library. Once we were seated side by side on one of the comfortably stuffed sofas, I curled into his arms and nestled close. He felt strong and solid. His heart beat steadily under my cheek. His scent filled my head, sharpening my awareness of every point of contact between us.

While Joshua gathered his thoughts, I placed my free hand over the ancient pendant and wondered if it had helped me see Joshua clearly despite Lucian's accusations.

"Someone really did move five hundred million dollars of foundation funds to accounts in the Cayman Islands." Joshua's voice startled me back to another facet of reality that simply hadn't seemed possible to me. "The accounts are all in Matthew's name, but they aren't his accounts."

"But who else could have access . . . ?" Silently, Joshua arched an eyebrow. "Oh, no! Not . . . Lucian? I can't believe he would do that!"

"As you say, who else? Lucian knew that even if you had
the expertise to crack your way into hidden files, your phobia
would keep you out of the basement."

"Does *everyone* know?" My cheeks stung with a sudden
blush.

He stroked my hair back from my burning face. "Yeah. It's
not exactly a classified secret."

Matthew wouldn't have told anyone without asking me first.
And I certainly hadn't told anyone. It had taken several of the
best kiddie shrinks in Connecticut and New York to get me to
talk about the ordeal at all. Since they'd pronounced me "recovered" from the trauma, I'd kept my posttrauma basement
aversion to myself.

I ignored his taunt. "That still doesn't answer the two most
obvious questions: If the accounts weren't actually Matthew's,
why was he flying to Grand Cayman? And if Lucian knew
about my basement . . . aversion, why would he set up *this*
basement as a postmillennium bug shelter for himself and me?
He would have known I wouldn't go down there willingly."

Joshua's gentle stroking of my hair stopped for a second,
then resumed. "First, Matthew really was going to Grand Cayman for the diving. And second, Lucian knew no one would
suspect you of being in your own basement when you disappeared."

"Oh, lord! Everyone *does* know!" My cheeks burned.

Joshua nodded against the top of my head. "You were too
young to read the papers, and Matthew said your parents
wouldn't let you watch the news in case you got traumatized
all over again. But the headlines were tabloid-style: 'Tiny
Heiress Missing'; No Call For Ransom. 'Charity Heiress Abducted?' 'Crank Callers Badger Family.' 'Toddler Heiress
Found Safe in Root Cellar.' Your family is too high-profile
not to have a file a foot thick at the Bureau."

His revelation left me feeling violated. Not that the FBI had
information about my family's activities; I had been raised to
understand the compromises between freedom and security for
anyone involved with the McMichaels Foundation. But that
there were total strangers who knew more about me personally
than I knew about myself, was disturbing.

Joshua must have sensed my discomfort. "Angela, I never
used anything in that file to gain any advantage over you. The

FBI doesn't assign agents to fall in love with potential witnesses. Granted, loving you is worth breaking a few regulations, but I'll be glad when this is a done deal."

There were still some questions niggling at my mind. "Go back to the theft of the foundation's funds. I don't understand why Lucian, if it even was Lucian, would do any of this. He comes from a wealthy ranching family, and has a generous salary and benefits package here."

"It *was* Lucian. You know it wasn't Matthew. He called us himself and was cooperating fully." Joshua shifted a bit, drawing me closer into his embrace. "First, you need to know that Lucian isn't who he claims to be. He's not the misunderstood son of a wealthy California family; he's never even been west of the Mississippi. He's just a poor kid from a wrong-side-of-the-tracks dysfunctional extended family in Pennsylvania. He's probably illegitimate, but so are most of his relatives."

Despite my profound shock at this description of Lucian, I felt compelled to defend him. "Being illegitimate isn't a child's fault."

"I know. But some folks treat those kids as if being conceived was their fault, not their parents. Unlike the rest of the family, though, Lucian is very bright, and he had greater ambitions than going on welfare or doing odd jobs for the rest of his life. So, he invented a new persona that would have a better chance to rise to his high expectations."

For a moment I mulled that information over, aching for that child who couldn't fit into his own family, but believed he had no other place in the world. "But if he went to all that trouble to steal so much money, why put it all back, then call attention to it?"

Joshua sighed. "Best we can figure out, he was testing his plan to take advantage of the possible confusion of the Y2K bug. Reporting the crime and restoring the money makes him a hero. If the theft had been discovered before he had time to replace the funds, he had everything set up to point the finger at Matthew. That's why he used Cayman Island accounts; he knew Matthew would be there at exactly the right time."

Again, I pondered Joshua's explanation. "But if Lucian wasn't planning to keep the five hundred million he moved back and forth, what *is* he planning to do?"

"Damned if we know." Joshua gave a short laugh that held

no amusement. Then he shifted so that we were facing each other, and looked intently into my eyes. "That's what I have to find out, preferably before, not after. Judging by his exit lines, he's definitely got something based on possible consequences of the millennium bug in mind. It also sounds like, until you broke the news of our engagement, you played a key role in his plans."

Sensing Joshua's frustration, I placed my hand on his warm, smooth cheek. "I'm sorry I interfered with—"

"You didn't interfere with my investigation, damn it!" There were angry sparks in his eyes; he looked so fierce that I had to resist the instinct to move away. "It's Drake's good luck you're out of his plans. If he tried anything, I'd—"

"Hush." I touched his lips with my fingertips. "It's Christmas, my love. Remember, peace on earth, good will toward men."

Joshua offered a contrite smile and kissed my fingers. "Yeah, I know. Turn the other cheek, and all that. But it's easier to honor the messenger for having compassion than the message of being compassionate ourselves, isn't it?"

His rueful observation echoed my father's own opinion of the modern commercialization of Christmas. And reminded me of a task I would have preferred never to face.

"Joshua, I was planning to hold a memorial service for Matthew before the new year. Will that interfere with the investigation in any way? Or vice versa?"

Try as I might, I couldn't quite control the sudden wash of tears welling up. The light seemed to fade from Joshua's beautiful blue eyes. He reached out and, cupping the back of my head in one strong hand, he drew me close to his chest again. Grateful for his empathy, his support, I wrapped my arms around him and clung.

"Damn, I almost forgot about that. My poor Angela. Can you postpone the memorial until after this is wrapped up? Security is tight, but if there's a leak to the press, accusations could tarnish Matthew's reputation. And the foundation's."

I wanted to argue, to refuse to change my plans for the memorial service for Matthew. It was my only way to say good-bye to my brother and, selfish as it might be, I thought I deserved at least that much. But Joshua was right; it would be a terrible injustice to Matthew's memory if the press alleged any wrongdoing against him. And that could damage the foundation's credibility, which would compromise our ability to help others.

Reluctantly, I took a shaky breath. "I'll talk to the minister about a date in the new year. And Joshua? Thank you for protecting Matthew's reputation."

He pressed his lips to my temple. "He was my friend, Angela, not just a case. I would be proud to call him my brother. Never forget that."

For a long while after that, we sat holding each other, lost in our separate solitudes. Finally, we shook off our gloom as much as possible. We spent the rest of Christmas Day quietly visiting with friends of my family so I could introduce Joshua and share our news. Grief for Matthew tempered the genuine joy my engagement to Joshua engendered; the prospect of our marriage helped alleviate the shared sorrow of losing Matthew.

It wasn't until much later, as we were climbing the stairs to my room, that Joshua reminded me that he would be working on the foundation's computer tomorrow. I assured him I had no problem with that. Indeed, I wanted answers quickly, too.

We made love sweetly, then lay curled together. Joshua fell asleep almost immediately, but I lay awake a long time, worrying. What if Joshua found evidence to incriminate Matthew?

What would that do to us?

Over the next several days, Joshua spent hours on end in the basement, working through the data stored in the computer. I had plenty to do to occupy my time, but no matter how much I filled my days, it was the nights in Joshua's arms that made me truly happy. I loved loving him. I loved feeling loved. This gave me the strength to push aside all the sharp-edged "if onlys."

As soon as the snowplows cleared the streets and our groundskeeper cleaned the driveway, I busied myself doing errands and checking in with some of the local charitable agencies on the foundation's support list. The days were brilliantly sunny and there was no more snow predicted until after New Year's Eve, but the temperature remained bitterly cold, even in the sun. I was particularly pleased to succeed in negotiating with a manufacturer for donations of winter coats, boots, and sleeping bags for shelters. Joshua congratulated me, but I ached to share my news with Matthew, too.

Olive was due to return early on December thirty-first. I
called her at her daughter's house to suggest she extend her
holiday break; after all, there would be no New Year's Eve
party this year for us. When she heard that Joshua and I were
engaged, however, she adamantly refused to stay away longer
than planned. We would greet the new year quietly, but we
would celebrate our engagement, on that she insisted. To be
honest, I was glad to let her have her way. She was all the
family I had left now, except for Joshua. I was really looking
forward to meeting his parents and sisters.

On Wednesday the twenty-ninth Joshua emerged from the
basement with a triumphant grin and a bottle of champagne.
He'd worked his way to the deepest levels of Lucian's hidden
files. Now he had all the proof needed for an arrest on charges
of fraud, theft, conspiracy to commit theft, and conspiracy to
damage public and private property. All he needed was to find
Lucian, which might not be as simple as he'd hoped; Lucian's
"aunt," whoever she'd really been, had disappeared with no
forwarding address, and there was, so far, no trace of Lucian,
either. That didn't seem to dampen Joshua's buoyant mood,
however.

"We'll find him. He probably isn't far away, and there are
three levels of law enforcement looking for him. We've alerted
the airports in Connecticut, Pennsylvania, New York, and
Massachusetts, but the chances are slim to none that he'll be
flying anywhere." Joshua flashed a wicked grin. "Drake's ac-
rophobic."

"He's afraid of heights?" A laugh bubbled up inside me.
"Oh, that's too rich! What a pity we don't have a roof garden
for me to hide in."

Joshua shook his head. "He's not likely to risk coming back
here now that he thinks you're consorting with his enemies."

He eased the cork from the champagne bottle with just the
proper amount of pop and, to his credit, no wasted froth. After
filling two of Mother's favorite antique crystal flutes, he
handed one to me.

"Here's to a peaceful end to 1999, and a disaster-free beginning to 2000." Looking very solemn, in contrast to his
faded jeans and a South Park sweatshirt, he tipped his glass
toward me in a formal salute, then sipped.

"Amen." My whispered reply was as fervently as if he'd

uttered a prayer rather than a toast. The chilled champagne danced on my tongue and tickled its way down my throat.

"You know what that dweeb was planning to do?" Not waiting for my reply, Joshua continued. "He'd hacked into banks in three states, as well as utility companies, to create his own carefully orchestrated millennium bug. Then, just in case those banks and utilities had solved the real Y2K glitches, his customized version was set to crash whole systems right after transferring a few hundred million into phantom accounts in his name. When the systems came back up, Trojan horse programs would have wiped the electronic evidence of his sleight-of-hand maneuvers. The accounts would look legitimate, right down to phony histories, and he'd be laughing all the way to the banks."

I was too stunned to speak, but Joshua was clearly excited enough for both of us. "Thing is, Drake was putting millions of people at risk by knocking out electricity along a lot of the eastern seaboard. January first with no heat, no lights . . . people freeze to death, or light fires and burn their houses down."

He tipped his head and studied my face. "That's where his plans for you and the basement came in. He set the place up like a cross between a love nest and a bomb shelter, with all the modern conveniences."

The thought of being dragged into the basement by a lunatic who imagined I was in love with him made me shudder. Even later, when Joshua held me in his arms and whispered about his own plans for us, visions of Lucian imprisoning me in my own house sent shivers of revulsion through me.

As if he knew how I was feeling, the last thing Joshua said before we fell asleep was, "Don't worry, Angela, you won't have to face Drake. I'm here to keep you safe. He can't hurt you now."

The next morning, several agents arrived with a van to remove the big computer system from the basement. Shortly before they expected to finish, Joshua informed me that he had to report to the FBI field office in New Haven for a few hours; he'd phone when he was on his way, and pick up whatever take-out food I wanted to order. I assured him that I had plenty to keep me occupied until he returned, and that I'd be home whenever he phoned. With a kiss and a reminder to set the alarm as soon as the other agents were done, Joshua drove away.

Dutifully I activated the alarm, although it felt like an over-reaction to do so in the daytime. My family never encouraged the fortress mentality wealthy and vulnerable people can develop, but it certainly wasn't a sacrifice to make Joshua feel more secure.

While I worked at my desk, preparing lists of tasks for my assistant to take care of when she returned from her holiday break, I listened to a Sarah McLachlan CD. Hearing the haunting lyrics of one of her songs brought thoughts of Matthew into sudden and achingly sharp focus. I cradled the star sapphire pendant in my palm, treasuring my last real contact with my brother. Was he, as I prayed, in the arms of the angels?

At my feet, the Yorkies stirred and growled softly. I assumed they were having doggy nightmares.

"Hello, Angela. Miss me?"

Lucian's voice came from behind me in the brief silence between songs. My heart leaped. My pulse raced. A cold feeling of dread settled in the pit of my stomach. With the pendant digging into my suddenly clenched hand, I froze in my chair. I was unable to turn around, unwilling to see that I hadn't imagined him here with me. How . . . ?

"How did I get in here?" He uttered a short, sharp laugh, then grasped the arms of my chair and spun me to face him. I had to release the pendant to grab the arms of the chair for stability. The dogs took matching aggressive stances and barked. Lucian's pale-blue eyes burned with indignation. Was he insane? Or simply immoral? I wasn't sure I wanted to know.

A sneer twisted his innocent choir-boy features. "You didn't seriously think I would let Matthew treat me worse than the groundskeeper, did you? If Zeke can have access to the house, with his garden dirt and oily rags and pesticides, surely I should. After all, I'm the brains of the foundation. Without me, Matthew would be lost." He paused, then snorted. "Sorry. Matthew is already lost. Too bad for you and Matthew. Lucky break for me. I couldn't have planned that any better."

His cruel words sickened me, but I tried desperately not to let my feelings show on my face. If Lucian thought I was still his ally, I might have some leverage.

"It's too late, Lucian. The FBI has the computer. They know what you were planning to do. You've been shut down. You might as well surrender. I'll . . . I'll arrange for an attorney for you, if you'd like. I'd like to help you."

With another snort of bitter laughter, Lucian grabbed my arm and yanked me out of my chair. The dogs barked shrilly. Off-balance, I staggered to keep my feet under me. As soon as I was steady, I closed my fingers around the pendant again, using it for a sense of security, as a child uses a favorite toy or blanket. Afraid Lucian might hurt the Yorkies, I tried to hush them.

"Shut them up or I'll toss them outside in the cold. And then you'll help me, Angela. You'll help me get away."

As if they understood, Laurel and Hardy sat quietly, staring at Lucian and me. Silently, I prayed that they'd stay out of harm's way. "The FBI knows about the basement shelter, Lucian. That's the first place they'll look for you."

He smiled. "That's the first place they'll look for both of us." His smile widened into a smug grin. "Give me credit for some intelligence, Angela. If I'm in a hurry, do I really need to have to overcome your claustrophobia to hide out?"

I admit, I was surprised by his response. "Then what are you planning to do?"

"There's more than one computer in the state, you know. It was more convenient and a lot more comfortable to do the programming here, in the lap of luxury, but backup is the lynchpin of safe computing. I've got another system ready to take over on the dot of New Year's Eve, and a cozy hideout suitable for a princess and her lover."

He smirked and caressed my upper arm with his thumb. I started to pull away, but something caught a beam of light, drawing my horrified attention. I froze. Lucian held a knife in the same hand he was using to touch me.

I didn't dare try to fight him now. It was like having a snake crawl over me, a poisonous snake that might strike if I moved. As if he could tell how uncomfortable his touch made me, he boldly stroked my cheek with his fingertips. Somehow, I found the fortitude not to shudder, but my skin felt as if something slimy had touched me.

"I've already packed a bag for you. Go get your coat and boots."

He caressed my cheek again, this time with the side of the knife blade. It felt cool and unforgiving against my skin. I began to tremble. I was petrified that he might cut me by accident, as well as on purpose, but I couldn't control my tremors. Lucian's grin told me I shouldn't bother; he didn't care if I was scared, now.

"We'll take your car. It's better than mine."

Joshua wouldn't be back for hours, but I decided to try to stall anyway. With luck, I might think of some way to leave a signal for Joshua and the police. I strove to make my expression neutral. Lucian's grip on my arm relaxed slightly, and he took the knife away from my face.

"So, where are we going?" I tried for a light tone; to my own ears, I failed, but Lucian's little smile indicated he believed I was cooperating. Unfortunately, unless I could think of some way to escape, that might be exactly what I ended up doing.

"You'll see." He gave me one of his boyish smiles that I'd always thought were so guileless; now it gave me chills.

"Can't you give me a hint?" Shamelessly, I tried wheedling. For the foundation, I'd charmed huge cash and merchandise donations out of people and corporations notorious for their tightfistedness. With luck, my skills of persuasion would help me now. "Is it in the mountains?"

"No mountains. No basements. Stop stalling."

His abrupt tone warned me I'd just lost whatever advantage I'd had. I'd forgotten his fear of heights. What else could I do?

"Fine. You said you packed a bag for me?" The thought of Lucian going through my things brought on more snake images. "I should check to make sure we have everything I need."

"Angela, we're rich. If I forgot to pack something, we can buy it." His fingers dug into my arm again, then gave me a little shake. Hardy growled softly; I shushed him. "Let's go, damn it! I want to get there before dark."

With the cool blade of the knife against my throat, I had no choice but to allow him to lead me to the closet. For once, the Yorkies weren't following me. Could they have understood the threat of that knife? I frantically calculated time and distance. The sun would be setting as early as four-thirty, and it was two something now; our destination must be about two hours' drive from here. Was there any way to use that to my advantage?

As I shrugged into my warmest coat, I tried another delaying tactic. "We have to stop for gas. I'm almost empty."

Lucian frowned as he handed me my boots. "I checked. You've got a full tank." He stood over me like an impatient parent with a recalcitrant toddler. "C'mon."

In desperation, I looked him straight in the eyes and lied. "I think my gas gauge is broken."

With an eloquent narrowing of his eyes, Lucian scowled and shook his head. "Forget it. I happen to know you just had the car serviced." He exhaled in a show of exaggerated patience. "Now set the alarm and let's go."

Twice, despite the press of the blade against my neck, I deliberately entered the incorrect code. Lucian snarled a warning before my third try. He squeezed my elbow painfully hard. I gritted my teeth and prayed Lucian wasn't desperate or crazy enough actually to use the knife.

Then I entered the incorrect code the third time, and all hell broke loose.

The alarms rang, the dogs barked, and Lucian shouted at me.

He also seemed to forget he had the advantage of the knife. With the hand that had pressed the blade against my neck, he reached for the front door and yanked it open. Still shouting into the chaos of the alarm bells, he tugged me hard toward the door. I realized that once he got me into the car, it could be hours before anyone realized I had been taken against my will. The police would assume someone had tried to break in while I was out doing errands. Joshua wouldn't be back for hours. It was now, or quite possibly, never.

Something warm pulsed against my chest. The pendant!

A flood of resolve washed through me. I pulled back as hard as I could, bracing my feet so that Lucian was forced to drag me, and only a few inches no matter how he tried. The clanging of the alarm bells was so loud my ears ached: the noise made it almost impossible to think, to calculate. I was so scared, I felt numb.

I stared at Lucian, still unable to believe this was happening. With a growl, he swung toward me. Cold fury sparked in his pale eyes, but the pendant pulsed warm near my heart. Time slowed, expanded, movements unfolded in slow motion. It felt as if I were watching myself struggling with Lucian. The knife in his free hand caught a glint of light. I raised my free arm, protecting my neck and face with the sleeve of my coat. The thick layers dulled the impact of his strike. I was fairly certain he hadn't stabbed me through the sleeve. I was stunned that he would try.

A blast of frigid wind blew the front door all the way open and nearly knocked us off our feet. Behind us, safe in the foyer, the Yorkies barked shrilly with the clanging alarm. I caught my balance and tried to assess the chances of escape. My car was parked at the bottom of the front steps, the motor running, ready for Lucian to take me away. The police would arrive in minutes because of the alarm, but by then we'd likely be on the road.

Fighting the wind, Lucian's next tug wasn't very effective. I didn't know what I could do, but I knew I had to keep trying.

Isn't that what faith is for? I heard Joshua's words as clearly as if he were speaking over the noise of the alarms.

I grabbed the doorframe and held on as tightly as I could with my free arm, fighting against Lucian's rough jerks on my other arm. He raised the knife and yelled at me to let go. Heat and ice flashed through me as I saw the knife flash in a threatening arc. Then I saw movement outside, behind Lucian.

As the knife came toward me, I let go of the doorframe. Lucian, still pulling on my other arm, yanked me down, out of the path of his knife. The force of his own movement pitched him forward, into the doorway, as I was falling in the opposite direction. But before I could hit the stone steps, strong arms scooped me up and out of the way.

By the time I'd registered that I was safely in Joshua's arms, I wasn't any more. Flanked by two solid local policemen who were holding me up, I watched two grim-faced men in dark winter coats fastening handcuffs on Lucian, whom they were holding facedown on the foyer floor. Joshua, his eyes locked on mine, stood over Lucian as he was hauled, snarling, to his feet.

Suddenly the alarms stopped ringing. Into the echoing silence, Joshua spoke in a tone all the more menacing for its deceptive control. "Lucian Drake, you are under arrest . . ."

He went on to list a litany of charges, including attempted kidnapping and assault with a deadly weapon. Then he paused until Lucian, still muttering, finally fell quiet.

"You have the right to remain silent, you sorry son of a—"

One of the men holding Lucian's arms cleared his throat. Joshua glared at him, but continued without embellishing Lucian's rights with his opinions. The entire time that Joshua spoke, Lucian stared at me with open resentment in his eyes. Yet despite everything Lucian had done, after Joshua finished reciting his rights, I spoke to Lucian the way I knew Matthew would have wanted me to. "Lucian, I'll send our family attorney to you."

A flash of uncertainty came into his eyes, and then his expression hardened to a sneer once again. "Sure. That's the least you can do. For ten years, I worked my butt off and watched your family dole out piles of cash to anyone else who asked. For ten years, I loved you, and you treated me like one of your damn dogs."

My heart sank at his words. "Lucian, was that why you did all this?"

His laugh was a short, sharp bark of bitterness. "No. That's the funny part, Angela. I did it because I could."

And with that, the agents escorted him off the porch and down the drive to where I assumed they'd hidden their cars. Less than a heartbeat later, I was back in Joshua's arms, with the Yorkies dancing joyously around our ankles. I clung to him, my knees trembling, and absorbed the warmth of his embrace, the familiar musk of his skin.

"Thank God you're safe!" His lips grazed my temple as he spoke in a hushed murmur. "We knew he didn't have a gun. We didn't think he would pull a knife. If he'd hurt you . . ."

"I'm fine, Joshua. Now. With you here." I tipped my head back to look into Joshua's now-pale face. To my amazement, he was trembling harder than I was. "I didn't think you'd be back for hours."

Joshua tightened his hold. "It was the weirdest thing. I heard a woman's voice, clear as a bell, saying, 'Joshua, my son, return now,' but there was no one in the car with me. I thought it was something on the radio, so I changed the station and turned up the volume. Then, I swear it, the voice said, right over the music, 'Joshua, return to Angela.' "

He gave me a sheepish grin that told me quite plainly that he wasn't the kind of man who believed in miracles, but I knew better. I had the pendant, warm and pulsing gently, to remind me that there were higher forces beyond our comprehension.

I couldn't resist teasing him, however. "A woodworker who also works miracles?"

Joshua did an actual double take before releasing a hearty laugh. Feeling a little giddy myself, I laughed, too, and hugged him as close as our thick winter outerwear allowed.

Finally, it occurred to me that we were still standing outside in the cold, although the wind had completely died down, Arms around each other, we went inside. I took off my coat and offered Joshua a hanger for his, but he shook his head. My heart sank.

"I'm still working, honey. We still have a couple of loose ends to take care of. I'll be back tomorrow in time to celebrate New Year's Eve in a very special way." He kissed me softly, and I felt his reluctance when he broke the kiss. But I smiled to reassure him, and he offered back a crooked grin. "Stay out of trouble, okay?"

I burrowed into his arms for a long, tender embrace. The pendant Matthew had given me pressed between us, and there was far more heat coming from it than it could possibly absorb from our bodies. After Joshua left, I cupped the pendant in my palm and studied it.

Was it really the magical star of the ancient legend, the gem a certain Infant, two millennia ago, had touched in wonder and endowed with healing, saving grace? Who could say? But the lovely, smooth stone in the center of the antique gold setting seemed to have trapped the light of a star within itself.

If only this talisman of hope and faith had the power to return Matthew to us. . . . Perhaps Joshua and I would someday be blessed with a son we could name after my brother, to keep him alive in our hearts.

The next morning, Joshua phoned to reassure me he would definitely be back that evening. He hinted at a surprise, but wouldn't let me wheedle it out of him. Olive returned from her daughter's home, and we busied ourselves preparing for a quiet New Year's Eve celebration. She was as shocked as I had been to learn about Lucian's duplicity; as we cooked, we tormented our memories trying to recall any clues, anything we could have done to prevent him from taking such drastic measures. Sadly, he'd fooled us both but, in the lingering spirit of Christmas, I was doing my best to understand and forgive him.

That evening, snow began falling, dancing like tiny stars in the streetlights, creating a hush that seemed to envelop the entire world. Although the third millennium technically didn't begin until the first moment of 2001, the first hours and days of 2000 would be the test of the so-called millennium bug. The agents had found and disabled Lucian's backup computer. Thanks to Matthew's information, if anything significant malfunctioned on the eastern seaboard tonight or tomorrow, it would be the fault of some other computer chip, not Lucian's sabotage.

It might not exactly be world peace, but it was still a good legacy for Matthew to leave behind.

When Joshua hadn't arrived by seven-thirty that evening, I was beginning to worry. I sat in the parlor near a roaring fire, Laurel and Hardy asleep at my feet. I was not reading the mystery novel in my lap, not drinking the sherry Olive had insisted on pouring for me. I heard a faint noise from the front of the house, and then the Yorkies, yelping frantically, tore away from the hearth and flew into the hallway.

I heard the muffled rise and fall of voices and the rustle of clothes, and guessed that Olive was greeting Joshua. Then I realized there were more than two voices out there. Joshua must have brought a friend to join us. The last thing in the world I wanted now was to share him, but I nevertheless fixed a welcoming smile on my face and rose, prepared to be the gracious hostess.

At the sight of the man following Olive and Joshua into the living room, my smile froze and my sherry glass slipped from my suddenly numb fingers. Dimly, I was aware of Olive mopping up the spilled wine from the hem of my velvet dress, and collecting the glass from the carpet at my feet. I felt Joshua wind a supporting arm around my waist. I stared at the man in the center of the room, only vaguely aware of two other figures flanking him and the excited dogs racing from person to person.

"Matthew?" I spoke in a whisper, afraid the vision of my

brother, alive and well, would disappear like smoke in the wind.

A second later, I was engulfed in my brother's familiar bear hug, and we were both laughing and crying. Laurel and Hardy, who adore Matthew, danced at our feet, yelping and begging for his attention. When I was finally able to think coherently, I turned to Joshua with no little bit of anger and indignation welling up beside my joy and relief.

"You lied, Joshua! You said you'd tell me everything, but you let me believe Matthew was ... that he had ..." I couldn't say the words for fear they would somehow become true.

Matthew arched a brow at Joshua and, grinning, stepped away a little. Olive mirrored my hands-on-hips pose, her expression as angry and hurt as I felt. Joshua raised his hands as if in surrender, but Matthew was the one who answered.

"Blame me, Angela. You know you're the world's worst liar. If you'd known the crash was a ruse and I was alive, Lucian would have known within two seconds."

Of course, he was absolutely right about my inability to lie, but I couldn't agree with his arrogant tactics. Still, I loved them both too much to stay angry.

"I forgive you. Both of you." I smiled at Matthew. "Thank you for my beautiful Christmas present." I brought my fingers to the edge of the pendant, which lay warmly on the neckline of my velvet dress. "Oh, and Matthew? You're grounded."

While laughter swirled around me, Joshua brought the other two arrivals closer to the hearth. A darkly handsome older man and a stunning young woman, they each scooped up an excited dog as they approached me.

"Angela, meet Special Agent Gloria Davidson, my little sister, and Special Agent Paul Vega, an old friend of ours. They were Matthew's baby-sitters while we had him hidden away."

So now I knew why Joshua had dodged my questions about his sister's career!

Matthew put his arm around Olive's shoulders. "And this is Olive, our long-suffering housekeeper, and the best cook in the country, if not the whole world."

To my amused surprise, Olive blushed. Was it Matthew's compliment, or the way Agent Vega looked into her eyes when he shook her hand? In the time it took for Matthew and me to share a wonderfully familiar conspiratorial glance, Olive had invited Agent Vega to help her set additional places in the dining room and he'd followed her out of the room.

Joshua drew the champagne bottle from the ice bucket and began unwrapping the cork. "I think it's time for a couple of pre–New Year toasts."

Matthew brought glasses and, as we gathered near the hearth, Joshua poured the champagne. Then he raised his glass and smiled into my eyes. I could have sworn the pendant grew warmer as I smiled back at him.

"To my future wife." His voice sounded raw with emotion.

Matthew tipped his glass toward us. "To my brave little sister and my future brother-in-law." Then he put his arm around Gloria's shoulders and cleared his throat. "And to *my* future wife, very Special Agent Gloria Davidson."

His announcement stunned me no little bit, but both he and Gloria were beaming at each other in a way that said they were head over heels in love. Joshua was grinning, as well.

I lifted my own glass to salute the two most important men in my life. "To the safe return of my brother, and to my future sister."

Gloria smiled warmly at me, then winked at Joshua. "To the dawn of the third millennium—peace on earth, and good will toward all. Even computers!"

"And to the Christmas star." Matthew glanced at the pendant glowing with its special inner light against the midnight blue of my velvet dress. "And to all the ladies who avert disaster by loving wisely."

After we'd solemnly sipped champagne, Matthew spoke again, his eyes suddenly sparkling with mischief. "I'd like to invite you all to join me on a diving vacation in the Cayman Islands."

"That's not funny, Matthew." I scowled. "Anyway, you're grounded."

"It's not meant to be funny, Angela. That pendant has a rendezvous with a fish, until the next time it's needed, and there are some *very* big fish in the Caymans."

I joined in with the general laughter, but I knew he was right. The pendant was more than a lovely piece of antique jewelry. The Christmas star worn by the Wise Man, Melchior, belonged to forces beyond mortal understanding, beyond mortal ownership.

After dinner, as we waited around the hearth to count down to the first second of the year 2000, I cupped the pendant in the palm of my hand. The star sapphire pulsed warmly from its magical inner fire. The melody of a Christmas carol unexpectedly began winding through my head. After all that had transpired, I decided that it certainly couldn't hurt to heed another hint this gem seemed to be making.

As soon as we'd finished toasting the new year, I went to the sound system controls and selected the CD I wanted. Gazing at the five people who were watching me with indulgent curiosity, tears filled my eyes. I'd never imagined such happiness, had never been so happy.

The lights had stayed on into the year 2000. Lucian's attempt to create darkness and chaos had truly been thwarted. My brother had returned, as if from the dead, and I was in love with a man who was apparently both a woodworker and a miracle worker. Was it the magic of the ancient Star of the Magi? Bemused but willing to believe, I looked into the center of the jewel. Perhaps it was my imagination, but the points of light seemed, just for a second, to flare even more brightly.

With perfect timing, the triumphant sounds of ''Joy to the World'' filled the room.